STILLWATER ISLAND

BOOKS BY GREGG OLSEN

Detective Megan Carpenter Series

Snow Creek

Water's Edge

Silent Ridge

Port Gamble Chronicles

Beneath Her Skin

Dying to Be Her

Lying Next to Me

The Last Thing She Ever Did

The Sound of Rain (Nicola Foster Thriller Book 1)

The Weight of Silence (Nicola Foster Thriller Book 2)

GREGG OLSEN

STILLWATER ISLAND

bookouture

Published by Bookouture in 2021

An imprint of Storyfire Ltd.
Carmelite House
50 Victoria Embankment
London EC4Y 0DZ

www.bookouture.com

ISBN: 978-1-80019-836-4
eBook ISBN: 978-1-80019-835-7

For Rick and Jennifer,
For making the trek from Tennessee to Washington to solidify a life-lasting friendship.

PROLOGUE

"Mommy, I'm scared."

"I'm right here with you, Bennie. We're fine." She's scared, too. Her thoughts are fuzzy. She remembers... what? What does she remember? She remembers she had awakened sitting against a wall with Bennie lying stretched out next to her, one little arm thrown over her thigh. She had put a hand on his chest to see if he was breathing. He's four years old and asthmatic. She felt it gently rise and fall. He was breathing. Alive. She was weak and wasn't sure if she could get up. It had taken all her strength to gather Bennie in her arms.

That had been an hour ago, two hours, maybe more. She still doesn't understand what has happened. Where she is. How she has come to be in this pitch-black place that smells strongly of mold and sawdust. What frightens her the most is a news story from a couple of days ago. A woman's body found recently, dumped, her two children's bodies were found hidden in empty oil barrels. The woman was pregnant. Just like her. But she and Bennie are still alive.

She blinks her eyes and listens to seagulls squalling. She can't tell where the sounds are coming from. She knows she must be near water.

Her thoughts shift to her son. Poor Bennie. She'd had to shake him hard before he'd stirred. Thinking about it brings her close to panic. She should have let him sleep. Maybe sleep was better than this cloying darkness.

The seagulls are quieting and she realizes it isn't completely dark. She can make out some of the shapes close to her. Something with hard, jagged edges runs from the floor at her feet to as far as she can reach above her head without putting Bennie down. It's cold like metal. A saw. A very big saw blade. She feels new panic rising in her and tastes bile in her throat.

"I need to put you down, honey. Can you stay right here for Mommy?"

"Where are we? Are we camping?"

"No, honey. But we're safe. I just need to get up and look around for a minute. Can you stay there?"

"No, Mommy! Don't go!" He clutches at her and buries his face in her chest.

She wraps her arms around his rail-thin body. "I've got you, Bennie. Mommy's got you. I won't go anywhere." She can feel the hitch in his breathing and knows an asthma attack is coming. "Slow breaths, honey." She breathes out and breathes in slowly. "Slow." She hears him mirror her and soon his breathing relaxes. He's scared and fear is one of his triggers. "That's right, baby. Slow. Slow." She has to be strong. Find out what is happening. Find a way out.

"I want to go home, Mommy."

"Me too, sweetheart. We'll be home soon, baby." He shifts on her lap, squirms, and tucks his hands under his head, his favorite sleeping position. He's so much like his father in some ways.

Her strength slowly comes back and causes a muscle spasm in her calf. She energetically rubs at it, and her hand brushes against something on the floor's gritty surface. A large plastic bottle and some other things. One is Bennie's inhaler. She shakes the bottle and hears a sloshing sound. Water. The other thing is small. Maybe three or four inches long. Hard like plastic. A shape. A figure. Maybe a toy. Maybe one of Bennie's toy baseball players.

She twists the cap off the bottle and sniffs. It doesn't smell like anything. She puts her tongue to the lip of the bottle and tilts it enough to get a taste. It is water. She takes a drink and waits a minute to see if she gets sick. It's okay to drink. She hadn't realized how thirsty she is.

"Here, baby. I have water. I'll hold it for you. Just sips, okay?" He takes several sips. "Bennie, I have to find the door. Can you sit right here and wait for Mommy?" He grips her like an anaconda and her heart breaks as she feels him tremble. "Okay. Mommy won't go anywhere. How about this? Why don't you ride piggyback on me like you play at home with Daddy?"

"Horsey?"

"That's right, honey. Horsey." He loosens his grip, and she gets to her hands and knees. He eagerly climbs on her back, arms around her neck, head against hers, heels digging into her sides. "That's right, baby. Just like that. Mommy's going to take you for a ride."

"I'm too big for horsey rides now, Mommy. Daddy says so." He loosens his hold but doesn't get down.

"Then it will be a piggyback ride. Like when I was your age."

"You were four?" he says like it's the funniest thing he's ever heard.

"If you're good I have something for you."

He freezes and she can hear an intake of breath. "What is it?"

She doesn't know what it is but it feels like a toy. "You have to hold on to me tight and be good."

"I'll be good." He kicks one heel into her side and clicks his tongue to urge her on.

She reaches up and pats his hands. "Hang on tight. Here we go." She makes it a few feet and is overcome with a wave of dizziness. Bennie relaxes his grip and begins sliding off.

"I'm sleepy, Mommy."

She is too. So sleepy. She lays him down and lies next to him.

The inhaler is in the pocket of her jeans along with Bennie's surprise. She closes her eyes and remembers waking up here feeling sleepy and a little nauseous. She's been drugged. But by whom? And why?

She fights the drowsiness, pulls Bennie against her and scooches back until she's against the wall. Bits and pieces of memory come back. Bennie not wanting to go to bed, insisting on wearing his Darth Vader pajamas. A gift from his father.

She'd found out she was pregnant. Ben was gone somewhere and she had made his favorite meal to give him the news when he came in. He hadn't come home until late that night.

She's having trouble keeping her eyes open and slaps her own face hard enough to hurt. It helps a little. She has to think. Stay awake. Her eyes feel like sandbags are hanging from the lids. She lets herself drift into another place. One where she and Bennie are together and happy. Somewhere away from Ben. But not here.

* * *

Someone stirs in the deep shadows of the room and stands over the sleeping woman and child.

"That's right. Sleep. It will all be over soon."

A door is unlocked and then bolted shut and locked.

The woman and small child sleep on.

ONE

2:00 a.m.

Police Dispatcher: 911. What is your emergency?

Caller: My wife and son are missing.

D: What is your name, sir?

C: *Ben. Ben Parker.*

D: Where are you calling from, sir?

C: *My wife and son are missing. Just send someone.*

D: Okay, sir. I'm going to help you. Can you tell me where you are?

C: *I'm at home. I'm at my wife's home.*

D: What is the address?

C: *21 Luna Ridge, Baker Heights, Port Ludlow.*

D: Are they missing from that address, or...

C: *Yes. 21 Luna Ridge in Baker Heights. Are you sending someone?*

D: Yes, sir. Stay on the line and talk to me. I have to ask these questions, sir.

C: *Okay.*

D: How long have your wife and son been missing?

C: *I'm not sure.*

D: How do you know they're missing?

C: *I talked to my son two days ago and I haven't been able to reach him.*

D: They've been missing for two days, sir?

(Pause.)

C: *I'm not sure. Maybe.*

D: Do you live at that address, sir?

C: *No. I mean, it's my house but I'm staying somewhere else. What does it matter?*

D: Does your wife or son have a medical condition?

C: *My son has asthma.*

D: What are your wife's and son's names?

C: *Marlena. Marlena Parker. My son is Bennie. He's four. They live in Baker Heights. I can give you directions.*

D: That won't be necessary, sir. Are you calling from your cell phone?

C: *Yes.*

D: Is there any sign of a break-in at your wife's house?

C: *I don't know.*

D: Stay on the line with me, sir. I'm sending a car now.

TWO

Twenty-eight-year-old Jefferson County Police Officer Burnett and Officer Paco have been riding together in car 42 for eight years. Paco, who is nearing retirement, calls Burnett "Sonny" because he still looks as if he were nineteen. With forty years on the job, Paco looks much older than his sixty-three years. He's been thinking about taking an early retirement for a year or so. He and the job don't see eye to eye any longer.

Officer Paco is riding shotgun and watching a storm gather over Mount Olympus, where in Greek mythology Zeus was the gatherer of clouds. He knows they won't see much of it. Port Ludlow lies in the rain shadow of the mountains, and Jefferson County receives the least rainfall yearly of any other county in Washington State. He's been looking forward to a little rain for his tiny garden—actually, Miriam's garden—but now that he's been dispatched on a run, he is glad he won't have to get out in the rain.

With the highest annual median income of any city in the United States, and nestled along Port Ludlow Bay, Port Ludlow is more of a bedroom community for the wealthy than a city.

"One day I'm gonna live like this," Officer Paco says. "Big house. Golf course in the backyard. Lots of money. A pool. No, two pools. One for each foot. You can come over and kiss my foot."

"In your dreams, old man," says Officer Burnett. "Unless you're related to Bill Gates and forgot to tell me."

"You're only as old as you feel, you young pup."

"If you hit the lottery, you'd better invite me and Cynthia and the kids over."

"I don't know if the gate guard would let you through. You look like a burglar, Sonny."

Sonny waves at the security guard and drives into the Baker Heights gated community. He turns down Luna Ridge and eyes the expensive homes whose back decks view a stretch of well-maintained seven-son flower shrubs, dogwood, magnolia, monkey puzzle trees, a private golf course, and Port Ludlow Bay.

"Have you set a date to retire, old man?"

Paco laughs. "Long before you do. With that baby face, you should grow a beard. Maybe people will take you seriously instead of offering you cookies and milk."

"My wife likes my face."

"She has to."

Paco shines a light on the house numbers. "Dispatch said there's a missing woman and four-year-old boy. Same age as my grandson." He squirms in his seat, thinking, *Man, I shouldn't have had that coffee. Now I gotta pee like a racehorse.* He turns the spotlight off. "That's it up ahead."

On the way there Paco pulled up the address on the car's data terminal and saw two prior calls for service involving domestic disputes. "Didn't we make a run here a couple of months ago? Neighbor called it in."

"Yeah. The guy was gone when we got here."

"That's right. He had just left. Wife said it was nothing. I remember the kid too. Little for four. And he wouldn't talk to me."

"That face scares kids, old man. Hell, you scared me until I realized you're just a pussycat."

They are quiet. They have made many calls for service of this type and hated it every time. The family is always in pain and thinks the worst. But most times the missing person isn't actually missing. They've gone off somewhere to visit a family member or a friend and haven't told anyone. With a history of domestic violence, this one may be different.

Sonny says, "I bet you they're not missing. If I remember right, the mom was a beauty. Classy. Rich. She's probably doing an overnight no-pajama party with some lucky young guy and the kid's with her rich aunt."

"You're too cynical for your age."

Paco worries about the young officer sometimes. Being a cop carries a lot of authority, and authority can be a big attraction to women. But the badge also carries a great responsibility. A sense of honor. He has known cops who have given up their honor for an affair. The cost is never worth it.

That makes him think about Miriam. The love of his life. They were married almost as long as he's been a cop. She died two years ago after losing a battle with a very aggressive cancer and he regrets all the time she spent alone, staying up, worrying about him until he walked in the door. At least she'd gone quick but there wasn't enough time to prepare. There never is when it's important. And he thinks about his grown daughter and his grandson. Kevin is the same age as the missing boy. He will have to rethink how much longer he'll stay on the job before he puts his badge away. He can retire now. Probably should. The job isn't like it used to be when he was sworn in. Hell, it isn't the same as five years ago. Sure, there are bad cops. But not all. Besides, if you get in a jam, who are you gonna call? Criminals don't usually help people out. Just last week an elderly woman in her eighties was pushing a shopping cart from the grocery store and had a heart attack. Two young guys robbed her and ran away laughing while she lay there dying. What's the world coming to?

A white truck, a Ford F-450 Super Duty, is parked on the wrong side of the street but the tinted windows are dark and they can't see if anyone is inside. The engine is running but there's no sign of movement. They wait for someone to get out but whoever it is just sits there. The husband called it in.

"You think that's him?" Sonny asks, and turns the spotlight on the truck's back window. The driver looks into the rearview mirror and shields his eyes but doesn't get out. Sonny flips the light off, and the man still doesn't stir.

Paco unsnaps his holster and puts a hand on his weapon. It's not unheard of that officers are lured into an ambush by crazies. Finally a door opens and a man steps out. He's about Sonny's age, around six feet tall, built solid like a weightlifter, not a bodybuilder but muscular. He's wearing too-tight worn-out blue jeans fashionably ripped at the knees, a skintight black polo shirt, and new white sneakers. Paco secures his weapon. No way the man is hiding a gun.

"Will you look at that?" Sonny says.

"What?"

"Those shoes. Holy cow, Paco. They're Jesus Shoes. Nike put water from the River Jordan in the soles."

"He's not walking on water now."

"He should be. Those go for around three grand."

Paco shakes his head. That's more than he paid for his first car. He grabs his metal clipboard. "We're not here for a fashion show, Sonny."

Before Sonny gets out, he says, "He doesn't seem too worried."

"Don't care," Paco says. "Let's get to it."

"I'll bet he says something like 'What took you so long? I pay your salaries.'"

"In that case he should give us a raise."

Sonny covers his mouth to hide a grin. The man waits for them to come to him.

"Are you the one who called, sir?" Paco asks.

"Yes."

"You're Mr. Benjamin Parker?"

"Yes."

"Dispatch said missing persons."

"Yes. My wife and son."

"We need to get some information, Mr. Parker."

"I've already given it to your radio person."

"Yes, sir," Paco says. "I still have to ask these questions. The missing persons are your wife and son. Is that correct, sir?"

"I think so."

"You think, or you know?" Sonny asks, and Paco gives him a cautioning look.

"Do you need my driver's license?"

Paco nods, and Parker retrieves it from a wallet stuffed with credit cards and hands it to Sonny.

Paco says, "Why don't you just tell us what happened?"

"Like I told your call center, I came over because they aren't answering the phone."

"You don't live here, sir?"

"We're separated."

Paco waits for Parker to continue, and when he doesn't, Paco asks, "Have you tried knocking on the door, Mr. Parker?"

The man gives him a blank look.

"Do you have a key?"

"No. I gave it to her when I moved out. We haven't been separated long. I've still got things here. I thought we'd work things out. You know, get back together. I have a son."

"Does your wife have a restraining order against you, sir?" He expects the question to ruffle the man's feathers, but Parker doesn't react. A restraining order might explain why the man wouldn't knock but it doesn't explain his absence of emotion. He sounds like he's reporting a fender bender.

"No restraining order. We get along fine."

"But you're separated?"

"Yes."

"Did you check with your wife's friends? Family? Call anyone?"

"I've called here a couple of times today. When I wasn't able to get an answer I came over and then called the police."

"Do you have any idea where your wife might be? Anyone she might be staying with? Friends? Neighbors?" He is thinking of the domestic violence runs to this address. He hopes the missing woman or a neighbor will come down the street and explain all this. But nothing is moving. No neighbors on the lawns like in the tighter-populated parts of town, where someone will call for help just to see the bubble lights coming.

"This is kind of embarrassing, Officer..."

"Paco and Burnett, sir. Anything you can tell us will help."

"My wife, Marlena, is having an affair. That's why we split up. But I thought we were getting past that. For my son's sake."

"What's the name?"

"The name?"

"Yes. The name of the person she's having an affair with."

"I don't know his name. She wouldn't tell me."

"Do you think she might be with this person now?"

"I don't know. We were talking about patching things up."

"Have you tried calling your wife's friends?"

"She doesn't really have any."

"Okay. What have you done so far, sir?"

"I called you. There's no one else to call."

"How about her parents? Your parents? Brothers and sisters? Employer?"

"I'm quite well-off, so my wife doesn't work. We're both only children. We don't have much to do with our parents."

"Start a report, Sonny. I'll knock on the door." Paco walks across the manicured lawn. A motion sensor light comes on near the front door and Paco notices two things: the motion sensor light on the side of the garage doesn't light, and there is another set of shoe prints in the dew on the grass. Leading toward the house like his but no prints coming back.

He rings the doorbell and recognizes the tune. The theme from a cartoon. Barney the Dinosaur. His grandson has it on the television, the cartoon channel, every time he visits his daughter. Now he'll have that tune in his head for the rest of the shift. He presses the doorbell again and waits. No answer. He tries the door. It's unlocked. He knocks louder and waits a minute before opening the door and calling out.

"Jefferson County Sheriff. Is anyone home?"

There's no response. He walks back into the yard and looks up at the upstairs windows. No lights and no movement.

"Front door is unlocked, Sonny. Is that usual, Mr. Parker?"

"It shouldn't be," Parker says, and turns his attention back to Sonny.

"Mr. Parker, do you give us permission to go into the house?" Paco asks. It's a formality. He's going in whether he has permission or not.

Parker nods. "Wait here, Mr. Parker," Sonny says, but Parker doesn't appear inclined to follow them.

"Check the outside, Sonny. I'll go inside."

They split up and Paco enters the house expecting the putrid odor of decay, but there's nothing except the mild smell of baked cookies. He calls out several more times and waits for Sonny to reconnoiter the house and catch up with him. He doesn't want to walk in on someone in the shower. Or get shot by a scared homeowner.

"Everything's secure, Paco."

Paco looks outside to see if Parker is going to come with them, but the man is on his phone texting and not looking in their direction. "You take the downstairs and the garage." He definitely doesn't want Sonny walking in on the lady in the shower or otherwise engaged.

They both have leather gloves on their belts and put these on before searching. Sonny flips the light switches on in the front room. Paco goes up the staircase that winds around to a hall landing with doors to the various rooms. At the top of the steps he finds the light switch for the sconces lighting the hallway and turns them on. The carpeting is a thick shag, cream-colored, matted in places where feet have trodden. He calls out again, "Sheriff's Office. Anyone home?" and gets no answer. He listens and can hear

Sonny's footsteps on the hardwood floors below. Sonny is also calling out as he moves from room to room. Paco looks in each room as he moves along the hallway, announcing his presence, turning on lights, making noise. The lights are off upstairs except for in one small bedroom where a night-light in the shape of Luke Skywalker is dimly lit. The bed is unmade, toys are scattered here and there. The door to the bathroom is closed. He looks in and it's empty and spick-and-span except for a child's toothbrush in the sink along with an open tube of Aquafresh Kids toothpaste. What appears to be a guest bedroom is orderly, bed made. He checks the closets in each room and finds nothing suspicious. The master bedroom is likewise spotless, the bed turned down as if someone were going to bed, the closet is open, a bookmarked Debbie Macomber paperback novel is on the bedside table. No one in the bathroom. Clothes all hanging in the closet. The tub and shower still show water spots. A single towel on the towel bar is still damp but not wet.

Paco goes to the top of the stairs and looks across to the front door. This place is a mansion compared to the two-bedroom, one-bath place he and Miriam bought after their daughter married and the house became too big for them.

Paco says, "I got nothing."

"There's a door from a mudroom leading to the garage and out the back. The back door was locked but the one to the garage wasn't closed good. There's a Mercedes in the garage."

"Did you get the wife's phone number?"

"I tried her already. It goes to voicemail."

"Try again."

Sonny calls the number. It goes to voicemail. He leaves a message: "This is Officer Burnett, Jefferson County Sheriff's Office. I'm at your house with your husband. Would you please call this number back as soon as possible?" He gives his cell number and disconnects.

"Start waking the neighbors. I'll finish the report with Mr. Parker." Better to apologize for waking them up than to delay. Paco gets the clipboard and goes outside to find the garage door is open and Parker has the trunk to the Mercedes open.

Parker looks up, startled. "I was looking to see if there were bags packed."

"How did you get in the garage, Mr. Parker?"

"The garage door opener is on my keys."

Paco keys his shoulder mic and requests a detective. "Mr. Parker, when was the last time you saw your wife and son? Give me a date and time."

THREE

I'm sound asleep and then wide-awake with an annoying buzzing sound and rattling on the nightstand—a thrift shop wooden chair, actually. A strand of loose hair is stuck to my mouth and I pull it loose, feeling around for the phone. If it's Dan, I'm going to brain him. Dan Anderson is the first true boyfriend I've ever had. The first man I've ever loved. He's built like a lumberjack in a Lisa Jackson romance novel but better looking and not a bit arrogant. Dan's just checking on me. He knows I've been a little stressed lately. A lot stressed, actually, after Dan and I were almost being killed by some psychotic bitch who had been in love with my bio-father—himself a serial killer. She's dead but so are a lot of good people that stood between her and me. Dan is in Maine at a marketing conference to get ideas for rebuilding the wood art business that she had destroyed, burned to the ground. I'm sure he doesn't remember the time difference. It's sweet of him to call, so I will forgive him. Unless he does it again.

The screen on the phone shows it's 3:00 a.m. It's not going to be Dan. I'm tempted to press the red button and roll over, but the caller display shows "Sheriff Gray." Green button.

"Megan, I need you to go somewhere."

I need *him* to go somewhere too. "What's going on, Sheriff?" I rub my eyes and comb my hair back with my fingers.

"Dispatch called for a detective. I'm sending Ronnie but you need to go with her. Missing person. A mother and child. Ronnie's never worked a missing person alone."

Ronnie Marsh shadowed me when she was a reserve officer going through the academy. Last year, while she was still a reserve officer, our boss, Sheriff Tony Gray, assigned Ronnie to me as an intern. Our first case was a floater. That's what we call a drowning victim. But this one hadn't drowned. She'd been beaten and strangled. Ronnie was a big help. I never thought I would accept a partner, because I'm used to working alone. Always have. But we've become a team. Ronnie is bright, intuitive, computer savvy, knows how to keep a secret, and is growing on me. I like working with her. *And* she saved my life not long ago.

There is no question as to whether I will help her. But why does Tony want me to go with her on something as simple as a missing person case? She's good at what we do. She can handle this. Most missing people are gone because they don't want to be found. Lovers' quarrels, angry teens, domestic spats—all making some kind of point and not caring what it costs the county to track them down to make sure they're alive. A mother and son would qualify for the deliberately missing category, but missing persons are my weak spot for very personal reasons. An unwanted memory of my mother comes to mind. When my mother was sixteen she was kidnapped by my biological father. She'd been beaten, raped, and tortured but managed to escape. I'm proof of what he did to her. The memory of what happened after that still makes my breath catch in my throat.

"I need to get dressed. Where should I meet her?"

"She's coming to you," Tony says. "Mindy will meet you at the scene."

Mindy Newsom was one of my first friends when I came to Port Townsend and is a forensic specialist, initially hired by the sheriff to manage our crime scene crew. But budget cuts ended that as a full-time position and now she does crime scenes on an "as-needed" basis. Now she owns a flower shop for full-time employment. In my opinion, the Sheriff's Department lost out and the flowers got the better end of the deal.

"What can you tell me?" I'd like to know if I need any special equipment. I keep climbing gear and other stuff in the trunk of my car. Also, I might need a thermos of coffee and some snacks.

"Ronnie should be at your place in about ten minutes. She'll fill you in."

I hang up and hear knocking on my door. My mind is still a little fuzzy. I get up, turn a light on, and see I'm wearing only one sock, boxer briefs, and a tattered Led Zeppelin T-shirt. There's an empty box of cheap wine and something resembling Chinese takeout on my desk. The food and wine go in the trash can and I go to the door.

Ronnie is wearing makeup, not a bright red hair out of place. I hate her. She starts to speak and I hold a hand up. "I need coffee first. Strong," I say, and trudge into the bathroom, where I take a shower in barely lukewarm water. The hot water heater is dying, finally. When I come out and peek into the kitchen, she's made coffee and toast and is sitting at my table.

"Thanks for the coffee, but I wouldn't eat that bread if I were you. It's moldy and I've been feeding it to the birds."

She stops chewing, gets up, and spits the bread into the trash can.

"That wasn't the moldy stuff. My bad."

"Not funny, Meg." I cringe every time I hear that nickname.

"Sorry," I say, but I'm not. That's what she gets for being perfect at after two o'clock in the morning while I'm still wrapped in a beach towel with wet hair. "Tony said you would fill me in. Let me get decent first. Then you can talk."

I take my coffee into my bedroom-slash-office. The coffee's good and strong. That's the only thing saving Ronnie's life right now. But if she calls me Meg one more time, all bets are off.

I finish the coffee before I finish dressing in my normal work clothes—black pants, white top, black boots—and go into the kitchen. Ronnie is nicely dressed in new designer blue jeans and a pretty white button-up blouse, moderately low-heeled shoes. I look like a vagrant she's picked up. I hand her my mug for a refill. It's handmade blue ceramic with a white anchor design etched on one side and "SIS" on the other, my special mug that my brother, Hayden, had it made for me.

I try not to get depressed looking at that mug but it's hard not to when hope is all you have. My little brother and I never had a normal life growing up. He was barely nine years old when I left him in Idaho with our aunt Ginger, who was a veritable stranger to both of us, when I went on the run. I was little more than a kid myself. Just sweet sixteen, but I knew that leaving Hayden behind was the only way I could keep him safe. I kept track of him and even have two photos of him on my home desk, one of him taken at Aunt Ginger's in Idaho while we were on the run together, the later one a photograph he sent me of him graduating high school. In the picture he has a smile on his face but his eyes don't look happy. On the back of that one is a handwritten note: "*Rylee, I'm graduating today. You are not here (as always). My foster parents are nice people, but they don't replace my family. Thanks for taking all of that away from me.*"

After graduation Hayden went into the army and then deployed to Afghanistan, after which I didn't hear from him for a very long time. I found out only recently that he'd been wounded twice. After a lengthy absence without any contact he surprised me when he showed up at my door. My heart felt like it would explode. A grown man stood before me but I could only see that wounded nine-year-old face. His lack of expression and his too-short visit told me his anger at me was clearly still there.

At first, I tried to patch things up but his anger would resurface and he would remind me of the wrongs I'd done to him. He has no idea of the things I've done to protect him. He didn't know what I had to do to find our missing mother. To avenge her and our murdered stepfather. He didn't and will never know. I can't allow that. If he knew the truth—about me, about our mom, about our real dad, and even about himself—he would never be the same. I've had to weigh the good that truth can do against the harm it might do to our relationship. Sticking with the lie wins each time.

Hayden's ignorance of the past has allowed him to keep a good relationship with our mother. I can't tell him she's a lying, back-stabbing bitch. He wouldn't believe me. He would definitely hate me more than he already does, and I don't think I could take that. So I continue the lie and take his little digs, feel the anger in his eyes, the things he doesn't say, like *I love you, sis*; *We're going to be okay, sis*; *I forgive you*. There's a hole in my heart only he can fill, and it keeps getting deeper.

I zone back in and Ronnie is saying, "Megan, are you okay?"

She's refilled our coffee. I take my mug and wonder if it's all I'll ever get from Hayden. "I'm fine. Just tired."

"Can I talk now?"

"Yes, you may, Detective Marsh." I try to smile. I'm not lying about being tired.

"Dispatch called for a detective and I was on the bubble," she says.

Being "on the bubble" is something Ronnie has heard in the station house. When you're next up for a case, you're on the bubble. I'll hate her if she starts using police jargon.

"It's a missing mother and son. Marlena Parker is twenty-six. Bennie Parker is four and has asthma. They live at 21 Luna Ridge in Port Ludlow. Ben Parker, the father, called Dispatch around two o'clock this morning to report them missing. Officers arrived and talked to him. They checked the house and no one was home. No sign of a struggle. The front door was unlocked. Her car is still in the garage. Officer Paco said something's not right. The husband wasn't much help and doesn't know how long she's been missing. Could be a few days to a week. They're separated, and he hasn't been home in a week or so."

I know Paco. He's an old-timer and a damn good officer. He has something he doesn't want to discuss on the phone. I'm beginning to feel like I've swallowed an ice cube. Maybe more coffee might melt it. I finish the coffee and make a show of washing the mug out in the sink, to show Ronnie I'm not a total slob. "Let's go."

"There's something else you should know."

I hate it when she does this.

"Marlena Parker is the sheriff's niece."

Now I'm awake! She could have led with that.

FOUR

Sheriff Gray had given Ronnie a take-home car, an eight-year-old Crown Victoria, beige, no hubcaps, that she has polished and cleaned to perfection. Armor All covers every vinyl surface, and a strong deodorant hovers in the air like a chemical weapon.

"I'm on call this weekend, but I didn't think anything would happen, so I cleaned the car," she explains.

I pat down the seat. It's still damp. "You did a superb job."

"I guess I spilled some of the freshener on the carpet. Is it too bad?"

It smells like a pine tree threw up, but I say, "It's fine." I open my window so I don't vomit.

"Too much?" she asks.

"Maybe just a tad." I resist hanging my head out like a dog.

Ever-efficient Ronnie has the address on her GPS and in no time at all we arrive at Baker Heights, where a gate guard is dozing off in his booth. He's barely sitting up and looks ninety years old. Ronnie flashes her bright headlights and honks to get his attention, then pulls up beside the gatehouse.

"I was just resting my eyes," he says, looking at her badge. "You here with the other cops?"

"Yes. We're with the police," Ronnie replies.

He bends and looks at me. "Her too?"

"Yes."

He looks at me a moment longer, then hits a button and opens the massive iron gate. I tell Ronnie to stop just inside the gate, and I motion the guard over. I can see he's having trouble getting off his chair, so I go to him. I show him my badge and say, "I'm dressed like this because I work narcotics."

Now he smiles and gives me a conspiratorial wink. "I know just where you're going too. I may be old but I keep my eyes open."

Ronnie chuckles. "Do you always work this shift?"

"I'm retired. When you're old as I am, you have trouble sleeping. I figured I might as well make some money. I really was just resting my eyes."

"You aren't that old," I say. It's what you say to the very old to be kind. He doesn't look a day older than dirt. "When did the police car come in?"

He rummages under a counter and pulls out a ledger. "I keep most of it in here. The other shifts used to keep this up, but now we don't have anyone on dayshift, and the mid-shift isn't regular, so..." He opens the ledger and says, "Two twenty this morning. Nice fellas."

"Do you take down information for the residents coming and going?"

"Not supposed to. They get a little cranky about their privacy."

"But you do anyway. Right? You seem like someone that pays attention." When you're not resting your eyes.

He gives me another wink. "Just in case the cops need to know if someone is here. But like I said, I'm the only one doing this now."

"Do you know the Parkers?"

"Yep. Sure do." He perks up.

I ask, "Do you know what the Parkers drive?"

"Yep. He's got a white Ford F-450 Super Duty. Big truck. Diesel and loud as all get-out. I'm surprised the HOA allows him in here. Now, the missus has a black Mercedes. Clean as can be and she's as sweet as pie."

He doesn't like Mr. Parker. Paco doesn't, either. I can't wait to meet Parker so I can join the club.

"Have either of their vehicles come in or gone out while you were here?"

"He came in about fifteen minutes or so before the police."

"Is that the only time you saw one of them come through?"

"Yep. Got it right here in the ledger."

"I trust your word. Thanks. I might need to talk to you later."

He starts shuffling pages.

FIVE

"Glad you're here, Megan," Officer Paco says with not quite a smile.

"Paco, this is Ronnie Marsh," I say.

"Heard good things about you, Detective Marsh," he says. She beams a dazzling smile at the mention of her title. She'll get over it and won't be so impressed after she's made a couple hundred calls for service. He looks at her and at me, then gives a mischievous grin. "Did they get you out of bed, Megan? Maybe rumpled is the new black."

"Yeah. You got me." *Now shut up your face.*

"Come with me," Paco says, and walks us a little away from where his partner is talking to a man who is dressed even worse than me.

"We got a missing person call. A woman and a four-year-old boy. He's the husband, Ben Parker."

"Ronnie said you have a problem with his story."

"When we arrived he didn't come to us. We had to pry information from him. He and the wife are estranged. He owns the house but he's been living in a cabin he also owns, for about a week. The address is in the report. He says they're on a trial separation and working on reconciling. He claims he last saw her when he moved out but he can't pin down the date. He last talked to his son on the phone about two days ago. He doesn't remember exactly what time of day but it was around suppertime. I haven't looked at his phone to verify any of this yet. I thought you'd want to do it." I nod and he goes on. "The wife is a stay-at-home mom with no friends he can name. The boy goes to preschool; also no friends he can name."

Ronnie and I exchange a look.

"Yeah. What I thought. So he says he tried calling her a bunch of times yesterday evening and again this morning but she wasn't answering. When she didn't answer he came over, saw the house was dark and called us. I asked if it was unusual, no light being on. He said she always kept a light on in the boy's bathroom. He's going through the boogeyman stage."

"What time did he call her this morning?"

"He said it was one o'clock. We got the call at two o'clock."

I'm not clear on why a detective was dispatched when there was so little proof that anyone was missing. Someone had to call Sheriff Gray and that means they knew the missing boy was the sheriff's relative. Doesn't really matter now. We're here. But still, one o'clock in the morning was a strange time for Parker to be calling the house with a four-year-old who was probably asleep. "Did he say what he was calling about?"

"I didn't ask. Parker was blank, Megan. He wasn't mad at us or yelling or crying. Said he gave her the house key when he moved out. He was just waiting in his truck when we got here. He hadn't called anyone, knocked on the door, or checked the windows or doors. I knocked on the door and rang the doorbell a couple times. No response. I found the front door unlocked. Parker said he hadn't gone inside. I didn't see him call anyone. But I saw him texting."

If it was me, I'd be calling anyone and everyone I knew to see where my wife and son were. Who was he texting at two in the morning when everyone's asleep? I have to remind myself every person handles stress differently. I also remind myself these are the sheriff's relatives.

"What have you done so far, Paco?"

"Sonny did another perimeter while I went inside. Sonny said it was all secure outside. He took the downstairs and I took the up. Nothing unusual. The kid's bed is rumpled but the wife's bed is just turned down. As far as I can tell, they were going to bed."

"Anything else?"

Paco turns so that Parker can't see his face. "When we came out of the house, Mr. Parker was in the garage, looking in the trunk of his wife's car. He said he forgot he had the garage door opener on his keys. He said he was seeing if she had any bags packed in the trunk."

"Maybe she got a call. Someone in the family is sick. Someone came to pick her up." I say it but I don't believe it myself. "Did you check with the neighbors?"

"Everyone's asleep. I noticed a few outside cameras but no one answered their door. Oh, yeah: the door from the mudroom to the garage was unlocked."

"Did he go through the house with you after you checked it?"

"No. I don't know how long he was in the garage. Or if he'd been in the house before we got here."

"Your impression?" I ask Paco.

I have to look up at him to ask. Paco's over six feet tall, lean, hard looking like he can chew nails and spit out bullets. His marine-cut hair is gray but he's always been the epitome of a police officer. Now he looks every bit of his sixty-plus years. His expression is one of concern and disgust and compassion when he says, "Megan, he's a lying piece of shit. I didn't see any blood or anything broken like they'd been fighting, but something sure smells here."

"He never called anyone while you were with him?" Ronnie asks.

"He might have, but like I said, I only saw him texting before me and Sonny went inside to check the house."

"Anything else I should know, Paco?"

"I made a rookie mistake and walked across the grass instead of the concrete driveway to get to the front door. Probably a good thing I did because I noticed shoe prints in the dew on the grass that weren't mine. They lead to the house and not away. They didn't look like they'd been there long. Might be his. Maybe not. And, like I said, the towels in her bathroom were still damp. She hasn't been gone long."

Luckily for Paco, I specialize in lying pieces of shit. "Ronnie, let's do our own walk-through."

SIX

She hears the heavy pad of something outside the tent. Then the ripping of nylon, the clatter of containers being knocked around. She can smell the damp earth and something else. Something animal. Sharp claws slice down the side of her tent, the dank animal smell of the beast is inside, its moist breath on her face, the damp nose against her flesh. It's found her. She'll be torn apart. It roars next to her face and suddenly she's in a wooden boat on the bay. Bennie is with her. He's trying to tell her something. Something about the boat. She feels something in the boat. Water. It's leaking. It's sinking. She can't remember if she can swim but she doesn't see land, anywhere to swim to. She can float, but what about Bennie? He'll be frightened. He's afraid of the water. She looks for him and sees his face under the water. She can't reach him. His mouth is moving, his eyes wide and pleading with her to save him, and...

Marlena wakes with a scream frozen in her throat and tries to reach the surface of the lake. She's not in the lake. She's on land. Somewhere. Her head is pounding; her mouth is dry. Her heart is racing. She was dreaming about the bear. When she was ten years old, she was on a camping trip. A bear came into the camp that night, drawn by a bag of potato chips someone had foolishly left out by the fire. The bear tore open the tent they stored provisions in and she had run to the lake. She hasn't dreamed about the bear since she was a teenager. But now thinks she can still smell the animal. In reality the bear didn't touch her tent, but in the nightmare she always dies. And then the dream turned into a true nightmare of water, a boat, Bennie drowning. The water is dangerous.

Bennie! Panic rises like gorge in her throat and she feels her heart pound a painful steady beat in her ears.

"Bennie!" She thinks she screams but the word comes out half-formed as if spoken from far away. She pushes herself up onto one elbow and feels the damp and gritty surface that pricks her palm and wrist and forearm. "Bennie," she manages to say with a force driven by panic. She gets to her knees and searches around her for her son. "Bennie! Oh, please, be here."

Her hand brushes something. A small arm. She seizes it and pulls him to her, first feeling for his face and then feeling his chest as it rises and falls gently. Tears flood her eyes and fall on to her little boy. "Thank you, God. Thank you." She pats his shoulder and rocks him gently. "Bennie, wake up. It's Mommy. Wake up."

She kisses the top of his head and smells his hair. She wants to scream. For joy, or fear, or desperation, all of these, but she doesn't. She has her son and he's alive. That's all that matters.

SEVEN

A rule of investigation is everyone is a suspect until they aren't. Also, the last person to see the victim is likely the doer of the bad deed. A soon-to-be ex-spouse is top of the list. Parker doesn't approach us to ask questions or tell us his story. He barely seems to be aware of our presence, and I don't want to talk to him yet, anyway.

A second rule is there has to be a crime or reasonable suspicion for a detective to start an investigation. All we have so far is a squirrely, disenchanted husband and nothing we can pinpoint as being suspicious enough to detain him. That's the law. I don't always pay attention to the nuances of the law but I'm cautious all the same.

We walk down the driveway and I shine a light on the grass. There are two sets of tracks leading to the house. The prints are not good enough to get a size of the shoe or foot that made them, but Paco's description is accurate. We put gloves on and go inside. Paco has left the lights on. We're in a foyer. A wide staircase with maroon carpeting and dark-stained bannisters leads to the upper level. To my left is a well-appointed living room with hardwood floors that would swallow my entire apartment. The furniture obviously didn't come from a thrift shop and probably has expensive brand names. My furniture has names like "desk," "bed," "chair," "stool," and sometimes, when I splurge, Ikea. But I'm not whining. I don't need much.

Ben is watching closely from the street, so Ronnie pushes the door shut and asks me, "Did you notice he's not once asked to speak with us?"

I did, but it may not mean anything. "Right now you need to see everything in here." She's a natural at recalling even the smallest details. I don't have photographic memory, where you can recall pictures or numbers or text in vivid detail. I have eidetic memory, which for a detective is even better. I can recall sounds, smells, and feelings with perfect clarity as if they were in the present.

"This is your investigation, Ronnie. What do you want me to do?"

"This is the first one of these I've done."

There's always a first time. And it stays with you forever.

Ronnie says, "Okay. I'll take the upstairs and you can have this floor. Then we'll switch. If there's a basement or an outbuilding, we'll do it together."

Ronnie goes up the stairs, and I take in my surroundings. A sense of déjà vu makes me lightheaded. The floor plan is laid out like my friend Monique Delmont's house, and I can smell the almond cookies she always baked for me, hear the chimes outside the picture window in the living room, and hear the clack of her high heels on the hardwood floor. It also brings back a memory of a friend who had experienced too much death in her life. I can hear her voice saying, "I had to give them to him. He threatened my daughter and grandson. I can't see you any more, Rylee. This is the last time we'll talk." The *him* she was referring to was the corrupt brother of my biological father. Also law enforcement. Also a killer. He'd somehow found out Monique was helping me hide, paying for my college. I could no longer be Rylee and became Megan Carpenter, detective with Jefferson County Sheriff's Office. My uncle is dead. But Monique was right to cut me out of her life back then. The next time I saw her, she'd been murdered.

Her death reminded me the past is never really past. Evil doesn't go away. It just passes from one person to the next like a mutating virus.

I force the thoughts away and still smell cookies. The living room opens to the kitchen, where stainless steel appliances gleam. Two china plates are in the sink with two juice glasses. Correction: one of the glasses has a cloudy coating. Milk. A baking sheet is on top of the gas range. It holds two huge cookies and shows the brown outline of six more. Pressing a gloved finger on one cookie, I almost expect it to be warm. It isn't but it's soft. It hasn't sat there for more than a day.

The bay windows of the breakfast nook give a view of the backyard. I imagine the family having breakfast or sitting together with the plates on the little table, coffee for the adults, milk for the tyke, who is staring with wide eyes at the warm cookies. His mom tells him he has to finish his milk to get a second cookie. These images of Bennie are so vivid, they remind me of my brother, Hayden. Our mother was gone quite a lot, so I had to be mother, father, and oftentimes a bitch to keep him safe and happy. I raised him more than my mother, but he still idolizes her. Boys do that.

A mudroom is off the kitchen, with a door leading outside and one leading to the garage. This room has a sink, coatrack, boots for mother and son set under a wood bench, a refrigerator—the new computerized type that tells you when you need something—and a large pantry. The refrigerator is fully stocked with groceries plus wine for the mom, juice boxes for the little boy. The pantry is full but neat and orderly. A half-full bag of cat food catches my eye. So far there is no sign of a pet.

The door leading outside is steel and locked with a sturdy dead bolt. The door into the garage is also steel and standing open. Neither door looks damaged or forced. In the garage sits a black Mercedes. I try the car doors. Locked. Parker must have a key if he's able to get in the trunk. The windows aren't tinted dark, so I shine a light around inside. A child's booster seat is in the back. A pair of child-sized sunglasses with fluorescent orange frames are on the booster seat. The car looks like it was recently run through a car wash.

Going back through the house, I check the dining room, a guest room, a full bath, and all the windows. The rooms are undisturbed. The windows are latched and have fully intact screens. A carpeted coat closet neatly tucked away under the staircase holds extra coats, jackets, and rain boots, a woman's and a boy's. Every inch of space is used.

I hear Ronnie on the steps, calling for me. She shows me to a bedroom. There's not much to see. The bed is turned down but not slept in. A tallboy dresser displays framed pictures of the family. One is of Ben Parker and his son. The boy is maybe two years old and holding a too-big baseball glove. Another photo is of the happy couple on their wedding day. Marlena Parker is glowing; Ben is barely smiling. She is almost as tall as her husband. Marlena's pretty, I suppose, but not a beauty. Ben is chunkier, flabbier, not as athletic looking and muscular as he is now.

A clothes valet is next to a standing mirror, with a tan blouse on a hanger and a pair of black slacks folded neatly on the seat. Cork sandals on the floor beneath. Mrs. Parker is not a small woman. The closet door stands open and the inside looks as orderly as everything I've seen so far. She has a four-year-old and still manages to keep a perfect house. I live alone and can't manage that. I console myself with the knowledge she doesn't work, but I know that's not why my house is messy.

"She's a neat freak," I say.

Ronnie takes a small, powerful flashlight from her pocket and shines the beam across the top of the dresser. I immediately see what she's looking at. The top of the dresser has been wiped clean of dust—and fingerprints. Ronnie shines the beam on the front drawers of the dresser and there are clean spots around the antique brass drawer pulls. This isn't a neat freak. Marlena would have used furniture polish on the entire dresser and not just wiped the pulls. Circumstantial, but attention getting.

Ronnie points at a dark square on the wall over the headboard of the bed. A picture is missing. She lies flat on the carpet and shines the light under and toward the head of the bed. I get down and see what she's found. A gold-colored metal frame sitting amidst broken glass. Something is in the frame. I crawl under to get a better look.

"A marriage license." I crawl out and examine the drywall where the frame was. The drywall is marred and concave.

"Come and see the boy's room."

She leads me to a small bedroom where a hand-painted mural of a baseball game covers one wall. In the painting the pitcher is bent over with a look in his eyes of total concentration. Under the picture the name reads: *Félix Hernández, 2005–2019*. I was never a baseball fan—or a fan of any other sport, for that matter—but I recognize the Seattle Mariners pitcher.

Hayden and I were homeschooled when my mother was around, but I ended up teaching him most of the time. I bought/stole some of his favorite action figures: Spider-Man, Batman, and some baseball figures I couldn't care less about. He had Lego blocks too. I remember him sitting on the sofa in his underwear, transfixed by some cartoon, playing with the blocks or figures and eating handfuls of Cheerios. I can smile at the memory now, but back then he was just a nasty little happy boy. I loved him no matter how gross. I just wanted to keep him safe.

The floor in the room is littered with Lego blocks made into unknowable shapes and tennis shoes and action figures of baseball heroes. All Mariners. Two plastic cubes sit on top of the small dresser. One has a signed baseball inside. The other is empty. A few baseball action figures are lined up on top of the dresser; others are on the floor like they've fallen off. Looking under the bed, I see the missing baseball and something long and molded plastic. A toy sword, a lightsaber from the Star Wars collection. On the other side of the bed, against the wall, I spot something and borrow Ronnie's flashlight. It's a black plastic helmet. Darth Vader's. I put the lightsaber back under the bed.

The closet and the bureau shelves are filled with little-boy stuff. On the floor is a vinyl bag covered with images from *Star Wars*.

Ronnie says, "I looked in the medicine cabinet in the mom's bathroom. There's a bottle of prenatal vitamins and a prescription bottle of Promethazine."

I know it's for nausea. Morning sickness. "Pregnant?"

"And there's an inhaler for asthma. The boy's. Filled two weeks ago."

Paco said the dad told him Bennie had asthma, but nothing about the mother being pregnant. How could Ben have missed that part when he talked to Paco and Sonny? My jaw clamps down hard enough to bite back my anger.

I say, "Let's talk to Ben."

EIGHT

Ben Parker is in the front seat of his truck when we leave the house. Ronnie taps on the truck window and he gets out and closes the door. "Ben Parker?" Ronnie asks, and offers her hand. He hesitates but takes it. She says, "I'm Detective Marsh. This is Detective Carpenter."

"Are you going to ask the same questions?"

"I'm afraid so, sir. Detective Carpenter and I work missing person cases," Ronnie says.

He runs a manicured hand through his short, thinning dark hair. He's prematurely balding. "Sorry, detectives. I'm not handling this very well."

"I understand you and your wife are separated and you don't live here. Is that correct?"

"Yes. But we were working things out."

"Were?" She raises an eyebrow.

"I meant to say we are working things out."

"Tell us about your wife, Mr. Parker."

"What do you want to know?"

"Everything. The more you tell us, the better chance we have of finding them. Start with how long you've been married and go from there."

He runs the hand through his hair again and looks away. "We met in college four, no, five years ago. Marlena is a good mother. Ben idolizes her."

I read between the lines. What he's really saying is Marlena isn't a good wife and the boy loves her because she's his mother. Just like my own mother is a horrible mother, but Hayden idolizes her. Ben won't look either of us in the eye. He cuts his eyes to the left again, so a lie is coming.

"Sorry. You asked when we married. We married October fourth, four years ago. We were still in school when she got pregnant with Bennie." He looks at my expression and says, "But we have Bennie and he was worth it. I love Bennie more than you can know."

"I know you do," Ronnie says. "I'm sure he loves you too. You bought him all those baseball figures, am I right?"

He gives a wan smile. She's patient and waits for his answer.

"I took him to a Mariners game in Seattle last year. The kid loved baseball. It cost a fortune but I got him a couple souvenirs."

He's speaking of his son in past tense. I can feel an icy fist forming in my chest and I want to put one in his face. I'm afraid for his family.

"I know this is a scary time for you, Ben. Can I call you Ben?" Ronnie asks, and puts a comforting hand on his arm.

He nods and looks at her anew. Her red hair gleams even in the subdued streetlights. He checks out her designer jeans and white blouse, his gaze ending below the neck.

"All we want is to bring your family home. We need your help, Ben. Do you understand?"

He nods again.

"Whose idea was it to name your son Bennie? Yours or your wife's?"

He looks at her curiously. "Both of ours, I guess."

"What name did you have picked out if Bennie had been a girl?" She uses the boy's name when she refers to him. It humanizes Bennie and reminds the father he's talking about a real person.

"I'm sorry. I don't see what that has to do with anything."

"I just want to get a feel for you and your wife. I want to see your family through your eyes, Ben. I can do that, you know. Let me tell you something about me that sounds crazy. I have a gift for reading people. They say the eyes are the doorway to the soul. Have you heard that?"

"I-I think so."

"Humor me, Ben. I'm trying to help you. I'll do whatever it takes to get to the bottom of this. You understand, right?"

"Yes."

"Do you believe me?"

He doesn't answer.

"You don't have to answer. I can tell you believe me. I'd know if you didn't. I can see it in your eyes."

He looks away but she's relentless. "I know it's hard for you to talk right now. I want to make it easy for you. I just want what's best for your son. You're a good man. I can tell. A good father. You love your son unconditionally. I wish I'd had someone like that in my life."

"I love my son. I would never..." His words trail off.

He stops and she waits.

While he's talking to Ronnie, I walk around his truck. The windows are tinted almost black. He starts to turn around, and Ronnie says, "You would never what, Ben?"

"I would never let him out of my sight. I just want to bring him home."

"And your wife. Marlena. You want to bring her home too. She's Bennie's mother and he loves her very much. But Bennie is the one we're worried about. His inhaler is still upstairs."

"Did you find it under the edge of his mattress? We always keep it there. And one in the master bathroom. He knows how to use it."

I say, "That's good. He sounds like a pretty smart kid." I'll have to go back upstairs and search under the mattress. "Officer Paco has put out alerts to every law enforcement agency in the state.

Those agencies are contacting their hospitals and clinics just like we are."

"Th-that's... good," he stammers.

"And we're canvassing the morgues too."

He doesn't react.

"It's just routine." I'm usually good at reading people.

"I'd like you to come to the Sheriff's Office with us so we can get more information, Ben," Ronnie says.

"If it's what you want."

"It's what *you* want. You want Marlena and Bennie to come home. Do you want to ride with us? We'll bring you back to your truck."

"I'll drive myself. I have to run by my place first. I'll come to the Sheriff's Office as soon as I can."

"Do you think they may be at your place?" I ask.

"I just have to get some things. I won't be long."

"Can I have your key to the Mercedes?" I ask.

He doesn't hesitate and hands me a ring of keys. Two of them are just plastic fobs. One for the truck and one for the car. A Mercedes emblem tells me which to use.

"Why were you looking in your wife's trunk, Ben?" I ask.

"I told your officers."

I wait him out.

"I thought if she went anywhere she would pack a bag. I guess it was silly to look in the trunk. I mean, the car's still here and she's not. She must have gone with someone. I probably shouldn't have called you."

"No, no. You did the right thing. Hopefully we'll hear from her soon and we can all breathe easier." Or we won't. "Why don't you ride with us so we can talk on the way to the station."

"I need to go by my cabin. I was upset when I left and don't know if I locked up or not."

"I can send a car by your cabin to lock it up for you," I suggest.

He stops and stares at me with piercing brown eyes. "Am I a suspect, Detective?"

Yes. "No. If you need to run home, that's fine with me. Keep your phone close. If we need you before you get to the station, we'll call. And if you hear from them, you call us. Understand?"

He nods.

"Do you know how to get to the Sheriff's Office?"

"I can find it."

"One more thing. I know the officers asked this, but I'm going to ask again. Do you have *any* idea where your wife is, where she might go, anyone she could be with?"

"I told them I didn't."

He didn't answer the question. Ronnie puts her hand on his shoulder again and gives him a pitying look. "We'll find them, Ben. We won't stop until we do. Not matter what."

He starts for his truck, and I say, "One other thing, Mr. Parker. Does your wife have any medical conditions we should know about?"

"I forgot to tell the officers she's pregnant."

NINE

We follow Ben Parker out of the subdivision. The guard is still at his post and waves.

I turn to wave. "I wish we'd both driven. I'd like to tail Parker and see where he goes."

"Do you think we should? He's a jerk."

"What do you think, Ronnie?" I'm still in teaching mode.

"I don't think he'll do a runner. He's headed in the right direction to be going home. It's too early to make him feel defensive. Let's see how this plays out."

"Your call."

She turns toward the Sheriff's Office. I call Tony to fill him in. Payback for my wake-up call. He sounds alert when he answers. It's just after four o'clock.

"Megan, please tell me you have something. My wife is on tenterhooks. I've kept her from calling her sister but she won't wait long."

"You should contact your sister-in-law, Tony. This kind of news will come better from family. We can't get much help from the husband. We don't know how long she's been gone, if she's actually missing or just having a tiff with her husband. Her mother may have a better idea what's going on and it may be nothing to worry about." I don't really believe there's nothing to worry about. My gut is screaming to get my attention. Sheriff Gray's an uncle-in-law to Marlena and a granduncle to Bennie. He's also a cop. He knows what it means if Marlena and Bennie aren't found soon.

"Okay. But you won't get much help there. Helen and I don't talk much. Heck, we're not even on the same planet. I can't tell you the last time she and Ellen talked. I doubt Helen's seen her daughter and grandson for a while. From what Helen tells me there's bad blood between her and Ben Parker. Of course I could be wrong."

Helen must be Tony's sister-in-law. I've never heard her name. Ellen is Tony's wife. She's a nice lady. Bakes brownies and muffins for him to bring to work. Some of them make it to the office. Some are sacrificed on the altar of appetite. I think I remember Helen and Ellen are twins. Or their parents had a mean streak. I've met Tony's wife and have had dinner at their house. But Tony keeps Ellen away from the office and out of the police business part of his life. We're alike in that. I keep my business to myself and have only recently shared my work with my brother, Hayden, and my boyfriend, Dan.

We met during a missing person case in Snow Creek that turned into a multiple murder case. I was interviewing neighbors and Dan had a cabin just down the road from the missing person. He took a shine to me and asked me out, but I wasn't in a good place at the time to even consider a relationship. Maybe a hit-and-run type but I had a feeling then that if I went out with Dan it would turn into more. I share very little with Dan and he doesn't pry unless I bring something up. But during the last murder case, one that involved a dear friend of mine, we were both taken prisoner, drugged, and threatened with watching each other be skinned alive before being killed. Dan was drugged more than I was so he hadn't heard all of her reasons for punishing me but he had to have heard something. Of course he claims he doesn't remember. I know he's faking it for me. That case was when I realized how deep my feelings for this man had become. I never thought I could admit it, but he's my first true love. I'd do anything for him, as I know he would do for me. That doesn't mean I'm by any means ready for him to pop the question. I'd rather face an armed gunman than deal with those scary feelings. What I've done in the past and what I do now would be a deal-breaker and I couldn't do that to him. I couldn't put his life in danger again, or cause him pain even if it meant my going away. Running.

The only people that know about my past—and they know very little—are Hayden, Ronnie, and Sheriff Gray. And my therapist, Karen Albright, and she's bound by confidentiality. But even she doesn't know everything. My dear friend, Monique Delmont, knew more and to punish me she was killed.

I don't ask what happened between Tony and Helen. It's not my business. Tony is my boss and my friend. One of a few that are left.

"Tell Ellen we're going to find them. I promise." I probably shouldn't promise, but he needs something to hang on to as much as anyone. "And there's something else, Tony. Does Ellen know Marlena is pregnant?"

"How do you know that?"

"According to Ben Parker, she's a couple of months pregnant. We just found out."

Tony sounds serious. "It's odd Parker wouldn't tell Dispatch or the officers that Marlena is pregnant. Maybe he's so upset he forgot to tell them. Or maybe no one asked. You know how some witnesses or victims can be."

I say, "Tony, we found prenatal vitamins in her medicine cabinet and a medication for nausea. Ben didn't tell us she was pregnant until we confronted him with it."

"Keep me posted. I'll call Helen. I wish I could help more. You'd think with Port Ludlow being so close I'd know more about my in-laws. My fault."

"You know better than that, Tony."

Tony has been good to me. I owe him more than I can ever repay. If anything has happened to his niece and grandnephew I'll make someone pay. Revenge is part of my DNA. I know how bad that sounds, and I'm trying hard to change that part of my life. I've always believed evil should be punished, and the only way to do that is to become evil. But living here, being a cop, having friends who care about me, a real boyfriend, and especially now that Hayden is close and I have family, I must change.

"Megan, thanks for coming in on this."

"Do I get overtime?"

He laughs and the line goes dead.

Ronnie glances at me. "I was thinking: maybe you should interview him when he comes in."

"We'll both do it. This is your case... unless you want me to take it."

"It's Sheriff Gray's family, Megan. I want you to take lead. I'll mess up."

"Okay. As lead investigator, I want you to do the questioning."

"Me?"

"I'll be watching on the monitor. He's not under arrest, so you don't have to worry about reading him his Miranda rights."

"You forget, I grew up with attorneys, Megan."

She's quiet until we pull into the Sheriff's Office parking lot.

I say, "There's nothing to be nervous about. I'll be watching and listening the entire time."

"Any other words of wisdom?"

"He's the one."

We go into the station to get ready. I'm sure Ben is doing the same.

TEN

Sheriff Gray has managed to get the county commissioners to loosen their death grip on our budget. Cameras and recording devices are installed in the interview room and on the outside entrances. Ronnie is meticulously checking and adjusting the equipment by having me sit in the interview room. I'll have her erase the recording after we're done here. I don't like being filmed.

Ronnie's finally done playing film director and sits across from me. I've put out Attempt to Locate bulletins to every law enforcement agency in Washington State, Oregon, and California. If anyone has any information on the missing mother and son, we'll hear about it. To be safe we've issued an Amber Alert on Bennie. If Marlena has legally taken him somewhere I'll apologize when I see her.

Mindy Newsom is working with two of our crime scene officers, going over every inch of the Parker house, Marlena's vehicle, and the surroundings. There's not much else we can do but interview the husband and then go back and interview all the neighbors. Ronnie was right about something she told Ben Parker: we won't quit until Marlena and Bennie are home.

"We need to get his fingerprints and a DNA sample before he leaves, Ronnie."

"I've got it taken care of." She fiddles with the camera. "I know you don't think we need to go to this trouble, but if he confesses to something, we'll have it recorded."

"Makes sense," I say. "Can I make a suggestion?"

"Did I do something wrong?"

"Let me ask you a question first."

She gives me those baby-blue eyes and I almost don't bring this up. But if we're going to this trouble to see his face, we should actually see his face. I say, "Are you sure you want to sit across from him? It might block the camera view." I always sit beside them. Close is better.

"I did some research on interviewing techniques."

Of course you did.

"According to a couple of them, like the Reid technique, I'm supposed to sit beside him, make him turn and face me and pin him in. There are lawyers who specialize in tearing that type of interview apart in court, saying you coerced or intimidated their client and they would admit to anything. I don't want to take the chance. And I don't want to get just part of his face. I'll make sure he's looking into the camera."

She's got me there. "Good thinking." *But I'll still do it my way when I'm in charge. The Megan technique.*

The buzzer for the lobby door sounds. He's here.

I answer the door and bring Ben to the interview room. Ronnie has pulled her chair out of the room, leaving him only one place to sit. I ask, "Would you like something to drink? Water? Coffee?"

"Some coffee would be nice. Cream and sugar, please."

"I'll find Ronnie," I say, and motion toward the lone chair. It's her show. She can be the waitress. I shut the door behind me and go to the little office where all the monitors are recording His Highness.

"He wants coffee..."

"With cream and sugar," Ronnie finishes for me. "The recorder is running. You'll come save me if I mess up?"

I'll superglue the door shut. I say, "I'll be right here if you need anything."

A minute later I see Ronnie enter the interview room with two ceramic mugs of coffee and a plastic bottle of water held against her chest under one arm. She says, "Can you help me?"

He gets up and takes the bottle of water. Fingerprints. DNA. Smart girl. "Thanks," she says. He smiles. She puts the coffee on the table. His eyes follow her as she shuts the door and adjusts her formfitting top. She's taken the jacket off between here and getting the coffee. If this is coercion, it's working. The smile is still frozen on his face.

"Mr. Parker... Ben... how should we begin?"

He looks surprised by her question. "Well..."

"You have all the answers, Ben. Just talk to me. Then I'll ask questions."

"What do you want me to say?"

"Whatever comes to mind. There are no right or wrong things to say."

"Well..." He is studying the tabletop.

"Okay. I'll start with some easy questions." She takes a notebook out. "What is your name?"

"Ben. Ben Parker."

She takes him through simple questions and writes the answers down. Date of birth, place of birth, height, weight, place of employment, how long there, home address... and then she throws in a blood type question. He is O negative.

"How about that? I'm O negative too."

She pushes the bottle of water closer to him and says, "That's for you. When I have to answer questions, it always makes me nervous. Water helps."

"Me too," he says, and smiles at this as if they've just discovered they both like rough sex. I could get to hate this guy. I wonder if Sheriff Gray has met him. If he has I'll bet he hates Ben's guts.

She closes the notebook and pushes it to the side. "I'm

recording this and taking notes so I don't get something mixed up. That's okay, isn't it?"

"Why are you recording this?" He's shifted in his chair as if he's going to get up.

"Two reasons. I might need to watch this later to see if I missed something important. Secondly, I know you don't have anything to hide, so you won't object to me doing this. It will help your family."

"Oh. Okay, I guess. I just want to bring them home."

"How long have you and Marlena been married?"

"Almost five years."

"Where did you meet?"

"We started dating in college."

"Washington State, right?"

"How did you know?"

"You look like a Cougars fan. Did you play baseball in college?"

He's not smiling. "I didn't make the team. The coach said I didn't have the attitude for it."

"Was he right?"

"The coach didn't like me and I didn't like him."

"Why is that?"

"He had a thing against rich kids. My father has big bucks. The coach was always taking jibes at me about it. I didn't even want to try out, but my father insisted. I just didn't measure up, I guess."

"I know the feeling. My dad is a big-shot lawyer. He wanted me to go to Yale like my older sister. I'm not Ivy League material. The black sheep."

Ben nods. "I guess that's what we are. Black sheep."

Ronnie reaches across the table and bumps knuckles with him and they both do that thing I absolutely hate. Make like their hands blow up. I cringe.

"Did you finish college after you got married?"

"I finished but it took a while. When Marlena got pregnant I did the right thing. I mean, I loved her, too, but with a wife and a baby on the way, I had to take on responsibilities. My dad gave us the house Marlena lived in. He was blown away with little Ben."

"I hear you. My sister will never have kids. Or a husband. She works for the family law firm and she's married to the job. She still lives at home. I'm making my own way. I don't owe him anything. But I know he wants little Marshes running around. Not because he likes kids necessarily, but he wants an heir to the throne."

I'm listening to Ronnie and hearing things she's never told me before. I know she resented her father bullying her to go to law school and he disapproved of her becoming a cop, but this makes me sad. She told me when he found out she was attending the police academy, he said, "The Marshes aren't that type of people." She may be lying about some of this to get close to Ben, but I don't think so. I guess I didn't realize how large the rift was between her and her father. In any case, Ben is buying it.

She asks questions about Bennie: what he likes to eat; if he goes to preschool; what his favorite place to go is; what Ben does with him for fun; if he's easy to raise; if he has a temper; and other things to test the dad's knowledge of the boy. He fails the test. He has very little knowledge of what Bennie likes, except for baseball and Darth Vader and his mother. He doesn't know Bennie's favorite place outside of the baseball stadium he took him to. He doesn't know his favorite food. He says he gave him piggyback rides sometimes and Bennie enjoyed it. He may as well be talking about a stray dog.

"Does Bennie like his grandmother?"

"Helen. Yeah, he liked her okay. Marlena took him over there sometimes but the kid always came home with a bad attitude. Marlena noticed it too and quit taking him so much."

With each past tense response he gives about his missing family my skin crawls. Ronnie waits for him to say more but he is finished. By the look on his face, there is no love for his wife's family. She changes the subject.

"I saw a Darth Vader helmet and lightsaber in Bennie's room. I'll bet he drives you crazy."

Ben's smile is genuine now. "I gave him those for Christmas. He would run around the house imitating Darth Vader's voice." He is silent for a moment and says almost emotionally, "I wish he would drive me crazy right now. I would do anything to bring him home."

I think about what he's said. He doesn't show feelings toward his wife. And he's still referring to his son in the past tense. Things like "He liked her okay" and not "He likes her okay." In my investigation class at the academy I learned about interviewees who would dehumanize the person or the victim by not using their name. It's also true of using past tense. That's a double denial that they've done anything wrong. This is especially true in a close relationship. I'm convinced he genuinely loves his son and I'm also convinced he has contempt for his wife, which may be jealousy over the fact his son idolizes her. I'll have to check with Helen to see if any of what Ben has told us is true. And to ask if there's a divorce in the works. There are many reasons for a man wanting to be rid of his wife and children: money, sex, freedom. I'm sure men would add boredom to the list. I won't rule out other suspects just yet, but my gut says Ben's the guy, the reason his wife and son are missing, the dangerous one no matter how preppy he acts. The big red flag for me was Ben forgetting to tell the police his wife is pregnant. Paco swore he asked him about any medical conditions.

The phone rings. It's my forensic specialist, Mindy.

ELEVEN

"Megan, I've got nothing that can help you. There are some kid's drawings stuck to the refrigerator door. Pretty scary colorings if a four-year-old made them."

"I remember the crayon drawings." One was of a house and a big green creature with a long tail towering over it, mouth open, showing sharp teeth. It was a child's depiction of Godzilla. I didn't see any other items in the kid's room indicating he likes monsters. Another was of a house on fire with a little face peering out of an upstairs window. No flowers in the yard. No other people. If this is what the kid feels his life is like, he's in a living hell.

"I know what you're thinking, Megan. But there is a drawing on top of the refrigerator. This one depicts a woman and a child standing in front of the house and they are smiling. No man in any of them."

Unless you count the monster. "Mindy, can you check something before you leave the house? Parker said his son has Darth Vader pajamas. He had the shirt silk-screened and it reads: 'Bennie, I am your father.' Have you run across anything like that?"

I hear her talk to the other crime scene techs and ask about the pajamas. "We haven't run across them but I'll look again."

"I might need you to meet me in a little bit. How close are you to being done there?"

"Thirty minutes to an hour. I found a nanny cam in the boy's room but no recording mechanism. It might be Bluetooth connected to a laptop, but there's no laptop here. I haven't found a cell phone, either. The house has an alarm system but it isn't armed."

"What about the doorbell?"

"I found that, too, but again no recording device."

"Nothing?" *Crap.* "I'll call you back with the address when I'm headed out." I won't call her until I've had a chance to go through Parker's cabin on my own.

Ronnie comes in and brings coffee. She says, "It's like talking to a wall. I take it back: a wall doesn't undress you with its eyes."

"Do you think you can keep him busy for thirty minutes?" I get up and put on my blazer.

"You going somewhere?" This is what she says, but I hear *Do I have to do this?*

The look I give her tells her where I'm going. To her credit, all she says is, "Be careful, Megan. I'll call if he leaves."

"Ask him to come back tomorrow. See if you can find out what phone carrier he uses so we can get a subpoena for the records. Have him show you the calls he made to Marlena. See what else is on his phone if you have time. And find out the family doctor's name." I give her my coffee.

TWELVE

Ben Parker's cabin is in a secluded stretch of waterfront property along Port Ludlow Bay. The GPS on my phone shows the address to be surrounded by a forest. The GPS is correct. I turn onto a hardpack drive that winds through the trees. A new growth of pine trees leads off to the east, and through the pines I can see the moon's reflection on the water of Port Ludlow Bay. The history of Port Ludlow was featured last year in the Port Townsend newspaper along with a pictorial history of the timber trade. Port Ludlow is now a bedroom community for the wealthy, but in the late 1800s it was a company-owned timber town housing sixty or so workers and their families. When I read the article I'd wondered what life had been like for those families. Community life where they shared experiences, both good and bad, and all had a common goal of having a better life but most had settled for survival. The world hasn't changed much. The poor still depend on the rich.

I round a bend and the back of Parker's cabin comes into view. Milled cedar with a Shaker roof. A deck surrounds the cabin with a view across the sound to Whidbey Island.

No other vehicles are parked at the cabin. I knock on the back door, hoping he doesn't have a killer dog. Alarm stickers and warnings are strategically posted on windows and the door to deter would-be burglars. For most people living in the boondocks, alarms are for show and doors are sometimes left unlocked. This one is no different. I enter, shine my flashlight inside, and announce, "Police officer." There's no answer or audible alarm and nothing bites me or licks me. The alarm pad near the door shows it is disarmed. I begin my walk-through, not stealthily but like I have every reason for being there investigating a possible crime, like a burglary in progress.

The living room is spacious and messy, guy messy, with clothes thrown around on the furniture, pizza boxes on tables, empty and half-empty whiskey and beer bottles. A couple of ten-pound dumbbells are on the floor by the sofa. He can relax and lift weights at the same time. He's obviously lived here for more than the week he said he's been here. My place isn't as dirty as this and I'm a slob.

Just off the kitchen is a small office with a floor-to-ceiling glass wall overlooking Port Ludlow Bay. The office is sparsely furnished and doesn't show any signs of use. No computer. And that begs the question: Who doesn't own a laptop in this day and age? Apparently Ben. Or maybe it's why he had to come here before coming to the station. A cable modem is lit up. He has Internet.

The front room has a breathtaking view of the full moon reflecting on the bay. By the door leading out to a large deck are two rolled-up sleeping bags. The large one is camouflage colored. The other is small enough for a child and imprinted with *Star Wars* stuff. I'm about to examine the smaller sleeping bag when headlights wash over the room. I quickly unlock the front door and then go out the door I came in and onto the rear deck, where bright headlights blind me. Tires crunch over gravel and the vehicle pulls up next to my car. Ronnie hasn't called so I prepare to lie to Ben and hold out my badge and draw my weapon. The best defense is a good offense.

The headlights go off and powerful flashlights come on and blind me. A voice yells, "Freeze!" Another yells, "Drop the gun." I want to ask which one I should do first, freeze or drop the gun, but I'm already on thin ice.

My gun goes back in my shoulder holster and I call out, "I'm Detective Carpenter, Jefferson County Sheriff's Office." I hear chuckling. The flashlights go off and Paco and Sonny approach me. Assholes for sure, but my kind.

"What are you doing in there?" Paco asks.

"What are *you* doing here?" I ask him.

"This is in our patrol area."

"Did you get an alarm?"

"No. You?" Sonny asks.

I improvise. "I was checking to see if our missing people made their way here. I found the doors unlocked and no one answered. It looks like a tornado hit the place or a bachelor lives here." It's not that messy inside, but it might be when I'm done looking around.

Paco says, "Yeah, that's why we're here too. I guess you didn't have time to look all through the house to be sure no one was in there?"

I say, "If you watch the front and back I'll finish checking the house."

"Good idea," Paco says. "I'll take the front." He whispers to me. "You should be more careful. It might not have been us."

"I don't know what you mean, Officer Paco." No need for stealth now so I turn on the lights. On the fireplace mantel there are at least a dozen framed photos of Ben. Ben playing baseball, Ben bowling, Ben beside a suspended sailfish. Ben piloting a boat. Ben in the cockpit of a plane. No pictures of Marlena or Bennie. None of older people, maybe parents. This is a shrine to Ben. Down a short hallway I find three bedrooms, a laundry room, and two full baths. One bedroom holds several racing bicycles and sundry biking gear. On a shelf are two framed photos of Ben. In each he's posing in biking outfits that look sprayed on. Again nothing of his family. The bathroom is unused.

The next bedroom has a California king bed against one wall facing a huge picture window looking over the bay. The ceiling is covered with mirrored tiles. I can see the moonlight shimmering on the waters of the bay and it looks dizzying from this perspective.

Suddenly a dark shape appears in the mirror and my heart jumps into my throat. I hear growling coming from outside the window. I reach for my gun and see a light illuminate the thing's face. Paco. I'm going to kill him when we leave. I try to ignore him but I can hear him laughing as he walks away.

The bed has been stripped, sheets and pillow covers missing. On the floor beside the bed are several unopened packets of condoms. The floor is carpeted. I watch where I step. The closet is open and devoid of hanging clothes except for two sport coats and coordinating slacks. The back of the closet is wall-to-wall shelving. On one shelf are dozens of pairs of blue jeans, folded knit shirts, bikini undies, and socks. The remainder of the shelves are lined with shoes of all kinds, some still in boxes. Maybe fifty pairs. There's no room to hide a body.

The en-suite bath is next. Droplets of water are on the glass wall of the walk-in shower. The bathroom smells of strong disinfectant and sweet cologne. Wet bath towels and a pair of blue jeans are wadded up on the shower floor. I check the jean pockets and find a matchbook. The cover says it's from a place called Gentleman's Club. Mud is caked around the hems of the legs. Wood chips are stuck to the denim. I use the matchbook to scrape some of the mud and chips on to another latex glove, roll this up, and put it in my pocket. The medicine cabinet holds men's hair products. Rogaine, some kind of dark-colored spray-on hair, hair gel. Also there is a tube of testosterone cream and one of toothpaste—I hope he doesn't get these mixed up. There's a prescription bottle for Viagra with two tablets left. I should call Ronnie and warn her, but she can take care of herself. The only real medicine I find is ibuprofen. There's no inhaler for the boy. Nothing for a pregnant woman, like vitamins.

I knew a guy in college, a wrestling jock, who took testosterone. He claimed it gave him extra stamina and strength. I looked testosterone up. Some of the side effects are enlarged breasts and prostate issues. I could use the enlarged breasts but I'm not that desperate. I have to wonder if Ben added the Viagra to the mix to enhance his stamina. The first bedroom I come to answers that question.

This room isn't being used as a bedroom. What gives it away is the trapeze bar hanging from the ceiling, leather whips, leather face masks, leather chaps, and an assortment of sex toys spread across what were probably once bookshelves. More adult toys are scattered around the room. One entire wall is a mirror. A massage table sits in the middle of the room. In the closet are several pairs of spike high heels and a pair of patent leather shoes with a ribbon bow on top. All manner of women's wear ranging from glittery evening gowns to a pleated plaid schoolgirl skirt hang like a menagerie of sexual fetishes. The clothing is all the same size: petite. The footwear is size six. Not Ben's size, so not his. Not his wife's, either.

I don't want to touch anything. As it is, I'll have to burn my shoes.

There's nothing here except for signs of illness and possible STDs. I go to the next room. Another bedroom. Messy like the rest of the place, but it contains a bed, dresser, lamps, side tables, and a closet. The bed looks like there's been a skirmish of warring tribes. There's no bed for his son. There's no spare inhaler for Bennie in this bathroom. Just more testosterone cream, lubricating gel, and a stack of magazines. Porn, of course. The toilet seat is up and his aim must be bad. When Hayden and I were younger, I would have to clean up the bathroom after he'd been in there. Why don't guys flush? Why leave the lid up? Why do guys have to pee on the floor around the toilet? Bad aim? Bad attitude?

Back in the front room a metal stairway winds its way down. As I near the bottom I see this is a game room with a walkout to a tiny deck. On the deck is a small glass-top table and two wrought-iron chairs facing the bay. Something brushes my leg. I jump and draw my gun, and over the blood rushing in my ears I hear a soft purring. My flashlight reveals an orange-and-tan long-hair cat wrapping itself around my leg. It's obese to the point it looks like a float in a Macy's Day Parade. "Hi, kitty," I say softly. "Is Bennie down here?" Something gleams in the fur around the cat's neck. A diamond-studded collar with a tag reading *Princess*.

I say to the cat, "Princess, are you being held as a sex slave?" No answer. The flashlight beam slides over a home theater system with comfortable seating and a half-wall flat screen with a projector on a stand. Under the stand are an assortment of Blu-ray discs. All porno. I hope Bennie has never stayed the night here. I hope he hasn't breathed the air in here. I hope he's okay.

A closet contains two quilted jackets and knit scarfs. One is Ben's size. The other is a small woman's. According to the description on Marlena Parker's driver's license, this one would never fit her, nor would the stuff in the upstairs playroom. This room is fairly orderly, considering the rest of the place. Maybe it's the appetizer and the main course is upstairs.

My phone vibrates in my pocket and I go back upstairs quickly, knock on the front window. and motion Paco to come to the kitchen door. Headlights are coming. I push the door wide open as Ben Parker pulls his truck behind the sheriff's car and gets out. Ben's expression is a mix of surprise and anger. And something else, too. Fear? Worry?

Anyone else would ask if something was wrong. He asks angrily, "What the hell is going on?" His next question gives away the reason for his fear: "How long have you been here?"

Sonny approaches him. "Mr. Parker, please stay back. We were patrolling and found your door open. I was about to call you, sir." God bless you, Sonny.

Parker is quiet. He's wondering if he left anything incriminating inside. He's worried I found his playroom and sex toys. "I must not have shut the door good when I left to come to your office. Thanks, but I'll be okay."

He keeps eyeing me as he says this. I should let it go and thank my lucky stars I was not caught red-handed. "It's no problem at all, Ben. I heard the officers' call about the open door and I thought maybe your wife and son had made their way here."

He's caught by surprise at my semi-confession and for a

moment he's at a loss for words.

"I called out for them but I didn't get an answer. Have they been here since the separation?"

The question is simple. The answer should be as simple.

"They haven't been here recently, but we stayed here a few times. Why do you ask?"

"I wondered if they knew how to get here?"

He says nothing.

"It's just that it's such a nice place. Why would you ever live in Baker Heights?"

"Marlena's idea. She didn't like being 'out in the woods,' as she called it."

"How long has this place been in your family?" I know he has to find it strange we're making small talk, me in his doorway, him standing outside by an officer. But he's recovered from the surprise and seems chatty. I've seen this before when I have someone on the hook and they feel they have to talk their way out.

"I'm not sure. My family has owned the property since I was little. My father had the original cabin replaced with this one."

"You must be very happy here."

"I can't complain."

No, you can't. You have a lovely lair. "Are you sure you don't want us to stick around and check to see if anything's missing?"

"I'm sure everything is fine."

Paco says, "Mr. Parker, both your front and back doors were unlocked. You should let us go inside with you to check things out."

"Not necessary," he says, and glares at Paco. "Now, if you don't mind, I'm very tired and I'm supposed to meet Detective Marsh again this morning."

"Of course. We'll get out of your hair, Ben." I don't ask if he's agreed to take a polygraph. He would agree to sell a kidney to shut Ronnie up. Been there.

"Thank you, Detective Carpenter," he says.

No. Thank you. Pervert.

THIRTEEN

When I return to the office I give Ronnie the items I've collected from the cabin, the matchbook, the mud and wood chips, and I tell her of the sex playground and the women's clothing. I fill Ronnie in on my activities, and she shivers.

I ask, "How did it go with Ben?"

"He agreed to another interview when we've all had some rest. The sheriff said K-9 and officers have swept the entire area and will do another door-to-door. It's hard to search when you have no idea where to start."

I say, "It's Tony's family so they will keep at it until he tells them to stop. What about the polygraph?"

"He said he'll take it, but I don't want lack of sleep to skew the results. He said he would come in around noon."

"That's good. We need some sleep too. Can you take care of the stuff I found?" Meaning the possible evidence I collected without a warrant. She agrees to give it to Marley Yang at the Crime Lab with her name on the request. Marley is short, compact, olive-complected, with a small amount of facial hair he's trying to shape into a goatee. He may think it makes him look more scholarly or attractive, but it's just not going to happen. At one time I thought he was going to ask me out, and that was never going to happen, either. Marley is the supervisor at the Crime Lab, exceptionally good at his job and, after a little pushing on my part, he's Ronnie's boyfriend. At first I thought it would be like mixing oil and water, but they've gone out for a while now. That's good for me, because it gives me an inside source at the Crime Lab.

I look at the time. Too late to call Tony. I'll leave him a note. I say, "Let's go home."

* * *

The first tendrils of morning light shimmer on the horizon when Ronnie drops me off at home. The sky is a deep red, a sure sign a storm is coming. *Red sky at night, sailor's delight. Red sky in morning, sailor's warning.* An omen? Or just a saying? Ben is scheduled for another interview at noon. As Ronnie leaves we agree to meet early.

My keys land on the table inside the door along with my purse. I go into the kitchen and peruse the fridge. There's some pizza and my stomach says it's time for food. But before I open the box, my phone rings.

"Megan. It's Tony."

"Morning, Sheriff. Did you get any sleep?" *Because I didn't.*

"Not a bit. Ellen was on the phone most of the morning with Helen. I would've come out to the scene, but there's nothing I can do that you and Ronnie aren't already doing and I don't want to get in your way."

His unspoken meaning is that he's too close to this. Tony sounds like he's hurting, so I push past my grogginess. "I was afraid to wake you up, but since you called, I'll tell you where we're at. Before I do, can I ask a few questions?"

Tony says, "Fire away."

"How well do you know Ben Parker?"

Sheriff clears his throat. "He's my niece's husband. Helen's son-in-law. I've never met the man but I know of him from Helen via my wife. There are some family dynamics involved, and I'd rather not say anything right now. But the family drama has nothing to do with Ben Parker."

Whatever he doesn't want to talk about is bad enough he stayed up all morning. This isn't an ordinary missing person's case. I knew that from the get-go. And not just because the victims are related to Tony. Tony's a good guy with a big heart. He's taught me about investigating—at least the legal part. But he knows when to look the other way, too. Lady Justice isn't just blindfolded, she's beaten and raped by criminals and attorneys and politicians who allow the unspeakable to happen. Sometimes Lady Justice needs a bodyguard.

"Tell Helen we're interviewing Ben again this afternoon. We haven't turned up anything positive, but we're hopeful. Ronnie did an excellent job with the interview, by the way." Praise where it's needed, but if she messes up I won't hesitate to throw her under the bus.

"Have you slept at all?" he asks me.

A yawn threatens to escape and I cover my mouth at the last second. "I was just getting there, Sheriff. We're starting in again at noon."

"Did you find anything at the house?"

I wonder for a second which house he's talking about. "Not at the scene." I'm not sure how much to tell him about his in-law, Pervert in Wonderland, but I know I'll have to eventually.

He says, "I brought in K-9. We'll search in shifts if needed. Helen is coming to stay with us until this is over."

He says this like a plea for mercy. I haven't met Helen, Ellen Gray's sister, but Tony has gone to great lengths to avoid her the few times she's been in town.

"We're going to ask him to take a polygraph today."

"So he's a suspect?"

"I didn't say that." *The hell I didn't.* "He's just not acting... you know... right. There are some inconsistencies in his story." Like his insistence that he and his wife are patching things up. His playroom tells a different story. But I'm not supposed to know that. Then there's his talk of his family in past tense.

Tony says the thing I don't want to hear. "A reporter called me at home."

"Sheriff, we don't have anything to give them."

"Megan, they may come in handy. More eyes and ears."

I don't like the news media, but he's right. Just not now. And the news media attracts the crazies. They want to take credit for the crime, or they give false information to get attention. We'll need extra manpower to answer the phones and try to sort through the calls. Tony will have to get the expense okayed and that means we'll lose some needed item somewhere else.

"Tony, I want to polygraph Ben and have a chance at a thorough interview before he sees this blasted all over the news. You know how that type of attention messes with an investigation."

"Megan, they brought up the case in Colorado."

I know of the case he's referring to. It led the news for days. A husband strangled his wife and two daughters. The wife was pregnant. The children were three and four years old. He dumped the children in oil drums and dumped the wife's body away from the children. The reason he gave investigators for the murders was he wanted to start a new life with a new woman. I feel a chill run up my spine.

Tony breaks into my thought. "Megan, if you need anything call me. I mean anything. Understand?"

"I do. And I will."

"I'll deal with the media," Tony says. "Maybe they'll have a heart and not put this all over television for a little while. The best I can get you is twenty-four hours."

"Understood." If they hold the information two minutes I'll be surprised. I'm sure one of the officers at the scene has blabbed to the media thinking they were doing me a favor. Some favor.

Tony says, "Megan, you and Ronnie need to get some sleep. I'll put the news media off if I have to threaten to arrest them."

If I get any sleep even twenty-four hours is pushing things, but

I'll take what I can get. We hang up. Right now I need a couple of hours' sleep. I really can't do much until I can get Ben into an interrogation room. And I'm dead on my feet. But the morning plays through my mind like a movie. In my mind I see Ben distancing himself from what's happening and at the same time practically drooling over Ronnie. There are many reasons why I don't like Ben Parker. The similarities to the Colorado case aren't lost on me. But I can't let my feelings distract me from finding Marlena and Bennie.

I kick my boots off but when I lie down, my mind spins like a top. I close my eyes and listen to the thunder in the distance. It sounds closer now, and I try to concentrate on the sound, imagine I'm watching the clouds roiling in the sky, but trying to relax is a joke.

They say if you are working on a problem, your mind will continue to work on it while you sleep. My mind is making connections, finding similarities, adding two and two and coming up with five. There's something I'm missing.

It's time to listen to the tapes. I keep a box of cassette tapes and a tape player in the bottom drawer of my desk at home. The tapes are from sessions I had with Dr. Albright, a psychologist, a smart woman, and a life raft for me when I was twenty and lost in a sea of indecision, anger, and fearing for my life. The tapes have served me well. I don't kid myself the tapes hold all the answers, but they help me make connections and decisions and help me understand. They've pointed me in the right direction several times when working a difficult case. I've listened to these tapes so many times, I know which one is which session and what I talked about, what I discovered about myself and my place in a very dysfunctional family. It's helped me realize there are lots of messed-up people and messed-up families out there and sometimes nothing can be done to help them. That sounds a little defeatist, but I've tried in my own way to limit the impact the evildoers have on society. I've saved lives. I know that. And I was willing to become evil to fight evil. Now I wonder if I made a realistic decision. I wonder if I can change and put it behind me. Live a normal life. But I'm not sure what normal is. I thought I knew, because I wanted that for my brother and was willing to give up any semblance to a normal life to give it to him. I've seen things, done things he must never know about. Has it really helped him in the end? Or did it just create a thick membrane of hurt and misunderstanding between us that I can't seem to claw my way through to reach him? We were so close once. I feel tears threatening and so I distract myself by getting up and going to the desk.

I've thought about having the tapes digitized. I can put them on my personal computer with a strong password. They'd be better protected than the cassettes in a box in a drawer. Dr. Albright assured me they are the only copies. The originals. But I'm loath to part with the physical tapes. I've kept them for so long they are a part of my working mind. Also, after seeing Ronnie's ease with computer manipulation and her hacking ability into systems that should be safe, I have put it off. There are things on the tapes, confessions I've made, that should never be in anyone's hands.

Ben said he met Marlena in college. She became pregnant. He said it as if she had done something to him. He said, "I married her" not "we got married," as if she were not part of it, or he was forced into marriage, which may be what he meant because Bennie was born shortly after. He might have been tempted to run and not take over the role of husband and father, but he stayed. That selfless act wasn't the Ben I'd come to detest. Was it love? Pressure from his rich father? Maybe he liked the idea of being a father. I have to admit, he seems to love his son. But it's very clear he doesn't love his wife.

I find the tape I want, insert it, and push "play." Dr. Albright's soft, kind voice comes from the small speaker. She calls me by a name I no longer use. A name I hope has been forgotten by everyone who knew it.

Dr. Albright: Put me there, Rylee.

Me: Courtney is my mom's real name. I'm not sure what my real name is any more.

I listen to my voice and it sounds so young. From a lifetime ago. I can hear the anger just below the surface, waiting for the catalyst that will cause the rage to erupt. I hear it because I lived it. Some of that anger has been tamped down over the years, but it's still there, not quite hidden.

Me: Courtney is my mom's real name. She hid that from me as well as everything else. Aunt Ginger said my mom was scrunched up in the hospital bed after she delivered me and wouldn't look at me right away, but Mom said she was glad I was a girl. My aunt Ginger told Mom to look at me. She said I was beautiful. My mom wouldn't look. She was afraid to look. Afraid that if she looked, she would see him.

Dr. Albright: "Him"?

My mom was glad she'd had a girl. Was Ben glad he had a boy? My mom was afraid to look at me. Afraid she would see my biological father's features reflected in mine. My aunt Ginger told me my mom was hiding from my bio-dad. She was afraid of him. Afraid for me. It was a lie.

I fast-forward the tape a little.

Me: So much of what happened in my life was orchestrated turmoil. Orchestrated by my mother to cover the tracks of one lie with another lie and another and another. I remember one time when we were watching an episode of Teen Mom *on TV and the girl who'd just had a baby was talking about giving it up for adoption.*

Dr. Albright: Your mom considered giving you up?

Me: Yeah. I guess she did. Of course, Aunt Ginger said it was to protect me from him. Mom pretended to be hidden from him for so long that he didn't know she was pregnant. It was all a lie. While we watched that show, my mom and me, I told her that I could never do that. Never give a baby up like that. She said if it was what was best for the child, it might be what's best for me. She said she knew people who had considered it because it was the only right thing to do.

Ben Parker claimed his wife was having an affair and that was why she was pregnant. Did he want the baby? Did they argue about that? He seemed certain Bennie was his son, but what would he do if he thought this pregnancy wasn't his? Did he want her to have an abortion, give it up? What would she do? Would she leave? Helen didn't know her daughter and grandson were missing until Sheriff Gray told her. Helen was concerned enough to stay with the sheriff and his wife. According to Tony, neither he nor his wife got along with Helen.

Ben, on the other hand, wanted to go to sleep. Answered questions but didn't volunteer anything.

Me: I asked Mom how ditching your kid could ever be right. I mean, they shouldn't have gotten pregnant in the first place. My mom just said mistakes happen sometimes. Sometimes pregnancies are anything but planned.

I switch the tape off and put the recorder back in the desk drawer. Marlena Parker didn't get rid of Bennie when she was in college and the pregnancy was inconvenient. Having been in her house, seeing the cookies and juice boxes, the crayon drawings, I'm sure she loves her son and was a good wife. Ben is a jerk. He was cheating on her. He was projecting his traits on her. Was the rift because of the new pregnancy? Did she know of his transgressions? Did she rebel? If that was the case, maybe she didn't want to be found. I start to select another tape but there is no need. I remember word for word the conversation I had with Dr. Albright. She asked if my life of being on the run seemed normal to my parents. Were there rules? I was seventeen while we were on the run and, knowing what I know now, my answer today would be different. I told her that seeming normal and being normal were at opposite ends of the pole. It was hell on us. I can still see the look on my stepfather's face when it came time to leave, change our names, and go on the run again. I feel his anxiety. See the way his eyes narrowed and sweat collected at his temples and he withdrew a little. He was worried each time that we'd be found.

Dr. Albright also asked how we decided where to go. My answer seemed stupid. Still does to this day. But it kept us alive for a long while. The night before we moved to another place, what my parents called "the switch," was done by filling a glass bowl with the names of towns written on small fortune cookie-sized pieces of paper. Whatever was drawn was the next home for our tiny little club. My mother explained the method as finding security in randomness.

Is that what Marlena Parker was thinking? Of running? How did she decide where to go? Did she need help? If so, why did she have to leave without telling anyone? What was she afraid of? Or who?

FOURTEEN

Two hours of sleep and I couldn't waste any more time. I get up, get dressed, and forego my morning coffee. The case and the news attention push me to get back to work. I can make coffee there. When I arrive at the station, Ronnie is already at her computer. I hear her punishing the keyboard as soon as I come through the door. She looks up, smiles, and goes back to torturing the keys.

"I couldn't sleep either. Coffee is made," Ronnie says.

"Thanks." I rinse my coffee mug out, fill it with black coffee, and take a sip, almost spitting it out. "What did you put in this? Lighter fluid?"

"Is it too strong? I didn't notice."

"Sorry," I say. "It's just right." I sit at my desk where Ronnie has left a stack of printouts along with evidence transfer receipts signed by Ronnie and submitted to Marley Yang. She has requested DNA, soil analysis, and DNA testing for the matchbook, mud, wood chips, and water bottle.

I ask, "Are we on the news?"

"Yes." Ronnie stops typing. "I'm the unnamed source and you're the detective that couldn't be reached for a comment. The reporter asked about the Colorado case. She must think police are like an ant colony and share memory. I told her I couldn't discuss an ongoing case and she should talk to the sheriff. My voicemail has blown up."

I ask, "What was on the news?"

"The usual hype. Mother and son mysteriously disappear. Husband is being questioned by police. Then they got into the Colorado case and tried to make a connection. They showed a picture of the suspect and murder victims from Colorado and then a picture of Ben and Marlena. They must have gotten them from their driver's license photos. And of course they said they tried to reach the detectives on the case but were told no comment."

"Have they talked to Ben?" I ask.

"I don't know. I hope not."

"Did they give names or descriptions, or ask people to contact us? Have we gotten calls from anyone but reporters?" I ask, and she shakes her head. I look at my cell phone and see I've had over a dozen calls that went straight to voicemail. All from two telephone numbers. Probably news media. "Tony said he'll deal with the media. We can't let them distract us from doing our jobs. What else do you have?"

"The matchbook is from the Gentlemen's Club in Port Orchard."

I say sarcastically, "Gentlemen's Club. Huh."

She sits on the edge of my desk until I give her a cautioning look that I hope says, *I'm tired. I'm hungry. Don't mess with me.* She remains seated. Good for her.

"I've got the contact information. Owner. Manager. Even some of the dancers. I thought we might want to talk to them in person."

"Good idea." It's just what I need. A bunch of naked women and slobbering drunks to start off my day.

"Marley said the wood chips are larger than from a chain saw. Some kind of industrial saw. Does that help?"

It doesn't hurt. I indicate the stack of paper and ask, "What have you got here?"

"Funny you should ask."

I hate it when she does that, but I go along. "So what did you find?"

"Ben's father is Cyrus Parker." She waits again, and I want to shake the words out of her. She sees the name means nothing to me. "He's what people in past days called a robber baron."

"He has a police record for robbery?" I know what a robber baron is, I think, but two can play at the stupid remarks game.

"No, Megan. John D. Rockefeller, Andrew Carnegie, J. P. Morgan, Henry Ford..."

"Did they have police records too?" I'm having fun. Now I need coffee.

Ronnie gives an exaggerated sigh. "Robber barons were captains of industry in the late-nineteenth century. They amassed fortunes through ruthlessness and questionable business practices."

Just like every politician, I think. I get up and walk toward the coffeepot. Ronnie follows. I'm not interested in robber barons, but I throw her a crumb. "You mean like Bill Gates or Mark Zuckerberg?"

"More like Jeff Bezos," Ronnie says.

"Who?" The fun continues.

"Never mind. The point I was getting to is Cyrus Parker has his hand in major businesses across the U.S. and beyond. Fishing, auto industry, insurance companies, corporate law firms, and—"

"Ronnie. I got about two hours of sleep. Just tell me, please."

"Okay. Sorry. Among other things, he owns or has owned most of the timberland and sawmills up and down the Washington and Oregon coasts."

"That's good work, Ronnie."

Ronnie says, "I called Ben's phone and left a message for him to come in early. If he got the message he should arrive shortly."

He makes me feel dirty just being around him. After being in his place, I can't bathe enough. "None of what he's said makes any sense. His behavior is way off. Maybe he's a sociopath and can't help being an insensitive prick. But we're on a timer here." Every hour that passes lessens our chances of finding his family alive. Port Ludlow lies within the Olympic Rain Shadow, so it receives half the rainfall of the other Puget Sound communities, but we're still not immune to nasty weather. The thunder last night raised a real threat to the search but fortunately the storm was a dud.

Ronnie says, "I've tried Marlena's phone and it goes to voicemail. Should we send a car to round Ben up, Megan?"

"If he doesn't call soon we'll go find him ourselves."

"I'll try his phone again," she says.

She calls and this time he answers. "Hi, Ronnie."

"Were you coming in to see me today?"

"I'm sorry, Ronnie. I wasn't paying attention to the time. I'll come now."

Ronnie puts the phone down, and I call Tony. "Sheriff, Ben's on his way in. I'm going to ask him to take the polygraph. How soon can we get an operator?"

"I've got an operator on standby."

I disconnect and ask Ronnie, "How did Ben sound?"

"I don't think he's been asleep."

That makes two of us. I slept, but it was full of dream memories from my past, and I woke with a knot of fear in my stomach. In the dream I was much younger, Hayden was a baby, we were in a car, Mom was driving, my stepfather wasn't with us. Mom hadn't met him yet. I didn't know who we were running from, but I was right to be afraid. There are real monsters. And not just under the bed or in the closet.

FIFTEEN

Earlier, Ronnie talked an officer into taking the evidence we'd collected to Marley Yang at the Crime Lab. Now she is gathering data on Ben and Marlena: school records, tax records, utility records, news clippings, and social media among other things. She calls it data mining. I'd done something similar when I was searching for my mother and my biological father. Not as thorough as Ronnie but it worked.

I make another pot of coffee and go over Mindy Newsom's report. According to Mindy, there is a doorbell camera at the Luna Ridge residence but it isn't active. Ben canceled the service two weeks ago. There was no sign of a struggle, nothing broken, no blood, no notes or an appointment calendar. The only thing Mindy thought was strange was the place on the master bedroom wall where a frame had been hung but was missing.

Officers canvassed the neighborhood again, looking for witnesses and outside video devices. Only one house had an operational device and hopefully had a view of the Parkers' house. The officers obtained permission for us to access their video storage archives. Of course, the home directly across from the Parker house had no such device but had a Rottweiler for an alarm system.

Mindy did not find the Darth Vader pajamas Ben described.

She didn't find any evidence Marlena had taken a trip. Several suitcases were in the closet. Bennie's overnight case, the one with Luke Skywalker on it, was still in the closet in his room. Jackets for Marlena and Bennie were in the downstairs closet. No empty hangers. Marlena's keys were hanging up by the kitchen door. Best case, Marlena had left in a hurry. Worst case, she had been taken.

The house had cable and Internet but no computer, cell phone, or recording device were found. Mindy collected the cookie sheet, the plate, the skillet and lid, and sent these to Marley for fingerprints and analysis.

"Have you read this?" I hand Ronnie Mindy's report.

"Yeah. It was on the printer when I came in."

"I saw two sleeping bags at you-know-where." She knows where I'm talking about. "When you have time, can you send pictures of the family to Parks and Recreation with a request to check all the park records for any mention of the Parkers? They don't have to launch a search or anything. Just have them check with the park rangers to see if they've seen the family recently."

"Already done," Ronnie says. "Parker is not in their system. I sent driver's license photos and they'll circulate them but don't expect to find anything. I agree with them. It's a long shot but has to be done."

"Ben told me Marlena doesn't like the outdoors. She's been to the cabin but not recently and didn't even like it there. When he comes in, ask him if they ever went camping and, if so, where. And how long ago."

Parker can easily explain the sleeping bags, but I still want to collect them. I'll need a warrant, but I don't think I have enough to get a warrant for the cabin. Or for Ben's truck. And I can't explain how I knew about the sleeping bags or the mud-encrusted jeans to a judge without admitting to searching his place without the warrant. I could lie. I'm good at that. But Paco and Sonny were there. They've already lied to Ben to cover for me. I don't want them to have to swear to the lie on a warrant. Ben Franklin said it best: "Three can keep a secret, if two of them are dead." But I'm not going to kill Paco's and Sonny's careers. Well, maybe Paco. But if Ben has done what I suspect and is a murderer, I can't chance doing anything to mess with the case. He'll have high-power attorneys and they know all the dirty tricks.

"Megan, I really think you should interview Ben. I don't feel comfortable."

She did fine with him before, but I get it. This went from a missing person case to a possible kidnap case or, worse, a murder case.

She says, "This is too important, Megan. If I mess up, something bad will happen."

I'm supposed to be training her. "You're doing fine." She gives me a look of uncertainty. I give in. "But I'll do the interview with you. I'll give him a break and we can get coffee and talk. Okay with you?"

She lets out a deep breath and I can see her relax.

"Don't even think I don't trust you to do this, Ronnie. You can." Not as good as me, but close.

Just then the front door buzzer goes. It's Saturday. It could only be Ben Parker.

Ronnie starts toward the front door to bring Parker back. I get a sick feeling in the pit of my stomach. We may already be too late. If the news reports of the Colorado case are correct, the wife and two children were dead for several days before the suspect confessed and showed police where he dumped the bodies. What kind of sick asshole could do that to a pregnant woman? To his own children? I remember him doing a press conference on television and he kept repeating he just wanted to *bring them home*. Ben keeps saying that exact thing.

"You ready?" I ask, and she nods. "Good. Now, go get him and we'll skip the water or coffee this time."

Ronnie goes to the front while I refill my coffee. Instead of Ben I hear Sheriff Gray coming in with Ronnie. His sparse hair is sticking out and his shirt is halfway tucked into his jeans. He's wearing flip-flops.

Before I can say anything, he stops me. "I know. I'm not supposed to be here. I just couldn't take another minute of that woman's mouth."

"What woman?" I ask.

"Helen." He gives a theatrical shudder. He's not carrying a grease-stained bag of food, and that worries me.

"Are you okay, Tony?" He has bags under his eyes.

"I'm good. I just need to change clothes. I've got a spare uniform in my office."

"Shoes?"

"Those too."

I find his mug, the one with Bugs Bunny on it. Bugs Bunny is saying, "What's up, Doc?" The mug is a gift from his wife meant to keep his stress down. I fill it with my extra-strong coffee, no cream, no sugar. He shuts the door to his office and I hear drawers being opened and shut, and not quietly. I knock on his door. "Sheriff, I have your coffee."

He cracks the door and reaches a hand out for the mug, takes it inside, and shuts the door again. A short time later he emerges dressed in a starched and ironed khaki uniform, heavy black boots, and a Sam Browne duty belt with weapon, with his hair combed, sort of, and a serious look in his eye. He would look like a badass if he didn't have a white plastic pocket protector from Dell's Auto Towing stuffed with ink pens in his right shirt pocket. I know it's from Dell's because it's written on the white plastic flap that holds it in the pocket.

The front-door buzzer goes again, and Sheriff Gray takes his coffee and heads for his office.

"I'll watch from my office. I don't trust myself around this... this..." His mouth clamps shut, and he goes in his office and closes the door.

SIXTEEN

Ben is dressed for an evening out, neatly shaved, hair slicked back, in tan slacks with a navy-blue knit shirt. The framed photos of himself in his cabin take on a new meaning now. The pictures are a pictorial history of his emergence from chubby-hood to manly muscular-hood. I can't deny he's a good-looking guy. A head turner. He smells nice. And he's smiling. Mostly at Ronnie. Perhaps imagining her in his playroom. Gross! But does he look like a distressed husband and father? Not by any stretch of the imagination.

I disabuse him of the notion we are at his Gentlemen's Club when I show him into the sparsely furnished interrogation room.

"Have a seat there." I indicate the seat in the corner against the wall; then I sit close beside him, hemming him in. Ronnie sits by the door, leaving no easy exit. He sits but his eyes blaze momentarily. He doesn't like being talked to like that by anyone. Especially a woman. He's bigger than I am. Bigger than Ronnie. He may be a killer, but so am I. I see sweat forming on his upper lip and I've not even asked a question yet.

"This is being videotaped," I say. He can refuse to be filmed but he says nothing, just casts a sideways look toward Ronnie. I say, "Look at me, Mr. Parker." His attention turns toward me. He smiles. It looks put on. He's trying for charm. I see it as smarmy. The smile fades when I say, "Mr. Parker, we still have no word on your wife and son in case you were wondering."

"I get it, Megan."

"It's Detective Carpenter," I correct, putting a stop to the familiarity. I'm in charge. "I'm not being unfriendly, Mr. Parker. I'm the one who is going to find your wife and son." I stop short of saying "and bring them home." The vibe I get from this guy is that coming home isn't possible. I push the feeling aside. I need to proceed as if they are alive and well and lost or confined. I have personal experience. My biological father kidnapped and chained me up in an abandoned water pumping station. My own father was going to rape, torture, and murder me. Why should this guy act any differently with his family?

I can see in his eyes the first glint of uncertainty as to who is in control. I make him nervous. Or at least I've stopped him from playing games.

"Mr. Parker, when was the last time you saw your wife, Marlena, or your son, Bennie?"

He doesn't answer right away. I give him a second. He looks directly at me when he answers. "That I actually saw them? One week ago. Last Saturday."

"And how do you know the exact date?" *Now.*

He doesn't shift his eyes but he crosses his ankles. "It will be on my phone calendar. I went to see Bennie and to discuss things with my wife."

"Do you always put things like that on your phone calendar?"

He blinks. "Mostly. Yeah."

I tell him, "Please give Detective Marsh your cell phone."

"Am I a suspect?" He doesn't reach for his phone and his eyes never leave mine.

"Mr. Parker, I know you're a smart man. You know we have to check your phone." He nods. "I also need to look inside your truck."

He says, "The first suspect is always the husband, right? I watch television."

"That's right. Let me do my job. I'm very good at it. I'll find your family. You've been very cooperative." *Not.* He seems to relax and uncrosses his ankles. He hands Ronnie his phone and his hand lingers on hers. She smiles encouragement. He sits back and smiles too. She leaves with the phone.

"I'll do anything to get them back home."

Bingo. The magic words. "Mr. Parker—Ben—where do you work?" He's already been asked this by Ronnie, so it should be easy.

"I work for my father."

"Parker Industries, correct?" He nods. "What exactly do you do for your father?"

"I'm one of his business managers."

"One?"

"Yes. My father has many business interests. Some here, in Canada, Italy, France, and other places."

"What do you do as a business manager?"

"Mostly, I handle his business affairs here."

"What do you handle here?"

"I'm on the company boards, but I go to the businesses and check up on things. I travel wherever I'm needed."

In other words you don't have a job. "Explain."

"Father is a major shareholder of a conglomerate of businesses. Some things he owns outright."

"Such as?"

"You name it. Grocery chains, casinos, steel production, communications, like radio and television and cell phone service. Shall I go on?"

I would say yes, but his head is so swollen with his own importance it might explode.

"Do you manage construction work sites? Refineries?" I leave the question open to let him elaborate.

"We have some construction companies. His oil industry holdings are mostly in Louisiana. I don't deal with any of that."

"How do you get along with your father and mother?"

"What does that have to do with this?" he asks.

"Family dynamics are important to get into your wife's mind." *And yours.*

"My father was all business when I was a child. My nannies and teachers more or less raised me. Mother sent me to boarding school. Quite a few of them, to be honest. My mother left when I was old enough to be on my own. I barely remember her. Then I was with my father. Sometimes more than I cared to be." He pauses. "You see, we didn't have a typical relationship, and being his son was, well... awkward."

"Is your mother still alive?"

He scoffs and looks away. "I haven't heard from her if she is. My father never talks about her. I don't ask."

"What kind of work does she do?" Being married to Midas doesn't lend itself to working.

"From what I gather, she does nothing. Stayed home and then she left. I don't have many memories of her. Why are you asking about her? She's not involved in what happened here."

Happened?

I ignore his question and ask one of my own. "Did Marlena know about your mother?" Talking about his mother agitates him. I drop it. "Strike that. How does your father get along with Marlena and Bennie?"

"Bennie thinks Cyrus is a superhero, and Father acts like Bennie is his own son and not a grandchild. Of course, my father rejects the idea that he's getting old. He doesn't allow anyone to call him 'Gramps' or 'Grandpa.' He's 'Cyrus.'"

When Ben says his father's name, his hand makes a little flourish in the air.

"How does Cyrus feel about your wife?"

"Marlena can do no wrong. After all, she's Bennie's mother."

"Do they see much of each other?"

"My wife and my father?"

"And Bennie?" I add.

"More than I do. I work a lot. My father rarely leaves his island."

"Island?" Why am I not surprised? "Which one does he own?" There are dozens of islands here.

"Parker Island. It's not huge. Maybe three square miles. He even built a small city on the island. Parkertown. No cars are allowed. Golf carts only. The only way on or off the island is by boat. His boat. He owns a section on the mainland where he built a dock and parking for the residents. But no one lives there now except Father and his staff."

Parker Island is not any island I've ever heard of. "No one lives there?" This is crazy, even for a billionaire.

"He decided he was tired of having neighbors. He held the mortgage to the houses, so he bought everyone out. They left."

Ronnie returns with Ben's cell phone and slides it back to him.

"You said Marlena and Bennie spend a lot of time with your father."

"He sends his driver for them. Sometimes they stay on the island for a week at a time. He has every convenience at Casa Parker."

"Excuse me for saying this, but you don't like your father, do you?" I ask.

He chuckles. "I can see why you made detective, Megan. I mean Detective Carpenter."

He thinks he's in control of the interview. His wealth and his father's power have made him overconfident. I'll let him think that way and run his mouth. "Call me Megan, Mr. Parker."

"You can call me Ben. Are we friends again?"

I wasn't aware we were ever friends. "Okay. Ben. Thanks." He turns in his chair and a knee touches mine. I don't like to be touched, but I resist punching his smug face in. "Do you think your father might have sent his driver for Marlena and Bennie? Are they on the island?"

A fire blooms behind his eyes but is quickly extinguished. "You'd have to ask Father. I guess it's possible. Are you going to go there with a search warrant? I'd like to see that."

The nut didn't fall all that far from the tree. "I don't think that will be necessary. Have you called him?" He doesn't answer. "You haven't notified him they're missing?" Again he doesn't answer. "Does he know of your marital issues?"

"Probably. He would like to rub it in my face if she left me and went to him. He thinks he'd make a better husband and father."

This is more than I can take in. I've seen sick, but this is like *Day of the Morally Dead*. "If Marlena is there do you think he'd let me talk to her?"

"You won't be able to reach him. He's better protected than the president and harder to reach."

"Do you like to camp, Ben?"

My sudden change of topics catches him off guard and I see his eyes narrow. He now knows I've seen the sleeping bags in his house and much more.

"I do. Commune with nature and all that."

"How about Marlena and Bennie? Do they commune with you?" He shrugs. "Do you go camping often?"

"Do I go camping?" He thinks on that for a moment. "Personally, I love to camp. Marlena has gone with me only once. Bennie seemed to enjoy himself."

"Did you and Marlena go camping alone?"

"Without Bennie?" he asks.

I nod.

"I wanted her to share my interests."

I notice he didn't say he wanted to share any of *her* interests. I ask, "Recently?"

"No. Not recently."

"Any special place?" After I ask that question I feel a shiver. Not long ago I was lured to a wooded area in Clallam County by a psycho who wanted me dead. I really hope I don't have to go back into the forest.

He cocks his head and gives me a knowing look. "Let me think on it. No, they wouldn't have gone anywhere like that. Their sleeping bags are at my place." A hint of a smile plays at his lips.

"Do you know where her cell phone might be?" I ask.

"I thought the police found it."

I say, "Does she always carry it? I'm almost glued to mine."

"With a job like yours I'm not surprised. You can get a call at any time. Marlena kept hers nearby but if you didn't find it at the house, it would be with her."

"Okay." *Unless you've taken it.*

He says, "I don't want to think this, but maybe someone took them and got rid of her phone. Or she could be with the guy that got her pregnant. Maybe she's with *him*. I know she keeps her phone close but she wasn't answering. And no, I don't have any idea who the man might be."

He's offering alternative explanations for Marlena's disappearance. I should keep him talking. Let him hang himself. But I want to do this slowly. Let him sweat. Make a mistake. "Would you care for some coffee? Water? Little boys' room?"

"Coffee would be nice. Yes, I'd like to go to the restroom if I can."

"You're not under arrest. Ronnie will show you where it is. I'll make some coffee."

When I stand to let him out, he brushes against me and not accidentally. He's dominating me, letting me know he's alpha. I'll be his omega if he doesn't watch the touching.

Ronnie points to the restroom, and I get coffee for myself and Ronnie. She takes her mug. I ask her, "So?"

She looks at me over the rim of the mug. "He's a train wreck."

"Agreed."

"What now?"

I tell her, "When he finishes putting his makeup on, bring him back to the interview room. He likes you. I'll interview him alone. Did you find anything on the phone?"

"Nothing we need to talk about right now."

"Round two is about to begin," I say, and pour coffee for Parker.

Ronnie leads him back to the room and shuts the door behind him. I motion to a chair.

Ben says, "I'm ready."

SEVENTEEN

She remembers waking in a dark place that smelled of sawdust and oil and the faint odor of fuel of some kind. She doesn't remember falling asleep again and this doesn't feel like the same place where she woke up the first time. The smell here is almost suffocating. Bennie had his inhaler before. She feels her pockets and is relieved when her hand closes over it. The toy figure is gone. She props the boy against her chest and gently taps his cheeks and shakes him until he stirs.

"Mommy?"

"It's Mommy, honey. You're with me. You're safe." She knows they aren't safe. The ground is dryer than before. The smell is different. Old, musty. She doesn't know where they are. Where they have been. How they got here. She only knows they can't stay here.

She feels a wave of nausea coming on and leans away and retches. Nothing comes up but phlegm. When her stomach settles, she takes deep breaths and thinks it may be the morning sickness. It was worse with Bennie. Tries to calm herself. She'll be no good to Bennie if she can't be calm.

She doesn't want to but she thinks about the dream. The boat was sinking. She didn't remember if she could swim, but the water was dangerous. She feels the ground around her and feels two plastic bottles. One feels empty. The other is half-full. A feeling comes over her. There's something about the water. Her dream was a warning not to drink the water. She and Bennie had drunk some water and must have passed out. She hadn't gone to sleep. She was too disturbed to sleep and she never sleeps heavily. She must have been drugged. She needs sleeping medication on a good night to help her go to sleep. "The water was drugged."

"Mommy? I'm thirsty."

His voice is sluggish. Weak. "We'll have a drink in a moment, honey. Mommy has to think."

"I'm thirsty, Mommy."

"I am, too, honey, but I think the water is bad. We won't drink unless we have to. Okay?"

"Okay, Mommy, but I'm really thirsty." He lies against her and his breathing slows as he drifts off again.

Someone *has* drugged them. How could they do that to a four-year-old? They've been kidnapped, that much is certain. But that they are alive is good news. The mother and her daughters who were missing and later found murdered had been strangled. Not left to die. The police suspected the husband. Or maybe he'd confessed. But she and Bennie are still alive and have been moved to a new place. That means their kidnappers want money. Not from Ben. He doesn't have his own money, and he probably wouldn't pay anyway. He doesn't love her. He made that clear. But he lives and breathes for Bennie. Or at least she thought he did. He was such a good liar. Was he pretending? Was he behind this? He'd beaten her before but he was a coward. Men who beat women are cowards. It would be like Ben to leave them here instead of divorcing her and having to tell Cyrus he'd failed at his marriage. The bastard.

EIGHTEEN

While Ronnie goes to pick Ben's cell phone information apart, I take Ronnie's vacated chair by the door. Let him think he's put me in my place. It makes my job easier. So far, Mr. Ben Parker has done well answering my questions. But he is easily drawn into deriding his father and mother. His resentment is on his face like a caul; it closes off his ability to get past slights done to him and threatens to smother him.

Interview techniques are easily available on the Internet, along with how to beat polygraphs. You can even find out how to make a nuclear weapon if you're so inclined. How to be a caring concerned human being is not. At least, I don't think it is. If I can get into Ben's computers, I know I'll find evidence he searched how to make convincing statements during an interview. Or how to dispose of a body. Ben is rich. Wealth has been his saving grace. He said he was teased in high school and college because of it. But I have to wonder if he wasn't overly sensitive and the ones who he claimed picked on him were only trying to get inside his defenses. I don't know if he's smart. Money can buy an education or a diploma, but he's not very imaginative or creative. He's always had his father or a nanny or a teacher to tell him what to do. If what he said is true about his father's relationship with

Marlena and Bennie, I need to start looking in that direction. If possible, I would like to find his mother. And I will have to talk to Helen.

"I've changed my mind," he says, and lounges back in his seat. "Will you get me a candy bar or something?"

I crack the door and tell Ronnie. She comes in a minute later with the master's request. He accepts it from her with a smug look back on his face. "Thank you, Ronnie. I owe you dinner."

She has a boyfriend, so don't get your hopes up. "Anything else before we begin?" I ask. *Like maybe a foot rub? Or I could shoot you in both kneecaps.*

"This will do. Where were we?"

"Your father owns an island."

"Parkertown. Yes. A little eccentric, but that's Father for you." He gobbles down the candy bar.

I say, "Maybe I should get him on the phone. Ask him to come down and sit with you. For support."

As I say this, I can see his expression revert to the old Ben Parker we met for the first time. He's the little boy who never had the love of a father. He's unsure. But only for a split second.

"He won't come here. He rarely leaves his island, like I told you. Besides, he'll expect me to handle this myself. My father doesn't suffer weakness or fools."

"I'm sorry, Ben. You've had a tough upbringing. I can relate." I may not like him or forgive him if anything has happened to his family. I'm not sorry for him. But I do relate.

Sharing something personal always pays dividends. "I never knew who my real father was until I was almost eighteen," I tell him. "My mother was absent a lot. My stepfather was murdered, so I more or less raised myself." I don't say anything about Hayden. I don't tell him my real father was a serial killer. I don't tell him *I'm* a killer.

"Well, you seem to have done well. Is your mother still around?"

"No. But the point I'm making is, even given your past troubles, your lack of a loving home, you still have to move forward. Do better than your parents. Do you believe that?"

He looks at me for a long moment. "Detective Carpenter, I didn't know you were such a deep person. Cops aren't supposed to have insight."

I try to smile. It helps me to not gag. "Yeah. That's me. Detective, psychologist, visionary."

This gets a laugh. I can be charming too.

"My father would like you. He liked Marlena because she was quick-witted like you."

Liked? *Was*? My skin crawls. "Will he know where they have gone?"

"I take it you don't think she was taken against her will."

"Just looking at all possibilities."

"He won't know and even if he did he wouldn't tell you because you would have to tell me. I doubt she told anyone where she was going. She doesn't have any friends or anyone to talk to. She liked my father but she wouldn't want to burden him with her issues."

"What issues?"

He looks at his hands. "I don't know why I said that. I'm not sure. I don't know. But if she left with a boyfriend, she definitely wouldn't tell my father."

Good answer. "Let's explore that."

"I already told you, I don't know the man. He's a stranger to me."

I start to press him when my phone buzzes in my pocket. I forgot the first rule of interviewing: Turn your phone off. I let it buzz.

"You'd better get that."

"It's not important," I say.

"Might be *your* boyfriend. I notice you aren't wearing a ring."

The phone is in my hand. The screen shows a telemarketer. I smile and power it down. "You must be clairvoyant. I'll talk to him later. Does your girlfriend call you at awkward times?"

"No," he says, and then realizes he's just admitted to having a girlfriend. "I have a friend, a lady friend, but she never calls me when I'm busy. Or hardly ever, anyway. I'm married."

"I'm sorry I said that." I'm not.

"It's okay. She and I are just friends."

"Does Marlena know your lady friend? Maybe your lady friend has an idea where they are," I say.

"No. I don't think so."

"What's her name?" I don't expect an answer, but I'll find out one way or the other.

"I don't want you to bother her. She's just a friend."

"Mr. Parker, I wouldn't ask if I didn't think it was important. Trust me to do my job."

"I do. I trust you. But it won't do any good to talk to her. She doesn't know Marlena. They've never met. I don't understand. Do you think I'm having an affair? Ridiculous."

"Look, Ben. You don't go to one of your board meetings without knowing everything you possibly can. Right?"

"Lucia. Her name is Lucia Simmons."

"How well do you know her?"

"We work together. She's my personal secretary."

I've gotten about all he's willing to give without scaring him away, so I change the topic. I trust Ronnie is surfing the net right this minute for Lucia Simmons and Cyrus Parker and Parker Island.

"Do you or your wife have enemies?"

"Everyone has enemies, Detective."

I'm "Detective" now. Not "Megan" or "Detective Carpenter." I've hit a nerve.

I ask, "Anyone in particular?"

"I've let a lot of people go from the company. Not every worker has a sterling reputation. On the construction end of things, we've hired a good deal of ex-convicts and work release participants, both men and women. I don't think my wife has ever run afoul of any of those types."

"If you had to pick just one of 'those types,' who would it be?"

"Uh, well, no one comes to mind in particular. I'm just saying they would be the only ones who might have a grudge against me."

"I'll need you to write down your work foreman's contact information. If you have several, I'll need them all. They can give me a list of workers that have been fired or left recently. Also, I'll need your personal secretary's contact information. In my experience, a secretary knows more than the boss thinks."

"Uh, okay. But I don't have my address book with me."

"No problem, Ben. I'm sure it's all in your phone contacts. Right?"

"Yes. I forgot about the phone." He looks uneasy. Good.

"We'll only use what we need from your phone." How can he refuse? "You said you don't know who your wife's lover is." He nods. "And you've never seen him or had contact with him?" He nods again. "So how do you know he exists?"

He says, "You just know. And she was pregnant. You know?"

Was? "I don't. Tell me."

"The fact she was pregnant is all I need to know. We've had a tough couple of months. And she was cranky all the time. Nagging. You know."

I don't, but I nod along. If he says it's her time of month, I'm going to strangle him.

"We haven't had a regular sex life since Bennie came along. She decided she didn't want any more children and wanted me to get fixed. I didn't want to. Still don't. So sex was almost out of the question."

He's telling a story now. He's having enough sex on the side to keep him satisfied. My bet is he's the one not wanting kids.

"When did you find out about the pregnancy?"

"We were arguing about several things and were talking about a trial separation, when she threw it in my face. That was last Saturday. The day I left. I knew what she was doing. I mean, how else could she be pregnant? We weren't doing anything. Besides, I always used protection. I asked her who the baby's father was and she wouldn't tell me. I told her I would be willing to go to counseling with her. I don't know if I could stand to raise someone else's child, but I wanted to keep my family together."

"That would be a hard thing to accept."

"I know all this makes me look like a suspect but I swear she wouldn't tell me who she was seeing. If I could bring them home, I'd forgive her. She's Bennie's mother. He loves her."

"Think carefully, Ben. Does your wife have any enemies?" He doesn't answer. He just sits there looking into space. "How much do you know about your wife's past?"

"Like I said, we met in college. I met her parents. She's an only child. They didn't want us to marry. Her father had something against me from the start, but her mother was the hateful one, derisive, haughty. Her father finally divorced the old witch, so I say good for him."

"Do you know any of her extended family?"

"I've never met any of them. We didn't have a big wedding. Justice of the peace. My father suggested a small wedding because Marlena was already showing. Marlena wanted the whole nine yards, but she did what my father wanted. Of course. And when Bennie was born Father gave us the house to live in. And the cabin."

I want to ask whose name is on the deeds but I don't want to sidetrack from what he's telling me. And I can find out through property records. "Can you think of anything else I haven't asked?"

"Well, there is one thing..."

Ben's "one thing" was a doozy. A peeping Tom. *How convenient. Bullshit!* We talked about this until I'd wrung him dry of what little he knew or thought he knew. Then I sent him home after I made him promise to come back for a polygraph.

NINETEEN

Ronnie is driving and her car has pretty much aired out enough that I don't have to carry a paper bag. We're on our way to Baker Heights to talk to the neighbor with the video. Our search of Baker Heights community and the surrounding wooded areas turned up nothing. K-9s came up with nothing. The one good thing was a second neighborhood canvass that turned up a neighbor's operational surveillance camera.

"Why didn't he tell us about the peeping Tom?" Ronnie asks after I fill her in on the bomb Ben had dropped at the end of the interview.

I tell her, "He said he was so upset about Marlena and Bennie he didn't remember it right away. And we didn't ask about a peeping Tom."

We give each other a look. Ben was anything but upset. And he'd had every opportunity to think of something like a peeping Tom. Of course it's bullshit. The neighborhood canvass never turned up an incident like that ever occurring to anyone else.

I say, "Ben told me just after their separation Marlena told him she was sitting in the front room with Bennie, when Bennie saw someone looking in the window. Marlena saw a shape and screamed. The shape disappeared. He went to the house to check on them and asked her if the police had found anyone. She hadn't called the police. He told Marlena to report it to the police but he didn't know if she ever did so. Ben thought maybe she saw a shadow or a dog running across the yard. He said Baker Heights is a gated community with a guard and nothing had ever happened there before. He thought she was making it up." I can tell by the look on Ronnie's face she's not buying any what Ben was shoveling. "He told me the very next night he was coming to the house to get some clothes and that time he saw someone running away from the side of the house. He chased them back toward the golf course but lost them in the woods. He said Marlena was frightened and told him someone had just been trying to get in the back door. She saw them through the kitchen window. He told her to call the police and she said she would."

Ronnie asks, "Why didn't he call the police?"

"Because he's Ben. I don't know. He couldn't tell me why he didn't call. It was all bullshit anyway. He called the guy an *intruder*. His word. His description of the person is Black, male, short, could be a teenager, dark clothing, hoodie sweatshirt. He wasn't sure they were Black but just felt like they were because those were the type of people that did things like that. He said they ran very fast."

"So Blacks run fast. That's a new one."

According to Ronnie's online research there has never been a police call to Baker Heights Police or to the Sheriff's Office regarding a peeping Tom or an attempted break-in. It was as if Baker Heights were paradise.

I remark, "Well, he referred to his blue-collar workers as 'those types,' so he's grown up privileged and biased. Anyone wearing dark clothes and a hoodie is a criminal."

Ronnie turns into Baker Heights and pulls up to the wide-open gate. No guard is on duty. "I thought they'd increase security, given the situation."

The residents would have to pay for extra security. Obviously they're not too worried. As we drive down the street I can see that most of the houses have cameras mounted somewhere visible. Our canvass teams said the house we're going to was the only one with an operational camera and the rest were dummies. The residents told them they thought the sight of a camera on their front porch would be deterrent enough. This is crazy in an area with million-dollar homes. If I had anything to steal, I'd have an alarm company on speed dial. Lucky for me, no self-respecting burglar will steal boxed wine and Cheetos. Even my Scotch is cheap. The only thing of real value are the tapes and I can't imagine anyone taking those. At least I hope not. Maybe I should buy a safe. An exploding safe. Punch in the wrong code and explode. I could sell millions of them.

I have a thought about Ben's peeping Tom story. He told us he hadn't seen Marlena since last Saturday, when he moved out. If he's telling the truth about the peeper, he was at her house on Sunday and Monday. Maybe it's nothing. Maybe he just forgot those facts too. In any case it's another tiny crack in his story.

As we come to Parker's home I tell Ronnie to pull into the Parker driveway.

Ronnie slows and says, "The house we want is about half a block down, Megan."

I can see the camera mounted on the front of that house but not where it's pointed. "I know. I want to see if that camera can see this driveway."

We get out and I look down the street to the house we'll be visiting. It's possible there will be something on the video, depending on whether it really works and if the camera is pointed this way. I can't see the camera, so it most likely can't see me. From what the canvassing officers told us, the neighbors around here kept to themselves and didn't want to be involved in a *marital dispute*. That tells me the neighbors suspect it was a marital issue, so there has been more going on than just an argument about Marlena being pregnant one week ago.

Was it even possible that Marlena and Bennie just went away, leaving medicine and coats and even her car behind? If Bennie still favored his Darth Vader pajamas, they were what he was wearing. None of the hospitals had record of an injured woman and boy matching their description. All the police agencies we'd contacted had nothing for us. It was like they just disappeared. I didn't believe it. I have to wonder why I'm willing to believe the neighbors but not Ben, when it was Ben that reported them missing. He could have kept quiet. Let someone else notice them missing and start an inquiry. And Ben's story about the peeping Tom seems convenient. Contrived. No one else can verify such an incident.

I start walking toward the woods behind the house and come to a clearing where I can see a golf course with a concrete track wide enough for golf carts and even service vehicles.

"Where are we going?"

I nod toward the track. "You go to the left. I'll go this way. Let's see where it leads."

Ronnie doesn't ask why. That's good. I'm not real sure myself. The track goes over a small rise and disappears and then reappears a hundred yards distant, where I notice some dirt churned up alongside the concrete. Tread marks where wheels have pulled off the track are uniform. Golfers are conscientious when it comes to destroying the green.

In the distance I see eight feet of churned mud and grass where a vehicle, not a golf cart, has strayed from the track. Someone has kicked the ridges made by the tires back into the mud. I stoop to examine it and can't make out a single tread mark. There are mud-colored streaks across the concrete where the vehicle crossed, but they've been mostly washed away. It must have rained here during the night—or day. I've slept so little, it's hard to keep track. I continue over another small rise and ahead of me I can see where the track crosses a street. Ronnie calls from behind me.

"I didn't see anything in that direction but a street."

Ronnie takes out her trusty cell phone and pulls up a map. "That's Mountain View, the street where I ended up. The one ahead of us is Luna Ridge."

I tell her about the tire tracks.

TWENTY

On our way to see Mrs. Green, the neighbor with the functional video system, I call Mindy and tell her about the tracks in the mud near the golf course.

"We found that, Megan. There was no clear tread mark to identify the vehicle that made it."

"So what's your opinion?"

"Someone ran off the track."

I think, *Smartass,* so I say it: "Smartass."

Mindy chuckles. One of us is having fun.

"I measured, and the concrete is barely wide enough for a car or truck. The maintenance crew probably."

Crap.

"I was going to call the greenkeeper. Do you want me to?"

"Yes." This opens new possibilities. Someone could have come in behind the house. But they would still have had to come down Luna Ridge to get there. Or Mountain View. Or maybe some other entrance.

The curtain in the front window of 28 Luna Ridge twitches and a second later a massive red door with leaded glass opens. The woman who comes out has walked out of the past. She's wearing a midcalf flower-print dress—roses, of course—shiny black shoes with low heels, short sleeves puffed up at the shoulders, and over this a lace-trimmed white apron. Her hair style is heavily permed and the chemical smell is worse than Ronnie's car.

"Mrs. Green?"

"I was hoping a detective would come by but I didn't expect two of you. And women at that."

She's about my height and in her early eighties to mid one hundreds. She might have marched in the 1913 Women's Suffrage Parade. "Women have come a long way," I say, and she smiles. "I'm Detective Carpenter and this is Detective Marsh."

Ronnie holds out her hand. "I'm Ronnie. She's Megan."

"Please come in. Where are my manners? I must be getting old."

"Thank you." We follow her into a spacious living room filled with antique furniture with red velvet cushions and upholstery and stained a deep mahogany brown. I'm afraid to step on the hardwood floors or touch anything. She sees I'm uncomfortable.

"It's all handed down from my great-grandmother. All the furniture, anyway. The figurines and keepsakes are mine, collected over a lifetime."

Boy, that makes me feel better. I never thought about amassing a lifetime collection of figurines, but I do now. I've never had the opportunity since we moved so often. We traveled light. Sometimes with nothing but the clothes on our backs.

"Have a seat and I'll put tea on."

Ronnie sits at one end of a magnificent sofa and I carefully sit on the other end, feet flat on the floor, hands in my lap.

Ronnie looks around and says, "My granny would like this."

I bet Ronnie's grandmother has a similar place.

Mrs. Green comes back with a silver tray, china cups, a vintage teapot, sugar, cream, silver spoons, and real cloth napkins rolled up in those silver rings. She pours daintily and we take the cups. The tiny, delicate handle on the teacup makes me worry I'll crush mine and be humiliated.

"Mrs. Green, you told an officer you had video surveillance of the street and front of your house."

She blows across the top of her tea and takes a sip. Her mouth contracts into a tight little bow. "That's much too strong. I'll make a fresh pot."

She starts to get up, and I rush to say, "Mrs. Green, that's not necessary. We had several cups of coffee on our way over and I don't think I can hold any more."

Ronnie looks at her cup and reluctantly puts it back on the tray. Mrs. Green looks disappointed. In my years doing this, I've found older people are the best source of information, gossip, whatever. But they are also generally the most in need of company.

I've never met my own grandparents. I'm not sure who they are or what their names are. I doubt they need company or if they are even alive, but all I know of them is what my mother and my aunt Ginger told me. My grandparents threw my mother out when she was sixteen and pregnant with me. It's probably all a lie. But I don't know how to find them to decide for myself what kind of people they are, and if what I've been told is true, maybe I don't want to know them. I've been disappointed enough.

"Just a moment," she says, and leaves the room again.

"I think you hurt her feelings," Ronnie whispers.

Mrs. Green comes back with an iPad, and I'm shocked to see the older woman with a modern device like an iPad. She touches an icon that looks like an old Polaroid camera and the screen turns to a list of files with dates in chronological order. She touches the one for today; the time is 02:30 and the picture is dark. The view is from her porch onto the street but not of the road in either direction. There is no sound. The video begins. Nothing. Then something with bright green eyes crosses into view. It's a cat. But while the cat has tripped the video, I can see headlights washing across the street the direction we came from. A vehicle would have to pass directly in front of the house to trip the camera.

This seems like a waste of time, but then the video catches something. The time on the screen is 06:13. A man in pajamas is walking into the yard, stoops over, picks something up, looks up at the camera and waves, then goes back out of camera range. The video is black and white but the man is obviously in his senior years. Mrs. Green stops the video.

"That's Mr. Burrage. He throws his newspaper in my yard and says the paper delivery guy is doing it, but I know he's got a crush on me. Don't tell my husband."

I say with a wink, "It's our secret, Mrs. Green."

"Mr. Green gets very jealous." She smiles, and I get the feeling she'll show the video to Mr. Green at first opportunity. "If you talk to Mr. Burrage, he likes to complain, so you'll get an earful."

"Would he have information for us?"

She gives a "Hmpff" and puts a finger to her temple, and whispers. "He's not all there, poor dear. You can't believe a word he says. But I didn't tell you that."

"Do you know the Parkers well?" I ask.

"I know everyone in the Heights. Ours was the first house built. What do you want to know?"

"Do you know what they drive?"

"Of course. He's got a big white truck. She drives a Mercedes. Black. My husband says the truck is too much for that one. Last year he had very loud mufflers. Mr. Green said he must have had them installed that way. We got up a petition and he fixed them."

I ask, "Is your husband here?"

"He's still in bed. We had quite a night." She gives me a look I don't quite understand and then I do and I throw up in my mouth a little.

I've gotten worse at hiding my thoughts, and she reads the look on my face correctly.

"You young folks don't think old people still have sex."

I try a smile and say, "Good for you." It sounds wrong even to me, but I'm stuck with it now. "We appreciate you taking the time to show us this." That sounds even worse.

Ronnie saves me more embarrassment asking, "Can you warm up my tea, please?"

I hold my cup out. "Me too."

Mrs. Green hands the iPad to Ronnie and begins pouring our tea. Ronnie scrolls through the files until she finds the one she wants. "Here's the morning before the Parkers were reported missing. Mrs. Green, do you mind if I copy this?"

Mrs. Green is mollified now that we're drinking the nasty brew. "Of course, dear."

Ronnie is finished in a jiffy. "All done. Thanks. Mrs. Green, you really should password protect your Internet."

Mrs. Green smiles and pours another round of tea for all of us. "Mr. Green says so too. But I don't want to remember a bunch of nonsense every time I want to watch my shows. I've got Amazon Prime on here. And I can get *The Voice*. I just love that show."

I turn a deaf ear while she and Ronnie talk about contestants and I drink the nasty tea. Finally they're running out of steam, and I say, "Can I ask you a question, Mrs. Green?"

"Of course, Detective Carpenter. You didn't come here to listen to an old woman prattling on."

She's right.

She has Ronnie outmatched in stream-of-consciousness talking. Telemarketers must hang up on her and take her off their lists. But I'll be brief and to the point and let her get back to her hubby, who is probably tied up and gagged in the bedroom.

"How do the Parkers get along?"

"We think the world of Marlena and her little guy."

That's not what I asked. "You don't like Ben? The husband."

She doesn't answer that, either. "We were excited to have a young family move in just down the street. And then the yelling started. All hours of the day and night. That poor child. He shouldn't have to live in that environment. We usually mind our own business, but we called the police one time when it got so loud and we heard the crashing all the way down here."

"How long ago?"

"Oh, months. The police came but he'd already gone. She and I were friendly, and Bennie would come down the street and sit on the porch with me, but I didn't know her well enough to interfere. The HOA provides lawn care for the community, but they don't cut the grass at the Parkers'. She told me she likes doing it herself, but I think her husband doesn't want anyone in their yard. He never helps her. He's gone a lot, and the times I've seen her leave, she's only gone a short time. Bennie goes to preschool. Every now and then a limousine picks her and Bennie up and they're gone for a couple of days. That husband of hers never goes with them."

"Did you talk to Marlena after the night you called the police? Did you find out what that was about?"

"No. I never had the opportunity. I feel horrible now. Maybe I could have done something. Do you think he's done something to them? I watch *CSI: Miami* and it's always the husband. Do you think they're dead?"

"Mrs. Green," I say in my most placating voice, "we don't know if Marlena and Bennie are missing but we have to investigate until we find they're safe."

"Just like on television," she says, and her head nods up and down.

I tell her, "There's nothing you could have done, Mrs. Green. From what you've told me, she might have just had enough and went to stay with friends."

"I guess it's likely but she didn't have any friends that I ever saw. I could tell she was afraid of him. She looked so cowed. Last week they were at it late at night. I have trouble sleeping and had gotten up to get something to settle me down. He was yelling at her and she yelled back at him for once. It wasn't as violent but I heard something break. She might have thrown a dish at him. I hope it hit him. Anyway, he came storming out of the house and roared away in that big truck of his. He's a coward. Anyone that beats on a woman is a coward. And that Bennie is just four years old and little for his age. No wonder the boy hasn't grown faster, living in that house."

"Do you know what the fights were about?"

"Not really, no. Although I suspect he was cheating on her. He always acted like he was God's gift to women. Tight jeans and muscle shirts. He was more God's curse if you ask me."

Ronnie asks, "Do you think Mr. Green might know more?"

"Nah. He won't say boo about a ghost. But he never liked the man."

"Maybe we can talk to him after we've looked at the video," I say.

"He won't be able to tell you anything I haven't already told you. I don't want to disturb him. He's tired from last night. He helped that man work on his beast of a truck once and came home laughing about how ignorant he was. Parker wouldn't know a spark plug from a butt plug, if you'll excuse my language."

"Mrs. Green, have you ever seen him hit his wife or the child?"

"No. But I heard her and the boy sounding as if they were in distress and the little one screaming, 'No, Daddy!' Mr. Green was going down there with a tire knocker. He would have just gotten hurt. That's the night I called the police."

"One other thing: Have you or any of your neighbors ever had a problem with strangers looking in windows? Taking things? That sort of problem."

"Not at all. Not at all. What kind of community would put up with that?"

"If you or Mr. Green think of anything else, please call us." We give her our cards.

"Find them," she says.

"We will."

This case has just gotten more interesting. Ben is not the concerned husband he portrays himself to be. If Mrs. Green can be believed and I do. I would normally insist on talking to Mr. Green but given the amount of time we've already lost looking for them, and the possibility that he may actually be 'tied up' I decide to get back to him if I have nowhere else to go.

TWENTY-ONE

My phone is on vibrate and I ignored a couple of calls from Sheriff while we were at Mrs. Green's. Ronnie gave me a crash course on how to operate the video function on her iPad. I plug in the thumb drive Ronnie copied from Mrs. Green's iPad and pull up the date file. I select the date when Paco and Sonny arrived and rewind about two hours. Midnight. I click on the video. The image is black and white but crisp and clean. I play it forward slowly until I reach the time Sonny and Paco arrived to meet Ben. The video is useless. A couple of times I thought I saw the ground light up faintly. One time would coincide with approximately when Ben arrived. The other with when Paco arrived. I'll hang on to the video. We know it doesn't show anything but Ben doesn't.

"Did you download the footage from Paco's dash camera?" I ask.

"I've got their body cams on there too. There's no sound on the dash cam."

The police dash cam starts where they are arriving behind Ben's truck. There is no movement for several minutes before Ben emerges. I freeze the frame and zoom in on Ben's face. He's not looking at the police car. He's looking off to the side. Toward the house. His face is expressionless. His posture is relaxed. His whole demeanor is of someone playing a part. I should know. My whole life has been playing a part.

The body cams from both officers show me the same thing. Paco's camera films from the front door outside to the truck, where Ben is busily touching the screen of his phone. Texting. He's not reading emails or he wouldn't be touching it so fast. He's not interested in what the officers are doing.

We're heading into the station, so I skip through the video from Paco's and Sonny's body cams until I get to the part on Paco's camera where he finds Ben in the garage with the trunk of the Mercedes open. I freeze it there and zoom in on Ben's face. He looked up when Paco approached but now his eyes are on the trunk. A look of relief comes over his face. Relief at what? Paco said Ben explained he was looking for luggage to see if they were planning to leave. Why? If the car was still there and they were not, why would luggage be in the trunk? What could he have been hoping to find? Or not find?

I've seen enough for the moment. I call the sheriff. His phone barely has a chance to ring before he picks up.

"Megan. Tell me you have something."

He sounds desperate and I can hear someone, a female voice, in the background asking where he keeps his "decent" coffee. Another voice speaks but I can't make it out.

"We may have something but I don't want to get your hopes up."

He exhales loudly and there's banging in the background. Good luck to them. We never buy good coffee. We just make it strong.

"Is that Helen?" I ask.

"God help me."

"We talked to a neighbor down the street from the Parkers. She has some video footage but it's not very good. We haven't had a chance to go through it yet. We didn't want to keep the lady tied up all morning." Although I'll bet the Greens have different plans.

Mrs. Green informed us she and Mr. Green have been married

for sixty-two years. The lesson I learned is sex keeps a marriage alive. Unfortunately, in Ben Parker's case, leather and whips and a willing lady friend didn't seem to do the trick for him.

"Nothing else?"

I want to give him good news. I want to see Marlena loading Bennie into a car and leaving on a video. It would mean she ran off and my stomach no longer has to be tied in knots.

"I can use some help looking through the video." It will keep him distracted, and Helen can watch too. There's nothing there except for Mr. Burrage.

"Are you coming in?"

My phone dings in my hand. It's Hayden. "Tony, I've got to get another call. We'll be there in ten."

"Please. If you need any help out there, I can come."

Nice try. "Thanks, but we've got it."

I disconnect and answer. "Hayden. What's up, McPup." I hear him let out an exaggerated sigh. He acts like he hates it when I call him that, but he likes it. We called each other all kinds of names when we were kids. Some not as nice. McPup is my favorite for him because he was as messy as a new puppy when he was younger. Peeing on the toilet seat and dribbling on the floor, leaving the water running. It seems natural to call him that name again. At least for me. He was as innocent as a pup, too.

"I was at Moe's this morning. Where were you?" Hayden asks.

Oh, crap! I was supposed to meet him for breakfast. "I'm sorry, Hayden. I got called in early this morning on a missing person case. A mother and little boy. This happened about two o'clock and I haven't really had any sleep." I realize I'm overexplaining.

"Kidnapped? Like what happened with Mom?"

Not even close. Mom was missing from our lives so much she might as well have been a ghost. Even with all she put us through, he's still in touch with her. I'd be in touch with her, too, but it might be with my fist.

"Listen, Hayden, how about I treat you to dinner? The Tides. We can catch up."

"You don't have to, Rylee."

He says "Rylee" low enough no one would hear it but me. It's not the name I'm using. It's not even my real name. It's a name that could get me in hot water. Rylee was a suspect wanted for questioning in the murder of my stepfather. One she, or I, didn't do. He's calling me Rylee to get even for standing him up.

"Did you have lunch?" I don't want to talk about our mother. I don't want to think about her. We've missed our lunch. I'll make up for it with dinner. I hope.

"I'm good." The phone is silent. Neither of us knows what to say. "Gotta go." Silence. He's hung up.

"Hayden's mad, isn't he?" Ronnie says.

"He'll be okay." *I* won't be okay. Life only gives you so many chances and then you're screwed. I've run out of tokens.

Ronnie parks next to the sheriff's truck in the lot. A brand-new Cadillac is parked near the entry door. Most likely Helen. We get out and make our way inside. I feel like I'm in trouble and about to get a dressing-down. Well, let her do her best. I'll neuter the beast.

I tense up as I go through the door but then I smell something wonderful. Cinnamon and coffee. The top of my desk has been turned into a table for Cinnabon-type pastries and cake donuts and the best-smelling coffee. A woman, close to the sheriff's age, sturdily built, plaid tweed kilt-type skirt, white puffed-sleeve blouse and black shiny brogues on her feet, is sitting in my chair. Gray permed hair surrounds her head and frames her face, making her look like Elizabeth, Queen of England.

Get out of my chair, Your Majesty. "You must be Helen. Pleased to meet you. I'm Megan. This is Ronnie." Ronnie offers her hand and I'm glad to see her grip has improved. In fact, Helen rubs her hand after Ronnie releases it.

Sheriff comes out of his office, no doubt following the smell of pastries, and stands by the desk. I notice sweat beads in his hairline.

Ronnie says, "The sheriff has said so many nice things about you," to which Helen breaks out in a sarcastic smile.

"This old buzzard never said a good thing about me in his life. But thank you for trying to pull his bacon out of the fire." She doesn't say this harshly. Rather, she is the epitome of class, with a pleasant demeanor. If I didn't expect her to bite someone's head off any minute, I might even come to like her.

"Tony tells me you are trying to find my daughter and grandson. He really has said all good things about you. He says you're his best detectives."

"Yes, ma'am." I called her "ma'am." I hate it myself and I hope she doesn't get upset, but I don't feel comfortable calling her Helen. The way Tony acts when he mentions Helen her last name could be Hun. Helen the Hun.

"Oh, please. We're all in this mess, so call me Helen." Her expression changes like magic from pleasant to anguished. "Tony said you might have news. Tell me you have something."

I see a vein throbbing in her temple. She was putting on a brave face, but she's barely holding it together. *Thanks a lot, Sheriff.*

"We have some video from the neighborhood... Helen. We haven't had a chance to go through it yet to see if it helps us." I cast a withering look at the sheriff, and he clears his throat.

Tony says, "Helen, I told you this might take some time. I don't want to tie up my investigators answering questions right now, but they might have some questions for you."

Helen forces a smile. "I made pastries and brought some decent coffee. Please. Have something to eat and drink while we talk. You too, Tony." She puts huge cinnamon rolls on two plates and indicates we should help ourselves to the coffee. We do, and she leads the way to the interview room. Tony puts two rolls on a plate and follows us. Helen doesn't get on Tony like her sister would have.

Ronnie and I take some extra chairs into the room and we all sit. Ronnie bites into the icing-covered roll, her eyes close, and she makes a face like she's having an orgasm. She's making pleasure-like noises, but her mouth is so full it sounds like she's choking.

She takes a breath, lets it out, and pauses, thinking. When she speaks it becomes clear she disapproves of Ben. Maybe "disapprove" is too weak a word.

"Okay. Ask your questions."

"I understand your daughter met Ben in college," I say.

"Yes."

"And she became pregnant."

A sad look comes over her face and she nods.

"Did she finish college?" I hope she answers with more than one word. This question hits a nerve and she scowls. It's a scary face and I understand why Tony is nervous.

She spits the words out. "He wouldn't let her. He completed his degree after they married but he wouldn't let her go back. Or even take distance courses. She's a semester away from getting her degree. She's such a bright girl. Bennie—that's my grandson—takes after her. Do you know he already knows how to use a computer and a cell phone, and he fixed my computer when I was having issues? Silly me, I was hitting the wrong key. He says, 'Hit this one, Gramma.' It worked. I hate those things, but it's the only way I can get pictures of my daughter and grandson."

I think, *That's a follow-up question.* But I let Ronnie get to it when she's ready.

"What was your daughter's major?" Ronnie asks.

"She was studying to be an interior designer. She already had half a dozen clients while she was still in school. She's so talented. You wouldn't know it to look in her house though. She can only buy what he approves of."

"Is she still doing interior design work?" Ronnie asks.

"Yes. But he watches her like a hawk. He controls the bank accounts, the credit cards—even watches how much phone and computer time she uses. The only thing she does is housework and raise Bennie."

"Does Ben love her and Bennie?" Ronnie asks.

I expect her to say no, but she says, "He's married to my daughter. I have to admit he really loves that boy. He'd buy the moon if Bennie asked for it."

This doesn't exactly fit with what Mrs. Green told us earlier about him yelling at Marlena and Bennie telling him to stop. But I won't tell Helen. It does, however, explain Ben's lack of concern.

"Did they argue?" Ronnie asks.

"Oh, you betcha. Sometimes, I think it's all they do. Marlena put up with him for the first year because of Bennie, but then she grew a spine and stood up to him. Fat lot of good it did. He controls the money. The house was a present from Scrooge McDuck. Sorry, that's what I call Ben's father. You're both too young to know who that is."

I'm not that young. It was a character from one of Hayden's cartoons. I might have watched some of those cartoons with him.

Helen says, "Marlena said Ben's father loves Bennie and it is mutual. She has nothing but praise for him. I think the only reason Ben married her was because of his father."

Ben himself told us he'd "done the right thing."

She takes a sip of her coffee and a dark look crosses her features. "I think the way Ben grew up, having a father that wealthy, he had to control someone like his dad controls him."

"Does his father control him?"

"Oh, yes. Very much so. Marlena told me if his dad says 'jump,' Ben gets out a parachute."

I have to snicker. I'm warming to her.

"Does he work for his father?"

"Have you talked to him?"

"We've talked to him," I say.

"Sorry. I forgot never to answer a question with a question. You'd think, being the daughter of a lawman, I'd know better."

Now I'm surprised. I had no idea Tony's father-in-law had been a cop. I guess there are a lot of things I don't know about Tony.

"Have you met Ben's father?"

"No. So I'm probably not being fair. I just imagine someone with that kind of money and power has to be a control freak. His name is Cyrus, but you probably already know that."

"Did they see much of Cyrus?"

"Oh, yes. He tried to buy their affection. People like that never have time for their families. They're too busy getting rich to notice their personalities have rotted. Bennie loves Cyrus because he has every toy known to man. He even has two wolfhounds. Bennie is scared to death of the dogs. Marlena loves dogs. She grew up with them."

"Do you think Cyrus let them come and stay with him? And didn't tell Ben?"

"Quite possibly. Have you called him?"

"Not yet. We just got his number from Ben a little while ago." Ben didn't think Marlena would be there, but I could kick myself for not contacting him yet. "Do you have a good phone number for Cyrus? Ben said his father is reclusive and we'll be lucky to reach him." Of course Ben might be lying.

Helen says, "Perhaps you two should split up. You can cover more ground."

Now she's getting on my nerves. "We're a team."

I look at Ronnie and see she is beaming. I'll never live the remark down.

"Sorry, I didn't mean to tell you how to do your job. I'm just scared. This has never happened to our family. I never thought I'd be at a police station looking for my daughter."

Welcome to my world. I never thought I'd be looking for someone I didn't intend to harm.

"Does your daughter or Bennie have any medical conditions we should be concerned about?"

"Marlena is pregnant but she's not far along. She takes prenatal vitamins. Bennie is asthmatic. He has an inhaler. The doctor thinks he'll outgrow it, but all the fighting at home is making it worse."

"Would he go anywhere without his inhaler?"

"No. Definitely not. Marlena is so careful to keep one with her. And he has one in his room. He knows how to use it."

"Are there any issues with your daughter's pregnancy?"

"It was unexpected. But Marlena was excited about having another child."

"What about Ben? Is he happy?" It's a loaded question, but I need to know how estranged he and Helen are.

"She was worried about telling him about the pregnancy. Their marriage has been in a bad place for several years. Since the beginning, really. They played at being a family, and I think Marlena always hoped he would fall in love with her, with the idea of being a husband and a father. She always made excuses for him.

"My ex-husband met Ben a couple of times, according to my daughter. She said her father was not impressed.

"I invited my daughter to bring Ben and Bennie to spend Christmas the first year they were married. Ben made some excuses and has never set one foot in my home. But Bennie and Marlena came every Christmas and Thanksgiving. I even managed to get Bennie for Easter last year. She always has excuses for Ben's absence. Last Christmas I went to her house and Ben was out of town. That's when I noticed the drabness of her house. It wasn't like my daughter to not decorate. She said she was still thinking about what to do with the house and couldn't make her mind up. I called Ben and offered to pay for whatever furniture and things they needed to spruce the place up. He was curt with me and must have been offended. I've never been invited back."

Ronnie asks, "So you don't see your daughter or Bennie very often?"

"She still calls me. But, no, I haven't seen her for several months. He hates me. He knows I disapprove of him and have from the beginning. You asked if Ben was happy about the new pregnancy. I don't know the answer. I haven't heard from her for over a week. She was nervous about telling him the last time I talked to her, but I told her he needed to know. And now..." Her voice trails off and her eyes dampen. "It's my fault. I'll never forgive myself if that bastard has done something to them."

I wonder if Cyrus Parker is aware Marlena is pregnant? Or that there is so much turmoil at home? But if Ben is telling the truth, Cyrus is close to Marlena and Bennie so he must have some awareness of the problems and the pregnancy. Maybe he's looking for some way to get custody of Bennie.

I ask the question. The big one. "Be honest with me. Do you think Ben has anything to do with their disappearance?"

TWENTY-TWO

Ellen has come to the office while we're talking with Helen. She's sitting at my desk when we leave the interview room. Why does everyone want to sit at my desk? She doesn't get up when she sees me. It must be a family trait. I sit on the edge of my own desk, and Ronnie gets coffee for us. I smile at Ellen but my mind is going over Helen's reply to my question of whether Ben had something to do with her daughter's disappearance. She had dabbed at her eyes with the backs of her fingers but was no longer on the verge of tears. She was mad. Watching her yo-yo between emotions I can't help but think of my therapy sessions with Karen Albright years ago. I was seventeen when my stepfather was murdered. My mother was kidnapped. Hayden and I were in grave danger. I took Hayden and ran. But I looked for my mother to free her. In the process I interviewed the families of other victims who had been taken, just like my mother. Hoping to glean some small clue as to where my mother was being held. I can still hear Dr. Albright say in her soothing voice, "How did it make you feel?" How did it make me feel? I've brought back the horrors of losing a daughter to these families. I can see the pain etched into their faces. The breathing becomes ragged from holding back tears and cries of anguish. I told myself I was doing all this to these poor innocent people to find my mother. To put an end to her kidnapper. To the killer of these poor people's daughters. But I was lying. To them. To Dr. Albright. To myself. I was putting these people through the wringer to satisfy my own anger and need for revenge. I can still hear the guilt barely hidden in my voice: "It's my fault."

My fault. It still weighs on me like a rock sitting on my heart. And I can see Helen is assuming that role as well. If she'd just done this … If she hadn't done that … But it wouldn't have changed a thing. I'm so caught up in the past, I hear myself saying to Helen the same words Dr. Albright said to me.

"Do you need a moment? I know this is difficult. You're doing fine. You are. We can stop if you want."

She answers with the words I said all those years ago to Dr. Albright.

"I'm not fine, but I want to finish this. I have to."

"Can I get you something?"

"No. I need to talk. To do something useful. I've never felt so helpless."

"Then just talk to me. Anything you want to say." I don't know if this will help, but when I was receiving therapy from Dr. Albright, I poured my soul out—at least, as much as I could. It didn't help right away but slowly, over time. I'm praying Ronnie will come back with the damn coffee, when Helen starts.

"Marlena is my only child. Things were different when she was born. The way people acted, the way they cared, just everything. Back then no one was allowed in the delivery room with the mother. They all waited in the hallway. Scared, excited, happy, expectant, guessing what the baby would be, guessing what it would be named. I knew she would be a girl. I don't know how, but I just knew. I hadn't even told my husband. We had discussed names but never told anyone else. I'd already decided it would be Marlena. We wanted another child, but it wasn't to be.

"She was smart and made friends so easily. Sometimes it was

like a Girl Scout troop had taken over our home. But they never got in trouble. No drugs. No booze. A good bunch of girls. When she went off to college, we never worried about her. She was very independent, able to think for herself. She was close to graduating when she called. She was pregnant. She didn't know what to do. It was the first time I heard her giving up. She said the boy wanted to marry her. Insisted on it. I didn't know then what he was really like. We met him and he was charming. My husband didn't like him right away. Thought he was a phony. I just thought Ben was nervous being around her parents. Turned out my husband was right, and I felt like a fool for not trying to get her to call the wedding off."

A tear runs down her cheek and her voice falters. "So it's my fault. All this trouble with him. My fault. If they're hurt, it's..."

There it is again. Fault. Blame. How can those words be so powerful? How can we think we're so important the world reacts to our whims or decisions or mistakes? "Helen, I hate to say this, but you've got to stop blaming yourself." She lets out a deep breath and smiles.

"Tony was smart hiring you, Megan."

I think so too. "He's a good guy. Let me ask you another question. How long have they lived in that house?"

"They moved in right before Bennie was born. It was too big for them. And he didn't want any more children."

"He didn't tell me." In fact, he'd said the opposite.

"Well, he wouldn't. When she told me she was pregnant this time, I thought, 'Uh-oh,' but I hoped he'd love the new one like he did Bennie."

The photos in his cabin crossed my mind. The only photos in my place are of Hayden. There weren't any photos of Bennie in his cabin. Everyone says he doted on the boy, so why didn't he have any pictures there? Not even a place for Bennie to sleep.

"Did you know they were separated?"

This takes her by surprise, but she tries to cover it up. "It must have been recently. We haven't talked for a week or so. Are you sure, or is that what he's telling you?"

Good question. We haven't had it verified by anyone. I change the subject.

"Can you give us the names of her friends and their contact information if you have it?"

"Her old friends probably wouldn't know much, but I can call them and put the word out. As far as recent friends, Bennie has a friend from preschool he's had playdates with. Never overnight. Just visits at each other's house. I can't remember his name right now and I've never seen him. Marlena thought he was a good kid. A boy Bennie's age. I remember Bennie talking to me on the phone. Wait a minute... Sean. That's the boy's name. Sean Hunter. I'm sure of it. The parents live not far away. Marlena is friends with the mother and they have coffee sometimes while the kids play. And there's a neighbor, an older lady, just down the street, according to what Marlena told me. They knew each other to wave at, but I don't think they were close."

"Did she like to camp?"

"He took them camping once but my daughter hated it. She had a scare when she was little. A bear came during the night looking for food. She stays out of the woods. Ben loves it. He goes for weeks at a time."

"Alone?"

Helen says, "I assume. Marlena never said. I know the only camping she and Bennie do is in the front room with sleeping bags. She makes cookies and some little picnic stuff for him. She wouldn't let him go with Ben; she worries about him being too far away with his asthma. Not that Ben would have wanted his son along. He could handle Bennie as long as someone was there to take over."

I show her the picture I took of the sleeping bags at Ben's cabin.

"That's hers and Bennie's. Were those in her house?"

I change the subject. "Where would she go if she wanted to stay somewhere overnight? Family?"

"My ex-husband died from cancer a few years ago. I'm all the family she's known. Ben came to the funeral but might as well have been on another planet. It embarrassed Marlena."

I'm storing all this in my head. I don't want to slow things down with a pen and notebook. So we have two friends for Marlena now. One is obviously Mrs. Green. The way Ben talked, she didn't make friends and he was the one trying to socialize. He was worried about the sleeping bags near his front door.

"Did Ben know about her friend from down the street?"

"She told me he knew about the playdate thing and disapproved. She didn't say why, but you can guess. He fetched Marlena and Bennie home from the friend's house. It embarrassed her to death."

Poor choice of words. "But he let her have a car."

"Marlena said he checked the mileage. He bought it just after Bennie was born. She was allowed to go to the grocery store and take Bennie to preschool. Things like that. I came over and took her and Bennie out or I brought them to my house when she would let me."

Checked the mileage? He's disturbed and paranoid. Paranoid about what?

"Helen, I have to ask this: Are you sure Marlena wasn't seeing someone?"

"Absolutely not. But if she was, I wouldn't blame her. We talked at least once a week until just recently. Usually while Ben was gone somewhere. She never gave any hints she was... No, she just wouldn't have. That's all. She's faithful to Ben. We talked once about her leaving him but she said she'd stick it out no matter what. She still loved him even though he treated her like a piece of furniture. But maybe it's just a mother's sense of things. She never said she was in danger or that he'd hurt her. She and Bennie had the bare necessities; a roof over their head, food on the table, she had her own car, but not many friends. I wouldn't blame her if she was seeing someone. Would you?"

I don't answer. I would never be in Marlena's situation. I grew up differently. The abuser would be the one missing.

"I'm positive she wasn't doing anything like that."

Tomorrow we'll go see Marlena's only friend, Mrs. Hunter. we'll both need sleep soon. We're no good this way but I won't be able to rest. Marlena, Bennie, and Hayden will haunt my sleep.

TWENTY-THREE

The Taurus engine rattles reluctantly, shuts down as I pull up in front of my place. I have sympathy for the car. It's acting like I feel. I called Hayden on the road home and he answered with "I guess you're busy again." His words are like a dagger in my heart. His apartment is not far from my own. I think about driving by. He answered the phone so he must be home. But I don't. It would look like I was lying when I called to beg off in the first place. I'd told him I love him. He didn't respond that he loved me like he always used to when we were younger and still a family. I've made a mistake not going to meet him. Maybe a bigger one not going to his place now. I've made a lot of mistakes when it comes to Hayden. Maybe I don't want to have family. Maybe it's a defense mechanism like my therapist tells me? Maybe I'm not deserving of his love?

I open the car door, the hinges creak and pop. I should put it out of its misery, but the choice is not mine. I trudge to the front door and let myself in to my darkened apartment. It's silent except for the yelling coming from the neighbors behind my place. I resist the urge to go over there, give them guns, and let them shoot it out.

My keys hit the table inside the house and slide onto the floor. Of course. My knees creak like my car when I stoop to pick them up. My bed looks like a life raft, but there's something I have to do first. I don't bother undressing or having my usual dribble of wine. I go right to my desk and pull out my pacifier, the box of tapes. The one I want seems to jump in my hand. I slot it in and take a deep breath, letting it out slowly before I hit "play."

Me: (I yawn and cover it with my hand.) Sorry. I didn't sleep much.

Dr. Albright: Bad dreams?

Me: Just tired. I kept waking and had trouble going back to sleep.

Dr. Albright: Tell me about the dreams.

I've said all this once before in another session but the words seem to spill out, force themselves out.

Me: They aren't so much dreams as they are memories from when I was younger. Hayden was still a baby. Not more than two or three years old. We're in a car and Mom is driving. My stepfather, Rolland, isn't with us. Mom hasn't met him yet.

I stop the tape. Rolland wasn't Hayden's father. Hayden was the product of the same sick serial killer as me. Mom lied about running from him after I was born. She'd been with him and along came Hayden. She ran away with us after that, but she didn't try to hide us. She kept in touch with our bio-father. She told him where we lived and that was the reason Rolland was murdered. I love her but I hate her for being so evil. I hit "play." All this isn't why I need to hear the tape.

Me: In the dream I didn't know why we were running or who we were running from. I only knew I was afraid. Sick with the fear I felt surrounding my mother. There were real monsters. Not just under the bed or in the closet. The ones that masquerade as people.

Dr. Albright doesn't say anything. She waits for the rest of the injurious words to be expelled. She taught me patience and I guess I love her for it.

Me: In the dream I look at Hayden in his little car seat. He's turned blue. Blood is spewing out of his mouth and his eyes are blackened and I scream at my mom to help him: "Stop the car! Hayden's dying!" When she turns her face toward me, I see she's not human. She's the monster. She's what I'm scared of.

My throat tightens and I feel that I can't breathe. Hayden's words have cut me to the quick. He doesn't know how much I love him. What is wrong with me? I put the tapes away and manage to shrug out of my blazer and shoulder holster and then fall across my bed before a wave of deep sadness rolls over me and I cry myself to sleep.

TWENTY-FOUR

The alarm clock didn't go off but something has awakened me. It's daytime judging by the sunlight coming through my bedroom window and I realize I've slept more than the hour I intended. I know that while I've been resting the Search and Rescue Teams have been out scouring the area, officers have been widening their door-to-door questioning of neighbors, everyone waiting for a call that they have been found safe. Or that the worst has happened. My sleep has been disturbed by the feeling that I'm missing something important. That I'm too late. But I'm not in my teens any longer and my body, even if not my mind, needs to shut down for a spell. My phone says it's 5:00 and I feel rested after nearly four hours of sleep. I also see there's a text from Dan, my boyfriend.

Megan,

I realize it's early there and hope I didn't wake you. I just had to touch base. I miss you. Do you miss me? I have several meetings today. Things are shaping up well. If this works out, I may open a franchise in Colorado and Maine. I know I said I never wanted to go this big. The offer is tempting but I don't like having my name on items that I haven't made myself. DAN'S CREATIONS. *How does that sound for a company name? If I take this on, I may have to hire Hayden full-time. He's good. Almost as good as me. Ha-ha. Do you think he's up for that? I hope he is, as I'm sure you'd love to keep him close. Anyway, my fingers are getting tired. You know I don't like to text, so that shows you how much I love you. If you have time this evening, please text me and we'll talk.*

Love,

Dan

I read the text twice and then once more out loud before I answer.

Who is this? I think you have the wrong number.

He'll get a chuckle out of that. But to be safe, I send another text telling him I do miss him and he can wake me up anytime he wants. As long as there's coffee involved. Or something else. I feel like a female Pinocchio. I'm turning into a real girl. He'd asked me out a couple of times after I first met him and I stood him up each time. I wasn't ready for a real relationship. Actually, I was scared to death of what he wanted. Just sex was doable if I needed it. But he was interested in all of me. I could see the look in his eyes, and the sincerity in his voice. I'd put us both through the mill before we finally settled into a smooth give-and-take relationship. He gave and I took. These days I find myself thinking about him quite a lot. If he's not careful I'll be the one giving and he can take for a change. I still have a ways to go.

Enough already. I hurry to shower and get to the office. I want to beat Ronnie there for once.

* * *

I don't. When I pull in, I see Ronnie's lavender-and-pine-scented car in its usual spot. I feel the hood of the car and it's still warm. Good. I stopped for coffee and donuts. I'll tell her I was here and went to get them.

"Help yourself," I say, and I have to make room on her crowded desk to set the booty down.

Ronnie absently takes a coffee from the tray and I take it back, giving her the other, three creams and four sugars. Mine is black. I'd inject caffeine if it wasn't against the law.

Ronnie is glued to the computer screen, and I open the bag of freshly glazed donuts and shake it under her nose. It's like smelling salts to us addicted people.

"Thanks, Megan. Guess what I've been doing?"

I'm not even mad she's teasing me. I'm in such a good mood from Dan's text, I can even put up with the sheriff's nosy secretary. But it's Sunday, Nan's day off, and so thank God I won't have to test the theory.

"Cyrus Parker owns companies that own companies that have banks that built subdivisions, including the Baker Heights community. He also owns a furniture manufacturer in Seattle and... well, there's just too much to go into."

"Too many to search?" I ask.

"Even if we used the National Guard. But I might have found something interesting. Right in Port Ludlow."

I'm starting to lose my mojo, but I'm still too happy to snap at her. Almost.

"I found several industrial sites in Washington, Oregon, and Colorado. I narrowed it down to the ones within one hundred miles of Baker Heights and kept chopping the list down until I came up with one very good possibility that would make a good place to hold a hostage."

Okay. Interesting.

"Ludlow Timber Works. It's nonoperational and has been shut down for twenty years, but I checked Google Earth and the plant is still there."

"What would we do without Google Earth," I say, and then add, "That's good work." I stuff a donut in my mouth to keep from being curt. And then I remind myself Dan said he loves me and misses me. I show Ronnie the text.

"Oh, Megan. That's so sweet. He's such a nice guy. You deserve each other. I hope you sent him a sweet reply."

I still have donut in my mouth, so I don't have to reply. I put the phone away, swallow, and wash the donut down with coffee that burns all the way to my navel. "I did. Now let's find Marlena and Bennie." And lock Ben up.

Ronnie stacks the papers into a neat pile and turns it all over on her desk. She's had Nan training. Nan is like a foghorn if she sees or knows anything, and even though she won't be in today, hiding things from her has become a habit. Of course, if Nan wants it, even a shredder will do no good.

* * *

We take my car. I'm not in the mood to smell the menagerie of cleaner and scents. "So what can you tell me about the old timber mill?"

"I told you it's been closed for twenty years, but Cyrus still owns it and pays taxes. I couldn't find any building permits filed, so I don't think much has been done to get it ready to open again. I think he's using it as a tax write-off."

Or money laundering, I think unkindly, and I haven't even met the man. But you don't get as rich as Midas by honest practices.

"We need to call Ben and see where he is."

Ronnie has her phone out and punches icons while she's driving. Scary. But she pulls up a screen and hands the phone to me. The screen is a map with a blue blip in the middle. I recognize the location as Ben's cabin. She's turned on "Find My Device" on his phone and we'll be able to track his movements somewhat.

"Nice. Now can you tell me what he had for breakfast?"

She laughs. I'm not kidding. What good is she? Ronnie takes

the phone back and thumbs another icon. She has the location of the Timber Works on GPS. Okay, I take it back.

The mill sits along a secluded part of the bay. The Parkers seem to love seclusion. Part of the mill is built over the water and held up by logs the size of telephone poles. A rusted chain-link fence blocks the entrance and is plastered with "No Trespassing" signs. More importantly it's chained and padlocked. The road leading to the gate is gravel pounded into the mud, and I can see tire ruts leading inside.

Ronnie looks down the fence line. "What do you want to do, Megan? It says, 'No trespassing.'"

Trespassing would be illegal. She's been around me long enough to know signs are just suggestions.

I've outfitted my car with some tools for just this type of situation. I get out and get in the trunk, take a claw hammer and pry bar to the gate, and beat the lock off. It's tougher than it looks and takes five good swings before it pops. On television a lock always opens right away. Or the lock is shot off with a single bullet that penetrates an inch of solid steel. There's never a ricochet. Ronnie gets out and we swing the gates open and go back to the car. I don't want to be caught in there by Ben or security. The lock and chain look new, so someone is concerned about intruders.

"I'll pull the car up and block the entrance. If someone comes, they'll have to honk. I'll say we saw the gate open and went to check for trespassers." It worked once.

Ronnie says nothing as we walk across the weed-grown lot and cross what was once light-gauge railroad tracks that more than likely transported the cut timber to the bay, where it was floated or loaded on barges. Most of the rails are missing now and the wood ties have been dug up. That explains the "No Trespassing" signs. An unusually shaped structure, easily thirty feet tall, that looks like a badminton shuttlecock. We get closer and it looks like a wigwam. The top is rounded and screened with a metal mesh. The entire structure is rusted. I see a large door on the side facing us that looks rusted shut.

Ronnie, who is the font of all knowledge, says, "That's a beehive burner. Some people call it a teepee burner because of the shape."

This reminds me of something Hayden said when he was about four years old. He'd probably heard it from my stepfather. He said, "Keep your peepee in your teepee." That was the only time I ever saw my mom yell at her darling perfect son. And then she laughed, because Hayden could do no wrong. If he smeared poop on the wall, she'd call it art and praise him for it.

"That's where they incinerate the sawdust and waste," Ronnie says, and points toward the teepee.

The thought makes me shudder. The smell of wood and grease assails my nostrils. The memory of Dan's burnt-out cabin and destruction of all of his wood carvings is still too fresh. I shove the sick feeling deep down but know it will resurface. Poor Dan. That tragedy must weigh heavily on him but he never brings it up. Never blames me for his losses.

The main building is a series of covered and enclosed bays with twenty-foot ceilings and conveyor belts of steel rollers I imagine fed the tree trunks into the saws. Ahead of me is what looks like an upright wagon wheel made of steel at least ten feet in diameter mounted on a huge hub/axle of some kind with a heavy saw blade disappearing into the plank floor. I examine the place where the blade goes below and can see nothing because of the grease and sawdust buildup around the opening.

Ronnie is on her phone and shows me a picture of something identical to what we're seeing. "It's a band saw."

I'd seen pictures of band saws in newspaper articles about these places. I can't begin to imagine how wide the steel saw blade had to be to fit these. The wood chips and sawdust are thick under my feet. When I pick some of it up, it has the same rough consistency as the stuff I found on Ben's pant legs at his cabin. Of course, wood chips are just wood chips. But the fact Ben owns a part of this place makes it worth exploring further. And the padlock and chain weren't rusty like the fence.

"Let's look around," I say. I think it's safe. The only thing I'll need my gun for is maybe a rat. But first I have Ronnie check Ben's whereabouts. He's still at the cabin. We split up and I go around back to see where the saw blade goes. There must be some way of getting down there to do repairs or whatever they do with behemoth band saws. This place would make a good haunted house tour.

On the back side of the mill, I see row after row of steel-framed windows with most of the glass broken out. A dirty canvas tarp catches my eye about midway down the side of the building. Lifting it, hoping rats don't scurry around my feet, I find a stairway leading to a solid steel door. The canvas is still damp underneath from last night's dew. The door has a hasp but no lock. On examining the hasp, I see where the rust has been worn away by something recently. My shadow disappears into pitch-blackness. The floor here is wet with mildew and covered with wood chips and sawdust. I shine my light around and see nothing at first and then the light glints off something in the sawdust. It's bottled water. Glacier Mist Natural Spring Bottled Water, to be exact. The bottle is empty except for some residue. I collect it and take it outside. All around is hard clay that's like rock from years of wood grit and oil ground into the earth by workers' shoes. There's no sign of my passage. Outside in the daylight the bottle looks fresh. It hasn't been there long.

Climbing down a mud embankment, I shine my light around the part of the mill that protrudes over the bay. Nothing. Two ramshackle structures are nearby. One looks like an outhouse. I open the door and see a hole in the floor. I go inside and shine the light down there. It hasn't been used in quite some time. It doesn't even smell, considering. Or maybe my sense of smell has been damaged by Ronnie's car.

The roof has caved in on the next structure, and planks have been pulled out of the sides. This one is small enough for a one-car garage, but it was probably a toolshed. There are still metal hooks on one wall. I go to see if Ronnie has found anything.

"Nothing but rats," she says, and I cringe. She sees I have something. "Where did you find that?" I tell her about the little room under the band saw and show her the bottle I found.

"There's nothing here. Let's go to the station." We go back to the car and I pull the gate shut and leave the padlock on the ground along with the chain. Vandals must have done that.

We arrive at the Sheriff's Office and the door is locked. Tony, Ellen, and Helen are gone. On top of my desk is a note written in the sheriff's perfect handwriting.

At Moe's. Join us.

Moe's is in Port Townsend. I'm glad he hasn't taken them somewhere fancy. We smell like wood and oil and other unsavory things. We'll fit right in at Moe's.

Grabbing an evidence form and some labels, we lock up the office and head out. This time I had filled out the details of the evidence I'd collected. I'd even signed it. Marley will be proud of me.

TWENTY-FIVE

Moe's started out as a breakfast joint, then progressed to hamburgers and fries for lunch and now has a full menu of junk food and beer. You don't have to know how to read French.

Moe comes out from behind the front counter wiping his hands on a dish towel. "Megan. Your usual?"

I wasn't aware I had a usual but just nod. "Same for her," I say, indicating Ronnie.

"Sheriff's waiting," he says. "He's got two hot ladies with him. Make that four."

Gag. "Do I need to wait to be seated?" It's a joke. He gets it.

Sheriff Gray and his two consorts are sitting in the back by the windows. He's already pulled up an extra chair. I grab the seat next to the sheriff and make Ronnie sit on the end.

"We just ordered," Helen says. Tony rolls his eyes. He usually has some grease with his sugar but his wife keeps a leash on his food choices. They met after Tony had a heart attack. She was his nurse. Still is, when he listens to her. If she saw the greasy bags of fast food he brings to work each day, he'd be in trouble. That's why he sneaks it into the office in the morning. He hides his food like an alcoholic hides his bottles. Burger-holic. That's Tony.

I don't want to ruin everyone's dinner by talking shop. Moe

comes with our food. Double cheeseburger bacon platters for me and Ronnie. Helen has two hard boiled eggs, avocado, and toast. Ellen and Tony have salads. Tony looks at our platters and I think he's about to cry. He looks like a starving dog. I want to sneak him part of my hamburger under the table.

We all get settled, and Helen asks, "Did you find anything while you were out?"

I don't want to tell her we found a plastic bottle. I don't want to tell her I broke a lock and trespassed on private property. She probably wouldn't care, and the sheriff knows how I work, but it seems disrespectful to say any of that in front of him as a lawman.

"We're still looking, Helen. Are you staying in town?" As I say this, I know it's not a good thing. Sheriff Gray gives me a cautioning look and I realize what I've done.

"If Ellen doesn't mind me staying with them another night, I'll still be here."

Ellen says, "You know you're always welcome at our place. Right, Tony?"

"Uh, right, hon. El can make up the guest room for you."

"Not if I'm a bother."

"No trouble at all. You're family," Tony says, and looks at his sad salad like the hell will never end.

"We have to take something to the Crime Lab, Sheriff." There's a handful of French fries on my plate. I slide it over to the sheriff and get a stern look from his wife. I don't care. I don't work for her. Ronnie hasn't touched the burger and only ate a couple of fries. She's watching her figure. If she doesn't start eating more, she won't be able to see it.

"Keep me posted," Tony says.

"By the way, Sheriff, how did you get the call that your niece was missing?" I ask.

He looks at his wife. "The dispatcher told me. I'm not sure how she knew but they seem to know everything. She got the call from Ben and dispatched a car and then called me."

My curiosity satisfied, we go to the car and the first thing Ronnie says is "You know she has him on a diet."

I know, but he was hungry. "Consider it a charitable donation."

"Helen's nice, don't you think?"

I say, "Yes. She's easy to talk to."

"I should call Marley and let him know we're coming."

She definitely needs to tell Marley *she's* coming. He won't be excited to see me.

* * *

I was right about Marley. He must have thought she was coming alone. He has that "puppy dog needs a pet" look on his face. I give him and Ronnie about two minutes alone before I get down to business. "What's the news on the things from the Parker house?"

"Which house? His or hers?"

He's guessing. Good guess. Ronnie steps in. "You're cute when you get all serious-like. You look like Robert Downey Jr. when he plays Sherlock Holmes." That's all it takes.

"You could be Gwyneth Paltrow in *Iron Man*."

I want to tell them to knock it off, but Ronnie's working him. At least I think that's what she's doing.

"Who do I look like?" I ask, and they both ignore me.

"I haven't been able to run DNA or anything. The machine is down, but I've got someone working on it."

My face drops and that makes him smile.

"Just kidding," he says. "But not about the machine. It's down for a little. However, I was able to pull fingerprints off the bottle Ronnie gave me from her interview and compare them to things from the house. You've got a match."

Good one. Way to go, science nerd.

Ronnie's face lights up and she hugs him. He blushes, and it's not easy with his complexion.

"Good job, Marley," I say, and don't hug him. That's what Ronnie is for.

When she detaches herself and lets him breathe, he says, "The DNA should be complete by tonight." He has a funny look on his face when he says this, and I brace myself for bad news.

"Ronnie can come back this evening to pick up the results."

It's not bad news. He's setting up a second chance to get a hug from Ronnie. Sly. *Way to go, Marley.*

"Which reminds me..." I say.

He holds his hand out and I give him the evidence bag and the completed evidence form. He reads it twice and looks at the signature.

"You did this?" he asks.

"You know I've always done my own evidence requests." He knows better.

He reads the document again. "You found this by an abandoned timber mill?"

"That's what it says, doesn't it?" It's not a lie.

He looks at me skeptically but signs the bottom of the form, accepting it to be tested.

"It's the same brand of water as the one Ronnie gave me. You want DNA and fingerprints?"

"Yes. Whatever you've got."

Ronnie says, "You're so good at this. I don't know what we would ever do without you."

He blushes again. "I'll try to have it for you, Ronnie, ASAP."

TWENTY-SIX

"Should I call the sheriff?" Ronnie asks.

"We'll have to get him away from the ladies. I don't need pressure from them."

"But this is good, right? I mean, how did Ben's prints get on the items found in the sink? He said he hadn't been there for a week."

Exactly. But he lived in the house. He'll say his fingerprints will be all over everything. If DNA comes back showing he used the glass or fork, we'll go after him. Hard. My gut tells me the plastic water bottle I found at the mill is gaining importance. Where there's water, there's life.

Ronnie is already on her phone, tapping like a madwoman. "Jon and Jennie Hunter. Thirty-two Mountain View, Baker Heights."

* * *

We're quiet, both thinking our own thoughts. I pull up in front of 32 Mountain View as a gold Honda Odyssey is backing out of the garage. The woman driving the vehicle sees us, stops, says something to a child in the back, and gets out.

"Mrs. Hunter?" We show our badges.

She doesn't look surprised to see us. "I suppose you want to talk to me. Let me get Sean. We'll go inside."

We hang loose while she takes a boy of four years old from the back seat. He's the spitting image of Hayden when he was that age. Skinny, a shock of blond hair, inquisitive eyes. I say, "Hi, Sean."

"You're a detective."

"That's right."

"Do you have a gun?"

Ronnie and I exchange looks. Just a kid and already mesmerized by guns. Jennie takes his hand and leads him up the drive with us following.

The Hunter house is beautifully decorated. She sends Sean into the kitchen to get a Fruit Roll-Up and tells him to sit at the table while she leads us to the sofa. She sits on an ottoman and gives us her undivided attention.

"You have a beautiful home, Mrs. Hunter," Ronnie says.

"I have Marlena Parker to thank."

"Do you know she and her son are missing?"

"Mrs. Green has told the entire community. I suppose she told you Marlena and I were friends. Our sons go to the same preschool."

Sean is back with a long strip of candy hanging from his mouth. He stands beside his mother and makes faces at us. I make one back and he giggles and makes a worse one. This can go on all day, but Mrs. Hunter turns him around and points him back toward the kitchen. "What have I told you about eating in the living room, Sean?" He trudges off to the kitchen.

"Marlena was getting a degree in interior design and should have opened her own business. I tried to pay her but she refused. She said company and coffee was all she wanted. Are you any closer to finding her?"

I change the subject. "We haven't told you our names. I'm Megan Carpenter and my partner is Ronnie Marsh."

"I'm Jennie." She takes our hands and squeezes tight with a

grip born from holding on to a four-year-old. "I've been worried sick."

Ronnie says, "Do you mind if I use your restroom?"

"Through the kitchen. Excuse the mess."

Ronnie excuses herself. She's going snooping. She learned that from me.

Jennie is in her thirties, short, shapely, and dressed in sweats. She sees me looking at her and says, "It's such a beautiful Sunday morning to go to the park. Sean's got a lot of energy."

I see Sean in the doorway to the kitchen looking like he's up against a force field with his candy. He's four years old. Same as Bennie. He makes a face at me and I ignore him. He turns and disappears.

"You say Marlena helped you decorate?"

"Well, I stood around while they delivered the stuff and she made it look like this. What you see here is all Marlena. She's magnificent, isn't she?" It's not a question. I could use some help decorating my place, but I don't like people coming inside. If I tried to put together pieces of furniture, wall hangings, curtains, tables, and the like, my place would look like it was hit by a tornado.

"Beautiful," I say, and I notice Ronnie is walking around the room, checking things out. Then I see her disappear into the kitchen. "Can I ask you some personal questions?"

"What would you like to know?"

I'd like to know where Marlena and Bennie Parker are. "How long have you known the Parkers?"

"My husband, Jon, bought this place for a wedding present. Ten years next week." She beams a smile at me, and I think, *That's what love looks like.*

"The Parkers moved in, let me see. Bennie's the same age as Sean. So that would be around four years ago."

"You've known them four years, then? You didn't know them before?"

"I didn't know her."

I raise an eyebrow.

"I met her when they moved here. We both had babies and it was nice to know someone else was learning the ropes. I'd never tell Marlena this. Anyway, before they moved here, I'd run into Ben Parker at a bachelorette party."

Now my eyebrow has grown wings and is flying upward.

"I know. Right? Anyway, a friend of mine was getting married and I was obliged to attend. I was planning on dropping off a gift and sneaking out, but Ben was in the bar with a couple of other guys. I recognized him when he moved down the street because of the leer on his face when he saw me. It was the same look at the bar. And he said something corny. I don't remember what it was now, but I remember thinking, 'What an asshole.'" She puts a hand over her mouth. "Excuse my language."

"It's your house," I say, and grin. I like her. I would have called Ben worse.

"I took Sean to the park one day in his stroller, and Marlena was there with Bennie. We got to talking and I liked her right away. Pure class. And smart. And funny. God, she made us laugh. Me and Jon. Jon teases me, saying that he should have married her. Jon absolutely fell in love with Bennie. When the boys get together, you would think Jon was the same age. I have to be the grown-up."

I feel my eyes moisten. The thought of having that kind of happiness. The kind of life where everyone is nice and not a killer or a liar or a psychopath. What would it be like? Who would I be right now? What I'm feeling scares me. Hayden had some of that life with his adopted family. No wonder he's having trouble letting me in. I wouldn't let me in, either. But I'll never stop trying.

Jennie is still talking and I've missed something. "Can you repeat that, please?"

"I'm just reminiscing. It's not important."

"Everything is important when someone is missing. Please?"

She smiles at me. "You're a very serious woman."

She called me a woman. I'm only thirty and a smidge. Am I getting old?

"I was saying I found out Marlena hadn't told Ben we were

getting together over coffee while the boys played. He knew the boys went to the same school, and he came over one time with Bennie and Marlena for a little party. He got angry about something and they left. Then one day while she and I were having coffee Ben just showed up at the door and told her to get her stuff. He needed her at home. Both of the boys were in preschool at the time and it was almost time to pick them up. I told Ben I'd take Marlena to pick the kids up. She looked... not scared, exactly, but cowed, beaten. I could see Ben wasn't going to let her go with me."

"What did Marlena say?"

"She didn't say anything. Just got her purse and left with him. He tried to take her hand and she pulled it away. That was a week before the blowup. I was glad when he moved out. She seemed happy for the first time since I've known her."

"So you knew they separated?"

"Oh, sure. I talked with Marlena shortly after he left."

Ronnie comes back from the kitchen with mugs of tea and hands them around. "I hope you don't mind me making myself at home," she says. "I just saw how cozy your kitchen was and it reminded me of home. When I was a kid I would make tea with my sister and we would pretend we were British royalty. Tea and crumpets." Ronnie looks sheepish. "The tea bags were out on the counter and I—"

"Ronnie, I don't mind at all. In fact, I should have offered."

Ronnie takes a seat and asks, "What did I miss?"

My lack of a life flashing before my eyes is what you missed. I say, "She was telling me about the time Ben came and took Marlena home from here."

"Didn't Helen tell us about that?" Ronnie asks.

"Yeah." To Jennie I say, "Marlena's mother, Helen, has been talking to us. Did Marlena talk to you about why Ben was upset with her?"

"She didn't. But he did. Ben picked Bennie up another day from preschool and tried to be charming when he saw me. He told me he had gotten off work early that day and was worried about them. He said Marlena is absentminded and he was afraid she'd forgotten about Bennie needing to be picked up. Then when I got home there was a message on my front door from Marlena asking that I call her the next day. Ben usually leaves around six o'clock in the morning and comes back after dark. Marlena told me he's gone a lot."

"Did you call her the next day?"

"I tried. Ben had stayed home that morning to take Bennie to preschool. I saw his truck and I waited to call. When his truck left, I called and he answered. I asked him what he was doing with Marlena's phone and he said he must have picked it up by mistake. He was driving because I could hear traffic. So I went to her house and she just cracked the door. She wouldn't let me inside. I could tell she'd been crying. She said Ben had taken her phone to get it updated at AT&T. That's not what he told me. He's such a liar."

"Was she okay? Did she look hurt?"

"I only saw a fraction of her face through the crack in the door but I could tell she was hurting. After that, I'd see her out in her yard and we'd wave to each other but I didn't see her again until he moved out. That was about a week ago. That day is burned into my mind. Our backyard is just a few houses down from theirs. The screaming and sounds of things breaking still gives me gooseflesh. I felt so sorry for her and that poor little boy. I had to keep my husband from going over there. I told him to let the police handle it. But before we could call them, I heard Ben's truck peeling out. We both went over and Marlena was upset but she didn't look like she was hurt. At least, not physically. Actually, she looked good. She said he was gone and good riddance. She asked if I would let Jon come over when Ben came back to pack his stuff. Of course Jon offered, but my husband is a little guy. Ben towers over Jon. I told her to call the Sheriff's Office, get a restraining order, file for a divorce, get a big mean dog."

"Did she do any of that?" Helen didn't tell us any of this. Maybe Marlena hadn't told her.

"I gave her the number for an attorney Jon knows but I don't think she called. Hold on." Jennie went into another room and came back with a card. "She didn't even file a restraining order. She said he would never hurt her or Bennie."

"That was a week ago?"

"The day he left. And now she's missing. But I've seen his truck in the neighborhood since then. Always at night. I think he was watching her. Creepy. You don't think he's done something to them, do you?"

TWENTY-SEVEN

We leave Jennie Hunter and I ask Ronnie, "Did you find his secretary's name in his phone contacts?"

"Lucia Simmons."

"What's her address?" She tells me. I know where it is. "I wish we'd already run her information down."

Ronnie digs in her purse and takes out her iPad. Of course she has everything on Simmons. Including some photos from Facebook. The girlfriend is strikingly beautiful.

"Her driver's license shows she's twenty-one years old, five feet two, one hundred pounds, brunette like Marlena. Her Facebook account shows she's single, no children, works at Parker Industries as a personal secretary, likes to camp, swim, and is an excellent dart player. One of her posts says she won the Yorkshire, England, championship last year."

"Any mention of Ben kidnapping his family?"

"She hasn't posted that. And Ben doesn't have Facebook, Twitter, Instagram, TikTok, or any other social media account I could find. But..."

I take the iPad from her. "Don't do that."

"What?"

"When you have something to say, just say it."

"Sorry."

Now I feel crappy. "No need to be sorry." *Unless you keep doing it.*

"Lucia Simmons has quite a social media presence. There are a couple of pictures of Ben with her. She's in a skimpy bikini. Some of the older posts came from him." Ronnie shows me a photo of Simmons and Ben on a beach. They don't look like she's taking dictation. There are several other pictures. On the deck of the Space Needle, in a hotel room, one of them having drinks and toasting, smiling for the camera. Several of Ben showing off his muscles and barely clothed. I'm surprised Facebook allows all this near nakedness.

"When did this begin?"

She looks at her notebook again. "Well, according to her Facebook page, the oldest post with Ben was two years ago. The newest was two weeks ago. They were in San Francisco having drinks. This has been going on awhile."

"But he doesn't have any social media?"

"He must have taken all his accounts down. But it doesn't take down posts he made on other people's account or any he's tagged in."

"Any way of finding out when he took them down?"

She shakes her head and I'm surprised my super-hacker can't get that information.

"I think we'd need a subpoena. But on her Facebook the posts from or about him stopped a month ago. He had a profile when he posted those, so that's enough to prove he had an account."

"Look up Jennie and Jon Hunter."

Ronnie finds it quickly. "Jennie Hunter has a lot of posts. Most from preschool, birthday parties, Sean making faces, Sean with Bennie, and the usual humorous cat and dog posts."

Someone should tell Sean if he keeps doing that with his face it will grow that way. Not me, though. I think it's cute. To a point. "Go back to the ones of Bennie and Sean." She does, and we go through them slowly. "Stop." I take the iPad from her and expand the video. "See that?"

"Ben and Marlena are in the background with a present. It must be a birthday."

I say, "What do you see?"

"The expressions on their faces. They've been fighting."

"What else?"

She looks closely and gives up.

"What is she wearing?" I ask.

"A turtleneck sweater and slacks. Her hair is down in this picture."

"What is everyone else wearing?"

"I see now. She's dressed too warmly for what's going on." She looks at her notes. "Sean's birthday is July seventeenth. If this was his birthday, it would be warm outside. The kids aren't even wearing shirts."

The turtleneck is almost up under Marlena's chin. I wonder what she's hiding under it.

"We need to call Helen and see who Marlena's doctor is."

"I'm on it." Ronnie calls the sheriff's phone.

"Ronnie. Have you found them?"

"Not yet, Sheriff. We just talked to a friend of Marlena's, Mrs. Hunter. Helen told us about her. She gave us some interesting information but nothing to indicate where they might be. Marlena hasn't contacted Mrs. Hunter, and I think they're close enough friends she would know if they left on their own. Also, Marlena isn't having an affair. Ben's lying. If she's pregnant, it's his baby."

"What do you need from me?"

"I need to talk to Helen. Is she there?"

Helen comes on the line and Ronnie puts the call on speaker.

"This is Ronnie. Do you know who Marlena's doctor is?"

"Dr. Krietemeyer is her family doctor. That's the Jefferson Healthcare Clinic in Port Ludlow."

"We'll find it."

"Do you think they're hurt? You do, don't you?"

"No, Helen. We're just covering all the bases."

She assures Helen again we will call when we have something. Ronnie's getting to be a pretty good liar. She should be. I'm her mentor.

I say, "Helen, can you put the sheriff back on?"

He picks up. "Did you get what you need?"

"It may be something. Can you set up a polygraph for Ben?" It will take the sheriff calling to get an operator to come in on a Sunday.

"What time?"

"Make it three o'clock. Ben said he would take a polygraph when we talked to him yesterday."

"Consider it done."

We hang up. I know where the clinic is, so I trade places with Ronnie and she rides shotgun. Then I remember the doctor won't be available until Monday. Shit. It's always better to talk to medical people directly. Sometimes a physical presence means a lot. And a pregnant woman sometimes talks to her doctor about things she wouldn't say to anyone else. Even a mother.

"Can you look up her doctor's home number?"

Ronnie gets the number and calls. The call goes to voicemail. She leaves a message and disconnects. "I'll try his answering service." She's about to punch the numbers in, when the phone rings in her hand.

"This is Dr. Krietemeyer. You just called my house?"

Ronnie puts it on speaker. "I'm Detective Ronnie Marsh with the Jefferson County Sheriff's Office. Detective Carpenter is with me on speakerphone. We're working a missing person case and we understand the missing woman is one of your patients. Marlena Parker."

"Is there a number I can call to verify who you are?"

She gives him Sheriff Gray's cell phone number. A minute later he calls us back.

"I'll tell you what I can, but you know about doctor/patient confidentiality and HIPAA."

"This is Detective Carpenter, Doctor. I have reason to believe your patient and her four-year-old son are missing and in grave danger. The boy has asthma and no inhaler. We've been told the mother is pregnant. I know about doctor/patient confidentiality but I promise I'll get her to sign a release when I find her."

"Sarcasm will get you everywhere, Detective Carpenter. I know who you are. Detective Marsh too. You've been in the papers. What would you like to know?"

Ronnie and I exchange a look. I pull over. This is easier than I thought. "First, we need to know how far Marlena is along in the pregnancy."

"Four weeks as of Marlena's last appointment, so that would make her almost seven weeks now. Is that important?"

I'm asking the questions here, bud. "We need as much information as we can possibly get, Doctor. We suspect she was taken against her will and time is important."

"Understood. What else?"

"Have there been any problems with the pregnancy?"

"Marlena is in good health, considering."

I don't like the sound of that.

"She's had some medical issues that affect herself and her pregnancy. I'm sorry I can't be more specific."

"Okay." *Not.* "Do you know her husband, Ben?" The line is quiet. "Doctor?"

"Oh, what the hell. He's not my patient. Yes, I know him."

"Talk to me."

When Ronnie disconnects, we've both gotten an earful. The doc didn't have anything good to say about Ben. Just the opposite. Marlena is on antidepressants and sleeping pills. Helen didn't even know. He talked about Bennie, and although he's not Bennie's doctor, he suspects the asthma was aggravated by some issues at home. He was Marlena's doctor from before she was married. After I promised him his opinions were off the record, he opened up even more. It was time to bring Ben in. Not quite enough to make an arrest, but enough to put him at the top of my list.

TWENTY-EIGHT

We meet Tony in the parking lot of the Sheriff's Office. I don't want to talk in front of Helen. Not yet. She doesn't need to know everything the doctor told us, and most of the important things he said were said in confidence.

The Taurus gives a rattle when I turn the ignition off.

"If you get Helen to go home, I'll give you a new car," Tony says. He looks exhausted. I want to find out what he has against Helen more than ever now.

"We talked to Marlena's doctor. What he told me is off the record." Unless I need it for court, and then he's on his own. "Did you get a polygraph operator?"

"On standby. Have you set it up with Ben?"

"Ronnie called. Ben will be here. I want him to think it's procedure." He's got Daddy's money to fight us, and I can barely afford a good Scotch on the money the county pays me.

"So what do you have that I couldn't hear in there?" he asks, hooking a thumb over his shoulder at the office.

Mindy's report is open to the page I wanted. "Mindy didn't find any medicine for Marlena or Bennie in the house, except for an inhaler and a bottle of prenatal vitamins in Marlena's medicine cabinet. Ben told us his wife was three months pregnant. The doctor said she was only seven weeks. He saw her three weeks ago. You can't tell Helen or anyone what I'm about to tell you." He nods. "Okay. The doctor said she's been on antidepressants for several years. He prescribed strong sleeping medication last year. He wasn't one of Ben's fans. He blamed Bennie's asthma on Ben's behavior. We didn't find sleeping pills or antidepressants in the house." Or Ben's cabin, although I can't say that.

"He gave us the name of Bennie's pediatrician to check on the inhaler situation and what pharmacy refills their medicine. If Ronnie gives you that, can you give them a call and see when it was last refilled?"

Tony looks thoughtful. "I'll have someone get on it. If there's no sign of her meds at the house it could mean she left of her own volition."

"True. But it could also mean someone was smart enough to remove Marlena's medicine. If so, they forgot Bennie's inhaler. If she's like most parents with an asthmatic child she would have a spare and she wouldn't have forgotten it. And the doc told us some things about Ben that match up with what the neighbor, Jennie Hunter, told us."

Sheriff sighs. "I heard Helen giving you the lowdown on Ben. I just thought she was being the typical mother-in-law. If it's bad, I'm glad you asked me to come out here."

It's bad enough. "Do you know his father, Cyrus?"

"I've met him. He's one of the county's benefactors."

Shit. Tony will warn me about going easy on him, but he won't make me stop. He knows I won't anyway.

"I'll give you the capsule. Both Jennie Hunter and Helen said Ben has isolated Marlena and Bennie. Bennie has a friend named Sean Hunter in preschool with him. We have a video clip of the Parkers at Sean's last birthday party in July. We saw something on the video we need to verify. The doctor swore me to secrecy but told me his opinion. Marlena came to see him the next day after Sean's birthday party. She was having stomach pains and had been nauseated for a while. He examined her and that's when she found out she was pregnant. She had a large bruise on her stomach and bruising on her neck. She told him she had dizzy spells and had fallen down. He asked her if someone was abusing her or her son. She said no but he didn't believe her. He suggested she see a counselor or call the police. She said she would."

"The bastard." Sheriff seldom uses strong language. I would have called Ben something else.

"Marlena told Jennie and Helen about the pregnancy but not about the injuries. Jennie said Marlena was concerned about Ben finding out she was pregnant but had decided she had to tell him. Jennie said she'd heard some very loud and angry arguing coming from the Parkers' house, Bennie in the background crying and saying something like 'Stop, Daddy.' Ronnie checked Jennie's Facebook page and found a video post of the birthday party. You can see Marlena and Ben in the background and he's staring daggers at her. Marlena is wearing a heavy turtleneck sweater. When we talked to Jennie, she told us it was hot that day and she worried he was harming Marlena. We saw in the video the kids were running around shirtless. The yelling started about a year ago but the worst was a week ago. Jennie hasn't seen Marlena since Ben left, but she said she put Marlena in touch with an attorney. She didn't know if Marlena saw the attorney or filed a restraining order. There is no restraining order on file, but it doesn't mean she wasn't doing the paperwork. If so, we didn't find anything at her house."

I pause again to see if he has questions. He doesn't. "In it was a water bottle that we gave to Marley Yang. He's comparing it now to the match we got from the bottle Ben used in the interview room and the items Mindy collected at the house."

Sheriff Gray says, "That's good."

I say, "Marlena's doctor said she was on antidepressants and Ambien to help her sleep. Ronnie's going to ask Marley to check the water bottle for chemicals."

Ronnie looks at me. "I am? Right. I am. I'm going to do it right now." She gets on her phone.

"Do you think the water was drugged?" he asks.

"What do you think?" I ask him. "I mean about Ben as a suspect."

He thinks about it for a little. "He's a good suspect, I'll give you that."

"But?"

"But it's not enough to arrest him. Not yet. You're going to need more."

"You mean like two dead bodies?"

"I didn't say that, Megan. Don't take an attitude with me."

I feel terrible. Tony has more at stake in this than I do. But he doesn't know that part of my history. How I searched for my missing mom and found her but we were both almost killed in the process. I didn't tell him about the three missing girls my biological father kidnapped, tortured, raped, and killed. How he dumped their bodies like so much garbage. How I made him pay.

"Maybe you can get a confession when we polygraph him," Tony says, but he doesn't sound any more confident than I am. Ben has lived a privileged life and won't just confess.

Ronnie gets off the phone and comes back. "You'll never guess." Then: "Sorry. Marley said he's run the lab tests on the bottle you found at the timber mill and the one we know Ben used. Ben's showed minute traces of alcohol and another drug he couldn't identify. The bottle from the timber mill contained zolpidem tartrate. That's Ambien," Ronnie says.

I turn to the sheriff. "That's the sleeping medicine the doc prescribed for Marlena."

Ronnie says, "Marley found residue in the bottle and suspects the pill had been crushed and mixed with the water. Marley said it takes from ten minutes to an hour for the medicine to kick in at a regular dose. There was more than a regular dose still left in the bottle."

When Marlena's house was searched there was no sign of a struggle or a burglary. The Ambien may have been the way they were taken from their home. Then they were held at the timber mill but the kidnapper decided to move them. So how did they get Marlena and Bennie to drink more water laced with Ambien?

I ask, "Fingerprints?"

Ronnie says with a frustrated grunt, "He said there were so many fingerprints on the bottle, he was unable to get a match to anything. They could be Marlena's and Bennie's or yours and mine. Except I know we didn't touch the bottles."

If the prints were even a partial match Marley would know because he had Marlena's and Bennie's fingerprints from the dishes and the juice boxes Mindy had collected.

Tony had told us he hadn't had any luck reaching Cyrus and that was one avenue we really needed to cover. "Tony, can you try to make contact with Cyrus? Maybe they'll answer if they see it's the sheriff calling. Helen says he was very fond of Marlena and Bennie. We may be spinning our wheels for nothing." *I hope.* But I don't really believe that. So far I have no reason to expect that Cyrus knows they are missing. And that makes me wonder why Ben hasn't notified his father. Talk about dysfunctional.

"I'll try. Maybe I'll send someone to track him down."

"See what you can find out and let us know."

"Gotcha. I'll make it happen. So, what next?" Tony asks.

"Ben's secretary. She has some pretty interesting posts on Facebook. Ben gave her name to Ronnie but he wasn't happy about us interviewing her. He claims she's not his girlfriend. Facebook begs to differ."

"That's good work. Now find the kidnapper. Make a case and arrest this bastard."

Or bitch. Kidnappers aren't exclusively men.

TWENTY-NINE

Ben's phone is still at his cabin. It hasn't moved any of the times we've checked. I drive to Lucia Simmons's apartment while Ronnie calls Ben. It goes to voicemail and she leaves a message she needs to talk to him. She asks how he's holding up. She says she understands how he feels and she's still working on finding his wife and son. She looks forward to talking to him. It all sounded very concerned, compassionate, complete bullshit. But he wouldn't know because his little head would be doing the listening. She disconnects and says, "Do you think we should call her first to give her a heads-up?"

"Surprise!" I say, and throw my arms wide.

"Do you think Ben has called and warned her?"

"I hope he has. What's he going to say? 'Hey, baby, the police are picking on me because my wife and son are missing, so lie to them about us.' Of course, she might be in on it with him. He's got big bucks. Maybe she'll tell us enough to pick him up and hold him." At least until his father's high-priced legal team gets him out and sues the sheriff and takes my Taurus.

Ronnie comes back with, "If he hasn't talked to her and warned her, she might call him about our visit and tell him what we asked about."

She's right. But her Facebook page makes her look like a soft mark. To make Ronnie feel better, I say, "For all we know, Marlena and Bennie are tied up in her closet. We might have to kick the door in and go in hot."

We brainstorm and come up with a workable plan by the time we arrive at the Bayview Racquet Club. From the looks of the expensive cars and the multitude of tanned bodies running around in their finery, not to mention the multitude of gardeners and golf carts, tennis courts and a golf course, I think the name should be Bayview Racket Club.

Ronnie spoke my thought. "How can a secretary afford a place like this?"

"Maybe she's independently wealthy." Neither of us believe that. We find her condo. It's easy, because her name is on the parking space where a new Mercedes is sitting.

Ronnie says, "That's an SL 550 Roadster. Retail is over a hundred and twenty thousand."

I whistle. That would buy a lot of box wine and pizza. I find a visitor's spot while Ronnie is admiring the surroundings and says, "This isn't the kind of place where you rent."

"I would never live here," I say. I mean "could," not "would."

"My sister has more money than God. How is a secretary able to afford this?"

I say, "Ben Parker is paying the bills."

"Maybe we should rethink this?" Ronnie says.

"We're here. You know what they say if someone can't take a joke."

"This isn't a joke. She's probably loaded. Has an attorney on speed dial."

So what if she's loaded? So is my gun, and it gets more respect than money. I can imagine her coming to the door and saying, "Do you know who I am?" And I pull my blazer back revealing my gun and say, "Do you know what *this* is?"

An ornate iron pergola covered with morning glories leads to a garden boasting a spectrum of colored flowers and shrubs and other plants I can't name. Some of these look like weeds to me. Expensive weeds, I'm sure. I look back at my Taurus and think, *The Beverly Hillbillies have arrived.*

A young woman, petite, wearing faded black sweats, with long brown hair pulled back in a ponytail, is sitting with her back to us at a wrought-iron table in a wrought-iron chair drinking something out of a cheap plastic cup. Maybe she couldn't find a wrought-iron cup. A bottle of Scotch is on the table. It's my brand. One of the Glens. She hears us and turns her head. Her face is pale, eyes puffy and red. She's attractive but not as attractive as Marlena. But then, she hasn't had one child and isn't pregnant with another. Not yet.

"Lucia Simmons?" I ask, and hold out my credentials. The gold badge looks cheap in this setting but, hey, she's drinking out of a plastic cup.

"I wondered when you would come." She motions for us to sit at the table.

"You knew we were coming?" Ronnie asks.

"Ben told me you would want to talk to me. He's pretty upset."

"You look like you're pretty upset yourself."

"I didn't know he had a kid until I saw it on the news. How's that?" She holds her cup out. "Want one?"

I'm wondering how many she's already had. This is going to be easier than I thought. "I'll take a small one. We're on duty."

She smirks and tries to get up, but Ronnie puts a hand on her shoulder and says, "I'll get the cups."

Lucia cocks her head toward the condo. "Glasses are in the cabinet over the wine rack."

I pick up the half-empty bottle. "That's one of my favorite Glens."

She manages a half-smile. "Glenlivet. It's my medicine of choice too. There's more expensive stuff inside, but I prefer something I don't have to count the cost of while I'm drinking. I'm a small-town girl."

"Same here. I'm Detective Carpenter. My partner is Detective

Marsh. I wasn't sure we'd find you at home. Sorry about not calling ahead." I look around. Maybe Ben is hiding in the bushes.

"No worries. He's not here."

"Ben?"

"Yeah. Benjamin Woodrow Parker. Son of a tycoon. Son of a gun. Son of a bitch."

I laugh at the lame joke. Ronnie comes back with two plastic tumblers. The kind you can use and throw away. Ronnie pours us both a teensy bit and sits again. I pretend to sip some of the amber liquid and give an exaggerated shiver. "Been a while for me. I can barely afford this stuff on a cop's pay. My boyfriend is my savior," I lie.

"Ben says detectives don't make shit. He's rich, you know. Really, really, really, really rich."

You've already told me that and you're on the express train to drunk.

"Have you talked to the old man yet? Cyrus. Who names their kid Cyrus? Or Woodrow? Tell me that."

It's really none of her business who I've talked to, but she's making sense. I'm surprised he hasn't already contacted me. Or the sheriff. If he's as close to Bennie as Ben says, he surely knows Bennie and Marlena are missing. Even if his asshole son hasn't informed him.

Her cup is almost empty. I repour it to the top. I'm helpful like that. "So, Lucia," I say, and she stops me.

"It's 'Luci,' if you don't mind. 'Lucia' sounds like some old maiden aunt. My mom had a sick sense of humor."

"I'm so sorry," I say. Not. "Have you met Ben's parents yet?"

"He's an only child. Mother's gone. Father's a real dick. And I'm Ben's secret."

"So, why did you ask if we've talked to Cyrus yet?" She gives me a blank look. Maybe it's the alcohol so I ask something easier. Something obvious. "You live here all alone?"

"Yeah. Ain't it a hoot. Place is big enough for a family." Her face bunches up and tears trickle down her cheeks. She asks me, "You got a family?"

"I have a brother."

"How about you?" she asks Ronnie.

"Yes. Do you?"

"A mom and a sister and a dad no one can find. He was a teamster. Truck driver. One day he got in his truck and just took off. My mom and sister live in New York where I'm from. We have oodles of nieces and nephews and uncles and aunts and cousins, and my mom and sister live there. The family crowds into an apartment about the size of my front room here. Christmas, christenings, birthdays, Thanksgiving. Food like you've never seen and drinking and singing." She looks up and cocks her head lost in the memory. "It's deafening. The noise in New York is... well, it's nothing like here. Seattle is the closest you get to Manhattan."

"Do you miss New York?" I say to keep her talking.

"Oh, you betcha. People are friendlier here, but I still miss it. I'm going to go home."

"You must be making good money working for Ben."

"What? You think I own this? I just live here. I had a studio apartment in Port Hadlock—no, Port Townsend. Hell, one of them ports. Why do they name everything a port here? Oh, well. It don't matter. Ben owns this place." She fills my cup to the top and empties the bottle in hers. "Would you mind?" She holds the empty bottle out to Ronnie. "Behind the bar. Some expensive stuff too. Wine. Brandy." She laughs when she says *brandy*. "Who the hell drinks that crap. Right?"

"Not me. I'm with Glen," I say, and she smiles at me.

"You're funny. You really a detective?" She's slurring again. "I never known a funny detective. Pricks. All of 'em."

Ronnie gives me a look and I nod. She takes the empty bottle and goes back inside. "I've had a few drinks or I'd find some snacks. Want some snacks?" She takes another drink and I notice her voice is getting louder.

"Not a problem. Luci. So you were saying Ben owns this condo?"

"Don't have to use this plastic crap. Real glasses in the monastery."

"These are fine."

Ronnie comes back with another bottle of Scotch. This one with an inch of liquor in the bottom.

"Did you call this a monastery?" Ronnie asks.

Luci picks up the bottle and eyeballs it, then waves it around at the condo and grounds. "All this. It's wonderful. I'm always alone. No one. No one to talk to. No friends. Ben don't like me having friends. Neighbors won't like 'em he says. Well, screw the neighbors. Friends don't like it here anyway. Too fancy-schmancy."

"Is the car yours?" Ronnie asks.

"Not even the car. I love that car." She looks around. "Where're my keys?"

"They're in the monastery," I say, and she grins.

"Had a Prius. But he gave me the car. Said the Prius embarrassed him. *Well, excuse me, Mr. High and Mighty.* It's all about appearances."

I can agree, but it's all about *his* appearance. Ben doesn't want a mistress who lives in a studio apartment and drives a Prius. I ask, "Did you break up with him? Is that why you're sad?" And drunk.

"Bastard's married." Her eyelids are sagging, her face turning to rubber. "He lied to me about having a kid. I don't belong here. Never did."

That came out like *doan blong here. Neffer did.*

She giggles and I smile. I have a hard time imagining Luci playing sex toys at Ben's cabin. To each their own, I guess, but whips and chains... I don't think so. Too much like torture and rape. I know all about that and what it takes out of your humanity and dignity. Did Marlena know this side of her husband? Did she participate? I didn't see a sign of it in the Parker residence. The thought is disgusting. I see Bennie's small face. I hear him yelling for Ben to stop. I take a drink of the Scotch. It burns my throat and takes my mind off the images of Ben and Luci in the playroom. The whips and chains. The schoolgirl outfits. The sickness in that room. I don't want to ask these questions but now is probably the best time, while she's still angry, hurt, drunk. I take the bottle and her glass away and pour it on the ground. If she keeps going, we'll have to take her to the emergency room.

"I had 'nuff. Huh?"

"I'm not going to take you in, so don't worry. We just need you to talk to us. We looked at your Facebook posts, Luci."

She shows a dreamlike smile and closes her eyes. "The beach. Yeah. Good times. Virginia Beach. My beach. He said he was gonna buy it. For me. Said he loved me." Her smile vanishes and now her eyes open and I can read the fury, the hurt, the sadness. Tears leak from their corners and her lips draw tight and quiver.

"We need to know about Ben. Ben's son is four years old and has asthma. The boy doesn't have his medicine. His wife is pregnant."

She pounds a fist on the table. "The bastard. I'll kill him. Off with his head! Off with his balls!" She laughs and lays her head on the table. The outburst is over as quick as it came on. Then she raises her face and there's spittle on her lips. "Bastard has a son."

I say, "His name is Bennie."

She cries and we sit with her. Ronnie goes back inside and makes strong coffee. We pour some of it down Luci but just when I think she's down the rabbit hole, she rallies and straightens up. Ronnie gives her another cup of coffee with a couple of cocktail ice cubes cooling it. She guzzles this and wipes her mouth with the back of her hand. Now I can see the pole dancer side.

"Said he was getting divorced. Never said nothing about no son." That explains why there's nothing of Marlena's or Bennie's at the cabin except for maybe the sleeping bags. "Said she left him."

I'm assuming we're still talking about Ben. I don't speak fluid drunk, but I get the drift.

"Said she stole a bunch of money."

I say, "You had no reason not to believe him." It's a good lie.

"Hell. He showed me papers from a lawyer. He didn't want her back. Said she can have what she wants. He only wants me." She leans toward me and lowers her voice like she's telling me a secret. "Talked about kids. Us. Having kids." She makes an ugly face but she's cried out.

"How long were you together?"

"Don't want to talk about this any more. Leave me 'lone."

We sit while Luci drinks another cup of coffee. She doesn't talk, just stares into space. No doubt looking at a life she's left for this. She can't even call this modern prison hers. She's sold her body and her soul for mere trinkets.

Luci takes a deep breath and lets it out slowly. "I'm okay. I'm just sorry for his family. If his wife didn't run off that is."

She can handle her alcohol. My first boyfriend, Caleb, used to tell this corny joke. "How do you handle your liquor?" The punchline is "One drink at a time." Not funny then. Not funny now. This girl has a problem and she's not going to find the solution in the bottom of a bottle.

Ronnie asks, "Do you feel like talking a little more?"

Luci's eyes aren't as glazed when she looks from one of us to the other. Ronnie pulls up a picture of Bennie on her cell phone. She holds it so Luci can see it. "That's Bennie. He's probably scared to death. He needs his medicine. Please help us."

Luci sits there staring at Bennie's picture for what seems ages, then lets out a belch and covers her mouth. "Sorry. Better out than in. What do you want to know?" She doesn't sound intoxicated. I've heard of people drinking themselves sober before but I've never seen it.

I ask, "When did you and Ben start seeing each other?"

"I guess you could say the day I was hired. Two years ago. I never understood why he hired me. I'd only done some part-time paralegal work before. Ben had posted a job on LinkedIn, and I sent an application. He answered right away and asked for a picture. The same day he asked if I would relocate to Seattle. Of course I would. Hell, the pay is four times what I was getting, and I wouldn't have to keep getting felt up by those geeks at the firm."

Now you just perform for Ben. But for more money. Moving up the ladder. Sick.

"When I got here Ben told me I would work from home when we weren't traveling. He had me hooked. We met at restaurants at first, then at nice hotels. All business. He didn't try anything funny. I thought he was a real gentleman. Charming. A nice guy."

I say, "But that changed."

"Boy, did it. I mean, he's attractive and, well, rich. And he wasn't wearing a wedding ring. He made me feel like a princess. Jewelry. Business trips in a company jet. We started sharing a room, my suggestion. I couldn't believe my luck. A good-looking guy that was successful and single. You know?"

Luci doesn't seem as talkative now, and I know the window Ronnie has opened is slowly closing. But then Ronnie asks, "Do you still have any papers or emails or receipts from these trips or hotels? If it was me I would have kept some mementos. But I guess you didn't."

"Are you kidding? We went to Edinburgh, Scotland, once. For New Year's. Stayed at the Caledonian and attended an honest-to-God Highland ball. He bought me a Scottish outfit. Want to see it?"

Ronnie says, "Later. Did you ever have misgivings? Anything about this bother you?"

"Well..." She looks at her hands, and I see a couple of rings that look expensive. She sees me looking and holds her hands out to show us a diamond ring, easily four-carat. "This one came from Tiffany's in New York." She's starting to sober. I resist the urge to pour more Scotch. "He said the rings were mine to keep as long as I was his to keep. That sounds corny now that I'm saying it. What a fool I was. But you asked if anything bothered me. Well, maybe the whole thing. It just didn't feel right. I'm a simple girl from a little place in New York City. I always thought I'd want to be swept off my feet by Prince Charming. When I finally was, he turned back into a frog. I missed my old life. My friends. Going where I wanted, when I wanted, wearing anything I wanted. He didn't have any friends. Or he didn't introduce me to anyone anyway. I thought it was strange that he'd take me on business trips all over the country and overseas and never seemed to do any business. I asked about his parents. I thought if he really loved me he would want to introduce me. Instead he yelled at me. Said never ask about them again. I figured his mom and dad wouldn't like to meet the mistress. If I'm the only one. Are there others?"

I say, "I don't know." *Probably*.

"He has some sexual issues."

Boy, does he. "And what are those?" I ask.

"He's into bondage and role playing. You know? He has bondage stuff at his cabin. A whole roomful of stuff. And he likes to record it. I would like to get those recordings back to destroy. Can you do that for me?"

"I'll try," I say. I didn't see any recording equipment.

"He had a movie camera set up on a closet shelf in the bedroom with the sex stuff."

It wasn't there when I searched—illegally—not that I want to watch him grunting and yelling safe words, but maybe he confessed to other horrible crimes on the video.

I ask, "What else did he have in there?"

"He liked me to dress up like a nurse and schoolgirl and stuff. He had whips. He liked to be whipped. He never hurt me and I tried not to hurt him, but now I wish I had. You must think I'm terrible."

Well, yeah. I say, "No, I don't. You were in love. Love makes you do funny things." *Like get chained up and whipped while wearing a grade-school outfit. Yuck.* "When was the last time you actually saw Ben?"

THIRTY

"Where to now, Megan?"

"Ben's cabin."

Ronnie is on her phone, searching motor vehicle records. "I can't believe I didn't find the other truck in his vehicle registration."

That makes two of us. "It's okay. We know now."

When Luci spoke coherently, she told us we had missed Ben's visit by less than an hour. According to Luci, he had come in a Chevy truck but he has access to two other trucks, another Chevy and a Ford kept in a garage within walking distance of his cabin. We hadn't searched the woods.

Ben bought the condo for her to stay in but they met at his cabin. Before that it was hotels. She thought he lived in the cabin. During today's brief visit he'd warned her when we talked to her we would try to turn her against him. He said he loved her and wanted to be with her. He admitted he hadn't filed for the divorce but that was because he couldn't find Marlena. He didn't know his wife was missing until the police contacted him. It was one of many other lies.

He told Luci to ask for an attorney when we came, because we would suspect her of his wife's disappearance. Ben came right out and said as his lover she had as much motive as he did to get rid of Marlena. He didn't mention Bennie. He promised to get her out of Washington State and take her anywhere she wanted to go if she didn't talk to us. He also said he would buy a house for them to live in together. She wasn't fooled and knew it was over between them. She would never live with a liar and a cheater. I'd asked if she had anyone that could stay with her. Hopefully to hide the liquor before she killed herself. There was no one. She'd never spoken to any of the neighbors and I could understand why.

I tell Ronnie, "Before we left, she asked if Ben was in trouble. I think she'll deny everything she told us. She's still in love with him."

Ronnie nods. "There are hundreds of vehicles registered to Parker Industries. I located his phone and it's still at the cabin. Maybe he has a couple of phones and switches them out."

We're too late. He's rabbited. He could be getting on his private jet right now. But Marlena and Bennie are still out there somewhere, and Ben is the only one who knows where. My instinct is telling me they were being held at the timber mill and when he didn't show up on time for his interview he wasn't sleeping. He was keeping them unconscious on sleeping meds and moving them. I can't imagine doing that to a four-year-old boy you profess to love. He's a psycho. A very rich psycho. He could hire someone to spirit them away. They could be anywhere by now. But I don't think Ben will want to give up control of them. He'll want them close. They belong to him. He's a very determined pervert. Ronnie is talking and I zone back in. "What?"

"I said, if we find him at his cabin, then what?"

"We offer him the polygraph and bring him to the station."

"Sheriff Gray doesn't think we have enough for an arrest."

"We won't arrest him. But he's coming with us. It's called investigative detention. We suspect he's committed a crime. Obstructing an investigation by telling Luci not to talk to us. We can detain him for a few hours while we search."

"Megan, I know how you feel. I want to find them too. I want it more than anything. But his father is beyond influential. He can crush us. We can't even get him to talk to us."

"I know that. But our job is to make Ben think we don't give a shit." And I don't. I don't think Ronnie does, either. She's being the voice of reason. She's the tasty carrot and I'm the stick.

She asks, "Do you expect him to confess? To take us to them?"

I honestly don't, but I have to try. "We'll see. In any case, if he keeps talking, he gives us more questions. It's harder to lie than tell the truth." I know that for a fact. Been there.

THIRTY-ONE

Ben's truck is at the cabin. We get out and I feel the hood. Cold. There is no answer at his door. Ronnie tries his cell phone and gets voicemail. I knock louder and for a long time. Usually that works. I'm not sure why, but it does. Nothing. I put my ear to the door and listen. All I hear are seagulls screeching out over the bay. The place feels empty but I walk around the front while Ronnie stays at the back. The blinds are shut. I try the front door. Locked. I knock loud and long and then shout, "Sheriff's Department". Nothing. I play with the idea of picking the lock again. I can always tell Ronnie I found the front door open. But I don't. Even a numbnuts like Ben wouldn't fall for that trick twice, and I doubt he's left any evidence behind this time.

Ronnie has soundlessly come up behind me and gives me a start. She says, "Google Earth shows some kind of structure about five hundred yards over there." She points into the thickly wooded area east of the cabin.

Now I wish I hadn't shouted. If he's back there I'd like to surprise him. We hike through the undergrowth and thick carpet of pine needles. It's almost like walking on a sandy beach.

"Luci said he had a couple of trucks nearby."

If it's on Google, it must be true. We work our way over some downed limbs, and I remind her, "Sometimes those pictures are old. Things change."

I no sooner say this than we come upon a path we totally missed. It leads to a clearing and a wood structure with a Shaker roof. It resembles a barn big enough to hold farm equipment or several vehicles. Deep tire ruts in the dirt lead away from the industrial garage type door. The door looks solid and looks like it must be controlled with a remote only. Walking around the building, I don't find windows, but there's another entrance/exit: double-wide hanging barn doors. A dirt trail bends back toward the gravel entrance to the cabin. The doors are secured with a heavy chain and a biometric padlock my little bolt cutters can't handle. The doors are on rollers and tracks. It looks solid and there are fresh tire marks in the soft dirt. I don't see any cameras or other security devices. It looks impenetrable without one of Ben's thumbs or a remote control. Next time we see him we'll get one.

Ronnie asks, "Do you think we can get a warrant to look inside?"

"Why don't you go back to the car and look for one. I think there's a blank warrant in the glove box. I'll sign the judge's name." She doesn't look happy so I say, "Listen, Marlena and Bennie could be in there. He never told us about this place. I'll take the heat. You can go back to the car and say you told me not to do it."

"Why don't you show me how to do it? I might lock myself out of my house some time."

Good girl. Or maybe bad girl. I'm teaching her bad things. I should feel bad, or ashamed, but I kind of like having a real partner.

Ronnie says, "Maybe we should try to raise someone's attention first," and beats on the rolling door with a fist, shouting the same thing I'd done at the cabin. She looks at me and says, "I think I heard someone calling out."

I've created a monster. "I can't pick this lock, but everything has a weakness." I squat and put my fingers under the edge of one door and start to lift. The door is heavy. "You wanted me to teach you so help me lift this." Both of us lift and are rewarded by the bottom rollers pulling out of the track. A stench of something rotten assails us. We try to ignore it and pull the bottom out far enough to crawl under the door. If I hear an alarm or sirens coming we'll use Ronnie's idea of someone inside calling out.

We glove up and I find a light switch beside the door. Rows of powerful LED lights dispel the gloom but do nothing for the smell. Ronnie puts both hands over her mouth and nose. The stench makes my eyes water. I put my arm across my nose and mouth and yell "Marlena" in a muffled voice. I call out again hoping to actually hear something and at the same time fearing what it means if I don't.

"I'll search it alone, Ronnie. No sense in both of us throwing up in here."

"In case it's a crime scene," she says.

"Right." No, I just don't want to trip over her when I rush outside to vomit.

"I'll stay." She wipes tears from her eyes and tries to acclimate to the rot.

"Use your shirt," I tell her. "No telling what kind of crap is floating in the air."

She pulls her shirt up over her mouth and nose. The inside is like any typical barn. Hayloft, straw and dirt floor, tools mounted around the walls. There's a Kubota yard tractor, a mud-covered Gator ATV, and a Ford F-450 dually truck, the same model as the one we've seen Ben driving but this one is midnight blue and a few years older. There's a space where the other Chevy truck could have been parked.

I take a quick tour inside while Ronnie runs the registration on the truck's license plates. There are no signs of a trapdoor, drag marks, or blood. The loft has a steel-rung ladder for access. It wouldn't be hard for a muscle-bound Ben to carry two bodies up there. I climb and the smell of decay increases with each rung. My eyes begin to water, partly because of the stench, partly because my heart is sick over what I might find.

"What did you find?"

"If you see me fall, you'll know I've found them."

I pause, holding the top rung, and push the straw away from the edge before going up high enough to see. The only sounds I hear are the wind blowing outside and my own heart pumping adrenaline through my veins. I steel myself and hold my breath before climbing on to the loft.

THIRTY-TWO

Sheriff Gray sits in his squeaky chair, pushes a bottom drawer closed, and brushes powdered sugar from the front of his khaki shirt. He came into his office alone, wanting to give his ears a rest from the constant chatter between the two sisters. He's thinking about the chocolate-filled croissants in the bag and jumps when Helen sticks her head in the door without knocking.

"What do you think is happening?"

"Helen, I'm sure if they found anything they would have called. They know what they're doing and how worried we are."

"Well, I *am* worried. I'm here, so where the heck is that husband of hers? Why isn't he here?" She means Ben but says it like He-Who-Must-Not-Be-Named. "You would think he'd want to be the first to know."

Ellen comes in and both women take seats.

Now there's no escape. He takes one last look at the drawer with the goodies and sighs. "I wasn't going to discuss this, Helen, because I don't want to make you think your son-in-law has done something wrong."

"Tell me what? I've been patient. Isn't that so, Ellen? Tell him I'm patient, for heaven's sake."

Ellen looks uncomfortable and says, "Considering Marlena

and Bennie have been missing for over twenty-four hours, she's holding up well, Tony."

"There," Helen says. "Now tell me what you've not told me. And don't sugarcoat it. I'll know if you're not being straight with me and you know it. I can always tell."

Tony leans back and rocks. It's a nervous habit. The chair doesn't know it's to calm him and screams with each movement.

"I agree Ben's behavior is not typical, but there can be any number of reasons for that. They're going through a rough patch and he may be feeling ashamed."

Helen waves the comment away with a snort. "He may be mad at her but he loves Bennie. Why wouldn't he help find Bennie? That's guilt, not shame."

"It may be guilt, but it doesn't mean he's done anything wrong. Criminally, I mean."

"So you admit there is a criminal aspect to their disappearance. Let me tell you what *I* think."

Ellen gives her husband a look of pity and mouths the word *Sorry*.

"I think she wants a divorce and he won't give her one. He's too proud to admit he's a failure as a husband. Or maybe he doesn't want to pay support. There have been other murders over that and you know it." Saying the words, letting the possibility see daylight, starts a flood of tears.

"Helen, we won't know anything until the detectives have had time to—" He stops short of saying *find the bodies*.

Helen's face is red and a rage is building. She gets up and leaves the office. Both Tony and Ellen let out a breath.

"She's going to explode," he says.

"Most people have no idea what you do, what you put up with, the heartache I've seen you come home with. I love you for being here for her. For me. You'll find them. I know you will."

Tony's eyes mist up and he blinks it away. He'll find them, but maybe not alive. "Thanks. I know it's not easy for either of you, and I promise to be as forthcoming as I can be."

"You can't say some things. Even to us. I'll make her understand."

Ellen leaves and shuts the door behind her. The sound of Ellen's softer voice is overridden by the urgent voice of her sister. Then it's quiet. He can hear the ticking of the Felix the Cat clock Ellen gave him for his birthday and insisted he put on his office wall to remind him to take a breath now and then. He takes that breath now. It doesn't work. He gets up to see what's wrong. That he would think something is wrong when it's quiet is a testament to his crazy job.

He opens the door just as Helen is coming in. They stand face-to-face for a moment, and she says, "I'm sorry. I really do appreciate everything you're doing. I'm almost out of my mind. She's my only child and he's my only grandchild."

"I'm as worried as you are, Helen, and I'm sorry too. We're family." He means what he's saying. He's always called her "Hellion" instead of Helen because of her short temper and judgmental attitude. But now they share something bigger than their feelings for each other. He would give anything to be out there with his detectives, searching, talking to people, doing what needs to be done. He knows Megan's not always appropriate in her methods, but she always gets results. He feels sorry for the devil if Megan goes to hell.

"I can call them if you want but it might be a bad moment for the phone to ring."

THIRTY-THREE

Ronnie mistakenly took my exclamation of surprise and disgust as something else and climbed up. Now we both smell like burnt coffee from hell. We climb down from the loft and my legs are trembling with relief when I call Tony and tell him what we found.

He says, "A family of dead skunks?"

I wonder how Ben put up with the smell. "Yeah. We think Ben has taken a different truck. His is still at the cabin. Can you do something for us?"

"Anything."

"Call your judge friend and get us a search warrant for the barn and his cabin and the other truck if we can find it? Ronnie will send you the particulars."

Tony asks, "I suppose when you smelled the decay—from outside of the barn—you entered the barn to check on the welfare of whoever? That's how it happened, isn't it, Megan?"

"Yes, it is," I say. That gives us exigent circumstances to enter without a warrant under the law. *Good thinking, Tony.*

"I'm sending some of the Search and Rescue people your way. And I'll pass this on to Mindy. She'll bring the warrant. Do you need me out there?"

"If you want to come out that's okay with me, but you're doing a lot of good there." And besides, I don't want Ben or some hot-shot lawyer claiming Tony's personal connection made him plant evidence or violate Ben's civil rights. In court it's not about the truth. It's about who tells the most convincing lies.

I tell him about our conversation with Lucia Simmons. "Ben had just left before we talked to her and told her to lie or lawyer up. She didn't really give us much except to confirm he's a selfish, controlling jerk and a liar. He never told her he had a son until the news reported them missing. She thought he was going to divorce Marlena. He promised her that if she lied to us he'd take her away and they'd live happily ever after."

Tony asks, "How did he explain his wife and son being missing? She had to wonder why he wanted her to lie."

I say, "He told her he was going to see Marlena to push for the divorce but the police called him." Tony's quiet. "Yeah, that's what I thought too. He's telling one lie after another. Anyway he showed Luci divorce papers from his attorney. He said he was trying to find Marlena to get them signed. Luci thought she'd hit the mother lode. He's been giving her expensive jewelry so she thought he'd marry her. Now she knows he's a bastard and she's going back to New York City, where she's from, but I told her to stay in town for a while until we sort this out."

"Do you think she'll stay put?"

"She's pretty sloshed right now and I don't see her going anywhere for a while."

"Can I do anything?" Tony asks. I love working for this man.

"That's it for now. We have to go home and change"—and burn these clothes—"and then we're going to see Cyrus Parker."

Now I hear his breath catch. "Are you sure, Megan?"

"Yes. And we're putting out an all-points bulletin for Ben Parker. He might have done a runner. I want to talk to his father to see if we can get his help in bringing his son in." And ground Ben's transportation.

"Is that it?"

"Oh, yeah: We'll need a search warrant for the timber mill the family owns."

Tony says, "It sounds like Ben's desperate. Too bad he's not coming in for the polygraph?"

"Oh, he'll come in. In a zipper bag, if that's what it takes." I don't realize I say this out loud.

"Be nice, Megan."

"Always. You know that." I hear him chuckle and disconnect. I say to Ronnie, "I'll never get the smell out of my hair or my nose. I don't have a change of clothes with me so I'll need to run by my place."

"I might be able to find some clothes that will fit you," Ronnie says.

"I appreciate it, but no. I'll drop you at home and pick you up." She's got two inches on me, a thinner waist, and all of her clothes have names. Besides, I make it a rule to never get naked in someone else's house. Unless it's my idea.

Thirty minutes later I'm scrubbed and back at Ronnie's. Her red hair shines and is styled like she's just left a beauty parlor. Mine is still damp and I have water in one ear I can't seem to get out. Someone told me to put a little alcohol in there and it will draw the water out. That's a waste of good Scotch.

"I found a different phone number for Cyrus Parker in Ben's contacts. It's for his personal security and I hadn't tried that one," Ronnie says. "I called ahead and arranged for us to see him. I hope you don't mind."

I did, but what's done is done. "Thanks. When will he see us?"

"His security chief said right now and asked if I thought Marlena and Bennie were okay."

"So he knows they're missing. Well, that makes that part easier." I'm wearing an identical outfit to what I had on earlier. I put the old one in a trash bag and sealed it with duct tape. The one I'm wearing isn't too far from needing to be pitched. I set the bag on the front step. Maybe someone will steal it and get a surprise.

Ronnie says, "I did some digging into Cyrus. The word is Cyrus is ruthless and has a temper."

"So." I've got a temper too. Ask my bio-dad. He's bio-dead.

"Just giving you a heads-up, Megan."

Now I wish I hadn't showered. I wonder how he'd like that. "I told Tony I'd play nice. I'll let you do the talking if you want."

Her face turns red. "No. You're the senior detective."

Damn right. "Let's just play it by ear." *He might like you. Most males between the ages of one and one hundred seem to.*

* * *

Cyrus Parker, magnate, tyrannical businessman, billionaire, lives in an appropriate place for someone of his station. His own island. We wait by his personal dock for a few minutes before we are picked up by one of his staff and ferried across to the island. I watch the island shore for any trees that had the word "CROATOAN" carved into it. The shore is deserted like that of the Roanoke Colony in 1590; no one is stirring not even a mouse. According to Ben, all the other living souls were bought out and moved on. Not spirited away mysteriously.

On the short boat ride I strike up a conversation with our ferryman—or ferrywoman, to be more exact. I had to ask for her name. Sissy. No last name. Like the artist formerly known as Prince. She's taller than Ronnie and me, with an athlete's build, fair-skinned, with short coppery red hair and green eyes like a predator's. I notice she's got "man hands": thick fingers, thick nails, strong. I'm glad we didn't shake hands. She's anything but a sissy.

She's Cyrus Parker's chief of security, which is a nice word for bodyguard, as well as his fetcher of visitors. Ronnie researched her, of course, and found out Sissy has a black belt in several martial arts and has competed in MMA tournaments. The scars above one eye and the side of her face prove it. Of course, the long white scar running down her cheek to her jaw looks like a knife didn't like her looks.

"How do you like living here?" I ask her.

"It's great. I live on the island. I have my own dojo. Cyrus has been very generous."

"Does he spar?" I ask as a joke, but she doesn't smile. Uh-oh. "Sorry, Sissy. I just went four rounds with a family of dead skunks and I've got water in one ear from trying to wash the stink off." I don't know what that has to do with my stupid remark, but she grins.

"I lost hearing in one ear from fighting. But it's okay. Here, let me fix it."

She takes my head and turns it to the side and rotates it slowly. I don't usually let anyone touch me, but she's got a black belt so I make an exception. The water runs out and I can hear again.

"I've got Ménière's syndrome. Medicine helps, but what I just did usually helps more than the medicine. Are you a boxer?"

I'm more of a Glock kind of girl. "No. I had some training at the academy."

"Your job can be dangerous. You should take it up. You'd be good."

"I don't want to scare people with my moves," I say, and she chuckles. I'm a charmer. I hope I don't have to fight her before I leave the island.

Ahead of us I see what looks like the stone spires of a castle peeking above the trees. She pulls up to the dock and ties off. We get off and she asks, "Are you hungry?"

"Are you the chef too?"

"You'd better hope not. I'd burn water. No, Cyrus likes his food. He has a kitchen staff that would make a three-star restaurant jealous, but he's a pretty good cook too. If you want it they can make it."

"If we eat, will Mr. Parker be joining us?" Ronnie asks. Nice segue.

"If you want. He's off stalking and will be back shortly. He said to make you comfortable. I'll radio him and let him know you've arrived."

"'Stalking'?" *Stalking who? Where am I?*

She smiles. "Hunting. There are deer on the island. Bears too. Cyrus doesn't allow anyone to shoot them, but he enjoys finding them and watching."

I almost say his son has other pursuits requiring leather masks and being beaten by a partner. I don't, because I've already made one stupid remark.

THIRTY-FOUR

Sissy gives us a tour of the downstairs of the mansion and then leads us into a small kitchen with a wood table and chairs. A red-and-white-checked plastic tablecloth is on the table with three place settings. The part of the house we came through was extravagant. This room is comfortable, utilitarian, and plain, and I like it more. I hear heavy footfalls and we meet the lord of the castle.

Cyrus Parker stands every bit of six feet tall. He's a sturdy man in his late fifties, but his hair is snow-white and there's lots of it, unlike his son's. He's wearing a brown leather open vest with a long-sleeve white shirt, beige canvas pants, and cowboy boots. He reminds me of an actor in one of those old Westerns on television.

Cyrus is a pleasant surprise. He welcomes us and takes our hands in a warm, friendly manner and looks us in the eye before letting go. He's your grandfather, father, and best friend all rolled into one. But I'm seeing the good side of him. His reputation is that of a ruthless, egotistical land baron.

He motions us to sit and goes to the cabinets. "That'll be all, Sissy." She backs out of the room, and he begins taking out boxes and iron skillets. "Sissy said you'd be hungry. I hope so. I make some mean pancakes and bacon. Or a wagon-wheel waffle with real maple syrup if you like. We get our syrup from the maple trees here on the island."

We both opt for pancakes, bacon, and eggs, which Cyrus makes and places in front of us. He regales us with stories of how Marlena has changed all their lives and how smart and talented Bennie is. How they come over every holiday and birthday but he wishes they would come more often. The way he says it makes me stop eating and ask, "Why don't you let them live here, Mr. Parker?"

"My employees call me Mr. Parker. Call me Cyrus, please." His face lights up and he says, "Bennie calls me 'Papaw Sy-wus.'"

I wait for him to answer my question. He doesn't. He's not going to. "You know why we're here, Cyrus." It's weird calling a billionaire by his first name. If he's trying to work us for information, he's doing a good job. Making us comfortable. Telling us a little about himself. Not asking questions directly, just putting the idea in our minds, winding us up and letting us spin. He isn't what I expected.

I play his game and wait him out. He gets up and brings an old-style copper-bottom coffee percolator and refills our cups. I sip my coffee and wait. Ronnie is following my lead, but I can see she's already a fan of Cyrus Parker. His coffee is hot and strong. It's good, but it's not why we're here.

He grins at me. "In answer to your question, Megan, I would have them living here with me if it were possible. Marlena wants to be self-sufficient. She has a degree in interior decorating. I don't suppose my son told you that. He wouldn't. If she'd have let me, I would have put her to work, or helped her start her own business. The girl is talented."

"We've seen some of her work."

"Have you?" He puts his coffee mug down and twists it around. "My son won't hear of it. He thinks I coddle them too much and undermine his place as a husband and father."

Every parent thinks they're doing what's best for their children. Except for my mother. She's a lying, sneaking, uncaring bitch. I didn't care that we never had money. I didn't care that we never had the best clothes or even a television most of the time. I didn't care that we moved at the drop of a hat and had to start all over again someplace new, with new names, a new house, new lives. All I wanted was for her to show an ounce of love for me like she did for Hayden. I was her servant, not her daughter. Cyrus treats his help better than that. So why does Ben dislike him so much? And Cyrus is skirting around the edges of dislike or disappointment with his son.

I say, "I asked Ben if he thought Marlena and Bennie were here with you."

Cyrus looks up. "If they were I would tell you. If I wanted them to be here, they would be no matter what Ben wanted. And I wouldn't have to hide them."

I believe him. "Do you have any idea at all where they might be or who they might be with?"

"I wish to God I did. That boy's not helping you find them, is he?" I don't answer and he lets out a breath. "He's my son. My blood. But he's not my son, if you understand what I'm saying."

Cyrus gets up and paces to the stove and back. "If I would have been home more, maybe..." His words trail off and I can see the emotion he's been expertly hiding.

"Can you tell me something about Ben that can help me know him? Reach him?"

An ironic smile plays at his lips. "He's a hard one to reach. Don't you think I've tried? But of course I wasn't around enough to see what he was becoming. I don't want to speak ill of my own flesh and blood, but he's an accomplished liar. He'll tell you what he thinks you want to hear or whatever serves his purpose."

Ronnie brings over his mug of coffee and asks him to sit. He does and looks off in the distance. "Unlike Ben, I had every disadvantage growing up. My father was a violent drunk. My mother had what we now call bipolar disorder. Back then they said she had fits of anger. We were extremely poor. But I was hungry for more than food. I seemed to have a talent for business. I've been successful, but to realize that success I was never present when Ben was growing up. I made sure he had everything he could possibly need or want. He went to the best schools, had the best tutors. He's bright enough to be anything he wants. What he wants is to punish his mother and me.

"His mother is—was—controlling. She demanded total allegiance, obedience, love, but gave nothing in return. I was gone much of the time. She sent him away to prep school after his eighth birthday. His grades were poor to begin with and eventually he was sent home. She hired nannies to be with him and paid the best tutors for private lessons. But after a few weeks his instructors refused to teach him. I saw a pattern and called some of them to determine why Ben was hard to teach. They were afraid of him. Or, more exactly, afraid of me. He'd bully them. Tell them I would ruin them if they didn't do what he wanted. I talked to him about it and he was sorry. He promised to shape up. He tried to be decent for a short time, but he hated his mother with a passion. He was creative in finding ways to pay his mother back for her lack of caring and total dominance and me for my absence. He took my absence to mean I didn't love him. I did love him. That's why I thought I was proving my love by giving him all the things I'd never had.

"You've been told, no doubt, that I own the island and had a community here at one time. When Ben was still young I thought his problem was a lack of affection. My business kept me away. He had no friends. I bought him a dog. A collie. It was gone in a week. Ben said he loved it but his mother gave it away. She denied it. I had the island searched and there was no sign of it.

"It was obvious Ben didn't want to go to school. I brought school to him. I had houses built and given to select people. I had a little one-room school built. I brought people with work ethics, skills they could teach, and particularly with children Ben's age. I had hoped Ben would make friends. But several of the families complained wild animals were killing their pets. They would find dead seagulls ripped apart on their back steps. Some pets disappeared and were never found. The parents stopped inviting Ben over; the children stopped coming around. The parents refused to tell me the reason they were leaving or made up excuses of job offers. I finally bought everyone out for their silence and they left. No one argued.

"Veronica, my ex-wife now, had already given up on him when he reached high school age and sent him away to a military academy. She thought it would give him some backbone. The trouble was he had *too much* backbone. But he was... what do the shrinks call it? Passive-aggressive. He thought the academy commandant was picking on him. The commandant's pet—a dog, I believe—went missing and was never found. They were convinced Ben had something to do with it but could never prove it. I now believe Ben had everything to do with it."

He got quiet, tracing one finger around the rim of his mostly empty coffee mug.

Ronnie stands. "Let me get more coffee for everyone." He lets her and she busies herself emptying the old coffee grounds and refilling the basket with ground coffee and the pot with fresh water. "My grandmother has a coffeepot like this. Revere Ware," she says. "I used to sit while she made tea and toast. She'd cut the toast into four squares and add butter and jelly and we had tea and—"

"Crumpets," Cyrus says, and gives her a surprised look. "Tea and crumpets. My mother did the same thing on a good day. The tea was just water, condensed milk, and sugar."

Ronnie smiles at him. "That's what my granny called it. She made it like that but said it was real tea. I knew the difference even when I was little, but I loved her so much I let her have her way. I was always comfortable sitting in her kitchen. The whole world was just us and our high tea."

"Is your grandmother still with you?"

"She passed a few years ago," Ronnie says, and there is great sadness in her voice. She turns the gas burner on and waits by the stove.

Cyrus goes back to circling the top of his mug with a fingertip. I recognize it as one of my mother's habits. When there was bad news or we were going to be packing once again, she would make coffee super-sweet with cream and let me and Hayden have a few sips when it cooled. While it was hot, she would trace a long, slender finger around the mouth of the cup, her mind lost somewhere in another place, maybe a better time.

Now I wonder if my grandmother would make tea or coffee and cookies and sit around with her daughters, peacefully enjoying each other's company. I doubt it. My aunt Ginger said their mother detested Mom. I wonder if my mother was a product of her environment. But I'm living proof a person can control who they are.

"Ben had a choice," I say, and both Cyrus and Ronnie look at me. "He could have been anyone he wanted. If he's strong enough to be controlling, he's strong enough to make the choice not to be."

Cyrus says, "Yes. He made his bed. He grew up without either parent. Without love. Without a sense of purpose. All of that was replaced with money and power over others. But he could have learned to enjoy life, to live among other people and use strength for good and not to dictate lives. My biggest regret is the time I spent away from my own son. Away from my wife. I didn't blame her for leaving me. And I don't blame Ben for hating me. And he does, you know. Hates me."

I say, "The past is the past, Cyrus. Things may turn around." If Ben hasn't done the unspeakable. Made his wife and son disappear like his academy commandant's dog. Like other people's beloved pets. He can't stand to see anyone else have what he can't have. So he takes what they love away from them. Permanently.

Cyrus must have read my mind. "He's troubled. But he wouldn't kill his family. In his own way he loves them. And he knows I adore them. He wouldn't do that to me, either."

Or he would do it for that exact reason? You never gave him what he needed. He's taking what you need.

"Do you know where Ben is?" I ask.

He shakes his head. "He stopped coming here ages ago. He lets Marlena and Bennie come. There's that."

"Did you know she's pregnant?"

He doesn't answer, but the look on his face tells me he didn't.

"When is the last time you talked to her? Or Ben?"

"They had a fight and I take it he moved out. She called a week ago. Sunday. She asked if I'd seen him. She told me about the quarrel and that Ben had stormed out of the house in a mood. I promised to talk to him if he contacted me. He never answers his phone when he's in a mood. Sissy said she saw his truck outside the cabin I let him use. That was a few days after I talked to Marlena. I didn't hear from her again, so I thought they'd patched things up. She should have told me. I would have insisted she and Bennie come here. I would have taken care of them. I know you're thinking I didn't do so hot with Ben. You're right. But I'm older and I've done everything I set out to do. I'm home for good." He stares into space for a moment, then says, "I'm going to tell you something no one knows but Marlena and me."

I nod and wait. He looks down at the tabletop. "He was never good for her. If it wasn't for Bennie, I'm certain she would have left him long ago. She's very faithful and she protects him, but I know he's never treated her right. I have Sissy keep an eye on them. I think Marlena had enough. She asked me if I would hate her if they divorced. I could never hate her. She's like my daughter. I told her to do what she thought was best. If she needed my help, a place to stay, lawyers, whatever, she could count on me."

Cyrus presses his eyes with a thumb and index finger. He is exhausted, ashamed, angry, defeated. "He's my son. I don't want to see him in pain. But if he's behind my daughter-in-law and grandson's disappearance, I'll disown him."

It would be like pouring salt in an open wound to tell him Ben believes the pregnancy isn't his. That Marlena was cheating. Or that Ben's the one cheating. We talk awhile longer and I get his ex-wife's contact information. I doubt she'll be much help. I doubt

Marlena is with her or has made contact. I write down Helen's contact information on the back of a business card and give it to Cyrus. Surprisingly, they have never met or even talked. Getting those two together might help them deal with whatever comes of this.

THIRTY-FIVE

Cyrus calls his son and gets his voicemail. He doesn't leave a message. He taps a button by the kitchen door, and Sissy comes into the kitchen.

"Sissy, can you find Ben's phone?"

She taps her cell and holds the screen where he could see it, then shows it to me. The dot on the screen isn't moving from his cabin. We already know where the phone is, but since Ronnie hacked his phone, we act surprised.

"Cyrus, does Ben own any of the businesses or any cabins, homes, that kind of thing?"

Sissy leaves the room. "Sissy will take care of you. You have my permission to search any place you think they might be. He owns nothing. The company, thus me, owns the cabin he's been staying in. Sissy says it's a pigsty."

I think, *So I'm not the only one breaking in.* Sissy comes back with a metal lockbox and an envelope. She hands this to Cyrus and he hands it to Ronnie. "The keys to the kingdom. And a list of all the properties around here that he might go to. The keys are marked. I've had my security people start searching all of these places, but I'll hold up if you want your people to do it."

We don't have the manpower. "Thanks for searching, Cyrus. If they find anything at all..."

"Sissy will have them stop and call you immediately."

Sissy hands me a business card. "My personal cell. If you need anything."

"Do you have other questions for me, detectives?"

"Not right this moment," I say.

"Sissy will take you back to your car."

We thank him and, once back ashore, make our way to my car. I give Ronnie the keys and make a call.

"Sheriff, you can forget the warrants."

"I just found a judge, Megan. What's going on? Where are you?"

"We went to see Cyrus Parker. Did I tell you he owns an island?"

"Parker Island. I was aware. Is that where you are now?"

"Port Ludlow. On our way to Ben's cabin. Listen, Ben doesn't really own any property. Or business. His father has him on a short leash. Cyrus has given us permission to search everything and gave us a list of properties and the keys."

"How many places are we talking about?"

"More than a dozen that I know of, but we have help. Cyrus has his own security firm. The chief of security lives on the island and is assisting us in searching all the properties. Even the abandoned timber works. I'm going back to the timber works first to see if I missed anything this morning when we found the place had been broken into." As good a lie as anything. "Can you have Mindy come to the cabin?"

"Do you need someone to sit on the cabin in case he comes back?"

"That would be great. If he shows up, tell them to detain him for questioning. We'll be there shortly."

"Crime Scene too?"

"Not just yet."

"I'll make some calls. Crime Scene will be on standby. I'll have an officer meet you."

"Tony. It's him." I give him a synopsis of what Cyrus told us. How animals disappear around Ben. How some turn up dead when he really doesn't like someone. How nothing could ever be proven. "I've got to go, Sheriff. I'll keep you updated."

"Good work, you two."

* * *

We go straight to Ben's cabin, where a marked sheriff's car is waiting. I pull in behind it and am grateful to see it's Deputy Davis. He's a couple of years younger than me, black hair, a porn mustache, chubby, and a people pleaser. Which I am definitely not. He's not yet jaded by the job and he has helped me with searches in the past.

Davis asks, "Are we searching the truck, Detective Carpenter?"

"Let's wait for Mindy, but I've got a key." I find the key in the box and hit a button. The door clicks. There's not much to see inside. But there is a bottle of Glacier Mist Spring Water on the floor. The same brand as the water I found at the timber mill. It'll wait until Mindy finishes with the cabin. Mindy's white flower shop van arrives.

"Megan. Ronnie. Deputy Davis," Mindy says. "I was nearby when Sheriff Gray called. Fill me in."

I do, and watch her expression change from pleasant to serious.

"Has anyone been inside yet?" she asks.

I don't want to lie, but Deputy Davis is standing there, and old habits die hard. "I was here the morning they were reported missing. To see if Marlena and her son might have turned up." Mindy isn't buying it. "The door was open, so I went inside and called out for them. Then Ben came home. By then Officers Paco and Sonny were here and we asked if he wanted us to check the house for him. He didn't."

She raises her eyebrows. I don't know if it's because she finds it as suspicious as I do or if she doesn't believe any of my story.

She says, "The mud and wood chips are from here?" She's onto me but she doesn't push it. "Do you have a warrant?"

"We don't need a warrant. Cyrus Parker is the owner. He gave me permission and keys." I hand her the key marked for the cabin and one for the car. "And there's a large building, a shop or garage, over there." I point in its general direction. "You can't miss it. Cyrus said we have his permission to force the door." He didn't say that, but I'm sure he would have. "And there's a truck inside the building." I find a key for the truck we saw in the barn and give her that too. She doesn't ask how I know the license plate of the truck.

"Good. I'll get suited up," Mindy says, and slides the side door of the van open to reveal a working crime scene vehicle.

Ronnie asks, "Do you have extras for us?"

Mindy pulls out white Tyvek coveralls and slips into them. "I'd like to go through first. Megan, did you see anything while you were doing a *welfare check* I should know about?"

I want to tell her, but the things I saw are obvious. If they haven't been destroyed. "Not that I recall."

Her eyes narrow and she slings a small camera around her neck, pulls on gloves, and carries paper booties to the door. She takes pictures of what she can see from the doorway and then enters. Ten minutes later she emerges and doesn't look nauseous, and so I assume all the toys are gone. Most likely the sleeping bags as well.

She comes over. "It smells of disinfectant. The place is clean enough to eat off the floor."

I can't help it. I say, "I was in there less than a minute and it was a total pigsty."

"Maybe he has a cleaning service?"

Bullshit.

"Maybe he was getting rid of stuff?"

Bingo.

I ask, "Did you happen to see camping gear?"

She shakes her head.

"Did you find a phone or computer?"

"No."

Standing beside Ben's truck, I dial his phone. I can hear a faint ringing coming from inside the truck.

THIRTY-SIX

It's pitch-dark in here but she closes her eyes and scoots back against a wall and tries to remember what she was doing before she was taken. She's still groggy. She remembers being at home and Bennie sleeping beside her. Nothing after that. She reaches back for older memories. She remembered being told by her doctor that she was four weeks pregnant. She'd been afraid to tell Ben not knowing how he'd react. She'd worked up the courage to tell him but before he'd come home she had a visitor. A woman that worked for Ben. She said she had to tell Marlena some things about Ben. She'd said horrible things and Marlena didn't want to believe her but when Ben finally came home late that night she'd been waiting downstairs and confronted him. She asked where he had been. She was still smarting, thinking about what the woman had told her, and when he lied about where he'd been she told him about the woman's visit.

He told her that the woman was crazy and thought he was in love with her. She had it in her mind that he was going to marry her. She'd asked Ben where this woman had gotten the expensive car she was driving. She described the woman and the car and the things she'd said. She asked if he wanted a divorce. He flew into a rage and began breaking things. Shoving her.

She was no longer afraid and told him she was pregnant. He was going to be a father again. To that he accused her of cheating on him. He said it couldn't be his child. He said they didn't have a sex life since Bennie was born. He was right about that because they didn't have a sex life unless he felt like it. When he wanted it, he was physically insistent and she gave in rather than fighting him. It felt like rape, but he reminded her they were married and she was obligated to fulfill his needs. That's how he put it. How romantic. The last time he'd forced her was consistent with how far along her pregnancy was. She reminded him of that time and he slapped her hard across the face. Ben said he wanted a divorce. He was sick of her. She was hurt and angry and said some things she wanted to take back. She'd told him she would give him the divorce but she was taking everything he had. And he'd never see his son or unborn child ever again.

He drew his hand back to slap her but Bennie got between them, yelling, "Stop, Daddy! You're hurting Mommy." Ben tried to calm down but he was so angry. Angry that he'd been caught, no doubt. He'd tried to talk to Bennie but Bennie had buried his face in Marlena's side and wouldn't talk to him. The last words Ben had said in that house were, "Your mother's a whore. You'll never see a dime. Go to hell."

She hadn't thought back then that he meant what he said. But he'd never come back or called her. Her face had hurt all that night from the blow. Poor Bennie had been upset so badly that he blamed himself for his daddy leaving. He wanted to call Ben and ask him to come home, but she hadn't allowed it. Bennie had been through enough already without having Ben come back with that little gold digger hanging on his arm.

Bennie had started seeing monsters in his closet. Sleeping with her most nights and even then would toss and turn or cry out in his sleep. She'd let him go to preschool, trying to make things as normal as possible. But then she saw drawings and colorings that Bennie brought home. Monsters, houses on fire, and other horrible things. These weren't the colorings of a happy four-year-old that drew cats and dogs and flowers and smiley faces. She was worried about him and had made her mind up to take him to a therapist. If Bennie was traumatized, she'd never forgive herself.

She didn't know how she'd gotten here or who had taken them, but she was sure now that Ben was behind it.

THIRTY-SEVEN

Ben's phone is under the seat and I bag it along with an empty water bottle. Ronnie receives a text, looks at the screen and puts her phone in her pocket. "The sheriff wants us right away."

"Does he have news?"

"The text doesn't say. Just to come in as soon as we can."

I don't like surprises. We're about fifteen minutes out, so I call him back.

"Megan, you need to get here as soon as possible."

"We're close. What's going on, Tony?"

"Ben and his attorney came in."

"Oh." *Shit.* "Be right there." I disconnect and off we go. "Ben has a lawyer with him. Call Cyrus and ask if he can come to the station."

Ronnie calls the number Sissy gave us. Sissy answers and hands the phone to Cyrus. "This is Detective Marsh," Ronnie says.

"Have you found them?"

"No, sir. But your son is at the Sheriff's Office in Port Hadlock."

"That's good. Does he know where they are?"

"We're not at the station, sir. We don't know if he's going to talk to us. He has an attorney with him."

"I'll be right there."

Ronnie disconnects. "Do you think he can talk sense into Ben?"

"Ben sees himself as the alpha male. His father is the only one who can trump that. I hope Helen hasn't taken a pound of flesh before we get there." I call Tony again.

Tony says, "I hope you're close. His attorney is impatient."

So am I. I ask, "Has Helen talked to Ben?"

"Ben and his lawyer are in my office. Ellen had taken Helen to our house before Ben arrived."

That's good. At least she didn't say anything that might put his back up. Yet. "Do you think you'll have a problem keeping him there?"

"His lawyer said they want to cooperate but made it clear he's not happy that we're harassing his client."

A person retains a lawyer when they feel threatened or have something to hide. Ben must have talked to Luci again. No amount of privilege or money will save him from his father. Or me.

THIRTY-EIGHT

Ben has moved from Tony's office to my desk and is sitting in my chair. A man I assume is his lawyer is standing next to him wearing a dark suit with silver pinstripes, gold cuff links, and a yellow tie. He's not looking at us. He's checking out the shine of his burgundy alligator leather shoes.

I reevaluate the attorney. He's tall, early thirties, with hair graying at the temples, sturdy looking, black Superman hair with that little twist of a curl down on his forehead. He's square-jawed, manicured, shaved. If he weren't an attorney, I'd think he was cute.

"Detective Carpenter," slick guy says, and holds out a hand. He's wearing a gold watch that probably cost more than I made last year. Who wears a watch any more? It's got to be for show. "Lincoln Mansoni. Mr. Parker's attorney."

I shake his hand just to get a closer look at the watch. He's a mugging waiting to happen. I introduce Ronnie and he turns a gleaming white smile on her while he checks her out. He trades a look with Ben and something passes between them. I have no doubt Ben has told Mansoni all about Ronnie's hotness. I'm not insulted. Ronnie makes good bait.

I ignore the lawyer. "Ben, you've not been answering your phone all day."

"What number have you been calling?"

"*Your* number." *Numbnuts.*

"Oh, you have my personal phone number. I've been carrying my work phone."

"Your wife might be trying to reach you. Would she know to call the work phone?" I'm incensed by his idiocy. He knows we don't know where they are. That worries me. He's confident enough to come in even knowing we've already talked to his girlfriend. He'll deny whatever she told us. She's not hard evidence. She was drunk. She can recant for the right amount of money. Not a smoking gun.

"I'm sure I called and left my number with someone in your office." He looks smug and takes one of my sticky notes and a pen. "Here, I'll write it down for you so you don't lose it."

"I never lose anything, Mr. Parker."

Mansoni clasps his hands. "So what are you asking of my client?"

"Mr. Mansoni, are you aware of what we're investigating?"

"My client has told me."

That's rich. A liar telling lies to another liar. Reminds me of a joke I heard at the police academy: "How can you tell an attorney's lying? His lips are moving." "We're investigating a report of missing persons. Marlena and Bennie Parker. Your client's wife and son."

He says, "Go on."

"We've interviewed Ben and he's agreed to take a polygraph. Did he tell you that?"

Mansoni's countenance changes. "I've advised my client not to take a polygraph."

"And why is that?"

"Because he's the victim here. He's a nervous wreck and that will affect the test."

Yeah. I can see how nervous he is. "Our polygraph operator is one of the best in the state." *I hope.* "She'll take that into consideration and will be very gentle and respectful of his worry and concern for the welfare of his pregnant wife and asthmatic son."

Mansoni's composure slips for just an instant and he almost looks human, then the lawyer is back in possession of his evil soul. Ben looks uncomfortable. *He hasn't told Mansoni about their medical conditions.*

"May I speak to my client alone for a minute?"

"Of course."

He looks at the surveillance camera by the entrance. "You will not record our conversation." It's not a question.

"Of course not," Sheriff Gray says. "You can use the interview room or my office."

Ben follows Mansoni into the interview room, casts a quick glance back at Ronnie, and winks.

"Did you see that?" she asks.

"I did. I'm glad Helen isn't here."

Sheriff Gray motions us toward his office. "Shut the door, Megan." He sits on the edge of his desk and his hands are trembling just slightly. I wonder how many cups of coffee he's inhaled. Or if he's trying not to commit murder after seeing Ben's behavior up close and personal.

He says, "I want you to be especially nice. Both of you."

"Not a problem. I can be nice when I want to. Ronnie is my witness."

His jaw tightens and he says almost under his breath, "Put this asshole away."

He could have led with that. "But we'll be nice when we do it."

There's a light knock on the sheriff's door. Ronnie opens the door revealing a big woman wearing a flower print jumper with cork high heels. She smiles at us. "Someone call for a liar detective?"

Tony makes introductions. "Louisa Layton. Meet Ronnie Marsh and Megan Carpenter."

Louisa is somewhere in her forties with blond hair pulled back in pigtails and bright red lipstick on generous lips. The cork heels look ready to explode. So does the waist of the jumper.

"You passed the liars on your way in, Louisa. Ben Parker and his attorney are in the interview room," I say, and Tony gives me a cautioning look. I turn my nice-o-meter up.

Tony says, "Use my office. Ronnie can keep me company out here."

I close the door, and Louisa says, "Fill me in."

I tell her everything she needs to know. She takes no notes, although I talk for fifteen minutes.

"Okay," she says, and gets to her feet. I notice her ankles are extremely swollen and she has trouble getting up. I don't ask, but it looks painful. She asks, "Has Mr. Parker's attorney agreed to the polygraph?"

We hear voices in the outer office. "We'll know in a minute."

We step out of the office, and I'm glad Ben doesn't look quite so smug. In fact, he looks constipated. Maybe because he's so full of shit. Mansoni does the talking. "Louisa," he says, and gives her an air kiss on the cheek.

What the hell?

"Lincoln. Good to see you. You're always good for business." She bats her eyes at him and he smiles tightly.

"My client has agreed to take the polygraph. He knows it isn't inadmissible in court."

Ben isn't under arrest, so I wonder why he thinks we'll be going to court.

Mansoni turns a shark's smile on me. "Why don't you go to the restroom, Ben. They'll come and get me when it's finished but you can stop at any time and have them get me. Understand?"

Ben nods and slinks off toward the bathroom, but Louisa calls after him. "Mr. Parker, please don't take any medicine. It will affect the test. You haven't taken anything today, have you?"

"No, ma'am." The cockiness is gone.

"Is this really necessary, Louisa?" Mansoni asks.

"Lincoln, you know it is. I'd rather he knows it now so it doesn't negate the test. I don't want to cost the county any more than necessary."

Mansoni says, "How good of you. I'm going outside for a smoke."

"Be sure you put yourself out," Louisa says, and slaps his bottom. He leaves, and she says, "I'd want him for my attorney. He's hot."

"You two know each other pretty well," Ronnie says.

Louisa laughs. "He's scared of me. He's never brought a truthful client to me yet, and I've known him for five years. Went to college with his momma. I liked her. Him, now... that's another story. But he is cute."

Ronnie giggles.

Louisa looks at me. "So, are we after a confession, or just a location of the missing persons?"

"You're the operator. I have to find them either way."

"Okay. If I start getting anywhere, I'll call you in."

"One of us, anyway. Ben's taken a shine to Ronnie."

"After seeing me? No way." She grins. "Let me get my equipment and set up in the interview room. Or did Tony turn that room into a breakfast, lunch, dinner, and snack room?"

"I'm right here," Tony says.

"So you are. Be right back." She leaves and Tony shakes his head. "She really is the best I've seen. She's gotten more confessions than Perry Mason."

"Who?" both Ronnie and I ask.

THIRTY-NINE

We crowd into Tony's office to watch the polygraph on the monitor. Louisa tells Ben to get comfortable and asks all the pre-questions about his medical condition, physical condition, psychological condition, and if he's had any coffee or other medicines today. He quickly offers that he had two cups of coffee. She notes that and the time the coffee was consumed. He doesn't tell her about the testosterone supplement he's been taking.

She connects the device to Ben and shows him how it works. She explains this isn't an interview and instructs him to give only yes or no answers. Then she asks a couple of easy questions to distinguish true answers from deceptive answers. Things like "Is your name Ben Parker?" to which he should answer with a yes. I've seen one of these given before and the readout looks like an EKG tape.

Is your wife Marlena Parker?

Yes. (He answers this with no hesitation.)

Do you love your wife?

(Hesitates.) Yes.

Do you love your son, Bennie?

Yes.

Are you separated from your wife?

Yes.

Is your father Cyrus Parker?

Yes.

Do you have a girlfriend?

I refuse to answer that.

Do you know where your wife and son are?

No.

He answers that question without hesitation, but his expression has changed. He looks tense. Unsure. The questioning goes on for twenty minutes before the front door buzzes. Ronnie comes back with Cyrus and Sissy in tow.

"Tony. How have you been?"

Ronnie and I exchange a look. Sheriff Gray seems to know everyone, from the poorest to the richest.

"Cyrus. I'm sorry we have to meet again under these circumstances."

"Marlena and Bennie. I love them like they're my own children. If there's anything I can do to help, say the word. I have resources."

Billions of dollars can buy a lot of resources. I don't think it can buy Tony. I know it can't. Tony is a stand-up guy. I hope Cyrus knows and won't try to interfere.

"I thank you for the offer, and we may take you up on it. Megan is the one who needs your help right now. I'll let her fill you in."

"Ah, yes. Detective Carpenter and Detective Marsh. Mansoni tells me my son is in with your polygraph examiner."

"He is," I say. "His attorney has been outside for a while, and..."

"You needn't bother with him. I've sent him on his way. Mansoni works for me and I told him Ben doesn't want his services."

He didn't tell us. But hey. A billion dollars.

"Oh, don't worry. I haven't violated any laws or constitutional rights. Mansoni was under the mistaken notion I had hired him.

Ben put the idea in his head and he was only too eager to go elsewhere when he realized he wouldn't be paid."

I'm really starting to like this guy. "In that case, I guess we can sit in the office and talk."

Sheriff Gray says, "No. Use my office. Cyrus can watch."

Good idea. He may even find some holes in what his son is denying. We go into Tony's office and Tony gives Cyrus the squeaky seat. Cyrus doesn't seem to be bothered. In fact, he sits very still, eyes glued to the monitor.

Do you have a girlfriend?

I told you I'm not answering such a ridiculous question.

Just yes or no answers. Do you understand?

Yes. But I'm not answering a question that is demeaning.

Does Lucia Simmons work for you?

Yes.

Is she your personal secretary?

Yes.

You and Marlena are separated?

Yes. (He sighs heavily.)

Have you been separated for a month?

No.

Have you been separated for a week?

Yes.

Have you and your wife fought?

What married couples haven't fought?

Please answer the question.

Yes. Yes, we've fought. But if you're trying to blame their disappearance on me, you're crazy. I had nothing to do with it. I haven't done anything to them.

Mr. Parker, confine your answers to yes or no. This is not an interview.

Okay.

Was the fight about money?

No.

Do you have a driver's license?

Yes.

Was the fight about infidelity?

May I speak?

Go ahead.

If you're asking about her infidelity, the answer is yes. If you're still pursuing the girlfriend question, the answer is no. We have never fought about my suspected infidelity.

Did you wife suspect you of infidelity?

I'm not going to answer.

Is your wife pregnant?

She said she was. It's not mine.

Is your wife pregnant? Yes or no.

I don't know how to answer that. She said she was. That's all I knew.

Has Marlena ever suspected you of infidelity?

I'm done here.

While Louisa disconnects Ben from the machine, Cyrus stares into space.

After a moment I ask, "What do you think about your son's answers?"

"He hasn't changed. Maybe I can get through to him."

I don't see how even Cyrus, especially Cyrus, can get Ben to be truthful. But I suppose it's what I had in mind when I asked him to come to the station. Now I wonder if it was such a good idea. Ben can just walk out of here, and I'm sure his temporary attorney told him as much. When he finds out his father sent the lawyer away, he may just leave. I can't afford that. I need him. He's most likely the only one who knows where Marlena and Bennie are.

Louisa comes out of the interview room. "I left the machine in there. He's lying about several things. He doesn't love his wife. He knows she's pregnant and that he's the father. He's the one having an extramarital affair. He almost came out of his skin when I mentioned Luci Simmons. Do you want to go in with me, Megan? I can tell him how he did. By the way, where's that stud attorney?"

Ignoring her last question, I ask, "Do you think he knows where his wife and son are?"

"I don't know. I thought the questions about his son would soften him, but he hates his wife so much, he doesn't have feelings for either of them. And did you hear the way he talked about them in the past tense?"

She noticed too. "Louisa, his father is here. I'm thinking about letting the two of them talk. What do you think?"

She looks at Tony and Ronnie and back at me. "You're the detectives. I'm just a detector for hire."

Tony puts a hand on her shoulder. "Come on, Louisa. You've been doing these things since I was a new deputy. What's your gut tell you?"

FORTY

She has searched every inch of their new prison. Bennie finally released her long enough to let her try to learn where they were. Her voice is hoarse from playing the Marco Polo game with Bennie so he would know where she was in the dark. She's found two more bottles of water nearby. Bennie's inhaler was in her pocket, so whoever took them doesn't want them to die.

"Mommy, I'm thirsty."

"We're saving the water, honey. Remember, it might be bad water. We only drink it if we have to."

"Mommy, I've got to pee."

She crawls back toward his voice. They're in a small building of some kind. A workshop, maybe. She felt tables with heavy tools mounted on them. Maybe a woodshop; that's why it smells like it does. She found a door in one wall. Steel by the sound it made when she pounded on it. She didn't find anything she could beat on the door with, so she used her hands and feet, and they hurt too bad to continue. She found a pile of sawdust near one of the tables. She takes Bennie there now to do his business. He can barely stand to walk. They're hungry and he's complained of having a headache. She's had one, too, but her hunger is worse. They need water. Dehydration can cause headaches and muscle weakness, hallucinations. She's not hallucinating yet, but who knows? Maybe this is all a hallucination.

Bennie pulls his pajama pants up and hugs her. "Mommy, when are we going home? I'm tired of Marco Polo."

"Soon." She leads him back to where the bottles are waiting for them to put them to sleep again. Maybe for good. She sits and cuddles him on her lap. "No more Marco Polo for you, mister. Let's think of the toy trains."

"I love 'em. I love Grampy."

"I know you do, honey. He's probably looking for us right this minute."

"Grampy told me he has a surprise for me."

Bennie never told her that. Cyrus never did, either. "What kind of surprise?"

"He said it won't be a surprise if I know."

"That's exactly right. You're too smart for your own britches, kiddo."

"Britches," Bennie says, and giggles.

"Oh, you think that's funny." She pulls him closer. "Just rest and then we'll have some water."

"I'm pretty thirsty, Mommy."

"Me too, honey. Me too."

FORTY-ONE

Cyrus says, "Hello, son."

Ben gets to his feet and takes a step back, almost tripping over his chair. Cyrus motions for him to take a seat. Ben looks at the door, but his shoulders drop and he sits.

"You should have told me."

"Why, Dad. So you could *help me*?"

"You're my son. I care about you."

Ben turns his head away.

"The police are trying to help you. Don't you want to find your family?"

"Don't you mean *your* family? Yeah. I want to bring my wife and my son home." He looks up at the camera. "I'd do anything to bring them home."

"Then why aren't you telling the truth, Ben?"

No answer.

"You're saying what you think people want to hear. Your mother did that."

"You don't need to talk about her any more, Dad. She's free."

"Of me, you mean."

No answer. Cyrus waits. Ben says, "Free of all of this. The drama. The feeling like a rich prisoner. She never had any real friends unless they were your friends. She—" He runs out of steam but his cheeks are red.

"We had a lot of the same friends. We ran in the same circles, Ben. How could we not have? We were married."

"*Were*. That's the key word. And I was your son. Did I have the same friends as you? How could I? You were never home. And when you *were* home, you were too busy haranguing me about school, or the neighbors, anything you thought was a weakness. You wanted me to be just like you. Did you ever think I didn't want to be like you? You can't imagine someone not wanting to sit at your feet."

Cyrus takes all of this calmly. He doesn't raise his voice or argue or defend his life choices. He does what he does best. Business.

"I've always loved you, Ben. I still love your mother. She did the best she could for you. For us."

Ben turns on his father. "She did her best means she was weak. Is that what you're saying, Dad? That I learned to be weak from her? She was with me a lot more than you. And you sent me to school after school where I never fit in. I was Cyrus Parker's son. People wanted to be friends with Cyrus Parker's son. I kept my head down until I realized it didn't make any difference. No matter what I did, I was going to sully the Parker name. Bring dishonor on the Parker empire."

"I admit I wasn't a good father, son. I regret it more than you can know. I'd like to make up for it if you'll let me."

I wait for the expected thunder after a flash of lightning. Ben's mouth is trembling; time has stopped. And right at that moment I have pity for him, pity for his father, pity for all the people who have been touched by the loss and animosity built over nearly thirty years of life. I imagine Ben as a young man, starved for attention and unconditional love, buried under the expectations of being someone other than who he really is. I see Cyrus, driven, a business genius, believing he's doing what is best for his wife and son, not seeing what his success at business is costing him at home.

I see myself in a similar position as Ben and Cyrus. Starved for attention, burdened with the past responsibility of raising a younger brother with absent parents, not allowed to be who I am, only who I'm pretending to be at the moment. I see how my life's events, my kidnapped mother, my murdered stepfather, the realization my biological father was a serial killer, kidnapper, rapist, sadist, have driven me with such focus that I have become the one thing I swore to bring to justice: a killer. I spent my teens and most of my twenties tracking down these animals and putting them down. My own form of justice makes me as bad as my real father. Is Ben just a chip off the old block? I know Ben's guilty of something. I'm just not sure what.

FORTY-TWO

Ben doesn't look up when I enter the room and sit. I say, "Long day." He looks up. His eyes are red. Tears have made salty tracks down his face. I feel a niggling but dismiss it and get into the zone. "Ben, I'm sorry I asked your father to come. I should have checked with you first."

He just looks at me with a blank expression. I watch his breathing and can see the tension, the slow drawing in of air, the quick release.

"He wanted to see you," I say. "He was concerned."

"Bullshit. He loves *them*."

"Ronnie and I met him. He spoke very fondly of you."

"Fondly. Did he? Let me tell you something. My father never loved me. He wanted to be as far away as possible. I think that's why he had such an empire. He would always have an excuse to escape from my mom and me."

"You never told me much about your mother."

"My mother." He snorts sarcastically but I can see tears hiding behind the disdain. "I barely remember what she looked like."

"You say that like she's gone. I thought she's still alive."

"Alive. Gone." He shrugs as if there is no distinction. "She sent me away. She was ashamed of me. She left me."

"My mother is gone too," I say. I wait. Curiosity killed the cat. He waits as well. But I win. "Is she alive?"

"Not so you'd notice." This gets a tight grin from him. "We moved around a lot. She was always gone and I had to take care of myself. I didn't even get to go to school. I homeschooled myself. Does it show?" That gets a smile.

"Not so you'd notice," he says.

I point a finger like it's a gun at him and we both laugh.

"So why did you become a cop?"

"My father was murdered." It's not a lie. I killed him.

Ben says, "That's horrible."

"And my stepfather was murdered."

"Yeah?"

"Yeah."

"There are worse things than dying." He looks away, and I don't know if he's talking about his parents or his wife and son. I feel a chill run up my spine.

"I've seen too much dying and death in my life," I reply.

"I imagine you have."

"It's not the same as on television. I can still see their faces. How they died. The smell." I'm watching him for a reaction to the grotesquerie. Nothing. "The nightmares that follow are of how they suffered. Alone. Dying. No one knows." Now I get a reaction.

Ben looks off into the distance. "Oh, I think someone knows. I mean, how could they not?"

Ronnie comes in with coffee and offers it to Ben. "How are you holding up, Ben?"

"I'm fine, Ronnie," he says. "Thanks, but I really have to go. My father reminded me I have some urgent business to take care of." He gets up. "Am I free to go?"

I want to put my foot in his ass, but I don't and just watch him leave.

Louisa and Tony come into the interview room and Tony says, "I thought you had him." Louisa nods, and Ronnie's looking at me like I'm a bug under a magnifying glass.

"Are you okay, Megan?" she asks.

"Is Cyrus gone?"

Ronnie hands me a cup of coffee. "He left while you were talking to Ben."

I take the coffee from her and take a sip, wishing it were Scotch. Lots of Scotch. I push down the anger and disappointment and say what they want to hear. "I'm just fine. He's the guy. Just like I thought. Anyone disagree?" No one does.

FORTY-THREE

Before I left to meet with Hayden I'm told what happened with Cyrus while I was interviewing his wayward son. Cyrus had offered to buy a new fleet of sheriff vehicles and refurnish our office. Ronnie told me Tony said he'd have to get approval from the county commissioners. They won't approve anything unless they get something too. Like new houses, cars, swimming pools, fact-finding junkets to Maui.

The good news is I might be getting a new car. The bad news is I might be getting fired after I drag Ben into the woods and beat the living shit out of him.

The Tides in Port Townsend is my favorite place to eat or drink—unless I'm in a mood like right now when all I want is a Scotch or three. I arrive at The Tides in record time because I've ignored the speed limit. It's my duty. To catch speeders, you have to think like one.

The parking lot at The Tides is full of vehicles and I scan them trying to guess which one is Hayden's. Without calling Dispatch and running registration of each one it's an impossible task, so I go inside and he's not there. Scotch time. I wonder if he's stood me up like I did to him: accidentally.

While I wait for the waitress to notice me I think about what

Cyrus had told the sheriff. Cyrus wanted to replace our worn-out desks, chairs, printers, computers, and video surveillance equipment with biometric locks on all the entrances. Ronnie said Cyrus's security chief, Sissy, was bringing an expresso machine to replace our Mr. Coffee. Tony told me Sissy was great and he wished she worked for him. *What am I, chopped liver?* All I need is competition. But on the other hand, someone like Sissy might be just what I need. Another hard-ass detective, a rogue, a rule breaker, a concrete cowboy. Stop it, Megan. I'm actually nervous about seeing Hayden. Do I apologize again for standing him up? That can be interpreted like I don't think he's important. He is important. But so is finding a pregnant woman and her small son. Not more important than Hayden, but... Why am I doing this? I'll just buy his meal or have a drink and be pleasant and try not to excuse myself for something I can't help. *Shut up, Megan.*

Hayden comes through the doorway. He's dressed in a new pair of black jeans, a white button-down shirt, black deck shoes, neat blond hair in a buzz cut—and my heart melts. He's grown into such a handsome man and exudes a confidence I never thought him capable of. He was always energetic and passionate as a child, into everything; he loved to draw and color and make things. Once he made a cabin out of Popsicle sticks and Elmer's glue and said he was going to build us our "forever house" when he grew up. The memory threatens to bring tears to my eyes, but I suck it up.

"Hi, Rylee. I mean Megan. Sorry. Can I sit?" He has a smile on his face and it looks genuine. It must be because Mom never taught him to hide his feelings. That training was reserved for me. *Or maybe it's his Army training. Or maybe he's just grown up.*

The waitress appears as if drawn by an electromagnet. She's a twenty-something blonde with long, skinny legs and large boobs, one of which sports a nametag that identifies her as SAM. She's almost drooling over my brother as she takes her order book out of her skintight jeans.

"We have a special on ribs, or if you like, you can have breakfast. Anything you want. Just ask."

Her eyes emphasize that Hayden can have anything. Anything? Seriously? There's no shame any more.

Without looking at her he says, "Just iced tea for me. I'm not much of a drinker."

Liar, liar, pants on fire. I can't keep alcohol in my place because of his search-and-drink missions.

"Sweet or unsweetened?"

"Sweet. Just like you," he says, and the waitress's face disappears in a smile.

"I'll take iced tea also," I say. And a barf bag. "Unsweetened, with Jack Daniel's in it. Or just make it a triple Scotch and shake some ice at it."

She's not listening to a word I say. She can't tear her eyes away from my baby brother long enough. She finally notices me and I order a Scotch yet again. I'll probably end up with a screwdriver. She walks away casting glances back over her shoulder. I've never thought of him as a babe magnet. I remember him telling me girls had cooties. Of course, I wasn't there when he had his first kiss. Or more. I should tell him girls like our waitress have worse than cooties.

"So you're working a missing person case," he says. "Mother and son."

I nod. "My sheriff's niece and her son."

"Maybe I can help, Megan." He emphasizes my name and grins. He's the same old Hayden. Teasing. Being a jerk sometimes. I love it.

"I appreciate the offer but I don't think so."

"You know I was in Army Intelligence."

I didn't know he'd worked in the intelligence field. The army must have recognized how smart he was. First in his class in high school. I have the picture on my desk to prove it.

He says, "Part of my job was tracking down people. Area and building searches. Research. That sort of thing."

His eyes become hard, challenging, and tell me he did more than track people and search buildings. I wonder how many he's killed. His eyes tell me he's seen more than me. I wonder if he carries that around with him. Or if he's become cold like me. Killing runs in the family. Our bio-father's blood runs through Hayden's veins too. When Hayden first came home he accused me of abandoning him. I wanted to give him my reasons—excuses, really—but I see what I hid from him as a kid just led to him finding better trainers in the art of killing.

Hayden's sweet tea comes, no Scotch for me, and the waitress leans over almost shoving her boobs in Hayden's face to serve him. He makes some silly remark, and she giggles like she's twelve years old. I have never giggled in my life. But I like what I'm seeing in my brother. Maybe he can fit in like I never could.

Daggers shoot from my eyes at the waitress until she leaves, and Hayden smiles at me.

"Can't I be protective of my baby brother?"

He smirks. "I'm not a baby anymore, sis. I'm all grown up."

I can see that. And so can the waitress. "Okay," I say. "Maybe you can help." I fill him in and when I finish, he looks thoughtful and downs his iced tea. The waitress materializes and refills it. Before she can disappear again I take her wrist. "My drink?"

"Coming right up. Sorry."

You will be if it's not here is two seconds.

"What did the crime scene tell you?" he asks, and I tell him about the results we have and the ones still being examined. He nods his understanding and I wonder how he can absorb all this so quickly. "You found an abandoned timber mill he's associated with and a water bottle in a secured room."

I hadn't told anyone about the locked room at the mill. Maybe he just assumed it. Maybe he knows me better than I thought. I tell him, "There were wood chips and greasy mud on some of Ben's clothes. He has access to two other trucks that he keeps in a building near the cabin where he's left his truck."

He asks, "Were you able to track his phone?"

He seems to know more than I wanted to tell him. "Yes. My partner turned on Ben's 'Find My Device' app."

"Your partner is Ronnie. Right?"

I nod. I don't want Ronnie to meet him and fall instantly and hopelessly in love. I've worked hard to cultivate her romance with Marley Yang, the Crime Lab supervisor.

Hayden strokes his chin. "When you went to see his girlfriend —Luci, right?" I nod. "Did you check on the whereabouts of the truck you saw him drive? The Ford?"

"That truck was still at the cabin."

Hayden looks thoughtful and turns serious. "Or at least his phone was. You found it in his truck later. Right?"

I expect any moment he'll exclaim, "Come, Watson. The game is afoot."

Hayden says, "He left this Luci woman no more than thirty minutes before you arrived. He may have even been in the condo, listening. How drunk was she?"

I say, "She got drunk pretty quick."

"And she gave him up right away?"

"She did."

He says, "She's lying. She knows more. Maybe where they are. Or were. They've probably been moved. She knew Ben was married and has a son. She knew his wife was pregnant. She's in love with him. She won't give him up. He's a gold mine."

I say, "But that would put suspicion on him."

The waitress comes back and stands holding a pad and pen. "Can I get your order. My name is Samantha, by the way." She says this and points to her overexposed chest.

Hayden offers his hand. "Hayden. Hayden Cassidy. I'll take the special."

I'm not hungry all of the sudden. "Samantha. Where is that Scotch coming from?" I get a blank look. Samantha has waited on me many times before but yet she can't remember what I always order. "Glenlivet," I say.

She tries not to smile. "We're out of Glenlivet."

"Any other Glen will do. Double. No ice."

"I'll ask the bartender what we have."

"Look, Samantha. Larry, the bartender, knows me. Just tell him the lady by the window with a gun wants a Glen. He'll know." I don't mean to be rude. Yes, I do. It's been one of those days and I'm taking it out on this lust-struck waitress. "Sorry," I say.

She scurries off and I see her whispering to the bartender. He grins and nods at me. She comes back with my drink. A triple Scotch, no ice. I wave at the bartender. He'll get a tip. She'll get a dirty table.

Hayden watches her walk away. "Wow, sis, you've still got a temper."

"Sorry. It's been a little stressful." And I'm showing you my bad side when I promised myself to be pleasant. "I'm not normally this way."

He laughs. He knows me too well. I ask, "So what do you think?"

"Ben is obviously confident you'll never catch him. But you will, sis. It's a puzzle, but he doesn't know you like I do. His arrogance will be his undoing. His dad said he has no friends, but you have friends and family to help you. You can pay." He smiles at me. I wish I had a camera. I'm surprised and proud of him and it feels good to be able to share my work with him. I'll have to do this more often. It won't make up for the earlier absence in his life but it's a start.

The ribs and my Scotch come. I try not to be snarky. Until I get her alone.

FORTY-FOUR

I pick Ronnie up at the office and we go to see Luci Simmons. Her car is gone.

"Maybe she's at the liquor store?" Ronnie says.

It's just after sunup. "I don't think the liquor stores are open yet."

Just then the Mercedes SL 550 Roadster pulls in beside us. We're parked in her neighbor's private spot and as we get out an older woman with too-black dyed hair and a face full of Botox comes out and glares at me. She's holding her silk kimono kind of robe together like she's got something to hide. All I can say is thank you. I hold up my badge but it means nothing in the face of true wealth. I don't care.

"Luci, we came by to see how you're holding up," I say as she slides from her low-slung seat. She has a paper grocery bag and the items inside are clinking. Ronnie was right.

She smiles and says, "I see you've met Mrs. Reagan." She gives the woman a finger and a smile.

"I didn't vote for her husband," I say, and Luci covers a chuckle with her free hand.

"Come in. Excuse my mess. I'm packing."

"We'll help."

"You don't have to bother. I've got it."

She's stone-cold sober now. We follow her and she instructs us to sit at the patio table while she puts the liquor haul away.

Luci comes back outside with three canned Diet Cokes. "I'm sorry. I'd offer you something stronger but I can see you're working. What can I help with?"

I take a leap of faith that my brother is right about her. If not, I'll have a lot of explaining to do. I take a laminated card from my badge case and hold it in my hand.

"Luci, I'm going to read the Miranda rights to you, so listen closely." The card is from a lock company. I found it stuck in my mailbox and kept it to shimmy doors. I start reading from the card. "Lucia Simmons, you have the right to remain silent. Anything you say can be used against you in a court of law. You have the right—"

She interrupts, her face is growing pale. "I haven't done anything wrong. What did he tell you?"

"You have the right to an attorney"*—and I hope you don't want one—*"before making any statements—"

"I haven't done anything. You don't have to do that. Whatever he told you, he's lying. What did he say?"

I'm not reading them in the correct order, but who cares? Ronnie leans toward her. "What do you think he said?"

A tear runs down her cheek and gathers on her trembling lower lip. "He's a bastard. But I don't know where Marlena and Bennie are. Honest to God. I swear I don't. He never told me."

I look at the fake Miranda card and hesitate a second before putting it away, leaving my badge case open on the tabletop. "What exactly did he tell you?"

Her shoulders slump. If she were a turtle, her head would disappear. I don't blame her, nor do I feel sorry for her. If she knew anything about them and didn't tell us, that makes her an accomplice.

"Okay. I'll tell you, but you have to promise he won't know it was me."

I shake my head and start to get the card out again.

"It was his idea. I tried to talk him out of it."

I feel a tingle of excitement and resist pumping a fist in the air. Later.

"Go on," Ronnie says in a comforting voice.

Luci dabs at her eyes with a cocktail napkin, then blows her nose. She sounds like a goose being tortured. "About two months ago he started talking about what his life would be like if he was single. He was tired of hiding out in the cabin. He hated keeping up the pretense that he was in love with her. Going home, making excuses to see me, trying to keep her from trashing his family name. He fantasized about her disappearing. 'Poof,' he said. But he was afraid his father would ruin it. He hates his father, but his father was close to Marlena and especially Bennie. Ben was jealous of the boy. He said his father never treated him like that. Spending time. It made him feel invisible. Like he'd just disappeared. He couldn't remember a time not feeling that way. Until he met me. He said our love had saved him. Made him a better man."

He's not a man. He's a monster. "Go on."

"A couple of weeks ago he started planning it for real. I thought he was all talk. He said he would find a reason to leave even if it meant living in the cabin for a while. He would come back and drug them both. He'd thought of a way to do this but he didn't tell me, and to be honest I didn't want to know."

"Did he talk about what he planned to do?"

"He said something about a timber mill. I was afraid. I thought he might hurt them. I made him promise he wouldn't kill them. He said he had other plans. He asked if I knew what human trafficking was. I didn't want to know and I told him to shut up. I didn't want any part of his sick plan. I threatened to stop seeing him but he just laughed and said I was already part of it. I'd go to jail if I said anything. He said he'd never let me leave, and if I tried, I'd disappear too."

She's done, but I know there's more. Hayden believed she knows where they are hidden. I do too. I start tapping my badge with one finger and looking directly at her. "Tell me where they are now."

Tears run freely now. Her lips quiver and she breaks out in a great bawling racket. Between blowing her nose and rubbing her eyes she says, "He texted me from the house when the police were there that morning. I can show you the text."

She digs in her pocket and pulls out an iPhone; the case is fluorescent orange. She touches some icons and hands it to me. It reads: *It's done. I love you.*

The time and date look about right. I surf the other messages. Ten in all from the same number, Ben's private phone. All the texts are similar, but none implicate him in a kidnapping. He says he can't wait to start life again.

"Ronnie, can you send these to me?"

Ronnie takes the phone and in seconds I hear my phone ding several times.

"You knew Ben had taken them to the timber mill and you didn't tell anyone."

She nods her head and wipes her running nose on the sleeve of what must be an expensive blouse.

"He said he owns an old timber mill. I've never seen it. Honest. But when he was planning this he said he was taking them somewhere near the bay. That seemed important to him for some reason. I hoped he didn't mean he was going to drown them. I didn't believe him about the human trafficking stuff. I mean, who would do that to a kid?"

A monster would. "Ronnie, do you have the pictures of the timber mill?" Ronnie gets on her phone and holds the screen where Luci can see it. Luci nods her head. It's the timber mill where we found the water bottle. I thought she said she'd never seen it. Still lying.

She realizes she messed up. "I guess I did see it the one time. I didn't know it was a timber mill, though. It's got some kind of big tower like a corn bin out there. He took me by there one night. He said he was going to tear it all down and build cabins."

"Was this while he was planning to kidnap his wife and son?" Ronnie asks.

"Yes. Oh my god! That's probably where they are. But you have pictures and you haven't found them. Have you?"

"You tell me, Luci. I'm not playing this game with you." I get out the fake card again, and she cracks.

"Don't do that. I'll tell you everything. You must know already or you wouldn't be here."

I slightly nod. "I'm going to read the Miranda rights to you, Luci. I can't promise you anything, but it'll go easier on you with the prosecutor if you cooperate one hundred percent."

"I understand. I just don't want to go to prison. Can you promise me that much?"

I can promise I'll choke the truth out of you if you don't work with us. "You know I can't. But I'll put in a good word for you. How's that?" *I won't.*

Her tears have dried completely. She's become a different person from the one we've seen thus far. This one is the real Luci. Cold, calculating, selfish, out for number one. I repeat the Miranda rights from memory, in the correct order this time, and Ronnie records her statement.

She looks at us with puppy eyes full of tears. "Am I going to jail?"

"Not immediately," I say. "But if we find out you've been lying to us again we'll be coming for you."

FORTY-FIVE

"Your arrest warrant for Ben is ready, Megan. You have to go to the judge to sign." Tony pushes back from his desk. The chair is silent. It's new. The desk is too. Cyrus doesn't mess around. The sheriff has called us into the office and I can see some relief on his face. We're finally getting some traction in this case. "Why aren't you arresting the girlfriend for her part in this?"

"Ronnie told her there was a tracking device built into her Mercedes. If it leaves her condo before we give her permission, she'll be arrested."

"And is there? A tracking device."

I look to Ronnie for the answer. "For one hundred and twenty grand, there should be rocket boosters and wings too. And yes, I was able to access her LoJack. She won't run."

"Well, you know what you're doing," he says to me. "You do know what you're doing?"

"Have I ever let you down before?" He's thinking. "Recently, I mean."

"You've solved some tough cases, Megan. I'll give you that. This time, please be more, uh, just watch your p's and q's. There will be a lot of media attention. The only reason it hasn't been front-page is... well, you know who can make that happen."

Cyrus must own the media. Of course he does. "I'll cross my *i*'s and dot my *t*'s, boss."

"Me too," Ronnie says, and gives a little salute.

"Get out of here, you two."

We make like Ben's neighbors' pets and disappear, but unlike those poor animals we're not dead. I pray that Marlena and Bennie aren't, either. This is one sick puppy we're dealing with.

My phone rings. I hand it to Ronnie. I need to watch my speed. The needle passes the seventy mark while I watch it climb. Ronnie puts the speaker on.

"Megan, Ronnie, you're not going to believe this," Sheriff Gray says. He's picked up Ronnie's bad habit.

"What is it, Sheriff?" she asks.

"Ben is sitting in the interview room. I'm keeping an eye on him, but you should get back here ASAP."

"Who found him?" I ask.

"He came in on his own. Apparently his girlfriend called him."

I should have arrested her, but the damage is already done. And this saves me a little time trying to track him down while everyone else is trying to hopelessly search all the places he has access to.

We park beside a newer white Chevy Silverado truck. Likely the one missing from Ben's barn. Ronnie is already running the license plates. If it's his or his company's, we'll seize it and search it. He's not going anywhere.

Sheriff Gray meets us at the door. "He just rang the front buzzer and said he needed to talk to both of you. Says he has some information."

"Did you tell him about the warrant?"

"I'll leave it to you. Is that truck his? The one you said was missing?"

Ronnie gets off her phone. "That's got to be it. Registered to Parker Industries. Should I call Mindy?"

Tony says, "I'll do that. And I'll get the video rolling. You take care of our visitor."

There's the old saying by Benjamin Franklin: "Guests, like fish, begin to smell after three days." Parker is a guest who is going to stink a lot longer than that. My heart accelerates as I enter the interview room and see him leaning back cockily in his chair.

"Ben," I say.

"Megan... Ronnie."

FORTY-SIX

We take seats across from Ben. Ronnie sets the legal-size manila folder that contains the copies of the warrant on the table. His name is printed on the outside.

"What did you want to tell us?" I say.

"You first," he says, and nods his head toward the folder.

"Guests are always first."

"I found a note on my truck's windshield."

Here we go again.

He takes a folded piece of paper from his shirt pocket, opens it, and lays it facing us. I swear I can see a smile hiding. It is a note and of course it's typed.

We've got them.

We'll be in touch.

"You shouldn't have handled it," I say.

"It was stuck on my windshield. I thought someone hit my truck and left their information. I always see the best in people, Megan."

As if I don't see the good in people.

Ronnie collects the note, and I ask him, "What does it mean?"

The side of his mouth develops a tick. I've pissed him off.

"What do you think it means? It means someone has kidnapped my wife and son. It means there is more than one kidnapper."

"Are you sure this isn't a fake?"

"Oh, for God's sake. Look at it. Who else would leave a note like that?"

"Is there anyone that would want to tweak your nose?" *Like your ex-girlfriend?*

"Oh, come on, Megan. Get serious. You have to treat this as a kidnapping for ransom. You're sworn to protect and serve. Two lives are at stake. They haven't asked for money yet, but I'm sure it will be an enormous amount. I'll pay whatever they ask. I just want to bring them home."

"You're right, Ben. Lives *are* at stake." *Do you really care? How will you pay if you don't have anything?* And then it hits me. Ben *doesn't* have anything. He's shaking his father down for money. He either has kidnapped his own family or he's taking advantage of the situation.

He reads my thoughts. "I love my family. I'll find the money somewhere."

"Where did you find the note?"

"I told you: under the wiper blade on my truck."

"The truck outside?"

He's impatient. "Yeah. The truck outside. I came right here after I found the note."

"This is a different truck than I've seen you drive. I just wanted to be sure."

"I have several trucks. I like to switch off sometimes. Is that against the law?"

I ask a question of my own. "Where were you parked when the note was put there?"

"I had gone to my bank in Seattle."

"Why were you in Seattle?" Ronnie asks.

"I had to go to the bank. That's where my bank is. Seattle. When I came out, the note was under my wiper. Does it matter?"

"Everything matters, Mr. Parker. How would the person know what you were driving if you switch trucks sometimes?"

"I don't know. You're the detectives. Figure it out."

"You say you have different trucks. What about the SL 550 Ms. Simmons drives? Do you also drive that?"

He doesn't miss a beat. "Nah. Not my style. That was just a perk for her. The company pays for insurance too. She's no longer working for me. The car is severance pay of sorts."

I ask, "Would she have left that note?"

A guarded look crosses his face. "You'd have to ask her."

I try to look stern, a little angry; I deliberately tighten my lips into a straight line before answering. "I talked to her and I take it you have too." I let that set a moment, and he starts rocking slightly, looking into nowhere.

"I did talk to her. She said you wanted to talk to me. And that you didn't like her."

She's right. "Did she call you?"

"I called her. She's been avoiding me."

"Did you go to her condo yesterday and warn her we would come?"

"You make it sound like I have something to hide. Yes, I went to see her and told her she might have to talk to you. I wanted to warn her that you thought we were having an affair. If I wanted to hide something, that was it. I texted her the morning the police were looking through the house for Marlena and Bennie and told her they were missing."

"Did she know you had a son?"

"Of course. I had her buy him gifts from time to time. Like the Darth Vader stuff. She knew it was for him. What did she tell you?"

"Did you tell her you were going to divorce your wife?"

He pauses. "We were having an affair. It got complicated.

Okay, I'm a jerk. I was stringing her along. But I never meant any of it."

"Why did you tell her your family was missing?"

"Well... she's my secretary. I didn't want her finding out some other way, and I'd have to tell her eventually."

"I mean why did you tell her they were missing when you weren't sure? We weren't sure right away. You hadn't even checked the house or talked to the neighbors or called her mother or your father."

"I can't tell you why."

"Can't? Or won't?"

"Can't. I can't because I don't know. I probably shouldn't have told her. It only made her think we were going to get together with them gone. She thinks I had something to do with it."

"Did your wife know about Luci?"

"She knew I had hired Luci."

"Mr. Parker..."

"Okay. Honestly. Luci was coming unhinged. For weeks she would make catty remarks about Marlena. She'd make remarks like 'If I was your wife...' sort of stuff. She had gone to see Marlena. I found out because Marlena told me. I planned to fire Luci, but she threatened to go to my father and tell him about the affair. If my father wasn't so much in love with my wife and son, I would have laughed in her face."

Asshole. "But you couldn't afford to incur Cyrus's wrath."

"You've met my father."

"When did these threats start? When did she go to see Marlena?"

"Marlena told me about it the night we separated. She was angry and I tried to tell her it wasn't all my fault. Marlena had been cold to me for a long time. I'm a man. I have needs."

I have needs too. I need to smash your face. "Did she talk to your wife that day?"

"She must have. I'm not sure. But I think so, yeah."

"When did you find out your wife was pregnant?"

"We were arguing about something. Nothing important. She was always mad about something or other. She started in on me and I got angry and yelled at her. She accused me of having an affair and I... well, I tried to deny it, you know? Then she told me Luci had come to the house. Told me what Luci had said. Asked if I wanted to divorce her. I lost my temper and said yes, I wanted a divorce, and I started picking up things to leave. I was so angry I didn't know what I was taking. Just stuff. She was in my face the whole time. That's when she told me she was pregnant. She said it wasn't mine."

I look skeptical. Helen portrayed an entirely different Marlena. Jennie Hunter too.

"I know you don't believe me, and I don't blame you, but what I'm telling you is the honest truth. I swear."

That proves he's lying as far as I'm concerned. I wonder how much to believe of anything he's said so far.

"I think Luci kidnapped my wife and son. It makes sense. She wanted me for herself and my family stood in the way. She had to know I'd never divorce Marlena. She knew I loved Bennie more than anything. More than her."

Past tense again. I feel a chill.

He puts a palm beside his head and rubs his temple and does a good impression of dawning suspicion. "Wait a minute. I remember seeing Luci with a Black guy a few times. Remember I told you I chased a Black guy away from the house once? Marlena said he'd peeked in the windows before. Luci might have someone helping her. That's why the note said 'we.' Luci told me she'd dated a Black guy in New York. She thought I would disapprove or get jealous. He might have been scouting the house—checking my schedule to see when the house would be unguarded. At first I thought it was just a peeping Tom, but now..."

His eyes widen almost theatrically. This guy should write for Netflix.

"Do you know any of Luci's friends?" I ask.

"Luci doesn't make friends easily. The ones she knew when

she moved here abandoned her. She seemed to think they weren't good enough for me. I didn't care who she was friends with. But there was one Black guy I saw her with at the airport one time when I took Luci on a business trip and then again in Seattle. They seemed awful chummy. He might be the one I chased. I'm sure it was him."

"Luci told us *you* were planning the kidnapping of your wife and son for several weeks."

"Of course she would say that if she was involved. Right? I know I didn't kidnap my own family, so it must be her and her Black friend. He looked kind of shifty. Maybe she was just coming on to me to get money and favors. God knows, I gave her enough. Maybe when she couldn't woo me away from Marlena she decided to do this. I just pray they're safe somewhere and we find them."

You're playing us again. It won't work. "Ronnie, I need you to do something." I get up and take her in the outer office and say loud enough for Ben to hear, "Make some copies of the note and then call the FBI." I'm shaking my head not to do that. I whisper, "Try to find Luci? You have her phone number." She grins for an answer. It's an evil grin. She's maturing nicely.

Back in the interview room, I ask Ben, "Is there anywhere Luci and her friend might have taken them?"

"I don't know."

"If you had to hide two people, where would you take them?"

"I told you—"

"Humor me, Ben."

He remains silent but his eyes watch mine. "Here's what I think, Ben. If I were a kidnapper, I'd keep them someplace they wouldn't be found easily. An abandoned warehouse, or an abandoned timber mill." He blinks. I've hit a nerve. "I'd leave them with my partner to watch. If I had one. Then I'd come up with a way to get messages to the family. I couldn't use my own phone." His eyes begin to drift away from mine but his expression doesn't change. I say, "If I thought the police were getting too close I'd move them to another hideaway."

Ronnie sticks her head in the door.

"Anything else you want to tell us?"

"Luci has a problem with liquor. She was sober when I saw her. I was there two or three minutes. I wish to God I'd thought about her being the one behind all of this."

"We'll find her. I want you to stay close and keep in touch with me."

"You mean don't leave town, like the cops say on those shows?"

Yeah. Exactly like that. "Nothing like that. I just need you to be available at a moment's notice. Maybe you could go home and hang around there today?" I hope Mindy and the crew are done with his cabin and the trucks. If not, tough.

"I have a couple of errands to run. I'll have to go to the house—our house—and tidy it up for when they come home. Marlena hates a messy house."

"Ben, do you any idea where Luci might be? Anything at all. A mall? A bar? A restaurant?" *An adult toy store?*

"No. But if she doesn't want to be found, I doubt you'll find her. She grew up in New York, in a bad part of town. She's pretty street-smart."

FORTY-SEVEN

"She's not answering her phone."

Ronnie has called Luci repeatedly as we head toward her condo. I have a sick feeling in the pit of my stomach. I should have insisted she leave the condo. Got her a hotel room. Ben knew she was a loose end. He came in with the note and admitted only what we already knew. It was a cinch to blame all of this on Luci and the imaginary Black guy. But only if Luci was no longer around to refute it. His remark about Luci having a partner struck me as important. What if Ben had a partner? If so, who would it be? His neighbors on Luna Ridge didn't care for him and he didn't have any friends outside of the perverted Luci. Cyrus told us as much.

"Should we search all the warehouses the company owns?"

"It would take a week to do that with our own people and we're spread pretty thin as it is. Thank goodness Sissy's crew are helping with that. Besides, if Ben told us about them, they won't be there. He knows we have Cyrus's help. He's got them stashed somewhere else." I don't have to say they may be buried or dumped somewhere. But Ben wouldn't just dump the bodies. He's too careful for that. The animals he made disappear didn't turn up unless he wanted them to. Luci may have disappeared the same way. Or maybe she's just done a runner. We won't know until we find her. "Let's see if she's home."

We go to Luci's condo and her car isn't there. "I'll go to the back," I say. "Look in the front windows." I'm hoping we don't have to talk to Mrs. Reagan and get an earful.

Down the side of the condo everything seems to be the same. Flowers. Several empty liquor bottles on the patio table and ground. The back door opens when I push it after knocking. Ronnie startles me coming up from behind.

"Sorry. I checked the front. All locked up. I knocked on the door and looked in the windows. The lady next door came out and told me Luci left an hour ago. No one was with her."

"How did you get her to talk to you?"

"I complimented her roses. They're beautiful. She knows my mom and dad." She giggles. "I'm supposed to tell them hello from Mrs. Reagan."

That would never work for me. I don't know squat about flowers. And the only people my mom knows are dead. "Fantastic."

"Maybe she's meeting Ben?"

"She may be running. What would *you* do?"

"Me? I'd be afraid of Ben. I'd run."

"Okay. What would a normal person do?"

I meant it as a joke but she looks offended. "I'm normal."

That's debatable.

"A normal person might believe that crap. But you and I are far from normal. We're the least normal people I know." Just like that, we're friends again.

"Are you going to call the FBI?"

"I don't think they'd be interested."

"They might because of who the missing are. Everyone knows who Cyrus Parker is."

I didn't. But she may be right. "I don't want to involve the FBI unless we have to. This will be bigger than the Lindbergh baby kidnapping. Press, cameras, sightseers, sickos crawl out of the woodwork. Besides, the FBI are too slow. They have to get permission to get permission and then get that approved. They'll bring in psychologists, negotiators, Santa and all his elves. It'll turn into a circus. Besides, I think Ben wants us to call the FBI. We would be off the case."

I call Tony. "Sheriff, can you spare someone to go by the Gentlemen's Club?"

"I can. What do you need to know?"

"We found a matchbook from there in Ben's cabin. See if he's a regular. Maybe someone there can help us out."

Tony says he'll get on it, and Ronnie asks, "What do you think Ben will do now?"

"He'll make up a second note."

Ronnie says, "I did some research. Washington has the fifth highest rate of child abductions. Family members account for ninety percent of the abductors, with mothers or female family members accounting for sixty percent of those. FBI figures show ninety-nine percent of those abductions end with the return of the child alive. But that's usually a custody squabble."

"No. Ben tried to make it look like that originally. When that didn't seem to work for him, he came up with the abduction scenario and then the peeping Tom scenario. Now that we know he's got a mistress, he comes up with the kidnapping for ransom. It's escalating every time we do something right."

"Megan, I hope we haven't pushed him into doing something horrible. He's not going to just take us to them or let them go. What if he kills them? I don't want to be responsible for that."

"What if we buy into the kidnapping-for-ransom crap Ben suggested? If they're alive, it might give them a little time. Getting the money together takes some time. Even for Cyrus it will take time if we coach him on dragging his feet." I've never been one to back down when I'm hunting. Searching for my mother is what got me here. Made me good at what I do. I can't stop. I have an idea that might buy us the time we need to find them on our own. "If Ben is after money, he'll enjoy watching his dad sweat."

"But there's no guarantee Ben will release them, Megan."

"We'll ask for proof of life. If it's too late we'll know and arrest him on the warrant we have."

Ronnie says, "The sleeping medication gives me some hope. That's probably how he got them. Why go to the trouble of knocking them out? Why not kill them in the house? He's keeping them knocked out. Why?"

"So that they don't try to get away. Make noise and attract attention."

Ronnie looks excited. "Or to move them without them seeing it's him. Maybe they don't know who has them. Maybe they're so drugged they don't know anything. If they don't, there's a reason to keep them alive. Get the ransom and let them go. Maybe that's been his plan all along."

"What do you suggest we do next, Detective Marsh?"

"He's involved Luci in this. We find her, bring Ben in, and put them in the same room. Let the sparks fly."

"Don't go all Clint Eastwood on me." I grin to let her think I'm joking. I'm not.

"Thanks for working this with me, Megan. I've learned a lot from you. If you ever need help with anything, anything at all..."

Her heartfelt pronouncement makes me a little embarrassed and I don't know what to say, so I joke, "I like you, too, Ronnie, but I won't sleep with you."

She punches me on the arm. "I mean it, Megan. You don't know how much this job means to me."

I do. It means as much, or more, to me. This job has given me a life I never thought possible. I'm helping people and punishing the evildoers. What more can you ask for? Maybe a new car...

FORTY-EIGHT

"Megan, I'm agreeing with you," Sheriff Gray says. "You did the right thing by not arresting Luci or Ben. But this is too big for us. You haven't notified the FBI yet. We *need* to notify the FBI. They have agents that specialize in this sort of thing. If word gets out the kidnappers are holding Cyrus Parker's daughter-in-law and grandson for ransom and we failed to call the FBI, I'll be looking for a new job."

"What about us?" I argue. "Our jobs are on the line too. We can do this, Tony. You can't give this to the feds. They can't do anything we can't do except to slow things down." *More than they already are. And it would take time to get them up to snuff. And they're by the book. They won't approve of my methods.*

Ronnie looks at him pleadingly but says nothing, so I call in a favor. "I bought you cinnamon rolls. I gave you my double bacon cheeseburger and fries. I've never told Ellen about your secret stash. I—"

"That's enough," he says. He's pissed. So am I. We sit that way for several minutes. Ronnie keeps stealing glances at the door. Running won't help. There's a time to stand and fight. This is it.

Ronnie surprises me and says, "If you don't trust us, maybe you should get some new detectives." My mouth drops open and I just look at her. So does Tony. And then she ruins the moment. "I'm sorry, Sheriff. I was out of line."

"No, it wasn't, Ronnie. You called us in on this, Tony. We're not quitters. We're good detectives. And we're women. What would the feminists say if you pulled us off and gave it to a bunch of guys with perfect hair and nails?"

Tony looks at me and I can see the struggle going on inside his head but misread it. He starts laughing. "Guys with perfect hair and nails." Soon we're all laughing. I didn't mean it to be funny. I was pissed. Still am. But it's either laugh or scream.

"So what do you say, Sheriff? Us or the guys from the beauty salon?"

He lies across the top of his desk laughing. I win.

Ronnie and I leave in my car before Tony changes his mind.

"Thanks for having my back in there, Megan."

"You owe me, Ronnie. Don't forget. I won't."

She chuckles and then stops. "You're serious?"

"I am. Tony has fired people for less. You've never seen that side of him. He threw a detective out the door for complaining about overtime."

"He didn't."

"No. But *I* wanted to throw the crybaby out." I can't stand whiners. Especially lazy whiners.

She calls Luci again. "No answer."

I tell her, "Call Mindy. Tell her to meet us for coffee."

Ronnie does and says, "She says to meet her at Moe's and you're buying."

Mindy's a cheap date.

"Why are we meeting Mindy?"

"I want to bounce ideas off her. I can't believe the county won't hire her full-time."

"See where Ben is first."

Ronnie pulls up Ben's phone and says, "His phone is at the Luna Ridge house."

"Call him."

She does and puts it on speaker. Surprisingly, he answers on the first ring. "Ronnie. So good to hear your voice."

I look at Ronnie and pretend to stick my finger down my throat and gag. "I'm here too, Ben," I say. *Is it good to hear my voice too, you jerk?* "Any news?" Ronnie puts it on speaker.

"I'm supposed to be asking you that, Megan. Did you find Luci?"

I pause thinking of possible answers. I guess it doesn't matter what I answer. "Not yet. We have everyone looking for her. Is there any place in particular she likes to go?" *Besides your playroom at the cabin?* "Any hobbies. Interests?" *Quit it, Megan.*

"I guess I didn't know her that well. We mostly talked about what *I* liked. I half expected her to call me. She'll need money."

"Ben, do you have her address or phone number in New York?" I don't expect him to have this and I'm not disappointed.

"I've got her application on file somewhere, but I'll have to call someone to get it."

"If you hear anything, call us immediately. Where are you?" I don't want him to know we're tracking his phone.

"I'm cleaning house for Marlena and Bennie. Your people left a mess with all that black powder. I can imagine what Bennie would have done with it."

His voice sounds thick, and if I didn't know what a feelingless jerk he is, I'd think he was on the verge of tears. "Ben?"

He clears his throat. "I didn't want to go back to the cabin. There's nothing there for me now. Nothing here, either, I guess."

I tell him to stay put and Ronnie disconnects but seems excited. "I don't know why I didn't think of this earlier."

"What?"

"Ben was wearing an Apple Watch the first time we met him. Luci was wearing one too."

"And?"

"I've never tried this before, Megan, but think I can find her Apple Watch. It's one of the devices that 'Find My Device' can track, but I need her iCloud password and some other data."

"Where do we get that?"

"Sissy might have it on file. She probably has to be able to get devices back when someone leaves the company." She finds Sissy's number and calls. It's a short conversation, and Ronnie takes out her iPad. She does things to the screen, then zooms in on a map. "Got it!"

Outstanding!

She's looking at the iPad and smiling. "I can't believe I did this."

I can't believe half the things you do. "Call Mindy and cancel. Tell her we've found Luci."

FORTY-NINE

Luna Ridge Loop Hiking Trail is the longest in the state of Washington at 5.5 miles. Ronnie has pulled up GPS coordinates for the Apple Watch along with Google Earth. There are three trailheads, each with visitors' parking. The Apple Watch is at the trailhead marked Luna Ridge Falls. The lot is empty but for one car. The Mercedes is pulled nose in under the low branches of a giant pine as if it rammed the tree. The brake lights are on and the engine is running. I can't imagine anyone deliberately driving an expensive car under limbs that hang to the ground. The license plate is right. We have permission from Cyrus to search it.

"Do you think she's passed out drunk?" Ronnie asks.

"Only one way to find out." My work clothes have seen better days, but this is the second set, and they're real comfy. No more skunks, please. I go to the trunk and slap my hand on the surface. No reaction. The inside of the rear windshield is covered with some kind of gunk, and the car is buried up to the passenger windows in pine limbs. I'll have to crawl to get to a window so I can see inside. I wriggle along the driver's side, knocking every foot or so on the metal, but nothing happens except my knuckles begin to hurt. I think I can get to the driver's door and it looks like there's room to get to the window or maybe pull the door partway open.

There are deep scratches and dents in the driver's door. The car is jammed in pretty good. I'm not sure it can even be driven out if the driver wanted. I put my face against the glass and can see someone is inside. I try the handle and the door comes open. I immediately wish I hadn't opened the door. There's a comedian known as Gallagher whose act includes the smashing of watermelons with a sledgehammer. This looks like that, only instead of a watermelon the exploded object is Luci Simmons's head. When I can pry my eyes away from the gore that once was an attractive face, I see the car is still in Drive and resting against the tree trunk. Her foot is on the brake, one of her hands is clutching the lower half of the steering wheel, the other lying across her lap with a bloody hole in the middle of her palm. The headrest is shredded, and brain tissue and bits of skull have peppered the back seat and rear windshield. Cracks like spin art surround a dime-size hole in the front windshield. The weapon was larger than the .45-caliber I carry. That much firepower would be as hard to silence as a howitzer, and in this case had the same result. There is little traffic back here. If there were witnesses they fled.

I work my way out from under the branches and meet Ronnie at the rear of the car. "Was she in there?" Ronnie asks.

Part of her. "She's been shot in the head."

"Are you sure it's her?" Ronnie looks queasy. I'm numb to this.

"Her face is gone, along with most of her head, but I'd have to say yes." Ordinarily, positive identification can be made with fingerprints, DNA, or dental records. Dental records are not going to help in this case. "We need Mindy and a wrecker. A flatbed."

"I called already."

"Call Mindy and tell her we have a body. I'll call Tony and the coroner."

Tony answers immediately. He sounds as exhausted as I feel. "Did you pick her up?"

"Yes and no. Ronnie was able to track her down to Luna Ridge Loop Hiking Trail. She's dead. Shot." I explain what I found, and the tiredness leaves his voice.

"I'm coming out there."

"Mindy and Crime Scene are coming. Mindy might need some help searching the area for evidence."

"What are you and Ronnie doing?"

"We're going to visit Ben."

"I'll send extra officers to secure the scene. Do you know where he is?"

"We did thirty minutes ago. Ronnie's checking now."

"I'm calling backup for you. Don't approach him alone, Megan. That's not a request."

"I promise not to approach him alone." I'm not lying. Ronnie will be with me. "I'll call for backup as soon as I get a location."

"Be sure you do," he says, and hangs up.

"Ronnie, find out where Ben is right now."

While she does this I try to picture where the shot was fired from. The killer must have been directly in front of the car due to the angle of the hole in the windshield and the missing head. The back windshield is intact, so the bullet may still be in the car. Luci's foot is on the brake. The gear is still in Drive. One hand is on the steering wheel, the other with a hole in the palm.

Luci saw the killer and was going to park. They were standing directly in front of her. She was meeting someone. Nothing was wrong at that point. Then she saw the gun. Too late. She reflexively put her foot on the brake and threw her arm up to protect her face. The gun must have been pointed right at her. It fired, the bullet went through her hand, her head, the headrest. The car rolled forward against the tree trunk.

When I crawled to the car door, the ground was thick with dead pine needles and sharp cones. I wasn't looking for a spent shell casing, but chances are it's not too far from the car. Unless the killer found it.

"Megan, I've got Ben's phone. It's still at Marlena's house. I tried to locate Ben's Apple Watch like we did with Luci and it's here somewhere."

"Here?"

"Right where we are."

We both start looking around, kicking at pine needles that are six inches deep. I get down on my hands and knees and start crawling back to the driver's door, when I hear a dinging sound and then a buzzing noise.

"Are you doing that, Ronnie?"

"I hear it too. You must be close."

I sweep my arm over the ground, clearing away what I can before advancing. The sound stops. "Do it again, Ronnie." A couple seconds later I hear the ding and buzz again. It's coming from directly in front of me but I can't see it. I'm not finding it.

"The screen should be lighting intermittently, Megan."

I brush more needles and twigs away, and there, in front of the driver's-side tire, is a black watch, buzzing and lighting like a lightning bug. I back out carefully. I don't know what other evidence I've crawled across.

"What is that doing here?" she asks.

"See if you can do that to Luci's watch?"

Ronnie hits a few icons and we hear a buzzing coming from inside the car.

I can hear Ben now, telling me his watch was stolen and Luci must have taken it. A lie for every occasion. That's Ben Parker.

"Find Ben's phone again."

"Twenty-one Luna Ridge," she says.

"I'd better call Jerry Larsen and give him a heads-up. He won't be able to climb back there with the body."

"I called while you were looking around," she says.

I need to get her a raise. Jerry Larsen is our part-time coroner and a druggist by trade. He and his wife run a pharmacy in downtown Port Townsend. He's in his early sixties, white hair, long, silky white beard, not fat, but his eyes are twinkly and he reminds me of Santa Claus. Think of Santa delivering dead bodies to the morgue. I can't think of a more incongruous job for a pharmacist.

"We have to wait for one of our guys to arrive to guard the scene," I say.

Ben has been my suspect almost from the beginning. He knew we were going to find Luci with or without his help. That's why he asked if we found her not thirty minutes ago when I talked to him. He was at Marlena's house at that time, not more than two miles from here. I replay my earlier scenario but this time with Ben as the killer. It all fits. He was going to let her keep a $120,000 car as a severance benefit, so what else was she demanding? One thing is in our favor. He doesn't know we've found Luci. But we have to hurry.

A marked sheriff's car pulls into the parking area followed by Mindy's flower van. Deputy Davis gets out of the sheriff's car. "Detective Carpenter. Detective Marsh. Sheriff Gray said to tell you to wait for backup before you go anywhere. What do you want me to do? Do you want me to go with you?"

"Someone has to stay here with Mindy and protect the scene."

"But the sheriff—"

"What if the shooter is still around here?"

He reflexively looks around. "But—"

"And I've got Ronnie for backup. Are you saying two female detectives can't take care of themselves?"

"No, Detective Carpenter. I'm just—"

"Deputy Davis, keep your radio handy and I'll call if we run into anything else. I've got to talk to Mindy and then I want you to start closing this lot off."

Mindy smiles at me. "You'll do anything to get out of buying me coffee."

FIFTY

On Luna Ridge Drive we see Ben's truck coming toward us. He jams the brakes and begins backing up, gaining speed and bouncing over the curb, spinning the truck around. His truck is sideways to us still partway on the curb when I slam my car into his passenger's side, pushing the truck into Mrs. Green's yard. My airbags don't go off and my ribs take a beating. Of course. But it's good the airbags didn't deploy, because I see Ben jump from the truck and start limping toward the golf course. I'm still trying to get my seat belt off when I hear Ronnie yell, "Stop, Ben, or I'll shoot!" I see her standing, legs spread, arms straight out, with her duty weapon trained on Ben.

He stops and puts his hands in the air. A handgun is stuck in his waistband.

"Get on your knees!"

He tries to get down but can't.

"I'm hurt, Ronnie. I can't."

"Put your hands on the back of your head, Ben." He does and starts to turn. "Did I say turn around? Look straight ahead and don't move or I'll shoot you. It'll hurt." She shoves him against the side of his wrecked truck.

I finally get my seat belt off and get out. She looks at me and says, "Are you okay, Megan?"

My chest hurts where the steering wheel caught my lower ribs, but I think I'm fine. I look at the Taurus and it's not okay. Steam is coming from under the crumpled hood, and the left wheel is turned at an impossible angle. "I'm fine," I say. "Cover me. I've got him."

I don't bother pulling my weapon as I approach. Ronnie is a crack shot. Ben is taller than me by about a foot, so I grab his belt and begin patting him down none too gently. "Where are they, Ben?" I say in a menacing voice. His head turns to the side to answer, and Ronnie lets loose a string of expletives that shock us both into silence. I've created a monster.

"Seeing someone with their head blown off makes her cranky. That Glock has been modified with a hair trigger and her hands are shaking. But I'm sure if you tell us where your wife and son are, she might calm down."

On cue Ronnie starts breathing hard and saying things like, "Hell with him. Move, Megan."

Ben's voice begins to break. "I don't know where they are. I swear I don't. Don't shoot me. Don't..." His voice trails off and I look back at Ronnie and make a cutting motion across my throat and hope she doesn't take it to mean kill him.

"It's not my gun," he says. "It was in my truck when I came out of the house. I swear to God, it's not my gun."

"Keep your hands on your head, Ben." I pull the weapon out of his waistband and stick the muzzle in my back pocket before handcuffing him. After I have him cuffed, I finish a more thorough pat-down search. "Do you have another weapon or anything sharp that might hurt me?"

"I don't have anything, Megan."

"Do you swear to God?" I can't help but ask it. Everyone always swears to God.

"I swear to God." Ben breaks out in wracking sobs, and I can feel them vibrate through his body when I take a fistful of his shirt in my hands.

"Watch him, Ronnie," I say. He's not faking the bum leg, but I want to keep him scared that Ronnie's lost it. I bring him to the back of my car and have him bend over the trunk as much as he can.

I pull my .45 and shove it into his temple. He quits. "Do you have something to say? Where are they?" I grind the barrel into his flesh and find he's become the other Ben. The cocky, arrogant, king-cock-of-the-walk Ben.

"My attorney will have a field day with this," he says. "You said there are cameras everywhere. I'll sue your asses off."

That's the only way he'll ever touch my ass. "What do you think will happen to you in prison? A good-looking guy like you. Your dance card will always be full."

Ronnie starts humming "Here Comes the Bride," and I feel the fight go out of him. Two sheriff's cruisers arrive and the officers take him into custody. I tell them to take him to headquarters and put him in the interview room. He hasn't asked for an attorney. Not in so many words.

The officer calls for another car to pick us up and for two wreckers. At least, this time we don't need the coroner. I use the time wisely and bag the gun I've taken from Ben: a Desert Eagle .50-caliber semiautomatic. Clint Eastwood would approve. I call Mindy and tell her about the gun. Then I call Sheriff Gray. He doesn't answer and I look up to see Tony's truck coming down the street.

He rolls his window down and eyes my smoking vehicle. "I told you to wait for backup."

"I'm fine, Sheriff," I say. "We're all fine. Nothing going on here."

He's angry and I don't blame him. "We'll talk about this later. Walk me through this."

Ronnie and I start to give an account, leaving out some of the things we said to Ben, when a voice calls from the sidewalk, "Tony!"

I turn and see Mrs. Green. The sheriff says, "Matilda?"

"I thought that was you."

"Been a while," he says, and his cheeks redden. I've never seen him blush.

Mrs. Matilda Green is wearing bright red lipstick and rouge and makeup so thick, it looks like she poured it in a bowl and stuck her face in it. She starts pushing her hair into place and smiles at Tony like he's something good to eat. I don't know if I want to know. On second thought, I definitely don't want to know. He gets out and walks her down the street toward her house, sneaking looks over his shoulder. Either at us or the smoking wreck. She hugs him and plants a kiss on his cheek. He's still red in the face when he returns sans paramour. "An old friend," he says, and clears his throat.

"None of our business," I say, and Ronnie nods but I think the conversation with her later will be fun.

"Never mind all that," he says. "Mindy's busy at the trail. You were walking me through this."

I show him the Desert Eagle. "Ben fled from us but Ronnie got him." I'll talk to her later about her language. "The gun was stuck in his waistband."

"He was running with it?" Tony asks. It comes out sounding like *I told you not to run with scissors* but I know he's just getting things straight.

"The trail is only a mile or two away. The last time we talked to him, he said he was cleaning the house because Marlena didn't like a mess. I think he was here to retrieve the gun, shot Luci, and then came back to hide it. We must have come up on him before he had a chance. Or he decided to ditch it somewhere else."

But it didn't make a lot of sense. Why didn't he just pitch it deep in the woods. Or off the side of the road on the way back. Why would he keep it?

"Think you'll get anything out of him?"

"We'll try, but he thinks he's untouchable." There's an old saying: "Bullshit walks and money talks." Given the situation, I can't imagine Cyrus helping him. "He's on his way to headquarters. I'll read the arrest warrant to him there, plus the murder and fleeing charges." And the assault on my little Taurus. Which reminds me: "I'll need a car, Sheriff."

"I'll see what I can do. Where to now, Megan?" he asks.

I'd like to go to headquarters and start grilling Ben and let Ronnie do a door-to-door here, but I know she'll never go for that. I don't blame her. If it wasn't for her quick thinking, we would still be chasing Mr. Wonderful across the golf course. "If you can have someone bring Ronnie's car to us, we'll do what needs to be done here and then come in and interview Ben. I think he'll keep."

"Sounds good to me. You'll need another crime scene crew. But, Megan?"

"Yes, sir."

"Try not to damage any more property. Ours or theirs. And I expect to see an accident report on my desk in the morning."

FIFTY-ONE

We are in luck. The first neighbor we visit witnessed the entire incident on the street and then some.

"Mrs. Lang, can you tell us what you observed?" Ronnie asks, and holds her phone up to record the statement.

"Like I said, I saw him come to Marlena's house about two hours ago and pull into her garage. He must have kept her opener. I never liked the man. He was smarmy. But poor Marlena and the dear little boy. They had to put up with so much."

She senses my impatience. "Anyway, he shut the garage door and was in the house a good while. I kept an eye out. He abandoned them. And now they're gone. I hope to God they're okay. Maybe they can come home now that he's locked up."

"Maybe," I say.

"I thought he might steal something, so I watched. Then I saw the garage door go up and he left in that loud truck of his. He wasn't gone for long before he came back and stopped in the driveway. He didn't go in the garage this time. He backed out and that's when he saw you, I guess. He tried to get away but you caught him good. I hope that wasn't your own car, honey."

"It wasn't."

"Well, that's good, then, isn't it?"

You don't know how good of a thing it is. "Yes, it is, Mrs. Lang. Now, did you see him with a gun any of these times you saw him?"

"Well, when he came the first time he was in the garage so I didn't see him except when he drove by. He was always in his truck. But then I saw you take the gun from him out there in the street. You two are so brave."

She looks at Ronnie's phone and indicates she should turn it off. Ronnie does and Mrs. Lang says, "I didn't want anyone else to hear this. I heard what you said to him and I don't approve of that kind of language." She looks at me and asks, "She doesn't talk like that to everyone, does she?"

Ronnie's face is on fire. "Mrs. Lang, I only did that to get him to... I mean we wanted him to tell us where his wife and son are. I don't normally talk like that."

"She doesn't. I made her do that," I say.

She seems mollified but only slightly. "Well, I guess I don't understand your job. And you were both so brave." She smiles. "And that man needed that after the way he talked to his wife. God forgive me, but I was halfway hoping he wouldn't stop. That's not very Christian of me, but there it is."

I wink at Ronnie and her cheeks are still red. "Mrs. Lang, is there anything else you saw?"

"I didn't know they were missing until yesterday. Is that what you mean?"

* * *

Crime Scene was going over the truck when we finished with Mrs. Lang. "Anything?" I ask the officer.

"One spent casing on the floorboard: .50-caliber. And there's a commemorative case for a Desert Eagle on the floorboard."

"Anything in the bed?"

"A shovel, two sleeping bags, a case of bottled water, two plastic tarps, and rope," the crime scene officer says.

Ronnie's car arrives and she meets the officer. I tell him, "Show me."

He takes me to the back of Ben's truck. The shovel looks new but there are bits of mud and oily wood chips on the rubber bed mat. The sleeping bags are the ones I'd seen earlier at Ben's cabin. There are several bottles missing from the case of water, and it's the same brand I found at the timber mill. The blue polyethylene tarp is dirty. Possibly taken from the floor of the building where we found the other truck. And the dead skunk family. The rope is a loose coil of the type used by boaters.

"Any bottles in the passenger area?" I ask.

"A couple of empties behind the driver. We're collecting them."

"Send them to Marley Yang as soon as you can. He'll know what to do."

"Will do. I won't be able to tell you anything about the gun until we get it to the lab, but I opened the bag and it smells likes it has been fired recently."

I thank him and get in the car with Ronnie. "Call Marley and ask him how quick he can go through the stuff we're sending."

"Slam dunk," she says.

"Yeah. Slam dunk."

"What's the matter, Megan. Was this too easy for you?"

"Maybe." The items in the truck fill me with dread. They could be dead and he was collecting the tools to bury the bodies. It nags at me that he would use a gun on Luci. Had he used it on his family? Why not dump them in the bay? His cabin is close. The timber mill is close. He's a dick. So why is this bothering me? It seems too pat. I was all geared up to take him down, and will, but we still don't have Marlena and Bennie.

"He's the guy, Megan. Everything fits perfectly."

Yeah. Perfectly. "Well, let's talk to him. But first I have to talk to you."

"Talk away, Megan."

"I have one big question for you."

"Okay."

"Did you really say you were going to shoot him *and* it would hurt?"

She grins. "I watched a movie last night: *Last Man Standing* with Bruce Willis. He's in a showdown with a dangerous mobster. It just kind of slipped out."

"Don't do it again."

"Okay."

"And don't curse like you did."

"Okay."

We're silent for a moment as Ronnie sulks.

"I'm just kidding," I say. "I loved it. But before you do it again, let me know you're going psycho."

"I thought it was effective."

"More like psychotic."

"Good cop, bad cop."

"Good cop, psycho cop."

We both laugh.

FIFTY-TWO

"Ben, can I get you something?"

"You can get me out of here." He smiles at me. Even faced with murder and kidnapping charges, he thinks he's charming. His looks and money have gotten him this far in his sad, pathetic life, so why change tactics now?

"You know I can't do that." He didn't ask if we found Luci. He knows we did. We're in the interview room alone. Sheriff Gray and Ronnie are watching on the monitor and waiting for word from Mindy and Marley. The evidence will sink his boat, and he has to know that, so why is he still being a jerk?

"I'll take coffee. And something to eat."

"How's your knee? Are you sure you don't want to have it looked at?" *Or would you rather I twist it?*

"Feels better. You rammed my truck. Do you know how much that truck costs?"

"It's not yours, so why are you worried?"

He grins. "You got me there. But it *was* a nice truck. Your car is totaled."

I know, jerk. "It was before I rammed you."

He grins again. "That's what I like about you, Megan. In another life we could have been great friends."

This state doesn't have coed prisons. "You might be right. But we have to deal with the here and now, Ben. You're here, and now I want to know where Marlena and Bennie are. Man up. Don't leave them out there hungry and scared. If you ever loved them, you'll help me find them. Just think how confused Bennie must be. He adores you. Wants to be you. How can you do this to that little guy?"

He's quiet for a moment. "I haven't done anything to them, Megan. I know you don't believe me—I guess I haven't given you much reason to believe me—but I'm telling the truth. I'm a horrible husband and father. I know that. But I love Bennie. I love my wife, even though I know she cheated on me."

He sees the face I make and says, "I know you disapprove. You've seen my rooms at the cabin. I know you did. You were in my cabin the night you claimed to have found the door open. You saw it all. And I lied to you about Luci because I was ashamed. But a lot of men do that. Cheat. My father would like you to think he's perfect but, believe me, he's not. That's why my mother left him. And she didn't take me with her because he had an army of lawyers. I talked to her once and asked why she just gave up on me. She said I was better off with him. She couldn't give me what I needed. The best schools. Cars. But she was wrong. I never wanted any of that. I just wanted to be with her. He passed me off to boarding schools. He was always gone. I'm surprised I even grew up to be a bad father. I admit I only married Marlena because she was pregnant. It was his idea. More like his unspoken command. He threatened to cut me off entirely if I didn't give him a grandchild. An heir to the throne. What would you have done?"

I would have done the right thing by her. Supported them. Let them have a normal life. But that's not the way Parkers do things. They buy people and whatever they do is right because of the money. They never feel bad about their decisions no matter what it costs others. It's why Cyrus felt the need to furnish our office. He wanted us to be in awe of him. Pity him for having such a son. Listening to Ben, I can see why he hated his father. Maybe his mother too. But how can he look in the mirror after treating his wife and son the way he has? Depriving them of friends, purpose, the life he claims he was denied.

"It's not my place to judge you." *You'll get that in court.* "My only concern now is with the disappearance of Marlena and Bennie and the murder of Lucia Simmons."

"Murder? Luci's dead?"

Nice try. "Do you remember the Miranda rights I read to you?" He doesn't answer, so I read them again. I also read the arrest warrant to him and he doesn't speak or change expression. "Is there anything you want to tell me?"

"I'm innocent, Megan, or Detective Carpenter, if you prefer. I told you I found the gun in my truck. Is that how Luci was killed?"

"Why were you at the Luna Ridge Loop Hiking Trail park?"

"I wasn't there. Who said I was?"

"The gun."

"I told you, I found it in my truck."

"You were at the house on Luna Ridge. It's only a mile or so to the park."

"I wasn't there. I've never been to that park."

"A neighbor saw you leave the house and get in your truck. You were gone about thirty minutes before you came back."

"I drove by Luci's place. I wanted to talk to her and see why she told you all those bad things about me. I wanted to know why she would lie. I was making a clean break and she didn't take it well."

"Did you talk to her?"

"I chickened out. I was mad at her but I would never kill her."

"Tell me about the gun."

"I came back to the house to finish straightening up and stopped in the driveway because the garage door didn't go up. It gets stuck sometimes. I found the gun on the floor and then I saw you coming down the street and I panicked."

"Why did you keep running after we wrecked your truck?"

"I told you, I panicked. Someone was setting me up. I was

afraid you'd arrest me for the gun. And with everything else, it would look bad."

"So you stick it in your pants and run?"

"I... I..." He looks at the floor.

"You what?"

"I was going to throw it away. Get rid of it."

"Who does the gun belong to?"

"I don't know. I've never seen it before. I don't own a gun. I don't even like to be around them. My father's bodyguard always makes sure I see the gun she carries. I thought you or Ronnie were going to shoot me. Guns scare me. My father is obsessed with them. It might be his gun."

"But you have access to his gun collection."

"I guess. If Sissy will let me in the armory, and I don't see that happening. She really doesn't like me. I think she sees herself as the next Mrs. Cyrus." He snorts. "Fat chance. She has nothing to offer. If she hadn't saved his life, he'd want nothing to do with her. Of course, he might be sampling the goods."

"Your fingerprints will be all over the gun, Ben."

"Well, of course they will be. I had the gun in my hands. But I didn't kill Luci. I could never."

Forensics will test his hands and clothing for gunpowder residue when they're not busy elsewhere. "We found a spent shell casing on the floorboard of the truck."

"What?"

"The gun had been fired. You stopped and picked up the spent bullet casing. Then you accidentally left it in the truck when you ran from us. What do you want to bet the casing matches the gun and the bullet matches the casing?"

"That's a lie. It won't match. I never saw the gun before I found it under the seat. I never touched the bullet or whatever." He gets a look of relief on his face. "You won't find my prints on the bullet because I never touched it. That will prove I didn't fire the gun."

I press on. "We found the water bottles in the back of the truck, Ben."

"What does that have to do with any of this?"

"We found a partial bottle of water in the abandoned timber mill that you took Luci to see. The same brand of water as the ones we found in your truck. The water had been tampered with. You drugged your wife and son with it."

"I never took Luci to a timber mill. She's lying to you."

I remind him, "Luci's dead."

"I didn't kill her. I swear I didn't. Why would I do that? I have enough money to make her go away." His eyes widen. "I didn't mean I could have her made to go away if that's what you're thinking. She was all about money. I could pay her enough to just go home to New York. Why would I kill her?"

"We know you were at the same timber mill Luci told us about."

"Okay. I admit I was with her at a mill. We own several."

My cell phone dings and I have a message. It's from Ronnie. The picture that Luci identified of the timber mill. I show it to Ben and his jaw tightens. "Do you recognize this?" I ask.

"That's the place I took Luci one night. I guess I was trying to score. You know. She was freaky and liked to do it in strange places. In public. Everywhere."

"Why this place? Is there something special about it?" I ask.

"Not really."

"Then why are your fingerprints all over the lock and one of the doors to a storage room?"

"We didn't go inside the fence that time. And we've only been there the once. I check several of the abandoned properties as a routine. I checked this one and vandals had cut the lock and trashed the inside with liquor bottles and stuff. I put a new lock on the gate. It doesn't keep them out but it's the best I could do."

"Have you seen the vandals? Maybe they're young, Black, and wearing hoodies like your peeping Tom."

"I didn't see them but the gate was wide open and I didn't want anyone getting hurt and suing us. Is there a law against that?"

He's so quick. "Does Marlena take any medications?"

"Yes. She told me she was taking a sleeping medication."

"Do you know what kind?"

"No. I don't need sleeping pills. I remember when we were in college she would take something at night. She said the classes stressed her and she had trouble sleeping. It wasn't a big deal."

"Have you ever looked around the timber mill? Checked all the rooms for damage or whatever?"

"No. I bought a lock and chain and locked it up."

"Did you ever take a water bottle inside the mill?"

"I told you no. I was there all of five minutes and that's been a while back."

"Did you take anyone with you?"

"No. I just found the gates open, got a lock, and locked it up."

"Luci said you took her in there one night and bragged about owning it."

"She's lying. She's never been in there. I brought her to my cabin, but that's all."

"Sleeping bags were in the bed of your truck," I say.

"Sleeping bags... Oh, yeah, the sleeping bags. I found them in my cabin and took them back to the house today. I forgot to take them inside. What about them?"

"You told me Marlena and Bennie didn't like to camp. Why were the sleeping bags at your cabin?"

"I told you *Marlena* didn't like to camp. Bennie was getting to like it, but he was a handful to take care of by myself. The sleeping bags were at my cabin from the last time we camped. When I decided to go and clean up the house, I remembered Bennie liked to sleep in his sometimes, so I was taking them back today."

"The adult-size sleeping bag is yours?" I ask.

"It was Marlena's. She left it at the cabin."

"Where is your sleeping bag, Ben?"

"I sleep on the ground. I don't need one."

"Why did you clean your cabin after the night I found the door open?" I knew what he was going to answer and I'm not disappointed.

"I was embarrassed for you to have seen it that way."

And that's why you cleaned out all the sex toys?

"Ben, look at me." He does. "I don't believe you. A jury's not going to believe you. If we find your wife and son dead, you are going to be in prison for the rest of your life. You may be able to fight the murder of Luci, but *three* murders? You'll be convicted of all of them. You'll go away forever. Unless you tell us where Marlena and Bennie can be found, I can't help you in any way. Are they okay?"

With tears in his eyes, he says, "I pray to God they are."

I pause a long time, looking directly at him. He looks away. "Ben, I know you killed Luci. I have proof."

"I didn't do it. You have no proof."

"Hold your arms up."

"What?"

"Hold your arms up." He does. "Where's your watch? The Apple Watch we saw you wearing every time you've been with us."

He stammers, "It must have come off while I was cleaning or something. I never use it. I didn't notice. You have to believe me."

He's lying. He's just realizing it came off when he killed Luci. I see beads of sweat forming above his lip.

"Did you find my watch? You must have or you wouldn't have asked. Where was it?"

FIFTY-THREE

An officer babysits a handcuffed Ben Parker while I meet with Tony and Ronnie in the sheriff's office. I get Mindy on the phone.

"Hi, Mindy. Did you find Ben's watch?"

"Yes. The band was broken. The pin that holds the strap on the watch was missing."

"Can you tell how it came off?"

"I haven't found the pin. I'll keep looking."

"Be sure you check for gunpowder residue in the truck. Crime scene will do the rest."

After thanking Mindy, I disconnect. It won't do any good talking to Ben. My phone rings in the outer office and the sheriff picks it up. I can hear him saying *We'll be right there*.

He's excited. "That was Cyrus. Marlena and Bennie are with him. He's found them. They're alive."

FIFTY-FOUR

Sheriff Gray stayed behind while Ronnie and I headed back to Parker Island. We met Sissy at the dock and on the ride over tried to question her about how this happened, but she would only say Cyrus would answer all our questions.

The mansion is lit up as we approach in Sissy's Jeep. Cyrus himself meets us at the entrance and ushers us into the kitchen.

"Isn't it wonderful? I can't believe they're here. And without a scratch. We have Sissy to thank for this."

"Can we see them?" I ask.

"Oh, I think the doctor will have to be the judge of that."

"You have a doctor here too?" I ask.

"Sissy fetched him. Don't know what I'd do without her."

"How long ago did Sissy find them?"

He makes a dismissive motion with his hand. "They're home. That's all that matters."

"We arrested Ben."

"Yes. Sissy told me about the murder."

Sissy excuses herself. I wonder how she knew about Ben's arrest. Or about the murder. We didn't pick him up that long ago, and I don't think there was time for the murder to be on the news. Maybe Tony told Cyrus when he called.

Cyrus motions us to take seats while he puts coffee on. "Would you care for some, or maybe something stronger?"

"If you want something, go ahead," I say.

We wait for him to sit down with his coffee.

"Tell us everything."

He gets back up and begins pouring two more mugs for us and puts them in front of us. "Sissy found them. She's been doing her own investigation. She assured me she wouldn't interfere with yours. She got a call from a woman claiming to have information on the missing persons."

"Lucia Simmons," Ronnie says.

"That's right. You knew about her. Of course you did. So this woman said she had information about Marlena and Bennie. She wanted a million dollars and protection."

"Who did she want protection from?"

"Ben. My son. She said he threatened to kill her because of what she knew."

"Sissy wanted proof and the woman got mad. She said Ben was going to kill them if she didn't hurry. Sissy wanted to know where they were so she could protect them. She promised the woman the money and protection too. Sissy agreed to meet her and told me. We were getting the money together when one of Sissy's crew called and said Ben had been arrested for murder."

"Sissy knew Lucia Simmons personally?" I ask.

"Simmons worked for the company. For Ben. Sissy had her checked out when she found out Ben was paying the woman, buying her expensive things."

"So how did Sissy find Marlena and Bennie? Did Simmons tell her where they were?"

Cyrus paused. "She said she had the island searched. She knew Ben wanted to punish me. She thought Ben might hide them here. You'll have to ask her how that happened, but it did and I'm very grateful to her. Marlena and Bennie are here. They're safe. Ben is in custody. You both are to be commended on your skills. If it wasn't for your tireless efforts, they might have died."

"Thank you for the compliment, Cyrus, but we'll need to talk to everyone involved in the murder and the abduction."

"I understand, Megan. Ronnie, I understand you're the one who caught Ben. And he was armed with the gun he used to kill that gold digger. I hope Tony gives you a promotion for bravery. In fact, I'll talk to him. Put in a word. Both of you deserve more than I can ever repay."

He answers some of my questions but doesn't reply when I ask why he didn't think to call me. After Luci called or after they found Marlena and Bennie. A doctor was "fetched." That would mean a trip to the mainland, and that would have taken some time.

"So where were Marlena and Bennie found?"

"The one place I never would have looked. Here."

I couldn't hide the surprise on my face. Ronnie spoke for us. "Here? Here in the mansion?"

"No. On the island. In one of the buildings. A woodworking shop, I think. I've never been in it. Couldn't tell you where it is. When I had the mansion built, I needed labor crews to stay here so they would work around the clock. I had prefab housing brought in for living quarters, a mess hall, along with a lumber yard and a mill. Anything I needed I brought here. I'm very rich, you know."

He smiles at Ronnie and says, "I've even had your father do some of the contractual agreements. He's a very talented man, your father."

Ronnie is surprised. She didn't know Cyrus was a client of her father's. I'm still amazed Ronnie didn't follow her sister into the legal empire of the Marshes.

"You say Sissy found them?"

"She and her security forces. She had them canvass the abandoned houses and buildings. She and one of her crew found them locked in a storage room under the timber mill."

I wonder what made Sissy think to do that. She and Cyrus had both said Ben hadn't been on the island for quite some time.

Now I have to ask: "When did you find them?"

"Several hours ago."

"Cyrus, you should have called me right away."

"When I saw the condition they were in, I sent for a doctor."

Still controlling things. "We would have taken them to a hospital."

"I didn't want that. I'm not letting them out of my sight. Your people didn't find them. Your people couldn't protect them. You couldn't even arrest my son. I did what I thought was best. I called you and here you are. And I thank you for finally arresting Ben. He'll go to prison and I won't lift a finger to help him. Not after what he did."

"We've charged him with murder."

He waves that away. "She was no better than a hooker. A gold digger. But it was my gold she was after." He grits his teeth and slams a big hand on top of the table, making both Ronnie and me jump. "I should have known he was guilty. I think I did know but I just didn't want to think my only child could be that vicious. He wanted a bigger part in the company but he wasn't up to it. I gave him what I could, but he was never content. He had a wife and son who adored him. Even that wasn't enough. He had to have a mistress too. He was sick in the head, from what I understand. Whips, chains, all that fantasy crap. He was never normal, but he was still my son. Do you have family, Detective Carpenter?"

So he knew about the playroom as well. Sissy. Must be. "Yes, I do."

"Do they ever disappoint you?"

Boy, do they. "Not too much."

"Well, you're lucky. I thought when Ben got married he would grow up."

I change the subject. "You have security on the island. How did Ben get on and off without you knowing?"

"Sissy watches what she can of the shoreline, but she doesn't have an army. Ben knows every inch of the island and would have known about the mill and workshops. He hurt me with their disappearance and it probably gave him pleasure to know they were hidden right under my nose."

"Is the doctor still here, Cyrus?"

"He knows you will want to talk to him." He presses a buzzer by the stove and a security guard comes in. "Take them to see the doctor."

"Yes, sir."

We follow him to a library. I want to actually see Marlena and Bennie, but I guess we'll follow their rules. It is his mansion.

"Wait here," she says to our guide, and he nods. "This place is like a medieval castle."

We enter and a man stands, shakes my hand. "I'm Detective Carpenter. My partner, Detective Marsh."

"Hello, Ronnie."

Ronnie says, "How are you, Dr. Svendsen?"

The doctor is in his mid-fifties, dark hair with a touch of gray at the temples and a three-day growth of beard. He's my height but thin and wearing tan chinos, yellow Caterpillar boots, and a red-green plaid shirt with the sleeves rolled up above the elbows. He must shop at the same place as my boyfriend, the Paul Bunyan store for men.

The doctor hugs Ronnie and his smile grows until I think his face is going to cave in. "I talked to your mother yesterday. She was quite concerned with you being in law enforcement. She worries about you."

"I know. She thinks I'll embarrass the family name."

"Oh, I doubt it. She's very proud of you. She said you're the only one in the family with true courage."

I can see Ronnie's head swelling. She'll need a cold compress if he keeps slathering on the bullshit, so I interrupt this happy meeting. "Doctor, how are Marlena and Bennie?"

"Quite right. That's why you're here."

We take seats on an overstuffed leather sofa and the doctor sits on a love seat across from us. "Both were severely dehydrated and hadn't eaten for some time. The young man was listless and possibly hallucinating. He thought Darth Vader had taken them.

His mother was only a little more cognizant and thought the water was drugged. Do you know what she was talking about?"

"We think she was given some strong sleeping medication," I say.

"That would explain their symptoms. An inhaler was found with them and I understand the boy has asthma. There were no physical injuries. I'm giving them both fluids and they are sleeping. If possible, I'd like to let them rest unless you have urgent questions."

"When were you called, Dr. Svendsen?"

"Two hours ago. A woman came to my house and said I was needed on the island. I knew of Mr. Parker and, well, she was very persuasive."

Had to be Sissy.

"Mrs. Parker is also pregnant. Two months, by her account."

"So she was coherent when you got here?"

"Only barely. She made the remark about the water and I think she wanted to talk to her husband. She called him Ben."

"I'll be sure to tell her husband as soon as possible." *I can't wait.* "Did she say anything else? Did she know who took them?"

"If she did, she didn't tell me. Have you talked to the woman who found them?"

"Sissy?"

"Yes. She was watching over them like a mother hen. Is she a relative?"

"She's chief of security for Mr. Parker."

"Oh. I see. Well, is there anything else I can answer for you?"

"Can you give my partner your contact information? We may need to talk to you later."

"Of course, but I'm sure she has it." He takes a business card out and writes on the back. "Here's my personal cell phone and office number. If you get my answering service, they'll know how to reach me. I'll be here for a while. I might want to have them transferred to a hospital."

"Thanks, Doctor."

Ronnie gives him a hug, and the guard shows us back to the kitchen. Cyrus is sitting with his head in his hands. He looks up and I see the business veneer has crumbled. He's aging before my eyes.

Ronnie puts a hand on his shoulder. "Are you okay?"

"No. I'm not okay."

"It's a lot to take in."

"Yes, it is."

I hate to be callous but I say, "We actually need to see Marlena and Bennie for ourselves, Cyrus."

"Of course. I'll have Sissy take you to them. Bennie would *not* be separated from her."

It hurts my heart to do this job sometimes, but their being found is a vital part of a missing person case, and I have to verify that with my own eyes. Then we need to talk to Sissy. As if Sissy were listening, she appears in the doorway.

"I'll take them up." The look she gives Cyrus is heart-wrenching. Ben hinted Sissy's in love with Cyrus. Possibly. The look on her face is pure compassion and empathy. Love.

FIFTY-FIVE

Sissy leads us up a sweeping flight of stone stairs and down a long hallway that projects the image of a castle even more so than from the outside. All that's missing are burning torches instead of electric wall sconces.

"Was the stone excavated here on the island?" Ronnie asks Sissy.

"Everything came from here but the furniture and appliances," Sissy says proudly.

"Is the timber mill still active?" I ask.

"Hardly. After Cyrus finished his home and the houses in Parkertown, he shut everything down. The workers were glad of the money while they had work and just as glad to leave. There was a car ferry until last year, but now we go by boat. It's a mile to shore. An easy swim."

"Have you done it?" Ronnie asks.

"What do you think?" This comes out snarky.

"She's asking a simple question, Sissy."

Sissy blows a strand of hair out of her eyes. "I've got better things to do than chitchat. If you don't mind, let's get this over with."

We come to a turn in the hallway and see an armed security

guard sitting in a chair beside a door. Sissy nods at him and he gets up, unlocks the door, and opens it. "Don't wake them. The doctor said to let them rest."

"Got it. We need to talk to you, if Cyrus can spare you."

"Cyrus needs me more now. I'm not going anywhere."

That's good. You don't have a choice. "Thanks, Sissy. I appreciate your help."

Both Ronnie and I step into the bedroom and I'm sure the faces match the photos I've seen. The bathroom door is partially open and the light is on. Bennie probably needed to see he was no longer locked in a dark place. I can relate to that. My biological father chained my mother and me up in a dark underground room where he intended to torture, rape, and kill us at his leisure. I still have a little trouble sleeping in full dark. For a very long time I would keep the bathroom light on and the door all the way open. I always excused this by thinking I wanted to find my way to the bathroom if I woke up. Then I progressed to having a night-light. Now I just have a Scotch or half a box of wine.

Marlena and Bennie lie on a super-king-size bed and Bennie has attached himself to her side. They're both wearing clean pajamas. I don't see any obvious injuries. I didn't realize my heart was pounding until it calms at the realization they haven't been tortured.

I whisper to them, "You're safe now." But I know from experience being safe is just a state of mind. No one is ever safe. Not ever.

* * *

Back in the hall, I pull the door shut and thank the guard. "Can we go back to the kitchen, Sissy?"

"The library might be better." She leads us there. She doesn't sit, so we stand.

"Sissy, we need to see where they were found."

She raises her eyebrows but doesn't respond.

"How about right now?" I say.

"Give me a minute." She gets on her cell phone. "Okay. Let's go." We follow her to her Jeep, and I notice two more security officers standing by the front door. There are two 4x4 ATVs there containing two guards each. They are all wearing black paramilitary outfits and carrying stubby weapons slung across their bodies.

"Machine guns?"

"MP5s. Licensed and legal."

We get in her Jeep and she drives down a narrow paved road barely wide enough for the vehicle and into a dense forest that soon swallows us up. She drives like me: fast and furious. She is wearing a shoulder holster with a large-caliber semiautomatic snugged down on the right side. She's left-handed. I notice this isn't the same gun she was wearing the first time we met her. But, given her career, she probably has an armory. And she has access to the armory and shooting range at the mansion.

"Sissy, does Ben have access to any weapons here?"

Without taking her eyes from the road, she says, "He does. He has access to everything on the island."

"Ben told me there's a shooting range in the lower level of the mansion."

"Cyrus is a hunter. He tried to teach Ben, but he wasn't interested."

"Was he any good?"

"Ben?"

"Yes."

"Fair."

"Does Ben own any weapons?"

"I'm sure he does."

"Do you know what kind of weapons he owns?"

"Cyrus gave him a new Desert Eagle when he was trying to teach him to hunt. It was more gun than he could handle."

"You saw this?"

"Of course. I take care of the weapons. I'm Cyrus's armorer."

"So you'd know what Cyrus gave his son."

"I told you. A Desert Eagle, .50-caliber. Ben dropped it the first time he shot it." She sounds disgusted. She thinks Ben is a weakling.

"Do you know if Ben still has the gun?"

"As far as I know." She slows and turns her head toward me. "Listen, I know you have questions, but I've worked for Cyrus many years. I normally don't discuss the family but I've made an exception, since these are exceptional circumstances. I'm not an idiot. It sounds to me like you're fishing to see if either I or Cyrus are involved. I can assure you we're not. Why would we be? If Cyrus wanted them they'd be living here. He's not a monster. It would be their choice. Me, I've got a good thing going here. So just ask your questions and stop trying to sneak up on it."

"Okay. What is your relationship with Cyrus?"

She stops in the middle of the road and turns to look at me. "If you're asking if I'm sleeping with him, you can go to hell. He's my employer and a very good man. Do I love him? You could say that. In fact, yes, I do love him. But not in the disgusting way you're implying. I'd take a bullet for him. He treats me like a daughter. I'm more family to him than Ben. And if either of you do anything to hurt him, you'll answer to me. Any other questions?"

I don't like to be threatened, but I wonder why she thought we suspected Cyrus. We didn't. Did she?

"How about Cyrus. Is he a good shot?"

"Why?"

"Sissy, this isn't going to be pleasant if you keep up with the attitude. You're a tough cookie. If we go after Cyrus, you'll come after us. We get it. We've got a job to do, same as you, and that crap's not helping."

I expect a fistfight but she says, "Sorry. I'm upset for Cyrus."

"Why?"

"Because he has put up with so much of his ex-wife's and Ben's crap. His wife only married him for money. She never wanted Ben. But Cyrus loved him. Ben was never a good son. He's willful, arrogant, lazy, and has no moral code. He doesn't treat Cyrus with the respect he deserves."

Tell us how you really feel. "How long have you worked for Cyrus?"

"Years. Before Ben and Marlena married."

"Did you spend time with Marlena and Bennie?"

Now she softens. Her hands relax the death grip on the steering wheel and she starts back down the road. "Cyrus adores them."

"Do you like them?"

"Why wouldn't I?"

"I understand you pick them up when they visit Cyrus."

"Yes."

"Can you tell us about that?" In more than one word.

"What do you want me to say? Cyrus asked me to pick them up. I did. Then I took them home. Sometimes they visited for the day, sometimes for a week. Marlena didn't work, so she could do that."

Don't strain yourself. I wonder where this resistance is coming from.

Ronnie asks, "Ben told us Bennie has a train set here. I'll bet it was fun watching him play."

Sissy looks in the rearview mirror. "Cyrus spent a small fortune on it. And it's not just a train set. It's an exact replica of a Swiss village, and the train and tracks are replicas of the train in the movie *The Polar Express.* What kid wouldn't be crazy about it?"

Ronnie says, "So you spent some time with Bennie. Was he a handful like Ben said?"

"Ben." She looks out the window before continuing. "Ben doesn't know anything about being a father. He doesn't know how to be a son. I've always wondered how a great man like Cyrus Parker could have contributed any of that DNA. Prison is the best place for him. It's better than he deserves."

"You and Ben have crossed swords," I say.

"Not really. He's not capable of having an argument or a meaningful exchange of words. He's a dick. Okay? Is that what you want to hear?"

"Hey, we're agreeing with you. You know him better than we ever want to. That's why I wanted to talk to you."

"Sorry. My job is protecting Cyrus. I take my work seriously."

"Got it. I guess you know the island pretty well."

"It's my home. I can't imagine being anywhere else. I bounced from one foster home to the next. Got in a lot of trouble. Ended up joining the army. It taught me family was who you loved, protected. I was closer to my unit than to anyone on the outside. Until I met Cyrus."

"How did you meet him?" I ask.

"Why do you need to know that?"

"Just curious." *Answer the question.*

"I saved his life."

FIFTY-SIX

Parkertown consists of a crossroad with four short streets. The homes are constructed of the same stone as the mansion and are identical. The lawns and greenery are still maintained and I expected to see the occupants milling around, playing in the yards, pets being walked on leashes, or at least an army of gardeners. At one time some of the homes had gardens in back. The outline of the gardens still shows, but nothing grows there any more. The gardens went away just as the people did. The pets are no more, having left with their owners or been killed by Ben. Rising above the trees is a green-painted water tower with PARKER ISLAND painted on the side in large letters.

I have a sad feeling as we pass Parkertown, knowing there was once life there and now it is a ghost town. A well-kept ghost town. We come to a gravel road as wide as a four-lane highway and turn left.

"Are you going to tell us how you saved his life?" *Or am I going to have to beat it out of you?*

"You don't give up. Okay. I was Special Forces. An IED took out a vehicle in front of us but it still rocked my world. Hearing loss. I was medically discharged, came home, hated civilian life, and went to work for Academi." She sees the dumb look on my face. "It's a private security company that used to be called Blackwater. After the Nisour Square massacre in Iraq they felt like a new name would change the reputation."

Now I remember. Blackwater was a private security service that hired ex-military, ex-police, or others from security services to provide personal protection in foreign countries. Many years ago a crew of Blackwater employees opened fire on civilians in Iraq and killed seventeen. I knew this because my ex-boyfriend Caleb loved to show me how intelligent he was. "I know of them."

"I mostly worked in Afghanistan, Somalia, places where businessmen were being kidnapped or knocked off by the competition. We were hired to protect Cyrus in Baghdad. One of our guys had been turned by the Saudis and tried to kill him. He got dead first. End of story."

"So Cyrus hired you away from the company."

"Here I am."

"How far to the site?"

"The timber mill is just ahead. It hasn't operated for quite a while. The old-timer who I replaced used to hide his car back here and drink. Cyrus doesn't allow staff to drink."

We come to a scaled-down version of the mill in Port Ludlow. She stops. "In there." She points to a set of concrete steps leading down to a heavy metal door. I can see the hasp is broken and hanging with a closed padlock.

"They were barely conscious. I took them to the mansion, and the doctor came."

Did Cyrus want to control this? Or was the delay Sissy's doing? Lucky for them Marlena and Bennie weren't in very bad shape, or I'd try to dream up a charge for both Cyrus and Sissy. They aren't exempt from the law. What am I saying?

I ask, "The doctor said Bennie had an inhaler."

"It was in Marlena's hand when we found them. And there were two full bottles of water."

"Did you find anything else?"

She didn't. The room was fairly dark even with the door open. They must have been frightened half to death.

"Were they conscious? Did either of them say anything?"

"'Ben.' That was all. She said 'Ben.' Bennie was out cold."

I pick up some of the grit by the door. It feels greasy, like what we saw in the back of Ben's truck. Like what I found on the legs of his jeans.

We get back to the Jeep just as Ronnie hangs up. "I've called Mindy."

"Sissy, can you post someone outside of that door until our guys get here? I don't want anyone coming near this place until my crime scene crew have a go at it."

She gets on her phone and arranges it. "I have something else to show you," she says, and takes a folded piece of paper from her shirt pocket. "I didn't tell Cyrus. He's been through enough. It won't make a difference anyway now, since you arrested Ben."

It looks like the same paper as the one Ben had in his pocket. The one he claimed was on his truck in Seattle. Ronnie puts gloves on and holds it so we can both see. It reads:

10 million in unmarked bills

no police or they're dead

FIFTY-SEVEN

The doctor has gone upstairs to sit with Marlena and Bennie. I can't drink another cup of coffee, so I ask everyone to gather in the library. Sissy takes up a position behind Cyrus with her hands on the back of the cushion. Ronnie is on the love seat this time. I sit beside Cyrus.

There are two armed guards outside the library door. Two more at the front door. I assume one is guarding Marlena and Bennie. And God knows how many more are out there to repel the Huns. I say, "Ben is in custody, Sissy. I think you can stand down."

Cyrus says, "I think it's under control, Sissy. I don't like all these guns in the house. Have them taken back to the mainland. They'll be rewarded handsomely. Let the police take it from here."

Sissy sounds incredulous. "Would you like me to leave also? Someone has to bring the boat back."

"No, not you, Sissy." He reaches back and pats her hand. "I'll always need you with me. But this is a police matter now and best left to the professionals. Have one of your people do it. They can stay and bring the sheriff here."

Sissy excuses herself and I hear her giving orders; then she comes back and takes up her position. Ronnie takes out the note

Sissy gave us and hands it to Cyrus. He reads it and looks up. "Where did this come from?"

"Sissy found it."

I say, "I thought we should discuss this together."

"Sissy?" Cyrus turns in his chair.

"I didn't want to upset you. That's why I gave it to them. The *professionals*." The last word comes out dripping sarcasm.

"You should have shown this to me. But I guess what's done is done."

Maybe. "Where did you find the note, Sissy?"

"It was on the boat."

"When did you find it?"

"Are you accusing me of something?"

Cyrus says, "Now, wait a minute. I don't like where I think this is going. You don't have to explain yourself, Sissy."

"I don't mind, Cyrus. I found it when I brought the doctor for Marlena and Bennie."

"On the mainland?"

"It was on the boat. I don't know when it was put there."

Cyrus turns to me. "She said she doesn't know who put it on the boat. Ben has been arrested. The note is moot now."

"Ben gave us a note like this one. Typed. Short. I want to try and establish a timeline for when these were found." And see who was where at what time when Luci was killed. I'm getting a bad vibe.

Sissy's phone buzzes; she answers and excuses herself. "Your crime scene crew are waiting on the other side. I'll take everyone across and pick them up. Unless you need me, Cyrus."

"We'll go with you," I say. I don't think I'll get much more from these two now that the damsel has been rescued and the dragon slain. "You'll need to work with my crime scene people here."

"Of course."

"I'll have to talk to Marlena when she's able to answer questions."

Cyrus just nods.

"Cyrus, do you have any other questions?"

He doesn't. He looks the way I feel. Beat.

FIFTY-EIGHT

Mindy and Deputy Davis are waiting with several hard-sided cases of equipment. Crime Scene is pretty stretched for officers. A dozen armed security officers leave the boat for a waiting bus.

"Hi, Mindy. This is Sissy. She's your ride to the island. She'll show you where the scene is."

"Hi, Sissy." Mindy offers her hand, but Sissy grabs some of the cases and takes them on to the boat. I notice how much bigger Sissy is. Not just in height but in overall mass. But I guess her size serves her well in a job like hers.

Mindy raises her eyebrows.

"She's okay," I say. "Ex-Special Forces. Not very talkative, but I guess she's not likely to go postal. She'll stand by with you."

"How are they doing?" Mindy asks.

"The doctor said they'll recover. They're sleeping now."

"So what's the billionaire like?"

"He's a good guy. He'll help with anything you need. Don't let him hire you away from us."

"I'm not working for the sheriff. I'm a contract employee. Maybe Mr. Parker will offer me a full-time position. I can just see myself lounging on the beach, grapes being fed to me by Julio. And I can get a real forensic van that doesn't smell like flowers."

"Dream on, Mindy. No vehicles are allowed on the island. Except for Sissy's Jeep, there are only some four-wheelers."

"How many people are on the island?"

"Cyrus Parker, Sissy, and a doctor right now." If this is the kind of life rich gets you, I don't want any part of it.

"I'm sorry about your car, Megan. Sheriff said it committed suicide. You're getting a new one. Or at least another one."

"Another junker is just what I need. I hope the door locks work."

Mindy chuckles and a marked sheriff's Jeep pulls up. It's Deputy Copsey. He's in his mid to late thirties but still in shape. He has strawberry-blond hair and huge biceps barely contained by his uniform. He would be a match for Sissy. His slight lisp is kind of charming.

"Megan... Mindy," he says, and opens the back hatch of the Jeep. "Sheriff said you might need some help. What am I doing?"

Mindy takes over and introduces him to Sissy. Ronnie and I get in Ronnie's car. I wave to Mindy and we start to head back to the station.

"Stop, Ronnie," I say. "Back up. I want to tell them something."

We get back to the other vehicles and Sissy comes over to the car. She says impatiently, "We're almost ready to go."

"Sissy, I forgot the most important thing. Marlena's mother has been worried sick about her and Bennie. I'd appreciate it if you can come back and get her in a bit. We'll bring her to the dock."

"Of course. Cyrus would insist on it. I'll have someone make up a room at the house for her."

"Thank you, Sissy. I'll call Sheriff Gray and let him know."

Before we can drive away, a truck approaches. It's Tony. Helen gets out of the passenger side and runs to me.

"Megan, how can I ever thank you." She wraps me in a hug.

"You can thank Sissy. She's the one who found them. Sissy, meet Helen."

Helen wraps Sissy in a hug and Sissy stands like a statue.

Apparently she doesn't like to be touched, either. The sheriff stays in his truck.

Sissy says, "We're taking good care of them. A doctor is there to monitor them, but he says they're fine. They'll be excited to see you when they wake up."

Helen says, "It's a miracle, Sissy. A miracle. You saved my daughter and grandson. Can we go? I want to be there when they wake up."

Sissy helps Helen on the boat, and Copsey gives her a thumbs up. He's ready to go. Davis casts off and then jumps in the stern. Sissy casts a glance back at me. I can't read her expression, but I don't think I'm on her Christmas list.

FIFTY-NINE

An officer is standing outside the interview room, looking bored to death. Tony tells him to take off and he wastes no time leaving.

Tony says, "Moe sent food over. I think he's sweet on you, Ronnie."

"Yay, Ronnie." I'm starving. There's a banquet of cold sandwiches and small bags of chips and pretzels laid out on my desk. I whisper to Ronnie, "Moe's not *too* sweet on you by the looks of this."

"I think it's very thoughtful of him."

Of course you do. You're a mouth-half-full kind of girl. "I do too. I'm just kidding." Not. But I eat my share, washing it down with fresh coffee, a Coke, and one of Moe's vanilla shakes. Then I gather myself for the confrontation with Ben. Sheriff Gray has taken all the leftovers to his office to binge on and watch the interview.

Ben looks up when we come into the room, but this time the arrogant smile is absent, replaced by one of defeat. We sit in our usual places and Ronnie opens a notebook in her lap.

"Ben, I need to remind you of your rights."

"You don't have to. I know them. I'm willing to tell you everything I know. It's over for me. My father will see to it that I go to prison, and he always gets what he wants."

"Make note he understands his rights." Ronnie scribbles something. "What have you been told?"

"I haven't been told anything but I heard the sheriff leaving in a hurry."

"Marlena and Bennie have been found, Ben."

Ben's face lights up. "Dear God, thank you. Are they okay? Where? Who? Did you catch the guy? Are they hurt? Please tell me they're alive. I knew you'd find them."

I wasn't expecting this outburst. "They're alive. Tell me what you know of their disappearance."

"Where did you find them? At least tell me if you've arrested someone. Was it Luci and her boyfriend? I'm so ashamed to have put Marlena and Bennie in that position. If I hadn't been a fool, none of this would have happened. Can I see them?"

Ben's facial expression is so real, it's hard to tell if he's being honest or acting a part again. My experience with him is that he's a liar. "Ben, answer my questions first."

He swallows so hard, I can hear a click in his throat. "Okay. I'll help any way I can so I can be with my family. Thank you for finding them. Both of you. I won't forget."

"What do you know of their disappearance? From the beginning."

Ben starts with trying to call Bennie and not getting an answer. He persists with the story he thought Marlena's pregnancy wasn't by him. He admits to a big blowout argument.

Ronnie plays the video of Marlena at Sean Hunter's birthday party where she is wearing a turtleneck.

"What was she hiding, Ben? The truth," I say.

"You have to understand, Marlena is a beautiful woman. Even in college she was popular with the guys. Everyone thought she was really hot. I've been with a lot of women, but when we got together, we really hit it off. I don't know if I was in love with her when she told me she was pregnant with Bennie, but I married her. I would have even if my father hadn't threatened to disinherit me and cut me off. Then Bennie came along and I knew I loved her. I didn't know what love was before then. I'd never had it. Before I met Marlena, I guess I was copying my father. He'd have one fling after another and none of them meant anything to him. I might have siblings all over the planet. My mom didn't seem to care. I thought that was normal, and since I was a Parker... well, when in Rome..."

He's off in his own world now.

"Even pregnant, Marlena turned every guy's head. I didn't like that. I felt it was disrespectful of me. So I had my father give me one of the homes in the subdivision his company had built, and we moved into the house on Luna Ridge. Marlena quit college and stayed home to take care of Bennie. I was a little overprotective of them. I tried to keep her away from the kind of people we don't associate with. Then one of the neighbors, the one from the party you showed me, started putting ideas in Marlena's head. Marlena started spending a lot of time at Bennie's preschool and over at that woman's house. Jennifer Hunter. Her husband was always leering at Marlena. Marlena thought it was cute, but I thought it was threatening my marriage."

"So what did you do about that?"

"We argued. I told her to stay away from the Hunters. She accused me of being jealous." He's quiet now, but he hasn't answered my question.

"What was she hiding under the turtleneck?"

He looks away and I don't think he's going to answer. I start to ask again, and he says, "Bruises. We were getting hang-up calls. She said she didn't know who it was, but I didn't believe her. It might have been Jennifer calling about getting together, but the phone always went dead when I answered."

"Do you have a landline, Ben?"

"No. I know what you're getting at. I was answering Marlena's phone. I wanted to know who was always calling."

"How did she get the bruises, Ben?"

"I might have grabbed her to make her listen."

"Did you hurt her after that?"

"I might have pushed her down when I left her. I told you we'd had an argument. A big one this time, so I pushed her away. I didn't hit her or choke her. I love her, but she resents having had to quit college. She seems to resent being married. Then she told me she was pregnant and my mind immediately went to that Hunter guy. It was the last straw. I asked her point-blank if it was someone else's baby. She denied it. I told her I'd had enough. She yelled at me and said she'd had it with me. She was sick of the way I treated her. I wasn't a father to Bennie. I was a ghost. A prison guard. She said the baby was someone else's. She wouldn't say whose."

I say, "Ben, I can understand your issues with Luci. Maybe you had reason to kill her. She was blackmailing you. You kidnapped your wife and son. What did you hope to accomplish by taking them? Was Marlena leaving you?"

"Marlena and I were having marital issues like every other married couple, but she wasn't leaving me. We were going to work things out."

I stare at him like he's an alien bug. He is. Ronnie is tapping her pen on her notepad.

"Don't look at me that way, detectives. I did not kill Luci. I did not kidnap my family. I lied because I was scared. Scared I'd be right here where I am now. I should have known the affair would end me. If my father found out, he would disown me and there would be no way to make things right with Marlena. I don't have a real job. I don't even know how to get one. We'd be ruined. That's why I lied to you. To everyone. Even myself."

"Tell me about the gun, and this time no lies. If you do, we're done here. You go to prison."

He looks at me, trying to judge if there is wiggle room. He decides I am serious. I am.

"It's my gun." He goes quiet, no doubt weighing how much that fact sinks him. "My father gave it to me years back. Before I was married. He's a gun nut. I told you the truth about the shooting range under the house. There's another range off in the woods just south of the house as well. He would make me go with him to the one in the woods even if it was pouring rain or snowing. We went once in a lightning storm and a lightning bolt hit a tree and uprooted it. I wanted to go back to the house, but he said it would toughen me up. He said my mother had spoiled me and made me too soft. He accused me of being gay and said if he ever found out I was, he'd kill me. Nothing can sully the Parker name.

"I was fairly good with the gun, but it was too much for me. He could barely control it himself. I left it behind when Marlena and I got married. She was pregnant and I didn't want a gun in the house. I haven't seen that gun from that day until I found it under the seat of my truck. I knew Luci was trying to frame me. I thought she had somehow put it there."

"You're lying, Ben. This conversation is over." I get up, and Ronnie closes the notepad.

"Okay. Okay. But if I tell you, you'll think I killed her."

I sit back down.

SIXTY

Ben takes several deep breaths and grinds the heels of his hands into his eyes. If a person could really sweat blood, his face would be red.

"I was at the house like I told you when you called me today. I was really putting things in their place. Trying to make the house okay for Marlena and Bennie when they came home. To be honest, I missed the place. Being there with Marlena and Bennie was the first time I felt I belonged. Had a home."

I lean back and look at the ceiling. "What were you really doing there, Ben?"

"I was looking around to see if Luci had left anything that would incriminate me. She could easily have made copies of all my keys. The house, the trucks. She called me. She said she didn't want me any more. For another million dollars she'd tell me who had taken them and I'd never have to see her again. She said if I didn't bring the money I'd never see *them* again. I was desperate. I told her I could get the money but she'd have to give me time. I swear that's true."

He pushes his chair back and looks at the floor.

"All of it, Ben." I look at the door.

"I got a text message asking me to meet her. It said she'd tell me what I wanted. I went to meet her and..." He trails off and licks his lips.

"And?"

"She was already dead."

He fidgets and starts again. "When I got there, her car was under a tree. I thought she'd had an accident. I crawled to the driver's door and it was partially open. My God, her face! Then I saw the gun on the ground. I knew it was mine. I thought she'd killed herself and was trying to implicate me. I panicked. I had to get rid of the gun. I knew it was mine. I thought I could hide the gun in the house. You'd already searched the house. But when I got there I thought I'd be better off throwing it in the bay or burying it in the woods. I was scared. You know the rest."

"Where did you meet her?"

"The park at the Luna Ridge Loop Hiking Trail."

"What did Luci mean by 'another million'?"

He looks from me to Ronnie. "I don't know. Honest. I didn't think about it then. Maybe Cyrus had given her money to go away." His eyes widen. "Do you think Cyrus had someone kill her?"

Tears run down his cheeks and his face contorts into a mask of grief. "Oh, God. I thought maybe she'd killed them already. My little Bennie. My wife."

I'm quiet. Taking this in. Trying to rearrange thoughts that are like a Chinese puzzle box that can be opened only by solving a puzzle. The pieces are there but there are so many combinations, it's dizzying.

"Luci was shot with my gun, wasn't she?"

I nod, and he hangs his head. "This can't be happening. I swear, I've never hurt anyone. I wouldn't kidnap my own family even if I was thinking about leaving Marlena. Listen to me. Why would I want to give my father ammunition to disinherit me? If I was going to kill them, I would have just done it. Luci took them. I told you. Check her phone. She called me about the same time you called me and then texted me. The text will be on my phone." He absentmindedly reaches for his pocket. "It's gone. I don't..."

"The phone wasn't in your truck? Where is it?"

"I don't know. I'm pretty sure I took it with me to the trail."

"What about your watch?"

"You had it already. You never told me where you found it."

"Ronnie, can we talk in the hall?" We get up and leave the room. Sheriff Gray meets us.

"I hate to say it, Megan: I know everything points to him, but I think he's telling the truth this time."

"I'm going to call Mindy."

Ronnie says, "I'll make more coffee."

"I'll make the coffee, Ronnie. You keep him talking," Tony says.

I go by my desk and find a sandwich Tony has missed. I take it outside to make the call. Mindy answers and of course I have a mouthful.

"Megan. Is that you?"

I swallow and say, "Sorry. I have a few questions."

"Okay."

"Did you find Luci's phone?"

"Yes. Davis found it in the woods. The battery was low, so I'm charging it."

"So you don't have it handy?"

"It's charging in Sissy's Jeep."

"Where's Sissy?"

"She's around here somewhere. Do you want me to find her?"

"Go check on the phone first."

"Hold on. I'm near the front door of the house. The mansion, I mean."

While she's checking, I ask Ronnie to have someone go to the Luna Ridge house and look for Ben's phone. Ronnie gets on her iPad. "It's still at the house. Or in that area." She calls Dispatch to have someone sent to the house.

Mindy comes back on the line. "The phone is gone from the Jeep, Megan. I know I put it on the charger. The Jeep is here but no phone."

"You didn't have a chance to look at the calls?"

"I did that, but the battery was so low I needed to charge it. I can tell you what I remember."

"I'm talking to Ben. He said he got a call from Luci's phone." I give her the approximate times. I give her Ben's phone number.

"Luci called Ben's phone around that time. And then she called a number I didn't recognize not a minute later."

"Did you check her text messages?"

"Sorry, Megan."

"Do you remember the number Luci called?" She'd made a note of it and tells me. I recognize it. "Mindy, I'm going to have Davis and Copsey come to the house."

"Why, Megan? What's going on?"

"Just get together with them. I'm going to call Copsey right now. Stay together and in the house."

"Megan, you're scaring me."

That makes two of us. "It'll be fine. Just wait there." I hang up and call Copsey's cell.

"Whatever you're calling about, I'm not to blame," he says. I've been teaching him how to have a sense of humor. He's still not funny.

"This is important. If you are near Sissy, just answer yes."

"No. I'm at the timber workshop. No one's here but me and Davis. What's going on, Megan?"

"Just answer. Have you seen Sissy or any of her security officers?"

"Sissy loaned us the Gator. Mindy just left on one to go back to the mansion. That was about twenty minutes ago. Have you asked her?"

"This is what I need you to do."

I give him instructions. He doesn't like them but he'll do what I ask.

He says, "You're telling me Godzilla's loose on the island and all I've got is a Bic lighter to wave around." At least he's joking, and that one is kind of funny. "If I get killed, I'm going to be really mad at you."

"Call me when you're set." I hang up.

Sheriff Gray has come outside and is standing behind me. "We might have a problem." I tell him what I suspect.

SIXTY-ONE

Sheriff Gray recognized the security officer who brought us all back across. He is a retired police officer from some little burg and is happy to take us back to Cyrus Parker's island. We meet Larry Pointer at the dock. He came by boat from Port Ludlow Marina. He is a hobby fisherman when he isn't doing security and is curious why we didn't call Sissy.

"She'll be madder'n a hornet at me for bringing you there. She rules with an iron fist."

Sheriff Gray says, "Officer Pointer, I'm deputizing you, so you have no worries about that. I'm friends with Cyrus and I'll take care of you."

We all climb aboard and Pointer casts off, backs the boat out, and heads toward the dock on the island. "Can you tell me what the big secret's about? Or would you have to kill me?"

He chuckles, but it's not all that funny. Sissy might really kill him. All of us, for that matter.

"You won't be staying, Mr. Pointer," I say. "Just get us there and take off. We'll owe you one."

"You'll owe me an explanation. I used to be a cop. I know when something's not right. If you need me, I got a gun on board. I can be some help."

I look Pointer over. He's all of five feet six inches and 250 pounds. At his age, a little past fifty going on retired, he would have a heart attack and I'd be taking care of him instead of business. But I'm touched he's offering. I say, "Once a cop, always a cop."

"You're damn right. So I'm coming?"

"No, sir. You need to stay out in the bay and watch for a signal from us. We're counting on you to come get us if we need to make a retreat." I'm laying it on, but he eats it up.

"You can count on me. Thanks for calling me, Tony. You won't owe me nothing. This security job isn't all it's cracked up to be. Sitting. Reading books, magazines. Wishing I was home watching television."

"You can always retire a second time, Larry," the sheriff says.

"The pay's too good to pass up. But if I get fired, I guess I'll stick with taking people out to beat the water with their rods. No one knows how to relax and fish any more. Too bad Sissy didn't have us come and search yesterday like I thought she was going to do. We might have found them sooner."

I put a hand on his arm. "What did you say?"

"I said we might have found them sooner."

"Before that."

"Yeah. Sissy asked me if I'd mind running the boat yesterday. She said she needed several of us to do something. She usually lets me know if she's going to need me because of my business. So I said sure, whenever she wanted me. She said she'd let me know."

"This was yesterday?"

"Yeah. I figured it had something to do with Mr. Parker's family missing. But she didn't call until this morning."

"What time?"

"Around eight o'clock, I imagine. We all went over around nine o'clock and just sat around waiting for something to do. Money's good, though."

I call Deputy Copsey's phone.

"I'm at the dock," Copsey says. "Davis went to the mansion. Where are you?"

I explain. "We found a boat to bring us across. We should be there in..."—I look at Pointer and he holds up a hand. I assume it means five minutes and not *Stop talking*—"five minutes. Have you seen Sissy?"

"No one. Davis hasn't called yet."

I asked that Davis call Copsey as soon as he was inside with Mindy.

"How long?"

"Thirty minutes. I was getting ready to go get him. He's not answering his phone and neither is Mindy."

"Wait there." I disconnect.

"Problem?" the sheriff asks.

"No contact with Davis. Copsey's at the dock." The dock is dead ahead and I see Copsey waving at us.

"What do you want to do?"

"I have a plan," I say.

SIXTY-TWO

Sheriff Gray nixes my plan. "I'm no babysitter. Excuse me, Larry. I don't mean I'd be babysitting you. I just don't want to be on the water if the shit hits the fan—excuse my language. Besides, that's my niece and grandnephew. And my wife's sister."

He doesn't call Helen by her name or even "my sister-in-law," but I'm glad he added her to the list. It shows character, given how he feels about her. I still want to hear that story.

We land and Ronnie goes over the side and ties us off, draws her weapon, and runs in a crouch to Deputy Copsey. She thinks she's Bruce Willis. I hope she doesn't get herself killed. I'd have to hook Marley up with someone else. But I have to admit, I'd miss her. She's growing on me.

I try Sissy's phone again. No answer. I call Luci's phone number and it automatically goes to voicemail. If Mindy had it, she would have recognized my number and answered. I call Mindy and it rings several times before she picks up. "Hello?"

Relief floods over me. All this drama for nothing.

She says, "How are you, Ronnie? I guess you want to know about the results on that knife."

I feel a little nauseous. Mindy called me Ronnie. She knows it's me. And she's talking about evidence that doesn't exist. I move up beside Ronnie and motion for everyone to be quiet as I thumb the speaker icon. I whisper what I want Ronnie to say.

Ronnie asks, "Is Deputy Copsey with you, Mindy?"

"He's here. We're in the kitchen. Cyrus has made hot sweet tea for everyone. He's such a nice man. Are you coming back?"

Copsey is standing beside me. He raises an eyebrow.

"That's why I called. Can you ask Sissy to bring the boat for me? I'm at the dock waiting for the boat. Megan's tied up at the office. Have you found Luci's phone?"

"When you talk to her tell her I found the phone but it must have gotten broken. It didn't take a charge. Sorry. There's no need to come back. The doctor said Marlena and Bennie are much better and Sissy can bring them back in a few hours. I have plenty of help here. You can head back to the office."

She's in trouble.

Ronnie says, "Okay. You're probably right. Sorry about putting a scare into everyone. Can I talk to Cyrus?"

"Uh, he's busy. He went to check on Marlena."

She just said Cyrus was making tea for everyone. I can't hear any of the normal sounds of conversation in the background. Ronnie says, "Okay. If you're sure you're okay there. Tell Cyrus we're taking Ben to lockup."

There's a long pause. I look around but can't see a camera on the dock.

Mindy says, "We're just having tea and then we'll go back to work on the scene. It may be a while but if I see him I'll tell him you want to talk."

The line goes dead. I'm sure Sissy's figured it out. I take the phone back and call Mindy's phone again. Sissy answers.

I say, "Hi, Sissy. I need to speak to Mindy?"

"Mindy can't come to the phone right now."

"Let me talk to one of my deputies."

"And I need all of you to get off my island."

"Your island? What are you talking about, Sissy?"

"Do you think I can't see you. Tell everyone to get back on Pointer's boat and leave. Not you. You stay."

"It doesn't have to be like this, Sissy."

"Of course it does. I knew from the moment we met it would end this way. Come to the house alone. Keep your weapon. If you win, they all walk out alive. If I win, I'm going to kill everyone here. What do you say, Megan? Want to play?"

Tony has his ear shoved against mine and is listening in on the call. Now he's shaking his head and motioning for me to hang up. I don't. I agree to her request. I'm sorry it has to end like this. I'm trying hard to change. I'm not Rylee any longer. I'm a better person. But I can't deny there's a part of me that wants to end her like all the other monsters.

Sissy says, "I knew it was over when Mindy found that damn phone."

"You shouldn't have kidnapped the Parkers. You killed Luci and sent the text to Ben from her phone. You made it easy for us to find Luci. You were the one who gave us the code to her watch. The thing I can't understand is why you set all this up."

She doesn't answer. I whisper to Tony, "See if you can go to the house without being seen. I'll use the Gator and keep her talking."

"Enlighten me, Sissy. Is this about money?" Copsey is leading everyone into the woods next to the road.

"I'm disappointed in you, Megan. You really don't have a clue. I could have gotten away with it, but oh well. It is what it is. At least I'll have the pleasure of ending things my way. Now tell everyone to go or you're going to regret it. Everyone here is still alive for now."

Ronnie is bringing up the rear and they are all out of sight. I go to the Gator. "You obviously wanted to keep them alive. Was Cyrus looking at hiring a new head of security? Did you think saving his daughter-in-law and grandson would make him more grateful? Like when you killed your partner in Iraq. You did that to impress Cyrus. I know about that. The Department of Justice is investigating you. I looked into your background and uncovered several lies, so I called them and guess what?" Now I sound like Ronnie. I hope it aggravates her as much as it does me.

"You don't know anything. Do you think this is a book where the bad girl tells it all at the end? You're so full of crap."

"If you live through this, you'll find out if I'm lying. I hope we don't have to do this. I don't want to hurt you." Not the truth. "Let everyone go. Do the right thing."

"Let me think about it. Uh. No. Come to the house. We'll talk. Or something."

"You're crazy. You know that, don't you?"

She laughs. "Not crazy. I feel I've just come alive."

I say, "You'll never leave this island. You know that too, don't you? One last chance." And I mean that. "Don't do this, Sissy."

"Don't you see? I have to find out."

"Find what out?"

"Which of us is the best. What do you say?"

"I say I'm coming for you. Like my partner says, it'll hurt." I disconnect. I can't believe I'm talking like Ronnie now. My phone buzzes.

"I want you to hear something so you don't chicken out." I hear a loud crack and a grunt. "Say something to her."

"We're okay, Megan. Don't do what she says." There's another grunt and the line goes dead. It sounded like Deputy Davis. He sounds hurt. I've given Tony and the others a good head start. They should get to the mansion a little after me. I want to get there first and distract Sissy. Get her away from the front to give them a chance to get inside.

I get to the mansion and don't see Sheriff Gray, so they are still in the woods. I hope they're close. Sissy is more dangerous than anyone I've come up against. There are no lights on except in the front entrance. She'll expect me to go to one of the other entrances so she's made sure they're all locked. I would. But I'm sure there are cameras all around the outside. I need to let her see me sneak around the side to get her away from any monitors. I go past the mansion and park the Gator in the back and hunch over as I head toward the mansion, gun drawn, thinking of how Ronnie did that.

There are two entrances. One is at the top of a set of stone steps to a back door. Another is at the bottom of a stairway leading down to a sublevel. I'll go that way. Four-foot-high concrete barriers enclose the entrance, creating a perfect place for her to snipe me. I come at the entrance from the side along the wall so I don't put myself in her line of fire. I keep my back against the wall and stand enough to see over the concrete. Helen sits on the top step, facing the door, gagged, arms tied behind her back. She turns her head and sees me and her eyes widen. I drop to the ground just in time to hear a bee buzz by my ear and feel bits of concrete strike me. I touch the side of my face and my hand comes away with blood.

I scrunch up against the concrete as tightly as I can. If she shoots down from the top, I'm dead. I didn't hear the shot. I was aware of being shot at only from the sound of the bullet hitting the concrete and the sting of fragments on my face and neck. She's close and using a silencer. She's back in the dark using Helen as bait. A human shield. I can't run. But if she's using the doorway to shoot at me, I may have a narrow field of fire to hit her. I just need to be sure she's in the doorway.

I say in a loud and what I hope is disgusted voice, "I knew you were a coward when I met you." There are several more coughs and some of the bullets hit the concrete just above my head and rain concrete bits into my hair. I look up and see Helen's head. Several more bullets whiz by me. Helen cries out and falls backward. I scooch forward so I can look over the landing. Helen is lying motionless on her side, facing away from me. I feel responsible for letting her come here.

It's dark now. I might have some advantage. Keeping one hand on the ground, I shoot around the side of the barrier several times. The muzzle blast from the Glock has got to be loud in that narrow opening, and I'm counting on the blast to temporarily ruin Sissy's night vision. I reach around and fire several times, hoping to hear I've hit her but the shots are loud. I wait to hear a sound and just then Helen struggles to her feet and takes a step forward.

"I warned you what would happen," Sissy says, and another shot rings out. Helen crumples to the ground. I'm sure she's dead or dying now. Sissy is an expert marksman.

My anger overcomes caution and I roll directly into the open area, firing until my gun is empty. I lie there expecting to be killed but nothing happens. Maybe I've hit her. I start to roll out of sight when a bullet plows a furrow across the top of my scalp. I don't stop but crawl behind my barrier.

"I could have killed you," she says. And I believe her. I'm outgunned and outmatched. She's playing with me.

The will to live is stronger than reason. I've trained myself to fight fear with rage. I'm building that rage as I reload and chamber another round. In doing so I forget to keep my eyes peeled for a threat. I look up and the barrel of a gun is in my face.

"I'll let you ask your question," she says.

I don't know what to say. All I wanted to do was give Tony some time to get in the house and free the other hostages. Helen is dead. I'll have to live with that. Or die with it.

"Are you in love with Cyrus?"

"He's dear to me."

"You took the Parkers so you could save them and be a hero again in his eyes. When were you planning to 'find' them?"

"After Ben was arrested. I gave you an excellent case against him. All you had to do was be satisfied with Ben, and Marlena and Bennie would have been free to live with Cyrus and me. But you've ruined that."

"Ben is innocent."

"Oh, he's guilty all right. He's guilty of breaking a great man's heart. Ruining any chance I had of becoming part of Cyrus's life. You asked if I love Cyrus. I do. But not as a lover."

I'm running out of things to stall with and she knows what I'm doing. She may be aware that Copsey, Ronnie, and Sheriff Gray haven't left. If so, she doesn't seem concerned. She's going to commit suicide by cop. After she kills me.

"You didn't tell me why," I ask.

"I have to admit, you did pretty good against me. You're a lot braver than most for not having been in war. I admire that. I can see why you've got the reputation as a hard-ass. I've got to tell someone, so it might as well be you."

I take a wild guess. "He'll never know you're his daughter."

I see her jaw clench and her gun hand tremble. "You couldn't have known that? How did you know?"

"I didn't. You just told me."

"Oh, you're good. It's too bad you won't be for long."

I say, "What's Cyrus going to think when you kill me? How are you going to explain all of this? The sheriff will come back with an army. You'll go to jail and maybe Cyrus will want to believe you are innocent, but eventually it will all make sense. He's not a stupid man. He doesn't know you're family. You should tell him before you do something you can't come back from."

Her voice softens but the gun doesn't waver. "My mother died a long slow death from cancer. She never married so it was just me and her. She told me who my real father was as she lay dying. I'd always thought he had been killed in a car crash. She didn't have any pictures because it was a lie."

"We have something in common after all. My mom did the same thing. I raised my little brother without any help from her. She moved us from one place to another, always a new name, new school, but my job was the same. I ran the house. She lied about my father. I thought he'd died in the war." I don't go as far as telling her dear old dad was a serial killer, or that I'd killed him when I found him, but I think we're bonding. Like psycho sisters.

Sissy is thoughtful, then says, "When she told me who he really was, I knew I had to find him. Not because of his money. I don't care about money. I wanted to belong to someone. Have a family. Mom told me it was just a one-night stand and that she'd never told him about me. I knew I had to find him and I fooled myself into thinking he would hug me and tell me he'd been looking for me too. Stupid. But when I found my father, I couldn't bring myself to tell him the truth about who I was. He's such a great man. Smart, generous, kind, and no one appreciated him. His wife left and his son... well, you know what a complete disappointment he's been. Cyrus was different from them. I got as close to him as I could, as close as he would let me be. He told me he loves me like a daughter." She takes a breath and her lips tremble. "He loves me. It's all I ever wanted." She lets the breath out slowly and the gun hand steadies. "It's too late now."

"Telling him would be the right thing, Sissy." I need to keep her talking until the sheriff or Ronnie shows up. But I think Sissy will shoot me anyway. I wish I'd thought to call Tony and left the line open. At least he could have heard her confession. "I've done bad things. Things I thought I had to keep from him. I was protecting him from the evil world and evil people. My lies grew like a cancer and I kept lying because it was easier than facing his disapproval and maybe lose his love. My little brother grew up resenting me because I had to be the parent figure. He loves our mother who basically abandoned us."

I'm losing her interest. I blurt out, "He was in Afghanistan." This gets a raise of one eyebrow. "While he was gone we grew apart and when he came home he wasn't the same brother that left. I blame myself. I wish I'd kept closer. I wish I'd told him the truth all those years. Told him that our mother was a bitch that ran out on us. Told him I loved him. And now I'm trying to bridge the gap. He's still a little angry with me but we're getting there. Now, after talking to you, I've decided to tell him everything. He's my only family. He'll understand. He may not like it, but he'll understand."

She's quiet and quiet's not good. I keep talking because it's keeping me alive. "Don't you owe it to yourself to tell your father the truth? He'd want to know. He told you you're like a daughter. You protect him and keep his life running smoothly. You're always there for him. Your mother let you down just like my mother did. But Cyrus won't. He's family, Sissy."

"I do protect him. I'll protect him from the ugly truth his daughter is a murderer. He's already lost his son. I don't think he can take any more."

I've run out of things to delay the inevitable and brace myself for what's coming. A voice comes from the dark behind Sissy.

"You're wrong, Sissy," Cyrus says, and steps up close to her. "You're wrong. I think I've always known you were more than a bodyguard. You saved my life once. And you've more than made up for Ben's failings. I've always felt your loyalty and respect and love. You treat me like a father and I will be proud to call you my daughter."

I hear his voice crack when he says this last and Sissy's eyes moisten but she doesn't turn toward him.

"Give me the gun, Sissy. We have so much catching up to do. I've dreamed of having a daughter like you. Someone to leave all this to. I won't let them arrest you. We can go away together. Start over. Anywhere you want to go. Don't do this. You have nothing to prove to me."

She takes a deep breath and wipes at her eyes with the back of her hand. I wonder if he's just telling her what she needs to hear but his voice is so sincere I think he means it. He has the money and resources to make her disappear, but where does that leave me? I'm a loose end that she might decide to tie up.

"I don't have any choice, Mr. Parker. It's too late."

Oh, shit!

Cyrus puts a gentle hand on her shoulder. "I'm your father. It's never too late for us. You're all I have now. Let me protect you now like you've always protected me. Please. If you ever loved me, please don't do this."

I'm about to die, but his passionate plea, the tears in Sissy's eyes, are catching and I find myself swallowing hard. My mother lied about my real father. So I understand some of what Sissy has been through, but I still hate what she's done and will gladly put a bullet in her face if given the opportunity.

Her finger tightens on the trigger and I scrunch my eyes shut so I don't see my own death.

"Come here, Sissy. Come here. I'll take care of you. Everything will be all right now."

I crack an eye open and the gun is gone. Sissy is wrapped in Cyrus's arms and her body is wracking with sobs. Cyrus holds the gun out toward me and I take it in shaking hands.

SIXTY-THREE

Tony kneels to check an unmoving Helen for a pulse. I give a start when Helen slaps his hand away. "Bitch shot me."

Tony and I look her over. I can't see any wounds. "Where are you hurt?"

Helen pulls herself into a sitting position and feels around. "I guess she missed. I must have fainted."

She had dropped on the ground so fast and so hard I know she's going to have some pain later. I'm shocked Sissy could have missed at that range. Even more shocked when Tony helps Helen to her feet and gives her a bear hug.

Ronnie comes up to me and hugs me, and this time I don't fight it. But then Copsey and Davis make it a group hug. Sucks, but what can I do. I hug them back. I'm alive.

"Are you okay, Megan?" Tony asks.

I'm trembling too hard to answer.

"We got here as fast as we could," Ronnie says. "It took some doing to get into the kitchen."

"Marlena and Bennie?" I ask when I find my voice.

"They're fine. Everyone's fine," Ronnie says.

Everyone but Lucia Simmons. May she rest in hell.

"We saw Sissy pointing a gun at you," Tony says. "We couldn't chance shooting her. Cyrus was with us and said he could stop her."

Ronnie says, "It was our only chance without getting you killed."

Her voice sounds a little thick, as if she's having trouble speaking. I hope she doesn't cry. It'll get me started and I have to keep remembering I'm tough. Sissy even said so. But I don't feel so tough now.

EPILOGUE

TWO DAYS LATER...

The Sheriff's Office isn't the most comfortable place to have a get-together with Helen and Ellen and Marlena and young Bennie, but it's safe and there's a child interview room where Bennie is entertaining himself by making Lego monsters and smashing them. The boy will need therapy after what he's seen and been through, but at least he's alive to get help.

Ronnie is with Tony talking to Helen and Ellen, and Marlena touches my arm and asks quietly, "Can we talk privately, Detective Carpenter?"

"Of course, Mrs. Parker."

At the mention of her married name her brow wrinkles in disgust. "Please, if I never hear that name again I'll be blessed. Call me Marlena."

"Okay."

We go out of the back door where the smell of old cigarettes permeates the air. "Let's go out front," I say, and she follows me around the building to a little grassy knoll just across the front parking lot under some trees.

"What can I do for you, Marlena?"

She smiles and I can see her face glowing. Two days have made such a difference that it's unbelievable. She looks healthy and doesn't have the haunted look that I'd seen the night we collected them from Cyrus's house and taken both to the hospital. Cyrus had started to object to them being moved and was about to say they'd be safer there, but when he saw the look on my face he shut up and let me do what needed to be done.

"First of all I want to thank you again for saving us from that crazy woman."

She'd already thanked us several times but I suppose she needed to do this. Maybe to prove to herself that she was free and that she and her son were alive and no longer had to fear Ben. "Marlena, Tony is the one you should be thanking."

"Mom was shot and you risked your life to save her."

I did. Not consciously. It's just what a cop does. "I'm glad she wasn't hurt too bad."

"My mom was shot, Detective Carpenter. That woman tried to kill her." Her eyes widen and I can see her composure slipping.

"It's Megan. And she was only shot a little bit." I grin and hold two fingers on my left hand an inch apart. It's true. The bullet Sissy fired at Helen had grazed her inner arm and ribs on the right side. I thought she was dead at that range, and given Sissy's military background it was a miracle that she missed. But to hear Helen tell it, she was at death's door.

Marlena chuckles. "You really are brave. All of you. Uncle Tony too. My mom has told me stories about him that I always wondered if they were true. You see, my mom and Tony don't get along all that well. I should have bridged the gap a long time ago but I wanted to keep peace with Mom."

"It's none of my business, Marlena, but what seems to be the problem there? You don't have to say. I'm just curious. Detective stuff."

She grins again. "I can see why you're a detective. You're even smooth when you're lying or prying."

I can feel my face flush. Caught red-handed.

"That's a compliment," Marlena says, seeing my discomfort. "Mom said Ellen told her many times about you. And your partner, Ronnie. Apparently Tony thinks you walk on water. Don't tell him I said that."

"Our secret," I say, but I'll use it to my advantage if needed.

"Okay, here's the issue in a nutshell: When Ellen got engaged to Tony my mother was married."

I knew that. Tony had only met Ellen about ten years ago. I nod to let her continue.

"My father was still alive and was in law enforcement. DEA."

Now that I didn't know and I say so.

"My mom didn't think Tony was good enough for her sister. She tried to talk her out of the marriage. When that didn't work she had my father do some digging into Tony's background. He didn't find anything, of course, but when Ellen and Tony found out there was an explosion. The sisters didn't talk for several years, and Tony did a good job of avoiding Mom or Dad."

"But that's kind of to be expected. I mean, for your mom and dad to want to find out if there was a reason Tony and Ellen shouldn't marry. How did they find out your father was looking into Tony's background?"

"That's the rub. Dad was looking in the system and talking to his law enforcement friends, quietly he thought. It wasn't so quiet. One of the county commissioners got wind of the inquiry, thought it was drug related because Dad was with the DEA, and Tony got called up on the carpet. He had to take a random drug test and word got around on that too. Poor Tony. I don't blame him one bit for being angry. But when Ben turned ugly I wished I had someone to go to for help. My mom would only tell me to move in with her and divorce Ben. My father was dead and Uncle Tony was distant. I know now I should have gone to him anyway."

So that's the barrier between Tony and Helen. I don't know what I expected but I might have reacted the same way. Or worse.

"How is Bennie doing?" I ask.

Marlena smiles weakly. "He's going to be okay. We're staying at my house. Cyrus signed it over to me solely. I don't need a restraining order for Ben. I think you scared him. Cyrus has threatened to disinherit him if he comes anywhere near us unless I agree. So far, so good."

"Get the restraining order," I say. "His word won't mean much. He can be arrested if he comes to your house. Also get the order to read that he has to stay a distance from you and Bennie. If he starts stalking you, call me and I'll be happy to arrest him."

She surprises me and gives me a hug. Not a small one either. "You're welcome to come and visit us any time. You and Ronnie. I hope to see more of my aunt and uncle too."

That raises another question. The matter of visits from or to Cyrus. When we were marching Sissy away under arrest, she had called out to Cyrus who was following us and looking worried and confused and a little out of it. She asked Cyrus to forgive her. His answer was both touching and exactly what I expected. He'd said, "I forgive you, Sissy. Now don't say another word until I've arranged an attorney for you. Everything will be okay."

Maybe in the world of a billionaire everything will be okay. Maybe Sissy will go to an honor camp, get psychological counseling, be cured, and get out to kill someone else. I ask, "You know Cyrus went to bat for Sissy and for Ben, right?"

Her smile vanishes. "Ben didn't get charged with any of the things you had on him, did he?"

"I'm afraid being an asshole isn't a crime in the state of Washington."

The smile is back. "Is Sissy really Cyrus's daughter?"

Cyrus thinks so. "I don't know," I say. "But she tells a good story. We know for sure she killed Luci Simmons and was holding you and Bennie prisoner on the island. I still think Ben kidnapped you. I think Luci found out and tried to make a deal with Sissy and got killed instead. I'm sure Sissy is the one that moved you from where Ben was keeping you to the island."

Marlena sighs. "I wish you could have proven Ben had something to do with this. But maybe I don't want that to be true. What will I tell our son? He already thinks his father is a monster."

"Get the restraining order. I'll go to the judge with you if you like. Or Tony can. He knows a sympathetic judge." One Cyrus can't buy. "If I can promise you one thing, I promise you this. Ben is evil. He is cruel. He's not going to change. I want you to talk to a friend of mine. Her name is Dr. Karen Albright. She's a therapist. She's retired but I'm sure she will talk to you. Don't get recycled and go through that whole abused woman syndrome. If you value your life and your son, get some help. And get a court order on Sissy as well. I'm sure when she goes to trial the judge will order her to stay away from you, but better safe than sorry."

She hugs me tightly again and this time I feel my shoulder getting wet. Sometimes I wish I would just keep my big trap shut. But what I've told her is the truth. Ben is evil. Scary evil.

"Let's join the others. Mom is going to take you all to dinner."

"Go ahead. I'll be right in," I say. After Marlena is inside I think back over the possibility of Sissy beating the charges. Cyrus will hire the best firm. Our prosecutor is good but he'll be outnumbered and out budgeted. Her lawyers can drag the trial on for years. Wait the sensational news stories out. Wait until the outrage from the public dies down. Then get her in a psych facility. I have no doubt that if she ever gets out I'll see her again. She's technically crazy, but she meant it when she said she wanted to see which of us was the best. I am, of course. But I may not see her coming.

And then I have another thought. I wonder if Academi will ever know she killed one of their people just to get close to Cyrus. Academi is not a company you want pissed at you. I pity the fool who sends them a letter giving them a heads-up about what happened. Hell hath no fury like a mercenary group scorned. I'll have to make sure the letter is untraceable and anonymous. It's the least I can do.

* * *

A few hours later, after the families have talked it out and gone their separate ways, Ronnie and I go to get coffee at Moe's. When we arrive Moe clears a table for us. We both get our usual. I have no idea what it will be today. We sip our coffee and enjoy the silence until the door jingles. I look up to see Cyrus coming to our table. Ben is standing outside, keeping his back to us.

Cyrus asks, "Do you mind if we talk?"

"Have a seat," Ronnie says, but he doesn't sit.

"So what's up?" I ask.

He clears his throat and his cheeks color. I hope he's not about to blast me for trying to keep Ben charged with obstructing a criminal investigation and assault with a deadly weapon, to wit, his truck. The sheriff reminded me nothing would stick because I had rammed him and that we were lucky Ben's not suing us.

"I don't know how I'm ever going to thank you two. I don't..." His voice falters and he struggles to continue.

Ronnie gets up, hugs him, and kisses his cheek. "It's okay, Cyrus. You can thank us by being a good father to Ben. Help him learn how to be a good person. He wants to love you. He's hurt and scared. You can't change the past, but you can change the future. The important thing is family. Ben, Marlena, and Bennie. And Sissy. And now Helen."

I'm amazed and proud of Ronnie. I'm at a loss for words, but she said the exact right thing. And meant it. I want to add that he should exile Ben to some foreign country but I don't want to make an enemy of Cyrus. Most likely Marlena will accept his presence. Bennie loves him. And I don't want to find blame in a man trying to protect his family. I killed for mine.

Cyrus holds Ronnie at arm's length and tears run down his face. "I owe you both so much. So much."

I do something I never thought was possible: I get up and hug them both and feel tears forming in my own eyes. My throat tightens. If this is what being a real girl is like, I don't know if I like it. It hurts. But it also feels good.

I hear the door to Moe's jingle again. "Hi, Megan. Did you miss me?" Dan is standing there and now I do cry. My family is growing and I'm growing as well. Just when I thought I couldn't be happier the bell over the door jingles and Hayden comes in. His eyes light up his face like he's just hit the lottery.

"Hi, sis."

Dan is grinning from ear to ear. He says, "Meet my new assistant."

A LETTER FROM GREGG

Dear reader,

I want to say a huge thank you for choosing to read *Stillwater Island*, the fourth book in the Detective Megan Carpenter series. If you did enjoy it and want to keep up to date with all my latest releases, take a moment to sign up at the following link. Here's a promise: Your email address will never be shared, and you can unsubscribe at any time.

www.bookouture.com/gregg-olsen

I loved writing *Stillwater Island* and wanted to explore the dark secrets within a family and their far-reaching consequences. Megan is always such a fun character to write—she's as feisty, smart and vulnerable as ever in this book and again, having to dip deep into her own personal trauma in order to solve the case.

I hope you loved *Stillwater Island* and if you did I would be very grateful if you could write a review. I'd love to hear what you think, and it makes such a difference helping new readers to discover one of my books for the first time.

I love hearing from my readers—you can get in touch on my Facebook page, through Twitter, Goodreads or my website.

Thanks, Gregg

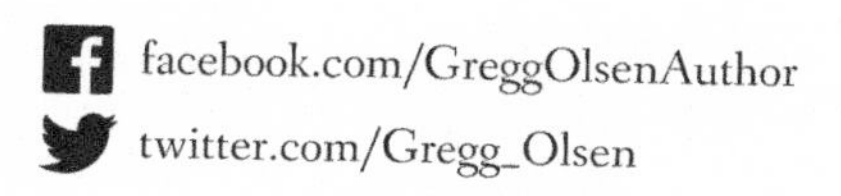

Made in United States
Orlando, FL
09 March 2025

59308414R00194